Read Between the Wines Cozy Mysteries Boxset Books 1-3

A SMALL TOWN FRIENDS COZY MYSTERY SERIES WITH RECIPES

DANI SIMMS

TRILLIUM SAGE
PUBLISHING

Book cover by GetCovers.com

Edited by L. Jackson, T. Collins

ISBN: 978-1-958118-13-9 | ebook

ISBN: 978-1-958118-17-7 | paperback

Murder at the Festival

BOOK 1

Chapter One

It wasn't often that the park looked as festive as it did during the
Winter Wine Festival. Avery hadn't been to the festival in many years,
as most winters she'd been in the city. That year Le Blanc Cellars had the
opportunity to represent themselves at the festival and Avery was proud to
see her vineyard such a success.

It was a big deal, and the few friends she had in town made sure to
remind her of it for the weeks leading up to the festival. Not only was it an
opportunity for Le Blanc Cellars to get some decent marketing, but Cellar
Vie Guest House was booked full for the week of the festival.

For Avery, it meant there was plenty to celebrate. And she was in the
right place for a celebration. The first day of the festival had been a success,
and the night was bound to be even busier. There was a popular band
scheduled to play, and the air was filled with the aroma of all the best street
food the city had to offer.

"Remember how we used to walk through this market looking for any
fallen coins so we could buy snacks?" Tiffany asked between sips. "It
always was, and still is, the event of the year!"

Memories of those days came flooding back to her. It was a time when
children could run freely through the festival without any concerns about
security. Avery wished she could go back to those days before she knew

what stress, grief, anger, or loneliness was. She remembered how carefree she felt as she would run through the fields, her head constantly bent down, searching for anything that seemed too shiny to be grass.

They would get completely hopped up on sugar, then go home and watch musicals until they eventually crashed. Everyone had fun then— Avery, Tiffany, and their parents. The memories were filled with laughter, music, and just the right amount of chaos.

Avery laughed. "I remember it all too well. I must admit, though, the festival is a lot more fun now that I'm old enough to drink the wine."

Avery was doing her best to take part in the conversation, but she was distracted by the beauty of the festival. It had come a long way since she'd last attended. She remembered it to be a couple of wine farms offering tastings and maybe the local karaoke bar would set up a temporary gig.

What Avery saw that night was vastly different. Strings with small lights wrapped through the air created a soft glow that could be seen from blocks away. Soft jazz filtered through the park, always at the same volume no matter where she walked.

The food was good, the atmosphere was refreshing, and she felt proud of something for the first time in a long time. She had put months of work into designing the Le Blanc Cellars stall. Everything about the wines, display, and wine-tasting experience had been perfected. And it seemed to be paying off.

To a certain extent, Avery had nothing to worry about. Her businesses were doing well, she had made friends, and she was healing from the death of her husband one day at a time. It was never going to be easy, but Avery had enough to keep her occupied.

She was about to say something to Tiffany when a stumbling man knocked the wine right out of her hand. Red wine spilled all over her and a nearby passerby. In fact, he had hit her hard enough that if Tiffany hadn't caught her, Avery would have fallen down too.

"She did it!" he yelled as he fell. "She's the one you're looking for!"

Avery stared at the man. He was a short, chubby man with pink cheeks and small round glasses. There was little about him that was attractive. He hit the ground with a loud thud, and a moment later, a small crowd gathered to help him up.

"What was that about?" Avery laughed as she inspected the wine stains on her shirt. "That, my dear, is the look of someone who has tasted far too much of what our vineyards have to offer," Tiffany replied.

When Avery glanced back, the man had been seated on a bench and left there to sober up. Tiffany and Avery headed to the ladies room in an attempt to clean out the wine stains that decorated Avery's shirt.

"Shall we wash it out with white wine?" Tiffany joked.

It was a good joke, good enough to have Avery laughing out loud. Her laughs echoed off the bathroom walls.

"Maybe if I just cover it with more wine, it will look like I dressed up for the occasion?" Avery suggested through giggles.

"Worth a try," Tiffany said.

"No, you can't be serious," Avery responded. She had been joking, but something in Tiffany's eyes said that she didn't think it was all that much of a joke. Tiffany led her back out onto the lawn, just behind the bathrooms.

Then Tiffany motioned for Avery to wait for her while she disappeared into the crowd, returning with two glasses of red wine.

"Now, hold still," Tiffany commanded.

Realizing that she really had nothing to lose and the blouse was already ruined, she nodded, giving Tiffany the go-ahead. Avery did her best to stand still between bouts of laughter as Tiffany threw two glasses of wine at her. The wine splashed, causing a huge mess on the ground at Avery's feet, but tipsiness had done a great job of dulling her embarrassment.

"That actually looks better!" Tiffany cheered.

"Except for the smell," Avery said as she blushed. "I smell like the bottom of a barrel."

"It's a wine festival," Tiffany whispered, linking her arm to Avery's. "Nobody will notice. Everything here smells like red wine."

"Isn't the mayor coming today?" Avery asked. "I heard some visitors saying something along those lines, and I thought I saw him earlier, but it was very brief."

Tiffany shrugged. "He usually comes on the first day of the festival, but I've been here all day and I haven't seen him yet. Maybe he'll come tomorrow."

3

"That's strange," Avery replied. "I was certain I had seen him. Maybe he only stayed for a bit."

"It's really great to see you having some fun," Tiffany said with a smile as she nudged Avery in the ribs. "Things have been hard on you. I'm happy you're able to let loose a little."

"Well, as of right now, I've decided to make it a habit to have fun," Avery joked, as she fixed her shirt.

It was the most fun that Avery had experienced in ages. They were lucky enough to make it in time to get a spot on the lawn and watch the band perform. To Avery's surprise, she knew the words to every song they played and sang along loudly with the rest of the crowd.

For a brief moment, she felt like a teenager again. The atmosphere was the same, and everyone around her was having a good time too. With the lights that ran through the park, the smell of food cooking over a fire, and live music, she felt like nothing could possibly go wrong.

It had been a long time since Avery had allowed herself to let loose like that. She realized that perhaps she had been taking life far too seriously, and made a tipsy reminder to herself to enjoy life a little more. She wanted countless nights like the one she was having, and she felt determined to make it happen.

∼

"Don't you have to clean up your stall?" Tiffany asked as they made their way to the parking lot.

The band had finished, and the crowd was leaving the park. Avery had always been amazed at how quickly a busy place can become completely empty. Soon, there would be nobody, and the lights would be turned off. The park would rest until the next morning when the second day of the festival would commence.

"Nah," Avery said, stepping carefully over the cables that led from behind the stage. "I've hired some young folk to do that for me. Best decision I've made so far," she joked.

Avery and Tiffany used each other for support to make sure they'd walk upright and neither of them would trip over anything in the dark. It was a habit they had formed after one too many bruises during their college years.

"Do you remember that time we tumbled down that hill after the art exhibition?" Tiffany laughed. "I bruised every single one of my fingers and eight of my toes."

"I remember!" Avery cackled. "That was tough to explain to your parents too. What a weird injury!"

"I have to admit, though, I can feel the age in my bones. I'm eager to get into bed," Tiffany confessed.

"Yes, please," Avery agreed. "I'd like to go home, too. I'm sure Sprinkles is worried sick about me."

Something about the last statement made Tiffany laugh so hard that tears were rolling down her face. Avery didn't really understand what was so funny, but then again, that was normal in their friendship. Before they made it back to the edge of the park, they noticed a large crowd had formed.

"What's going on there?" Avery asked, tugging on Tiffany's arm. "Let's go see."

They wormed their way through the crowd, and Avery couldn't help but notice that many of the faces she passed were pale and concerned. That's when she saw the police tape. It was the drunkard from before.

His limp body sat exactly where he had been left when he'd been helped off the ground hours before. There were murmurs traveling fast through the crowd as police did their best to do their job, ignoring the questions of the spectators.

The man's wife was screaming on the sidelines, reaching for her dead husband through loud wails. For a brief moment, the woman tried to fight one of the police officers before collapsing to the ground and sobbing loudly into her hands.

"How terrible," Tiffany whispered.

One of the officers gently lifted her from the ground and ushered her away from the bench. That's when Avery understood precisely what was going on. She recognized the woman's behavior. She'd been there herself not too long ago.

The man was clearly dead. He had hardly moved since he had been placed there. The police tried desperately to usher the crowd away, and

5

Avery took one last glance before respecting their request and walking away.

As she looked at the man, she realized he was tightly grasping a stone in his hand. She could just make out the word *Heron* painted on it in what looked like red lipstick. It seemed like a bizarre thing to reach for in his final moments.

But she had seen him when he fell, and she thought that she would have remembered him clutching onto something so odd.

"Do you think it's possible to drink yourself to death like that?" she asked, suddenly concerned for her own health and safety. "If so, then I need to start taking things easy."

Tiffany scoffed. "Not at a festival like this one, surely. Although, if you ask me, death by wine tasting doesn't sound like a bad way to go. Maybe he bumped his head when he fell?"

"How hard can you bump your head against a soft lawn?" Avery asked, frowning as she thought it all over.

The women walked in silence for a moment before Tiffany shrugged. "Maybe he just had a heart attack or something."

Avery thought it over for a moment, and then decided that a heart attack was her favorite explanation for it. It still didn't really make sense, given the man's behavior before he fell and the fact that a wine festival hardly seemed like the place to have a heart attack. Then again, Avery was no medical professional, and she couldn't think of anything else that made sense, either.

Everybody around them seemed to be discussing it, talking about the dead man and giving their own explanations for what had happened. By the time they reached the car, there were hundreds of theories traveling through the town gossip.

"A death at the wine festival," Tiffany said quietly. "Talk about a buzz kill."

It was a good joke, but Avery had a hard time laughing at it. Tiffany always had the worst timing when it came to humor. She didn't often tell jokes, but when she did, there was a strong chance that the timing was completely inappropriate.

The women hopped into a cab and headed home. The cab driver had already heard the news about the dead body. One of his friends who had attended the festival had phoned him to tell him about it. The gossip really was traveling fast.

Avery groaned. She knew that it meant the following day would be a tough one. She'd likely have to answer the same questions over again, considering that there wasn't often anything new to talk about. She didn't like getting involved with town gossip, but she needed to make some sales. She was running the vineyard, so she needed to make sure that anybody interested in their wines knew she was equally as interested in them. So, she didn't have a choice.

Chapter Two

T he sun cast a bright golden glow over the wintry vineyard. Outside, Avery could hear the sounds of the bustling guesthouse as her guests started waking up. It was a noise that she found comforting. Coming from the city, often the vineyard felt too quiet for her.

The moment she moved, she was aware of the pounding in her head and the dryness in her throat. She swallowed hard, hoping she'd had the common sense to leave a glass of water out for herself before she went to bed. No such luck. "I guess past me doesn't care much about future me... or should I say, present me," she joked.

She moved slowly through the house as she prepared for the day. It had been a long time since she'd last been hungover, and she couldn't quite remember what she was supposed to do about it.

She drank some water, had some coffee, and then decided that her best bet was just to pretend that the hangover simply wasn't there. Although, she wasn't certain it would work.

It wasn't until she spotted the red lipstick in her makeup drawer that she remembered the events from the night before. A man had died at the festival.

As she crossed the damp lawn toward the tasting room, she wondered if, in the history of the festival, anyone had died before. It certainly would be a lot to keep the minds and mouths of the townsfolk busy for the next while.

"Good morning!" Charles' voice sang as she entered the tasting room.

"Shhhh," Avery hushed him as she pressed her fingers to her temples.

"Ah," he chuckled. "I guess you enjoyed the festivities then?"

"A little too much," she admitted. "I didn't see you there, so why do you look so tired?"

Charles poured Avery a cup of coffee and slid it across the counter toward her. She gratefully accepted it, rejoicing as the warm liquid poured down her throat, warming her belly. Charles knew exactly how she liked her coffee. In fact, most days, he made it better than she made it for herself.

"Well," he sighed. "I was getting some pretty decent sleep when I was called in to consult on a dead person. The case is a bit of a mystery."

"Oh," Avery said. "Yes, the drunk guy."

Charles looked at her with a frown on his face. It took her a moment to realize that perhaps referring to him as 'the drunk guy' seemed a little insensitive.

"He bumped the wine out of my hand right before he drunkenly stumbled onto the lawn," she explained. "Completely ruined my favorite blouse."

"How rude of him," Charles teased. "Sorry about your blouse."

"It's okay; we fixed it," Avery said, waving her hand through the air so Charles could continue with his story.

At that moment, Avery remembered how she had stood so that Tiffany could shower her in more wine as a feeble attempt to make the blouse look better. *How embarrassing.* She sunk her head into her hands and wished she could simply sleep the day away.

"Well, they needed me last night because half the police force had attended the festival and was far too unfit to deal with the scene."

Charles had been a police officer before working for Avery at the vineyard. And although she loved having him around, she had often wondered if he missed his job. But now she wondered if he missed it enough to go back to it. She didn't like the thought of that.

Avery chuckled. The mental image of a drunken police force somehow cheered her up enough to lift her head back up and give Charles her full attention.

"So, you consult for them?" she asked.

"Have been for a while," he admitted. "I realized there were some parts of the job that I missed. The best part about consulting is that I don't need to do any paperwork."

"And you don't have to quit your job here," Avery said sternly. "Honestly, I don't know what I would do without you."

Charles took a large sip of his coffee and smiled. It made sense to her now. She had been wondering why he seemed to be more cheerful the past few weeks. She also couldn't help but notice that he'd been in better shape.

"So, you had fun last night?" he asked, changing the subject.

"Yeah, it was alright," she said. "The concert was great, but...you know...a dead body making an appearance is enough to kill any good vibe."

Charles nodded in agreement.

"Who knows, though? Maybe he just had too much fun. It's not a bad way to go," Avery continued.

Charles placed his cup on the counter. "I don't think he died from having too much fun," he said.

Avery perked up. She looked at Charles and immediately knew that there was something he was keeping from her. She knew him well enough to know the sparkle in his eye meant that he had information that she didn't. "What do you mean?" she asked as excitement bubbled up in her belly.

"I mean, I have more information on the dead person than the rest of you, so I can tell you that it wasn't all the fun that killed him."

"So he didn't have a heart attack?" Avery snapped.

Charles sipped his coffee silently as he shook his head. Avery sat upright, swallowing what was left of the coffee in her cup before shuffling her chair closer.

"Give me the details," she said, clasping her hands in front of her.

"I don't know if you want to know," Charles laughed.

She knew he was teasing her. She didn't care. If he had information that was in any way interesting, she wanted it. She had a pretty boring day ahead of her, and she would take anything that could make it more interesting.

"Please, Charles," she begged. "I'll give you half a day off if you tell me."

The bargaining worked. Charles put down his cup and took a step closer to her. "Well, first, the stone seems to have everyone baffled," he said. "It doesn't appear to have any meaning, and they just about had to break his fingers to pry it from his hand."

"Okay, I mean, that's something, but I wouldn't say that's anything particularly interesting," Avery said, almost disappointed.

"That's not all," Charles continued. "They tested the stone for fingerprints and found none. We have no idea where it is from."

Avery sighed. "Okay, so the stone is a bust and a dead-end. I get it. I'm not really sure this information is worth an entire half a day off."

"Well, there's always the suspected manner of death that might prove to be a little interesting," he teased.

"Tell me," Avery said with a bright smile.

"Well, it hasn't been confirmed yet," Charles explained. "But at the moment, it is suspected that the man has been poisoned. He had no obvious signs of a heart attack or any other natural cause of death, but a certain yellow tint in his eyes might point in the direction of poison."

The gasp that escaped Avery was so loud that it echoed through the empty tasting room. "He was murdered?" she asked. "At the festival?!"

Charles leaned back, satisfied with her shocked reaction to the information. "At the moment, it looks that way."

It was too much for Avery to immediately comprehend, and she didn't have the time to ask any more questions. A quick glance at her watch told her she needed to hurry up. It was the second day of the festival, and she needed to make sure everything was ready.

The second day of the festival had a vastly different atmosphere from the first. Whispered rumors about the dead man that had been found circulated unfiltered through the crowds. By the time it was late afternoon,

Avery had heard nearly twenty different theories about how and why the man had died.

As usual, rumors had spread fast among the crowd, and the poor man seemed to be the main topic of discussion for the day. Almost everybody that came to taste the wines of Le Blanc Cellars had asked about him or claimed to have new information on the case.

One man even theorized that the poor man had been a spy that had been taken out for finding out some sensitive information. When Avery asked the man who would be worthy of spying on in such a small community, he simply claimed that he was not at liberty to divulge such information.

By the time the second day of the festival had come to a close, Avery felt like a walking zombie. Her feet were aching in her shoes, her brain was throbbing in her skull, and her eyes were burning in their sockets. But that night, she had signed up to help with the cleaning. So, it was still a while before she could go home and place her head on her pillow. She walked aimlessly, picking up empty wine cups and discarded paper napkins. Her only focus was to get it all done as quickly as possible so she could go home.

She found herself standing in front of the bench where the dead man had been sitting the night before. She wondered what his last moments might have been like. Knowing that he was potentially murdered, she contemplated all the reasons why somebody might have wanted him dead.

She remembered his distraught wife as she cried over her husband. Avery knew the pain the woman must have felt at that moment and felt pity for her. As she stared at the bench, she pictured the woman at home without her husband, knowing he'd never be coming back.

Avery knew well enough what it meant to lose a husband. Her husband, James, had also died, and she had reacted the way the woman at the festival had. Disbelief had poisoned her mind, and she had refused to believe that he could truly be gone. And as soon as she accepted it to be true, grief made its presence and nested itself so deep in her heart that she felt it might never beat the same again.

The memories of Avery's own pain came flooding back too quickly for her to bear. So she turned away from the bench and carried on with the task at hand. She looked for other things to focus on, hoping that all thoughts of the dead man would soon leave her and she could carry on in peace.

She was paying little attention when a small stone caught her eye. It didn't seem out of place, only that she could spot a small red mark on the back of it. Carefully, Avery lifted the stone up and turned it around. The word *The* was written on the stone in the same red that had been spotted on the stone in the dead man's hand. Avery's heart sank. She took a step back and felt a large bump beneath her feet. When she looked down to see what it was, she found another stone. On that stone was written the word *Follow*. She picked it up and held the stones side-by-side. Her heart was pounding as she stared at them, wishing it was only a dream.

"Follow the heron," she whispered.

It wasn't until she looked up from the stones that the situation became even more terrifying. They were lying right beneath the bench that the dead man had been found on. It looked as if they had simply fallen there.

"This can't be good," she whispered as she swallowed hard.

Chapter Three

A very had abandoned all attempts at carrying on with the clean-up of the festival grounds. Instead, with the stones placed neatly on her passenger seat, she raced toward the police station.

"Follow the heron," she said. "What does it mean?!"

As it would be, she was stuck at the world's slowest traffic light, and her thoughts raced ahead of her. *What if that visitor at the stall had been right all along? What if the dead man really had been a spy? Were the stones a message to him or the police?*

She had been so deep in thought that she hadn't realized the traffic light had turned green until an impatient driver in the car behind her honked their horn.

By the time she finally made it to the station, she was breaking out in a sweat. She'd imagined that now that she'd found the stones, she would be in danger, and perhaps that car behind her was following her, and she'd be the next one found dead on the festival grounds.

She slammed the stones down on the counter, causing the police officers on duty to jump.

"Ah, Avery," said the officer. "What brings you here this evening?"

"I-I was doing the clean-up thing at the festival, and I found these two stones," she said, out of breath.

The officer reached for the stones and lifted them up. The moment the red writing was visible, every officer in the room stood up and took a few steps closer. They looked at the stones and then at each other. Then they looked back at Avery. They continued through that cycle a few more times before one of them finally spoke.

"Where did you find these exactly?" he asked.

"They were just lying there," she explained. "I found them by accident while I was cleaning up."

"Yes, I gathered," he said sarcastically. "I mean, where did you find them exactly? Was it near the bench where the man was?"

"Yes," Avery answered. "I found them directly beneath the bench that he was on. How did you not see it when you were there?"

"Forgive us, Avery," he said even more sarcastically. "But when we're dealing with a random death that hasn't been ruled a murder yet, we're not exactly looking for stones. Are we?"

There was silence as the police officer wrote the information down. Then, he pulled out some paper, drew a vague map of the park, and asked Avery to circle exactly where she had found them.

She did so, and the officer showed the rest of them and then put the paper on the counter. Avery immediately felt as if they weren't taking it seriously enough. Nobody was scrambling to make any phone calls or asking for a formal statement. It was nothing like she'd read in her husband's books or watched in a crime series.

"I saw the stone that he had in his hand yesterday. With all three of them, it reads Follow The Heron," she explained. "I figured it would be important to the investigation since they look kinda the same."

The police officer smiled. "Yes, thank you," he said before handing the stones to another officer to tag as evidence. "You did the right thing."

"What do you think it means?" Avery asked, tears welling up in her eyes. "Do you think it has something to do with who murdered him?"

"Who said anything about murder?" the police officer asked with a frown.

Avery rolled her eyes. Every time she had ever dealt with the police, they had been nothing but completely unhelpful. Still, they were the only choice she had. "You literally just mentioned it earlier," she said with a straight face.

"Yes, you did," the officer's colleague chirped from the background.

"Oh," he replied sheepishly. "I see."

Avery had to be careful how much she said. She didn't want to get Charles into any trouble. She had seen how his face had lit up when he spoke about consulting for the police again. She didn't want to do anything to jeopardize that by blurting out information she wasn't supposed to have. She knew she couldn't mention anything about the poisoning. She wasn't supposed to know about that.

"Look," the officer sighed. "Thank you for bringing these in; we've put them in as evidence, and I'm sure we'll look into it."

"You're sure?" Avery asked, her voice wavering slightly from the stress. "You don't seem all that convinced."

"Where you found these stones doesn't make any sense," the officer explained. "At the moment, the likely scenario would be that he simply found the stone and was coincidentally holding it at the time that he was... um...he died."

"What do you mean they don't make sense?" she blurted out. "He had one in his hand, and these were right below where he was seated."

"You have to let us do our jobs," the officer said, unamused. "We're the ones with the training."

Avery knew that it was the end of the conversation. She could tell by the way the officer kept glancing toward the door that he didn't want to answer any more of her questions.

"Thank you for bringing these in, Avery. We'll be sure to look into it," he said. "Just one thing before you go. Please don't get involved in any of this. I've read your husband's books. They're fiction. It's good you brought these to us, but it's up to us now to follow it all up."

Avery sighed and left the station. On the one hand, she understood that perhaps the dead man really had just found the stone and that none of it meant anything. On the other hand, she knew there was something odd about a man potentially being poisoned at the wine festival. None of it made any sense to her, and she didn't entirely like the way the police were handling it. But she was no professional detective, and her hands were tied.

Still, as she drove home, the words *Follow The Heron* replayed over and over in her mind. The words seemed so carefully chosen. They made no sense when put in any other order, and they formed a complete sentence. They were purposefully spelling something out. It seemed like an odd thing to leave lying around.

It didn't seem like the kind of phrase a child would use, either. She replayed the conversation with the police in her mind, too. She couldn't quite decide whether or not they were taking it seriously enough, according to Avery. Then again, how much could they really do?

She felt her eyes start to burn as she considered the grieving wife. She remembered how cold the empty space in her bed had felt when her husband, James, had died. She knew the dead man's wife was going through the same thing.

Avery understood that perhaps she was taking it all too personally out of empathy for the grieving woman. When she thought about it, she could still feel how the tears had burned her cheeks after countless days of crying. It was a dull headache that lingered for weeks, and she knew that the woman she'd seen sobbing on the ground was going to go through all of it. She wondered if they had let the woman know that her husband had potentially been murdered.

By the time Avery got home, she was completely fed up with her own thoughts. Still, she couldn't help but feel that the police should be doing more.

Maybe Charles can help. She looked at the time. It was very late. But she needed to clear her head, and he was the only person who could help her do it. So, she reached for the phone and dialed his number.

"Avery, do you know what time it is?" his sleepy voice answered.

"Yes, Charles, I'm sorry," she said. "Do you have a minute to talk?"

On the other end of the line, she heard the familiar sound of ruffling blankets and the sound of a light switch.

"What's up?" he asked. "Everything okay?"

"Yes, well, kinda...I don't know," she answered. "I was doing the clean-up at the festival grounds tonight when I found two stones with red words on them."

"Like the one the man was holding?" he asked, his voice suddenly sounding much more awake.

"Exactly like those," she answered. "The one read *Follow*, and the other read *The*."

There was a moment of silence before Charles answered. "Follow The Heron?"

"Precisely!" Avery was almost excited when she heard Charles say it. "I took them to the police to hand them in for evidence."

"You don't sound too happy about it," he said.

"Well, I am because I know it was the right thing to do," she said. "And they said they would do what they can."

"But?" Charles asked, anticipating Avery's complaint.

"But," she sighed. "They seem to think that maybe it means nothing at all and it is just coincidence then that he was holding the stone. I was hoping you could nudge them to look into it a little more."

The silence on the other end of the call carried on for a short while. Avery wished she could hurry Charles up. She was sleepy and just needed him to help her so she could relax enough to get into bed. But she also knew that she had woken him up at a ridiculous hour, so she gave him time to formulate his response.

"Where did you find the stones?" he asked.

"At the edge of the park," she answered, realizing that he was asking all the same questions as the first officer.

"You know, Avery, I'd love to help you here, but I'd have to agree with the police," he said. "It is probably just a coincidence."

Avery sighed. "Do you really think so?"

"Well, the words don't mean anything. It has nothing to do with anything at all. It could just be parts of a children's game, and he might have found that stone just the same way that you found the other two."

"Do you know if they have tested for poisoning yet?" she asked.

"Yes," he answered. "Our suspicions were right. The coroner confirmed this morning that he died of poisoning. We're waiting to hear back about exactly what kind of poison."

"So then someone was after him, and the stones could mean something?" Avery pressed.

"If this were a James Bond movie, perhaps. But this is a small-town wine festival. It could have still been an accident."

"So you agree with the police?" she asked bluntly.

"Yes, I agree with them. Now get some rest; it's very late."

"But if it is a murder like we know now," Avery continued, "then surely you have to think the stones are a message of some kind and that they hold some kind of meaning?"

"What exactly do you think they could mean?" he asked, annoyed by her persistence.

Avery thought about it for a while. "I don't know," she answered sheepishly.

"Precisely. It doesn't make sense," Charles snapped. "Now get some rest. I'm going back to bed."

Avery ended the call feeling even more frustrated than she had before. The one person she relied on to take her side was Charles, and he had done nothing to help her. She wasn't really sure why she felt so frustrated about it, either. She knew that they were right.

It did seem kind of odd and as if it meant nothing. But she knew what the dead man's wife was going through, and she knew the grieving woman would want the police to take it a little more seriously.

Chapter Four

A very awoke after a restless night to discover that the sky was gray and overcast—much like her mood. She had spent many hours of the night imagining all the things she could have said to Charles that would either have changed his mind or made him at least as frustrated as she was.

Sprinkles snuggled up to her feet, convincing her to spend just a few more minutes in bed, and she obliged, of course. Besides, Charles was due to stop by and collect some more wine before dropping it off at their stall at the festival, and Avery was in no mood to see him.

Her bed was nice and warm, and Sprinkles did a decent job of keeping her company when she went to sleep. Still, as she stared at the empty space beside her, she couldn't help but feel pity for the dead man's wife.

She remembered the first few mornings after James died and how strange it felt not to hear his soft breathing or cheerful greetings if she'd slept in late. She wondered if the grieving woman she'd seen that night at the festival was feeling the same way. *Of course, she is.*

Avery dragged her feet through the house to start her morning routine. Feed Sprinkles, have some coffee, eat breakfast, and have another cup of coffee. Then, she would probably stare out the window for a few minutes before speeding through a shower to get ready. There wasn't enough coffee in the world that day that could fix her mood, but at the very least, she was caffeinated and had a full belly. Eggs and smoked salmon always hit the spot just right.

Avery needed to work one more day at the festival, and then Charles would take over the stall. She very much looked forward to finishing her responsibilities there. She could feel the tiredness seeping into the center of her bones, and all she wanted was a day off to sit and do nothing.

A pile of books had been taunting her for weeks. She'd been threatening to read them, but all of her time had gone to prepare for the festivities, and now the large pile of books just seemed like a tedious task on her to-do list.

Normally, her morning routine included a stop at the wine room to greet Charles and make sure he was prepared for the day. But not once had he actually needed anything from her, and she was certain if she went to see him, she wouldn't be able to bite her tongue.

She had been so certain when she phoned him the night before that he'd take her side and see things from her perspective. But he didn't and it irked her. She also couldn't shake the thought that she had annoyed him somehow.

Then, the thought of him finding her annoying only made her even more upset. The combination of all her twisted emotions toward the entire situation made her feel confused and further frustrated and only worsened her mood.

As Avery watched through the window, the gray clouds kept rolling in, and the sky only got darker. She wondered if it would mean a quieter day at the festival. If it rained, then the day might be a complete bust, and she wasn't sure she could handle something like that. They had been doing so well; she was eager to keep that ball rolling.

She thought about all the feet that had walked through the park recently and how many of them could have spotted the stones she had found. If they were left there by somebody else, then somebody would know something about it. Surely it wouldn't be too hard for the police to simply ask for more information on the stones? Of course, they wouldn't, as they'd already decided that the stones were simply a coincidence.

Frustrated and eager to let it go, Avery decided to shower and prepare for the day. As she washed her hair, she tried desperately to rinse away all thoughts of the murder and the stones. She had other things to focus on. But it was no use. By the time she stepped out of the shower, she had already envisioned multiple false scenarios and conversations, and she was only more irritated with Charles and frustrated with the entire situation at hand.

"That's it," she mumbled. "I'm just going to have to prove him wrong."

With a determined stride, she marched over to her laptop. It took her a few minutes to choose the right font and font size, but by the time she was done printing the notice, she was pleased with it.

"If the words *Follow The Heron* mean anything to you, come and see me at Le Blanc Cellars," she read out loud as she held the page up in front of her. "Ha!" she cheered. "This is ridiculous, but it just might work!"

She read it through a couple more times before placing it carefully on the passenger seat of her car and making her way to the park. She smiled the entire way as she drove. She was impressed with her plan and certain that it would yield results that would force Charles and the entire police force to eat their words.

You're his boss. You could just instruct him to believe you, and he'd have to do it...no, that would be stupid. Why do you care so much about what Charles thinks? She forced the question from her mind. It had been replaying for hours, and she didn't want to take the time to determine the answer. Mainly because she was certain the answer was a reality that she was not yet ready to face.

Avery scanned the notice board at the festival to find the perfect spot for her poster. She wondered first how many people actually looked at the board. She knew that she hadn't looked at it once since the festival began. Most of what was up there were advertisements for music lessons or snake removals, things of that nature. Her notice would seem completely out of place. But perhaps that was best.

She was about to pin the page to the board when another thought crossed her mind. *What if the police see this? Could I get into any kind of trouble?* Avery scanned the field around her, looking for any sign of their blue uniform. She took her time, too. She wanted to be absolutely certain that no police officer saw her putting the sign up. When she was certain the coast was completely clear, she neatly pinned the sign to the board.

She took a step back, admiring her work. She'd printed the letters in bright red, similar to those that had been written on the stones, and the words *Follow The Heron* were in bold. A wide smile crossed her face as she read through it a few more times.

"And now we wait," she said quietly.

At that moment, a familiar voice called out to her. It was Tiffany. Avery swung around to find the source of the voice and spotted Tiffany waving at her from the line at the coffee cart.

"Can I buy you a cup?" Tiffany asked as Avery approached to greet her.

"Oh, please, I'm dying for another cup," Avery answered cheerfully.

They waited together until they had their cups of coffee. Avery was about to sip hers when an unexpected and intrusive thought popped into her head. *What if he'd been poisoned by the coffee?* She hesitated for a moment, but when the rich aroma of the dark roast coffee filled her lungs, she decided it was worth the risk and eagerly took a large sip.

"Has the mayor been by your stall yet?" Tiffany asked.

Avery shook her head. "No, I haven't seen him at the festival at all," she answered.

"Hmmm," Tiffany responded. "That's odd. He's never missed a year. Do you think he's maybe ill?"

Avery shrugged. She didn't know, and she didn't care. The mayor's presence at the festival meant little to her. As long as she was making sales, she didn't really care.

Hours had passed and every time somebody approached the Le Blanc Cellars stall, Avery got excited. She kept waiting for one of them to say that they knew about the stones or that they had some information she was looking for.

But they all just took their sips of wine and left. With the overcast weather threatening to rain them out, it was a particularly quiet day at the festival. The crowd was small, and most of the people who attended were only there to socialize. So, sales were low too.

The time moved by slowly as she waited for someone to come and give her the information she needed to prove Charles wrong. Eventually, she felt like she should simply give up, pack up her stall, and call it for the day. It was by far the quietest day they'd had since the festival started. But then it dawned on her. What exactly was she expecting them to say? If they did, in fact, have any information, why would they be willing to share it with her?

That's when an even more terrifying thought danced around in her mind. *What if the stones really are part of the murder? Now I've put up a sign that practically tells the world I know about it. Will they poison me next?*

A wave of nausea washed over her as she thought about it even further. It had been so foolish of her to think something like that might have worked. She could have gotten herself into heaps of trouble, not only with the police but with the actual murderer.

The whole thought of it made her dizzy, and she rushed over to the notice board. She ripped the sign off, hoping nobody had seen her doing it, and stuffed it in her pocket.

"What were you thinking?" she whispered as she walked back in the direction of her stall.

By the time she made it back to pour the next wine tasting for the newest eager visitor, she had decided without a doubt that it had been entirely Charles' fault. He was the reason that she was being so foolish about it all.

If he had just agreed with her and taken her side, then she wouldn't have been so determined to prove him wrong. Avery knew it was unreasonable to put the blame on Charles, but it made her feel better.

Then, it only made her more upset.

How dare he push me so far that I do something so daft? It was an absurd thought, and she knew it. And yet, it made sense to her. Charles was the reason she was behaving this way. If he had only done a better job of supporting her beliefs, she would have slept better, behaved better, and probably made more sales that day. That's how she felt, anyway.

Chapter Five

The coffee shop was packed, and Avery was having a hard time speaking over the noise of the crowd. It had been years since the town had been that busy, and Avery and Tiffany had walked all over just to find a restaurant with a table available for them.

Inside the restaurant, music was filtering evenly. The entire space was filled with green plants, and the smell of coffee hung in the air. It made Avery feel relaxed, and she was happy for a little bit of privacy among the plants. She could catch Tiffany up on everything that had happened.

"Where did you find the other two stones?" Tiffany asked in horror as she listened eagerly to Avery's story.

"On the outskirts of the park; that's why everyone seems to think it's just coincidence or whatever," Avery answered between mouthfuls of her delicious lunch. "If you ask me, it's the furthest thing from a coincidence."

"You know he's just doing his job, right?" Tiffany asked. "He's acting like a police officer."

"That's fine," Avery said. "But he's supposed to be my friend too. Couldn't he just take my side this one time?"

"He's always been on your side," Tiffany laughed. "Honestly, I don't know why this has you so upset."

"I don't know either," Avery sighed. "I guess I just think there's more to this than they want to admit. It doesn't make sense for it to be a coincidence."

"It doesn't make sense at all, in any sense," Tiffany agreed.

"Do you think I've overreacted a little?" Avery frowned as she reached for her coffee. "I haven't spoken to Charles again since."

"Maybe a little," Tiffany said with a shrug. "But that's normal. You care about each other, and you wanted him to hear you out. I get it."

We care about each other.

Tiffany was absolutely correct. Avery cared too much about what Charles thought. That's why she had been so upset. It should have been obvious to her, but it wasn't. She just wanted him to take her seriously, and when he didn't, it made her feel foolish.

Why doesn't he just listen to me? Surely he doesn't think that I am too stupid to understand it all? We've known each other some time now, at the very least, you'd think he'd properly look into it for me.

She was about to voice this revelation when Tiffany suddenly spotted something to her left and pointed at it with her knife. "Isn't that the guy's wife? The one that was crying so much? She was screaming like mad, remember?"

Avery brushed past the insensitivity in Tiffany's voice and glanced over to where she had been pointing. Tiffany was right. The dead man's wife was sitting at a table not too far from them. She paged through a design magazine, flipping cheerfully through the pages. Then, she received a phone call and answered it. Avery watched in awe as the woman joked and laughed with whoever was on the other end of the call.

"She seems a little too cheerful for someone who just lost her husband," Avery commented. "I mean, now isn't the time to be cracking jokes."

"Maybe that's how she copes? With jokes and stuff," Tiffany said.

"Trust me," Avery whispered. "I've been where she is. Nothing is funny when you've just lost the love of your life."

Tiffany cast her eyes downward and put her knife back down on her plate. "You're right; I'm sorry," she said.

Avery looked back at the woman who continued to flip through the magazine while she spoke on the phone. From what Avery could hear, she was discussing an upcoming holiday to the Maldives. The entire scenario made Avery's blood run cold. Nothing about it seemed normal or right to her.

The woman then lifted her hand and pushed her sleek blonde hair off her neck and over her shoulder, revealing a tattoo on the back of her neck. Avery stared at it for a while. She could make out the shape of two wings that wrapped around the back of the woman's neck.

"It's a heron," Tiffany said sternly. "Look."

"No, surely not," Avery said with an uneasy chuckle. "It could be any kind of bird, honestly."

"Look closer; I'm telling you it's a heron," Tiffany pressed.

Avery narrowed her eyes in an attempt to focus on the tattoo. But she knew that Tiffany was right. The dead man's wife had a large tattoo of a heron on the back of her neck. That could not possibly be a coincidence.

What Avery felt was a mix of excitement and panic. She had stumbled onto information that was potentially groundbreaking to the case, and it made her feel bad for the dead man. Then again, it was enough to prove Charles wrong.

"What do we do with this?" Tiffany asked. "Do we go to the police? Should we call Charles?"

"I don't know. We need to know more before we accuse her of anything," Avery said. "Let's run this past the Stammtisch."

"I'm on it."

Tiffany was the newest member of the Stammtisch, and the group had only gotten closer over the last few months. They were a group of women who all loved wine and had very few things in common, but they got together regularly and had a good time anyway.

A few hours later, Avery's living room was filled with the group of women, who listened eagerly as she filled them all in on what had happened.

It was the classic, perfect mix of characters. Eleanor was the founder of the group. She was feisty and had no problem speaking her mind. Deb, married to a wealthy vineyard owner, spent most of her day visiting with friends. She was a walking tabloid for anything that was happening in the town. Camille was often present, but most of the time, her mind was somewhere else. Still, she joined in when it seemed to count. Tiffany was the newest in the group. She was Avery's childhood friend, and she just seemed happy that she had a reason to be social.

"Why haven't you told Charles yet?" Eleanor asked. "About the lady and her tattoo?"

"Well," Avery searched for the right answer. "He's working at my stall at the festival today, and I need more proof. I mean, we only think it was a heron on the back of her neck. It could have been a crane or something."

"Pfft," Deb scoffed. "Please, Avery, you know better. You need to trust your gut."

"I'm pretty sure it's a heron," Tiffany added.

"Well, I just think I need to be absolutely sure, and besides, I want to slam some really solid evidence in Charles' face. I can't wait to see his reaction," Avery said excitedly.

"Why do you care so much about what he thinks?" Camille asked. "Just go tell him, and let the police do their jobs."

"I have to agree with Avery," Tiffany stepped in. "Before we accuse the woman of being involved in her husband's death, let's just be sure about it first."

The women spent the next few hours going through all sorts of possibilities in excruciating detail. They discussed her body language at the restaurant while one of them googled what it all meant. They looked up photographs of herons as Avery and Tiffany tried desperately to remember the details of the tattoo.

"What was she like when she learned of her husband's death?" Eleanor asked.

"She was screaming and crying and on the ground," Avery said, exasperated at that point.

"Crying?" Eleanor asked. "Were there any real tears? Or did she just look like she was crying?"

Avery thought about it for a while. "Now that you mention it, I saw her scream and put up a fairly decent fight against the police. But then, she just stopped and let them take her away."

"But were there actual wet tears, though?" Eleanor asked again.

"Honestly," Avery answered. "I was a little too distracted by the dead guy to be paying close enough attention."

The sun was already setting when one of them finally asked. "So what should we do about this?"

"We need to gather more information, but where do we start?" Eleanor answered.

"We don't even know where to find her," Deb added.

The group of women fell silent for a moment as they all thought it over. Avery enjoyed the brief moment of silence; it had been a busy few days, and she was tired.

"The festival," Avery finally clicked. "Tomorrow is the last day...the day of the auction. Everybody goes to the auction."

"You're right!" Eleanor cheered. "We'll all go and keep an eye out for her. If we spot her, we wait until she leaves and follow her to know where she is staying."

"That's an excellent idea!" Camille agreed.

With that, it was decided. The group of women would have their own little top-secret operation. Once one of them had determined where the woman was staying, they would let Avery know. She would then go and speak to the woman, offering her support and condolences. Hopefully, she would be invited in for coffee, and then she could get as much information about the woman as possible and ask about the tattoo on the back of her neck. She would then be able to take that information and rub it in Charles' face.

There was still so much that didn't make sense to Avery. She thought about how her late husband would write his crime novels. There was just too much missing information when it came to the woman with the heron tattoo that she couldn't seem to piece together anything logical. For one thing, there was no motive. Unhappy marriages end in divorce, not murder. Still, she knew she was on the verge of getting the information she needed.

That night, she struggled to fall asleep. She spent most of the night fantasizing over all the ways she might take the evidence she was certain she'd gather and show it to Charles. She imagined what his face might look like when he learned that she was right and he was wrong.

She hadn't spoken to him again since the phone call about the stones. Some part of her missed him through all of this. He had a way of guiding her to the right answer—even when she didn't want to hear it.

The women of the Stammtisch were a great support, but they easily got carried away, and they were a lot of energy to deal with all at once. At least when she went to Charles, he was always calm, quiet, and eager to listen.

But still, the way he'd so easily taken somebody else's side had her unreasonably upset. Their plan had been solidified, and she knew exactly what to do. The next time she spoke to Charles, she'd have a little more than just speculation, and she'd hopefully convince him to believe her.

In the meantime, she would take instruction from some stones and follow the heron.

Chapter Six

It was a beautiful sunny day when Avery opened her eyes again. With a plan of action, she found it easier to drag her tired body out of bed and get prepared for the day. That evening was the auction, and she was determined to follow through with their plan. There was only one thing that she was nervous about. She needed to figure out what exactly she would say to the lady with the heron tattoo when she got the chance. She knew she needed to somehow get something out of her that would pass as evidence.

But what would that be exactly? Perhaps she only needed to prove that the woman wasn't all too sad about her husband's passing at all. She wasn't sure yet, but she needed to come up with something. If the woman really was involved, she couldn't say anything that would make it obvious that she knew about it. That could put her own life in danger or the woman could simply skip town, and the entire thing would be a bust.

It felt as if she was on one of her favorite crime shows or perhaps part of one of her late husband's crime novels. Part of it was exciting, but it mostly made her nervous. She would have preferred to have no part in it, but she was far too stubborn for that.

By the time the evening rolled in, and the auction had begun, Avery still didn't know what she would say, but she had run out of time. At any minute, the lady with the heron tattoo would make an appearance, and the plan would be set in motion.

She couldn't concentrate on anything else as she scanned the sea of people over and over again, looking for the woman. She realized that it might be more difficult than she'd anticipated. Everyone had dressed up for the auction, and she wasn't entirely confident she knew what the woman's face looked like.

Without the heron tattoo visible, she couldn't even be certain if she had the right woman at all. If the woman had her hair down, how would they know it was her? These were all things they had not considered when they had made the plan, and it was only making Avery more nervous.

The auction had turned out to be a rather extravagant event. The section of the park where the auction was being held had been decorated with balloons and red velvet chairs. There were waiters carrying trays with wine and bubbly. It seemed to be the event of the year. To one side, a violinist in a flashy black dress covered in sequins played smooth jazz. There had even been a makeshift cigar lounge set up in one place with large leather sofas and a Persian rug.

As she looked through the crowd, she spotted the women of the Stammtisch also glancing through the auction attendees. They were sticking to the plan.

Who knows? Maybe I'll get lucky, and she'll have her hair up. Avery took a deep breath and tried to stay as focused as possible. She walked around the back of the crowd, slowly inspecting every blonde woman she could spot. Most of them she knew, so that took them out of the lineup automatically.

Later, after the auction, it was time for everyone to socialize. Then, it became even more difficult to look for the woman with the heron tattoo. People mingled and walked around each other constantly. Many people stopped Avery to have a conversation with her, drawing her attention away from the task at hand.

By the end of the evening, the ladies were all defeated. It seemed that the woman with the heron tattoo never made an appearance. This meant that their plan had not worked, and since it was their one and only plan, she no longer knew what to do. Which, in turn, meant that she'd have to go to the police and Charles, tell them about the heron tattoo, and hope that they'd see it the way that she did.

Just to be certain, Avery waited at the sidelines as everyone left the field, hoping that perhaps she'd simply missed the woman. But by the time Avery was the last one standing, it had become clear that there was no hope.

The lights that hovered above the festivities were switched off, tables and banners were packed up, one final cleanup was done throughout the park, and the festival officially came to an end.

To Avery, it was a bittersweet moment. It had been a successful festival. But she had hoped to be able to take the days following to relax and simply enjoy the quiet time. Instead, she knew that she'd be agonizing over the dead man and his wife with the heron tattoo.

When she got home, she poured herself a generous glass of wine and fixed herself a plate of hot food. On her own, she celebrated the success of it all. Le Blanc Cellars had done really well in festival sales, the guesthouse was still fully booked for a few more nights, and the business was generally a success.

Her home was her favorite place on Earth. She'd spent weeks decluttering it of anything that had belonged to previous owners or her parents who had lived in the house before her. She had bought decorative items to make it feel more like her own place. Avery had rearranged almost every piece of furniture until the spaces were barely recognizable. At home, she hid away from the rest of the world and was allowed to do whatever she wanted. This mostly consisted of eating, reading, and watching movies.

It felt odd to celebrate alone, but the only person she felt she should celebrate with was Charles, and she still hadn't spoken to him. She wouldn't know what to talk to him about other than the woman with the heron tattoo, and if he didn't react the way she wanted him to, it would only have made things worse.

After her wine and meal, she got ready for bed but not before checking her phone. She saw a few text messages. Some were from her parents, telling her about the latest political and sports news. There were messages on the Stammtisch group thread saying nobody had spotted the heron tattoo. There was also a message from Charles. She considered, for a moment, ignoring the message but found herself clicking on the chat anyway. Thankfully, the message was positive.

Excellent work! The festival was a great success. You should be proud.

She was about to respond when she saw another message come through from Camille. It was late, and she had just caught the first words when the message popped up at the top of the screen. It was enough to catch Avery's attention, and she switched instead to the chat with Camille.

I found her.

The message was followed by a location pin. Avery's heart skipped a beat. She was so certain that the woman hadn't attended the auction. A few messages back and forth with Camille answered all of her questions.

Avery learned that Camille had spotted the woman grabbing takeout at a local restaurant. She followed her back to where she was staying and immediately texted Avery. She wasted no time letting the rest of the Stammtisch women know that the woman with the heron tattoo had been found.

Then, Avery found herself opening the chat with Charles again. She felt that she had to respond to him somehow. But she didn't know what to say. She typed message after message, only to delete each and every one of them.

In the end, she just closed the chat and said nothing. She knew it wasn't the right thing to do and it likely might upset him. She just needed to wait a little while longer until she had gotten enough out of the woman with the heron tattoo to talk to Charles again. Without it, she knew that she might snap at him, and she really didn't want to hurt his feelings. She didn't want to put him in an uncomfortable situation either if she pressured him about the three stones that were linked to the murder case.

For a while, she did her best to sleep. But it was no use. There was too much on her mind, and she was too excited. Instead, she watched movie after movie in an attempt to speed up time until she eventually fell asleep on the couch with Sprinkles pressed tightly against her legs.

Chapter Seven

A very and Tiffany parked the car just across the street and a few doors down from where the woman with the heron tattoo was apparently staying. It was a pleasant night, and Avery couldn't help but think she would rather be at home, sipping wine out by the garden. Instead, she was sitting uncomfortably in her car, waiting for something to happen. It seemed silly, but she was stubborn and determined to prove herself right.

"What will you even say to her?" Tiffany asked. "It just seems odd. I mean, I get why we're doing it, but where do you even start?"

"I've been wondering the same thing," Avery answered. "What exactly are we trying to get from her? What would be good enough evidence?"

The two women were clearly not qualified to be staking out any person or home, yet they would both see it through to the end.

"Maybe you just need to find out more about what their relationship was like?" Tiffany suggested. "If she tells you it wasn't a happy marriage, then you have a motive. Wouldn't that be enough?"

"I don't know," Avery said. "Let me think about it. I don't think I'll get any answers soon, though. I might have to just wing it once I get in there."

"That's if you can get her to let you in."

Tiffany was right, and Avery felt like she was in way over her head.

"We don't know if she's the actual one that did it, but I do think she's involved," Avery added. "The stones only said to follow the heron, not that she did it."

"Still," Tiffany said quietly. "She might have done it."

Avery didn't want to think about that too much, considering she would have to go and have a conversation with the woman and hopefully convince her to let Avery into her home.

"Should I have brought binoculars or something?" Avery asked quietly.

"Binoculars?" Tiffany asked. "What on Earth for? I thought you were just going to talk to the woman!"

"I don't know," Avery laughed. "I have no idea what I'm doing!"

Now that they were there and actually watching the woman's house, it occurred to Avery that they might be breaking a bunch of laws themselves. If they got caught, she was certain that they could be charged for something. She was only moments away from calling the entire plan off when Tiffany's eyes lit up.

"Wait! There she is!" Tiffany said, pointing at the house where the woman was staying.

The woman walked to her car. She was dressed up in a short dress with high heels. She had her makeup done and her hair up, exposing the tattoo on the back of her neck. She was not dressed for a quiet night at home and most certainly not dressed like a grieving widow.

Avery was certain that by now, the woman would have heard from the police that her husband's death was a murder. It should be a devastating blow to any woman. It required sweatpants and an oversized shirt, not a form-fitting dress and stilettos.

"Where do you think she's going dressed like that?" Tiffany asked.

"I don't know. But I think we should follow her."

They waited for the woman to get ahead a little before turning on their car. Keeping their distance, they followed her through the streets of the town until they stopped at a gas station.

"She didn't dress up to get gas, I can promise you that," Tiffany joked.

They waited a while until they spotted her leaving again. Then, they followed her a little further through the town.

The town was fairly quiet after the festival. Most of the tourists had already left, and those who were residents were likely resting. It was easy to follow her, and they had little risk of losing her, so they were able to keep their distance.

"This feels a little silly, doesn't it?" Tiffany eventually asked. "I feel like I'm in a detective show, like those on television."

"I know," Avery laughed. "We're being absolutely ridiculous. But I don't know what else to do."

"I should have brought some coffee. I didn't think it was going to take this long," Tiffany teased.

"We'll stop for some wine when this is over. I'm sure I'll need it," Avery promised.

"If we ever find ourselves in this situation again, promise me you'll pack some snacks," Tiffany said.

The two women laughed at the thought. Avery hoped with every fiber in her being that they would never find themselves following a suspect in a murder case through the small streets of their hometown ever again.

Then again, too many strange things had happened since she moved back from the city. She couldn't guarantee that it wouldn't happen again.

"Do you know what's been bothering me?" Tiffany asked.

Avery shrugged. "I'm no mind reader," she answered sarcastically.

"Do you remember when that man bumped you? And it spilled all the wine?" she asked.

"You mean the dead guy?" Avery laughed. "A little hard to forget."

"Well, do you remember what he was saying when he fell? He was rambling on about something, saying that *she* had done it," Tiffany continued.

"I vaguely remember that," Avery replied. "I think I was too upset about my blouse."

"Well, don't you think that's some evidence right there?" Tiffany said. "Think about it. He rambles on about this *she* that has supposedly *done* something. Then, a few hours later, he's found dead."

"I think I see where you're going with this," Avery mumbled.

"So, what if he didn't fall because he was drunk like we originally thought?" Tiffany continued. "What if he fell because he was poisoned, and he was trying to tell everyone who had done it?"

The thought made Avery's blood run cold. She gripped the steering wheel hard as she thought about it. Tiffany was right. He might have been trying to tell them what was going on, and everyone had simply treated him like a drunk tourist.

It was a terrible thought. Perhaps the man was trying to ask for help. Who knows how difficult it might be to actually talk when there is poison in your blood? She didn't like that thought one bit.

"I feel terrible," Avery said as they rounded another corner.

"Me too," Tiffany said. "I can't imagine what that must have been like for him."

"How awful," Avery whispered. "He might have been a nuisance, but he still deserves justice," Avery said. "We need to get this evidence so we can make this right."

"She's stopping," Tiffany said. "Isn't that the mayor's house?"

They stopped a few houses down and turned off their lights. Avery was no expert in following others, but she'd watched enough crime shows to know she needed to turn the lights of her car off if she didn't want to be spotted.

They watched as the woman with the heron tattoo spent a moment in the car fixing her hair and makeup. Everything about her behavior was odd to Avery. She couldn't quite figure out what the woman was doing.

"What is she doing?" Tiffany asked.

"I don't know. But I don't have a good feeling about this."

When the woman finally stepped out of the car, they noticed a bottle of red wine sticking out of her purse. Avery knew from the seal on top of the bottle that it was a red wine from Le Blanc Cellars. She hated the idea that a woman who was potentially involved in the murder of her own husband would favor the wine from her winery.

She rang the doorbell at the mayor's house.

"You can see the tattoo pretty well. Maybe you should take a photograph," Tiffany suggested.

Avery hurried to get her phone out of her bag and zoomed in as far as she could. She had the woman's head and shoulders in the frame and was about to take a photograph when the mayor pulled the door open. Avery snapped the photo just as the mayor pressed his lips to the woman's.

The two women gasped loudly as they watched the situation unfold in front of them.

"Hardly seems like a grieving widow to me," Tiffany said.

The kiss was no ordinary old-people-greeting-kiss either. Neither of them was old enough to warrant one of those, and it lingered for a solid few seconds before the mayor snuggled into the nape of her neck.

"Please tell me you got that on camera," Tiffany said with a hint of excitement in her voice.

"You bet I did. I got a great shot." She presented Tiffany with an image of the woman and the mayor kissing, with the tattoo clearly in view.

"Ha!" Tiffany cheered. "Busted!" Tiffany's excitement quickly fell, and a frown crossed her face. "That scoundrel," she mumbled.

The women sped off, leaving the mayor and the tattooed woman in the distance. Avery wasn't sure if the mayor had spotted them leaving, but she didn't care. She had enough evidence to give the woman a solid motive, prove herself right, and prove Charles and the police wrong.

She felt odd for feeling so smug about it, but she didn't care. She simply needed people to know that there was more to her than meets the eye and that the next time she came with what she felt was important information, they should take it more seriously.

"I'm too excited to sleep," Tiffany said when Avery dropped her back home. "I know it sounds ridiculous because we're talking about the death of a man here, but maybe I should change careers. Suddenly, being a cop sounds like fun."

Avery laughed. "Don't get ahead of yourself. You forget how bored we were for eighty percent of that experience."

She told her best friend goodnight and headed home. Avery's head was swimming with theories and thoughts that she had no control over. Then, a familiar sinking feeling hit the pit of her stomach.

What if the woman wasn't simply involved somehow? What if she is the murderer? What if they saw your car leave? What if they recognize your car and know that you've seen them? What have you gotten yourself into, Avery?

Chapter Eight

The vineyard was dead quiet, and the only source of light came from Avery's living room. There, she scrolled between the photographs, admiring every detail of them. She relived the events of the night over and over in her mind, trying to comprehend it all.

It had been a remarkably successful stakeout. She felt as if she were watching one of her late husband's crime novels playing out right in front of her eyes. She had been like one of his characters that night, and the adrenaline had not yet worn off.

It was a little before midnight when Avery eventually reached for her phone and sent Charles the photographs. She had intended to wait a while before showing them to him, but she couldn't sleep and didn't want to wait any longer. There were too many thoughts plaguing her mind, and she couldn't keep them all to herself any longer. Once the photos were sent, she got up and headed for bed. Her plan was to sleep so that she could speed up time. She had assumed that Charles would only see them in the morning, but a few minutes later, her phone rang.

"I assume you got the photographs," she answered.

"What the hell is this?" he asked.

That was it. There was no greeting, no excitement from him. Instead, he sounded annoyed. Avery had never heard him talk to her like that before, and she didn't enjoy it one bit.

"I took them myself, if you must know," she said. "Did you see the tattoo?"

"Yes, it's a bird. Is that the mayor?"

He spoke to her the same way her teachers had spoken to her in school when she just didn't understand the lesson.

"It's a *heron*," Avery said quite proudly. "So, I followed it. Just like the stones suggested." It sounded ridiculous when she said it out loud and not nearly as cool as she thought it would, which caused the frustration to build and created a small localized headache on the left side of her head. She raised two fingers to her temple and massaged her head in a circular motion.

There was a brief silence on the other end of the line. A part of her hoped that he wouldn't say anything else. But she knew that it was wishful thinking.

"You didn't answer my question," he said. "Is that the mayor?"

Avery sighed. "Yes, that is the mayor...who is quite clearly in a relationship with the dead guy's wife. If you ask me, that's a motive for murder." Avery smiled. She felt quite pleased about it all. She was certain that Charles would be grateful for the evidence. They didn't have a lot of time to solve the murder before the victim's body was supposed to be returned to his hometown. Now, she could help them somehow.

"Avery, please tell me you didn't sneak outside the mayor's house and take photographs of him without his consent." Charles almost sounded like he was begging; he was so desperate for it not to be true. And Avery hadn't looked at it that way. She had just assumed that she was doing the right thing and wanted to shove it in Charles' face.

"I guess when you put it that way, it doesn't sound too good."

"I don't have to tell you that it is illegal to do that without the necessary paperwork. Surely you know that? You're not a police officer, Avery. Why didn't you tell me that you were going to do this? I would have advised you against it."

Avery sighed. "You didn't even believe me that the stones had anything to do with the case in the first place. Why would you have believed me about this?"

"It's not that I didn't believe you, Avery. It was just that the police officers made a good point. At the time, there was no reason to believe the stones were all that relevant to solving the case," he explained. "But if you had told me that you found the victim's wife with a heron tattoo, I definitely would have suggested that they look into it."

"Well, I saved you the trouble," Avery said proudly.

"What if you had been caught?"

Avery couldn't believe it. He was still arguing with her about it. Better yet, he was upset about something that might have happened but didn't. So, he was really upset about absolutely nothing.

"I didn't get caught, though," she said smugly. "And you're welcome, by the way."

"I can't do anything with this, Avery," he said. By that point, it sounded as if he wanted to shout from frustration. "If I send this to the police officers, they're going to ask me where I got it from, and you'll immediately be in trouble. Besides, you're going in the wrong direction."

"Not according to the stones," she said, feeling smug.

"It's precisely the stones that I'm referring to," he explained. "We found where they probably came from."

"Oh?"

"They're a type of pond stone," he said. "There's one shop here that sells them, and apparently they've only ever sold them to one person. The postman."

"So is he a suspect?" she asked.

"Yes, and the police would love to look into him," Charles said, annoyed. "But all this with the mayor is a problem, Avery. You've really made a mess now."

Avery didn't know how to respond. She understood what she did was wrong, but she never realized that it might have been for nothing. She just wanted to show off to Charles and prove to him that it was worth taking her seriously. Instead, by doing that, she had interfered with a case, and none of it even made a difference.

"Alright," Charles eventually said after a long silence. "This is good evidence, Avery. It needs to be sent to the police, but they can't know it came from you."

Avery smiled a little. "So what do we do?"

"You can put in an anonymous tip with these photographs. I'll send you all the information on how to do it."

"That's a great idea," she said hopefully. "So then it isn't all for nothing? Do you think they'll arrest her or something?"

"I don't know," Charles said through a loud and annoyed sigh. "But if this doesn't work, and they discover that we both have seen the photographs...Avery, if they know you took this, and that I knew about it and didn't say anything... It's not that the police would do anything, but the mayor could take legal action against both of us."

"Do you think he'd do that?" she asked foolishly.

"Wouldn't you?" he snapped. "Please tell me that you understand how reckless this was?"

"Yessss, Charles," Avery whined as she rolled her eyes.

"Why didn't you just tell me?" he asked again, this time with more desperation in his voice. "You haven't spoken to me in days. Is this what you've been up to?"

"Well, yes and no," she answered. "There's been the festival. I suppose me and the girls did spend about two days on this plan," she admitted.

"You and the girls?"

"Yeah, the ladies from the Stammtisch. They helped me track down where she was staying."

Charles let out his longest, breathiest sigh yet. Avery could hear him grinding his teeth on the other end of the call. "Just hope none of them talk about the photographs around town because then it will certainly lead back to you," he said.

"Not all of them know about the mayor yet. Only Tiffany. She was with me," Avery said.

"Well, tell her to keep quiet about it," he snapped. "She's a smart girl; she'll understand how illegal this is."

Avery frowned. Had Charles implied that she wasn't smart? After all, she hadn't considered the legalities of it until Charles had mentioned it only a few minutes earlier. Her cheeks got warm as she started to get angry again.

"Alright, I'll tell her. So, what do I do now?" she asked, unable to hide the irritation in her voice.

"Don't worry about it. I've thought about it some more, and I'll send the anonymous tip for you. I'll keep you posted if anything happens or we've been found out," he said.

"And what about the postman?" she asked.

"Oh no," he said. "I'm not giving you any more information about this. You'll only get involved and cause me even more trouble."

Without saying goodbye or goodnight, Charles hung up the phone. Avery couldn't believe it. He no longer trusted her at all. He didn't even think she could handle putting in an anonymous tip. How hard could it be?

Still, her conversation with him had made her feel nervous. He was right. She had essentially stalked a woman and taken inappropriate photographs of the mayor. What was she thinking? How had she allowed herself to become so irrational?

After a couple of cups of tea and a few hours of thinking it over, she decided it was Charles' fault. He was the one who had made her so irrational. Avery hadn't quite worked out why she had reacted so extremely, but she was satisfied that he was at fault.

With that, she climbed into bed and rolled around for hours, agonizing over all the ways she could have handled their conversation differently.

When morning finally came around and the vineyard came to life, she dragged her near-zombie body out of bed. Avery could feel the bags under her eyes every time she blinked and did her best not to cry when she saw her exhausted reflection in the mirror.

She was so consumed with trying to get her concealer right that she almost completely ignored the sound of her phone buzzing. However, when she saw Charles' name out of the corner of her eye, she dropped everything she was doing to read the message.

Anonymous tip was well-received. They're bringing her in for questioning. Don't forget—nobody can know it was you.

Avery was so pleased that she did a little dance to celebrate. She was right, and that was all that mattered. The stones had indeed meant something, and now there was proof of it. As she turned to face her reflection again, she wondered if Charles had slept at all.

She imagined him staring at his own tired, stressed-out reflection in the mirror, and her heart dropped. She had caused him a lot of trouble, and he had every right to be upset with her. Yet, she felt that she was the one who deserved to be angry, simply because he didn't react exactly the way she would have liked him to.

Avery understood better the arguments that she and her mother had when she was growing up. When her mother had expected her to be apologetic, she had been unbothered. Those were the biggest fights her family had ever had.

It turned out she was more like her mother than she'd hoped.

Chapter Nine

No amount of pacing or distractions could stop her mind from agonizing over it all. She had gone to the wine room to speak to Charles and see how he was doing, but he seemed entirely uninterested in having a conversation with her. He had kept it professional, of course, but Avery could see that something was wrong. She had put him in a difficult position, and she didn't like the idea of that one bit, but couldn't he just forgive her? She wanted them to joke and tease like they used to.

She didn't have time to think about any of it anymore. That night was the barbecue social event for everyone who had taken part in the festival. Charles would be there, and at first, Avery had thought maybe they could travel together. But she didn't think it was worth asking him anymore.

So, she slipped on her best barbecue dress and waited for the taxi to arrive to take her.

The event was pretty uneventful. There were people talking in small groups. The men gathered around the fire like moths while some of the women chatted about salads. Avery couldn't help but notice that no matter where she was in the space, Charles was on the opposite side.

There was light jazz playing and fine wine all around. For the most part, the wine was all that got Avery's attention. Everyone had gotten together to celebrate the success of the festival. Avery was about to call the taxi to take her home when she spotted a familiar face arrive at the barbecue.

The mayor walked in hours late. He looked exhausted as if he'd had a particularly tough day, and Avery was sure she knew why. *Probably took you by surprise when they came to arrest your girlfriend.*

Despite her better knowledge, Avery found herself approaching the mayor rather confidently. "Mayor Oswald," she said. "It's lovely to see you here. My name is Avery, from Le Blanc Cellars."

The mayor flashed her a bright smile. "It's lovely to meet you, Avery. Your chenin blanc is my favorite, I must admit."

"I'm so pleased to hear that," Avery said, doing her best to sound as friendly as possible. "You're a little pale. Are you alright?"

He was going to answer, but Avery didn't give him the opportunity.

"You know, I was expecting to see more of you at the festival. I was worried that perhaps you would be ill."

"Ah, yes," the mayor said. "I believe this year's festival has been one of the most successful yet!"

"You know who else I noticed was missing?" she continued. "The postman. He's such a friendly man, I was hoping to get the chance to speak with him and get to know him."

She knew how ridiculous it sounded, but she couldn't get the idea of the postman being a murderer out of her head. He was a perfect criminal. He knew enough about everyone in the town to know what their weaknesses were.

If it were one of her husband's books, he'd definitely have been the kind of character to get away with murder.

"Well, luckily for you, he's a friend of mine," the mayor answered. "I'll let him know to knock on your door next time he delivers the post, and the two of you can chat."

At that moment, someone decided they wanted to make the fourth toast for the evening. Avery wanted to kick herself. She should have just left when she was going to. Now, she had to suffer through yet another thank-you speech and cheerleading session for the upcoming year.

She was exhausted, and all she wanted to do was sleep, but she couldn't tear herself away from the opportunity for a conversation with the mayor. Besides, Charles still wasn't talking to her, so she didn't have many other people to talk to.

Almost ten minutes later, when the speech was finally concluded, Avery turned immediately back to the mayor. She knew by the look in his eyes that he wanted to leave just as badly as she did and that he was in no mood to talk with her. She wanted to see exactly how much information he would give her, though, and how much information he knew.

"Would you like to walk with me?" she offered. "I heard that there is a lovely duck pond at the end of the property. Besides, between you and me, I'm afraid they might start another speech." Avery chuckled. The mayor checked the level of the wine in his glass, looked despairingly at the group of people, and agreed.

"Yes, the festival has been excellent. The best sales we've had in years. I look forward to the next one," Avery said.

"That's good news!" the mayor said, forcing a cheerful tone.

Avery had always pitied people that had gone into politics. She'd always felt that she wasn't a good enough actor for it. She had a problem where her thoughts would often be accurately displayed on her face.

Politicians didn't have that problem. They had a manner of speaking which could make bad news seem like something worth celebrating. She recognized that same tone in the mayor's voice as they walked slowly across the grass.

The sound of the barbecue was growing quieter in the distance.

"It's just a tragedy about the dead tourist," she said, choosing her words carefully.

"Yes," the mayor said. "I've heard all about it. I believe the police are doing the best they can."

"So what's it like being friends with the postman?" she asked, pretending it excited her. "He must have so much information on all of us."

"Well, if he does, then he doesn't say," he answered. "In fact, I had dinner with him just the other night, and he hardly mentioned any of the townsfolk at all."

"I'm part of a stammtisch, and let me tell you, we discuss all of you all of the time," Avery joked.

The mayor chuckled. "I must admit, I am a little worried about him. He didn't seem like himself the last time I saw him."

The mayor's statement sent Avery's mind into overdrive.

Perhaps he didn't seem like himself because he was preparing for murder. Still, there was one thing that bothered her. If the stones came from the postman's pond, how did they wind up in the hands of the victim, with a clue scribbled on them?

Avery watched as the mayor's fingers fidgeted nervously with the stem of his wine glass. He kept his eyes downcast as he spoke, putting on yet another performance.

"To think, while the rest of us enjoyed the concert, singing our hearts out and having a blast, he simply sat on that bench and waited as his final minutes ticked by."

Mayor Oswald stumbled a little at those words but did an excellent job of regaining his balance. Avery was watching him closely, wondering if his body language was a sign of how much he knew or simply just because he was clearly quite tired.

"Unfortunately, I couldn't attend the first day of the festival," he said.

That was a lie. Avery was certain of it. Although it had been brief, she knew she had seen him that day at the festival. She thought back on every minute of that first day, trying to remember every small detail or something she might have missed. It didn't make sense for the mayor to lie about something like that. She had seen him, but where? It had been somewhere odd, that much she could remember. She knew that as fact because she had made a mental note of it.

"That's a pity, I suppose," Avery said. "The poor man's wife. She looked so distraught. The police had to practically drag her away."

Mayor Oswald's expression didn't change, as if his face had been set in plaster. Avery knew instantly that he was trying too hard not to look as if he had any emotion toward the mention of the dead man's wife.

"Yes, I can only imagine," he said in a deadpan voice.

They had finally made it to the end of the path, and the mayor was looking back up at the barbecue as if he suddenly wished he was among the crowd.

"My apologies, Mayor Oswald, I've chosen a rather uncomfortable topic of discussion," she said.

"No, that's not a problem at all," he said with a smile that seemed almost genuine. "I suppose the event is playing on all our minds, and I'm sure everyone has a lot of questions."

"It's an odd thing to have happened at an event like that," Avery said, keeping a close eye on his body language. "But I have faith that you've got it all under control."

In the distance, Avery could hear the sound of yet another fork being tapped against the bell of a wine glass and let out a sigh of relief, knowing that it was a speech she would be lucky enough to miss.

Avery looked out over the pond. The ducks moved slowly over the water, which reflected the light of the moon. In the darkness, she could hear the water as it lapped against the edge of the pond. She closed her eyes and breathed in the fresh air.

"Ducks are peaceful when they're like this," she said. "Other times, they're nippy little creatures."

She looked at the pond and thought about the postman again. She wondered if maybe he did do it. Charles had given her so little information. But what would his motive be?

The mayor chuckled. "I've had my fair share of duck pinches."

"You know, I'd have to say that ducks are not at all my favorite bird," Avery said. "My favorite bird would be something more like a graceful swan...or perhaps a sparrow."

The mayor stared into the water and smiled. "I'm not sure I know many people who would say ducks are their favorite bird."

"I suppose not many people ask that kind of question anymore," Avery chuckled. "It seems like something that children ask each other."

"Well," the mayor said cheerfully. "Perhaps that's what is wrong with the world. Grown-ups have stopped asking about each other's simplest interests."

"I don't follow," Avery said blankly.

"Children get to know each other, you know?" he explained. "And not on a business level, like grown-ups do. Adults want to know what you do for a living, where you plan on traveling next, or how things are going with your great-aunt."

Mayor Oswald looked out over the pond with the ducks. "Children don't care about all those extra things. They just want to know about *you*. They ask about your favorite color, food, or bird," he said.

He wasn't wrong. And Avery suddenly found herself questioning whether or not she knew anybody's favorite color. Or even whether she knew her own, should anybody ever ask her.

"Well, Mayor Oswald," Avery said, turning to face him. "What is your favorite bird?"

The mayor tapped his nail against the side of his glass as he thought about it for a while. Then he perked up as if the answer had suddenly come to him. He smiled at Avery. "My favorite bird would have to be a heron."

Chapter Ten

A heron. Avery couldn't believe that would be his answer. Well, she could believe it. She just didn't want to. Then again, he had no way of knowing that she knew about the heron tattoo. He must have figured it was a safe topic of discussion.

Avery wished that somebody else had been there to hear it. She knew she shouldn't pry any further, but her curious nature was stronger than her self-control.

"Why do you pick a heron?" she asked, trying not to let her excited energy be too apparent in her voice.

"Why do you pick a swan? Or a sparrow?" he asked, challenging her.

Avery thought it over for a moment. If she wanted him to be forthcoming with her, she would need to make him believe that she was being honest with him. To do so, she figured she might as well speak honestly.

"Swans have been my favorite since I was a little girl," she explained. "They used to remind me of ballerinas, and I've always been a terrible dancer. So, I was somewhat jealous of the swans."

Mayor Oswald let out an amused snort. "And the sparrows?"

"The sparrows remind me of my late husband," she answered honestly. "We went away for a week once. It was one of the only times when he wasn't writing toward a deadline. The place where we stayed had a nest full of sparrows. My husband and I sat for hours watching them, doing absolutely nothing. It's a fond memory."

Through the darkness, she was certain that she'd spotted the corners of his mouth turning ever so slightly upward.

"So, why do you pick a heron?" she asked again.

"Well, they do only ever what we expect to see of them. I like the simplicity in that," he answered. "They're graceful creatures...but mostly they remind me of someone important to me."

Avery's heart sank with horror at the same time that her heart fluttered with excitement. She didn't know what to do or say. Grateful for the cover of darkness, she closed her eyes and took a moment to compose herself.

He had no idea that what he was saying to her was dangerous to him. Then again, perhaps it wasn't dangerous to him after all since there were no witnesses to hear what he was saying. *Surely I am a viable witness?*

She couldn't stop then. She needed to find out a little more. Whatever was going on between the mayor, the woman with the heron tattoo, and the dead man was more sinister than anyone had expected, and the mayor was somehow involved.

Avery wanted to know exactly how involved he was and exactly how forthcoming he was expected to be.

"Did you know the man that died?" she asked before realizing that the question came seemingly out of the blue. "Sorry, it seems silly, but I've just realized that I've been talking about it, and perhaps you knew him. That would make it a difficult conversation to have, and I don't want to have crossed any boundaries or stepped on any toes," she continued, recovering only slightly.

"No need to worry," the mayor said calmly. "I didn't know him at all. He was a tourist, I believe."

Avery wasn't entirely satisfied with that answer. It did nothing to quench her curious thirst. Instead, it only left her feeling rather bored with the conversation. "His poor wife," she sighed. "Some of the locals seem to know her. Do you know her at all? The poor thing."

The quacking of the ducks nearby briefly interrupted them, and a small part of Avery wished it would continue on a little longer. She had no idea what the mayor would say, and she had no idea what she really wanted him to say either.

"No, I can't say that I know her. I believe she is quite distraught."

Avery wanted to gasp, but she couldn't. She did feel a little dizzy, though, because she knew the truth, and she hated that he'd lied. She hated even more that she wasn't surprised that he'd lied. She wanted to push him into the pond and let the ducks attack him. She wanted to kick him in the shins and shout at him for being a liar. But everything she knew was supposed to remain anonymous. So, she had to keep quiet. If not for her own security, she had to do it for Charles.

"So, which days were you at the festival?" she asked. "Because I thought I saw you on the first day, but you say that you weren't there. Must have been your doppelganger."

"No, I wasn't there on the first day," he answered.

Once again, she was certain he was lying. Not only that, but he was avoiding her question. She was about to give the mayor a piece of her mind when she decided to rather change the topic of discussion.

"So, what's the postman like?" she asked. "If he knocks on my door, what can I offer to him for tea?"

The mayor shrugged. "The funny thing about our postman is that he really isn't all that friendly," he said. "And still, he is a sensitive creature. He nearly quit his job right before the festival. He said some tourist had been just awful to him. I had to beg him to stay. He's been the best postman we've ever had."

"There you are," Charles said, canceling Avery's opportunity to further her prying. "I was wondering where you disappeared to."

Avery turned to face the origin of the voice and saw the silhouette of Charles, illuminated by the lights from the barbecue.

"You missed some great speeches," he said coyly. "Ah! Mayor Oswald. How good to see you again."

"Hey, Charles," Avery said, unamused. "We came to look at the ducks and get some quiet."

"Yes, that sounds lovely," he said calmly. "But unfortunately, I must let you know that the mayor is expected at the party. It seems they have a gift for you, Mayor Oswald."

The mayor excused himself and made his way back to the festivities, leaving Avery and Charles alone at the duck pond.

"I'm so glad I missed the speeches," she joked. "They can be so tedious, and there were far too many of them. I was afraid that I might be expected to make a speech."

She had taken a step to walk back toward the party when she felt Charles' fingers grip her sleeve, keeping her back. For a brief moment, she wished that he'd taken her hand, but then instantly, the idea made her wish he'd never touched her at all.

"What were you talking to the mayor about?" Charles asked sternly.

"We spoke about the ducks and our favorite birds," she said dryly. "He says his favorite bird is a heron."

"And what else?"

Charles wasn't buying her attempt at downplaying the conversation. She knew he wouldn't approve of it, and she wasn't in the mood for yet another argument with him.

"We spoke about the murder, but he doesn't know that I know it was a murder," she said. "I asked him if he knew the dead man or the man's wife...and a couple of questions about the postman. They're friends."

"You are unbelievable," Charles said as he started walking away from her.

"He lied to me," she argued, following him back up the path. "He said he didn't know either of them. He's willing to hide it all."

Charles spun around to face her. "I'm going to assume that you've had too much to drink tonight," he said angrily. "You need to go home before you create any more problems for me."

"Problems?" she said. "How have I created any kind of problem? He had no idea what my questions were about. I promise you, I made them sound super casual."

"That's not the point," Charles said. "Say goodbye to everyone. I'm driving you home."

With that, Charles spun on his feet and headed back toward the party. Avery watched as his silhouette grew smaller the further away he got. Then, she let out a quiet and frustrated growl. It was loud enough to cause the ducks to erupt into chaos again.

Doesn't he know I'm just trying to help?

She wondered if she and Charles could ever be friends again. Everything she said and did seemed to upset him. She liked it better when he wasn't involved with the police force. Then, he seemed to just let her be and do whatever she wanted.

By the time she made it back to the party to say her goodbyes, Charles was waiting impatiently for her in the car. Somewhat out of spite, she took her time.

It didn't bother her that she was leaving. The party was coming to an end, and most of the attendees had had too much to drink. People were hanging on each other, and a few tears were being cried. It was only a matter of time before someone would wind up dancing on the tables. Avery noticed the mayor seemed to be avoiding any real conversation with anyone.

Avery stood in the parking lot, wondering which direction she needed to walk to find Charles' car. It didn't take her long to find him, though. He was flashing his headlights at her impatiently.

"Took you long enough," Charles said as she climbed in.

"You said to say goodbye to *everybody*. So I did."

Charles clenched his jaw as he turned the key in the ignition. "We need to talk," he said gruffly.

Avery was having none of it. She was tired, her social battery was low, and she didn't like how Charles was behaving toward her. She wanted things to go back to normal. But, instead of saying that, she chose sarcasm. "What would you like to talk about?" she sang. "I'm so excited to share yet another cheerful conversation with you."

Chapter Eleven

The streets were quieter than they had been for weeks as Charles drove her home. With the festival over, most of the tourists had left, and the town was finally the quiet place Avery had grown to love.

Charles drove slowly, and it was agonizing. Avery didn't want to spend too much time in the car with him. She wanted to go home, sleep, and talk to him when she'd had enough time to think all possible conversations through. It felt like it was gearing up to be a conversation she needed to prepare for.

Still, she was stuck in the car with him. She had learned early on that it was best to get difficult conversations over with. It had saved her many days of sour feelings before, and she figured now would be the best time to talk.

"Forgive me if I'm more than a little frustrated with you," Charles said. "I'm sure I'm well within my right to be, considering you're doing everything in your power to screw this case up."

"Screw it up?" Avery said, shocked. "I'm trying to help. You don't need to be so stressed out all the time."

Charles had been correct when he implied that she'd had too much to drink. She was tipsy but far from drunk. She had just enough alcohol in her system, though, to remove any filter she once had over her words. Liquid courage is a dangerous thing.

Charles was about to say something when Avery saw the flesh beneath his eyes settle. He was beyond the point of being angry. He was tired of her. It didn't make her feel good.

"You're being completely reckless," he said helplessly. "All of what you're doing could be dangerous. Not only to the case but to you."

His knuckles were white from gripping the steering wheel, and she knew he was working hard at not completely losing his temper with her. At that moment, she pictured what he must have been like when he was a police officer.

"I can take care of myself," Avery said, turning to look out the window.

"That's not the point," Charles responded. "The point is that you keep sticking your nose where it doesn't belong. Not only do the police feel it is none of your business, but I'm also pretty sure the murderer feels that way too."

"The murderer?" she scoffed. "We don't even know who that is!"

"That's precisely the point," he pressed. "It could be any of a number of suspects. If the murderer realizes you know too much or feels like you're prying, you could be the next victim."

His words scared Avery enough to silence her.

"Besides," Charles continued. "There is no *we*. This is for the police department to handle, and you're not a police officer."

"Neither are you," she said under her breath.

"You're right." By that point, Charles sounded completely exasperated with Avery. "But I am your friend, and I know a little about how these things work. I'm begging you, please leave it alone and let the police do their jobs."

They were quiet just as the car passed the mayor's house. Avery wondered if he was still enjoying the party or if her conversation with him had ruined his mood entirely. Perhaps he was having a drink to forget about the woman with the heron tattoo or even his conversation with Avery earlier. It hadn't occurred to her that she could be getting herself in trouble. She understood that she could be stubborn, but she was learning that she was easily the most stubborn person she knew.

"I'm sorry," she eventually said. "I just want to help."

"Please tell me you didn't talk to anyone else about it," Charles said. "The last thing we want is for the murderer to get spooked and leave town. The victim deserves for this case to be solved."

When he said it like that, she felt truly terrible. Still, she didn't like how Charles was speaking to her. It felt like she was in trouble with one of her parents, and she certainly didn't see Charles as a parental figure.

"So," he continued. "Would you please tell me about the conversation between you and the mayor? On the off-chance that there is something useful in there."

Avery sighed. "It wasn't much. He said his favorite bird was a heron, which I find interesting. Then he said he didn't attend the first day of the festival, which is weird. He also said he never knew the dead guy or the dead guy's wife."

"I don't even want to know how you managed to work all of that into one conversation and make it seem natural," Charles started. "It's just—never mind. Why do you say it's weird that he didn't attend the first day? Maybe he just had other plans."

"Because I saw him there, I'm sure of it," she explained. "He was sort of keeping to one side, but I am certain that it was him. He's the only person I know who wears glasses like that. He's the mayor; he's not that hard to recognize."

Charles hummed thoughtfully, "Hmmm."

"See? I think that's a little weird, don't you?"

"Well, if you saw him, then others surely saw him," Charles said. "And if he says he wasn't there, then perhaps he has an alibi, and you saw someone else."

"Yeah, but other people don't know what I know, so they'll think nothing of the fact that he was there that day. Or that he lies about having been there that day. I also learned that the postman had been complaining about a rude tourist, so I think there's a motive there," Avery rambled. "Also, how hard is it to fake an alibi? Most of us have friends who are willing to cover for us."

Charles glanced at Avery with a knowing look, and she sank back into her chair. She felt like a teenager who'd been caught drinking at a friend's house or something. It was bizarre. She was an adult, and still, she was in trouble.

"I wasn't doing anything illegal by talking to him," she defended herself.

Charles decided to ignore that statement completely.

"Do you remember what time you saw him?" Charles asked, taking more interest in it than Avery expected.

"I couldn't say, but it was somewhere between the grape-stomping competition and the concert."

The car fell silent again as they approached Avery's driveway. As usual, Sprinkles was outside waiting for her. Avery got out of the car, feeling completely defeated by the events of the day.

"Thanks for the ride home," she said, keeping her eyes on the ground.

"I thought you should know that Daya will likely be released," he said before she could close the door.

"Who's that?"

"The victim's wife," Charles said as if her name had been common knowledge. "We've questioned her, and she's not saying much. Without any concrete evidence, we'll have to let her go within the next twelve hours."

"Ah," she answered, raising her eyebrows. "Well, good luck."

Avery closed the door and left Charles in the driveway. She wasn't certain how she felt anymore. But she knew that the emotion was somewhere between disappointment and frustration. Coupled with that, she felt a small amount of guilt.

As Avery washed the smell of smoke off her body, she contemplated every word of her conversation with the mayor. Perhaps there was something he said that could be used to keep Daya detained for just a little while longer.

She wondered if it would have been different if she had waited to talk to Charles before following the woman to the mayor's house. She wondered why the mayor hadn't also been detained. She assumed it was because there was no proof that he had any knowledge of Daya's husband, to begin with.

If that were true, it would have been a much bigger shock to him than Avery had realized. And her bizarre choice of conversation would have been an awful reminder of his reality. Perhaps the mayor had been betrayed by her, just like she'd betrayed her husband.

Then she thought about the mayor at home again. Only, this time she wondered if he was completely heartbroken. She remembered the bags under his eyes and how late he was to the barbecue. Then, she pictured having to behave as professionally and cheerfully as he had, despite having just found out his lover was potentially a murderer.

"Oh, geez," she whispered as she covered her eyes with her palm. *How could I be so distasteful?*

It was, of course, easier to see it that way now that she had sobered up a little. She also understood Charles' behavior. Avery had spent too much time thinking of the suspects and hardly any time thinking of the victim.

She dragged herself out of the shower and put on dry clothes. Then, she sat down to craft a message to Charles. It took her some time because she didn't quite know how to put into words what she was feeling.

I'm sorry. I should have been more respectful. I should have checked with you first.

She deleted it. She didn't like the tone, and it sounded too impersonal.

Charles, you've always been a good friend to me. I'm so sorry if I've crossed the line. I promise it won't happen again.

She hit the delete key again. She couldn't make that promise. She was learning how stubborn she could be and couldn't be sure something like that wouldn't happen again.

It was irresponsible of me to do what I did; you're right. I was only trying to help in the way that I knew how. I never stopped to consider that perhaps nobody needed my help. I can't fix it, but I can promise to do better. I do hope that the police find the evidence they need to keep Daya detained. Keep me posted.

She hit send. Avery figured it was the best that she had to offer. Still, she wasn't sure it would do the trick. She would simply have to wait until she saw Charles again to know exactly where they stood. She waited for his response. But it never came. And she couldn't sleep because of it. She didn't know if he had seen her message and read it and was ignoring her. Perhaps he was asleep. She wondered if he was at the police station, reporting back to them on the conversation she'd had with the mayor.

She had no way of knowing and it was driving her completely nuts.

Chapter Twelve

As usual, Avery's thoughts had kept her awake all night, and she had even darker bags beneath her eyes. She hadn't even bothered trying to cover them up with makeup. It had reached a point where they were so bad, makeup would have only made things worse.

When the doorbell rang, she was grateful to see her father's smiling face greet her. He would be the perfect distraction for her.

"How about some coffee, then?" her father asked. "It sure looks like you need it."

"Thanks, Dad," Avery said sarcastically. "Don't judge the bags under my eyes before you've seen your own."

"Pffft." Her dad waved away her remark. "Those are nothing. They've gotten way better since the doc gave me those sleeping tablets. Do you want some?"

"No, thank you, Dad," Avery laughed. "I think I'll need to have my brain removed before I'll be able to get a decent night's rest."

"Something on your mind?"

It was a beautiful winter's day in the vineyard, and the guest house was quiet. For the most part, everything was under control. So, Avery and her dad headed out to walk in the vineyards as they sipped their coffee.

"You've really done a great job of getting the farm back on its feet," her father said. "I've always said you belong here. Not in the city."

"I miss the city sometimes," Avery said. "There, the drama all seemed far away from me. I mean, of course, there is worse crime and certainly more drama than here. But it seemed as if none of it affected me at all. It was just nothing more than stories in the news."

"Drama?" her father asked. "Has something happened?"

"Forget it," she said.

There was no way she could catch him up on everything that had happened over the previous few days. It was too much and too complicated. It would only make her parents worry. That was added stress that she couldn't afford. So, they walked in silence some more, but it didn't last very long.

"You never did tell me what's been bothering you so much that it keeps you awake," her father said.

Avery rolled her eyes. Her father never forgot anything. Even in his old age, it seemed his memory had only gotten better. Which only meant that as an adult, she got away with far less than she did as a child. At least back then, he had other things to occupy him, so most of what she did went unnoticed.

As an adult, with her parents living on the other end of the property, she couldn't get away with anything. He had nothing better to do, so he noticed everything.

She knew that she couldn't tell him everything. She had promised Charles she wouldn't, and if her father told her mother, which was likely, then it wouldn't be long before the entire town knew about it. Avery needed the perfect subject matter to steer the conversation away from what was on her mind.

"Hey, before I forget," she said cheerfully. "I met the mayor last night."

"Ah, yes," her father said with a smile. "Mayor Oswald. I know him quite well."

Avery looked at her father in shock. "You do?"

"Yes. We've both lived in this area equally as long. He and I met in the library many years ago. Well before he was the mayor here."

She couldn't imagine what it must have been like to live in such a small town before the invention of the Internet or television. Even now, there was little to do, and Avery relied perhaps a little too much on technology to keep her entertained.

She'd never met anybody in a library. In fact, even her books were online. It had been many years since she had last set foot in the library.

"Well, we didn't get to talk much. All I learned is that his favorite bird is a heron," she said.

She hadn't considered that the best way to get more information about the mayor might have been to ask somebody who knew him. It was even more perfect that the person was her father because he was less likely to find her line of questioning strange.

"A heron?" he asked. "That seems interesting."

"Interesting?" Avery laughed.

"It's just an odd choice," her father said, unknowingly agreeing with her. "Most people's favorite birds are parrots or flamingos or something like that, you know. I've never heard of anybody's favorite bird being a heron."

"Well, maybe it reminds him of his wife or something," Avery said, hoping to find out more about the mayor's past life.

"Oh no, Oswald's never been married," her father explained. "It seems a pity since he is so likable. He's the only mayor I know that insists people refer to him by his first name."

"His first name is Oswald?" Avery asked in shock.

"Oh yes," her father laughed. "Did you not know that? It's a family name. His surname is Peters."

"Now that seems backward," Avery chuckled. "So he was really never married?"

"No, he focused on his career his entire life. As far as I know, he lost his parents when he was quite young. He's really only ever relied on himself. Which makes his achievements all the more impressive," her father explained. "I don't know what I would have done without your mother by my side."

"That's how I felt about James," Avery commented. "And yet, here I am."

She motioned to the vines around her. She couldn't help but relate to the dried out branches that she saw ahead of her. The stems seemed just as twisted and heavy as her thoughts. Although the parts of the vine that lay above the surface were all but dead, what happened below was nothing short of remarkable.

The most important person in her life had died, leaving her as nothing more than a shell of the woman that she had been. And yet, every other part of her had seemed to fall into place.

"Here you are," her father said with a sympathetic smile.

"So how do you think he did it?" she asked. "How do you think he made it through everything alone?"

"It's that military training, I tell you," her father answered.

"He served? He doesn't seem the type." Avery thought back to the man she had spoken to at the side of the pond. He had seemed so soft and quiet. She was having a hard time imagining him in his uniform, wielding a weapon.

"The man he is today is nothing like the man he once was," her father explained. "I've seen the medals in his house. That man has done more than most to protect this country. Besides, from what I hear, he's a really good man. Every month he goes over to the postman's house to help him in the garden. He's the only friend the postman really has."

"How does one go from serving in the military to being the mayor in a town like this one?" she eventually asked.

The ground was damp beneath her feet as they walked side by side. The steam from their coffee cups wafted clouds in front of them, and every time she took a sip, the warmth would burn the tip of her cold nose.

"Well, it wasn't quite as easy as you make it sound," her father chuckled. "When he could no longer stand fighting in the war, he decided to do something to more directly protect the people. He joined the police force."

"Mayor Oswald Peters was a police officer?" Avery asked, stunned.

"I'm not sure why this surprises you so much," her father shrugged. "Many police officers find themselves going into politics."

Avery wondered what it meant for the case. It was probable that more than a few people had worked on the force with the mayor at some point. It would make it incredibly difficult to look into him properly as a suspect. And his close friendship with the postman made it impossible to look into the postman as a suspect too. It certainly explained why Charles seemed so convinced that the mayor was a victim.

"So, how did he wind up here exactly?" she asked.

"He was serving on a force in a larger city. He had even been offered a promotion to detective. But then, one day, he got called out to a pretty rough scene. Something changed in him, and he simply couldn't face it anymore."

Her father paused to take a long sip of his coffee, peering into the bottom of his cup when the sip wasn't quite as big as he'd hoped. Avery turned them back toward the house. Her cup was also nearly empty, and she was certain she would need another.

"He declined the offer for promotion," her father continued. "He asked to be transferred somewhere with a lower crime rate, hoping for a quieter life."

"I see," Avery said softly. "I didn't know any of this about him."

"I didn't know that his favorite bird is a heron," her father said. "So why are you so interested in our mayor anyway?"

Her father raised an eyebrow at her like he often had when he was insinuating that perhaps there was more than met the eye.

"I'm just trying to make some more friends," Avery said before rolling her eyes. "Besides, I didn't even tell you the best part."

"Oh?"

"He says that the Le Blanc Cellars chenin blanc is his favorite," Avery said with a proud smile.

Her father smiled, too. He tapped one of the vines as if to congratulate it on producing a wine fine enough to be the mayor's favorite. "Then we should name the wine after him," her father said.

Avery laughed. "That seems a little drastic," Avery said. "Besides, you never know if he was just simply trying to be polite."

"Then perhaps I should give you his address. Send him a case of it," her father suggested.

It wasn't a terrible idea, but Avery shuddered to think exactly how upset Charles would be if she did that. It would be completely inappropriate, given the circumstances. She could just hear him telling her that she was once again crossing the line.

"Better yet," her father continued. "Why don't I set up a time to have coffee with him? I've been meaning to catch up with him for quite some time. You can come with me, and we can give him the bottles personally."

"Oh, no, thank you, Dad," she said. "I think I'll pass on that one. But if you do see him, please give him my regards."

As soon as they stepped back into the warmth of her home, she poured them both another cup of coffee. They sat at the kitchen table as they often had when she was younger and sipped their coffee in silence.

She was grateful for her father's visit. Not only for the pleasant distraction from her own thoughts. But he had told her so much about the mayor that she hadn't known before. But none of it had answered any of her questions. Why had he lied about being at the first day of the festival? And why did he not mention that he knew the wife of the victim?

"You know, your mother has been talking to the women of the book club," her father said suddenly. "She says the one woman has a niece whose good friend is currently shacked up with a police officer. She told your mother that the dead man from the festival had been found with large stacks of cash in his shoes."

Avery stared at her father with a knowing look.

"I didn't believe it either," he laughed. "But I thought it was interesting to see exactly how far the rumors had already traveled. I won't be surprised if soon there's someone claiming that he's half-robot."

If only he knew that she held the most precious information of all regarding the case. On her phone, she had photographs of the town's beloved and decorated mayor kissing the wife of the dead victim. And she would never tell a soul.

"I just hope they find the culprit soon," her father continued. "The whole thing has your mother very stressed out. You know how she is when people die."

Avery nodded. "I remember after that time when one of the chickens met an unsavory end. She nearly got an armed guard up in front of the coop!"

Her mother had a way of taking even the smallest situation and making it into a very big deal. She remembered it all too well and shuddered to think what her mother would make if she knew the truth about the dead man.

Her father nodded and laughed. "Precisely! Now we've got a man dead at the wine festival, and your mother is too afraid to have a second glass with dinner in case she drinks herself to death!"

If only her mother knew that the man had been poisoned. Avery wondered if perhaps then her mother would refuse to drink anything at all.

Chapter Thirteen

By the time her father left, Avery was eager for some quiet time alone. She'd been happy about his visit, but he had a habit of staying just a few minutes too long and talking just a little too slowly. At first, she thought the visit with her father would clear her mind of the repeated thoughts about the dead man and his cheating wife. Instead, she had only learned more about the mayor, which steered her thoughts in a completely different direction—direction she wished she had never been steered in. *What if he's in danger? What if she intends to do it again? It could be an insurance scam...I'm sure the mayor has excellent life insurance.*

Her thoughts were running entirely out of control, and she needed a way to reel them back in. At times, when her thoughts ran away from her like that, she understood why her mother sometimes went overboard in response to bad news. Perhaps her mother was acting out on her own chaotic thoughts.

It was clear that Oswald was a man who had dedicated his life to the service of others. It is a rare quality to find in a person. She wondered how much he knew about the case. Given that he had been in the police force before and was the mayor, it was likely that he'd been given a fair amount of information. But he also happened to be in a relationship with the victim's wife. So, perhaps they hadn't told him all that much information because of that.

Avery tidied up the coffee cups and wondered what she would do for the rest of the cold wintery day. She needed to do something to keep herself busy. One part of her brain was telling her to get to the mayor and warn him about the potential danger that he was in. Nobody wants to know that they are in a relationship with a murderer. But still, it is better to know than not to know.

He's a military man and a police officer. He can take care of himself, certainly better than you can protect him. You're just being silly. Calm down. That thought temporarily put her mind at ease. She hopped in the shower and got ready for the day. Still, when she was clean and fresh, she had nothing to do for the day.

Then, another thought undid her mind once more. *He's in love. He will be blind to it all. We've all made stupid choices in the name of love. And he is only human, after all.*

She'd had enough of her own thoughts and panic. She was stressed about a man that she barely knew. A man that she had promised Charles she would not speak to again regarding anything to do with Daya.

She needed a better distraction. So, after a quick few messages, it was arranged that the women of the Stammtisch would be getting together at her house for lunch. But that was still hours away.

Avery made the cold walk over to the wine room. It was decorated for winter, with small crystals hanging from the rafters. She quite enjoyed the effect that it had, casting little rainbows throughout the room every time the light streamed in.

She only caught a glimpse of Charles. As she walked in, he had darted off toward the storeroom. She hated going into the storeroom. She had no idea what was going on in there; everything was piled up so high, and it felt like a tiny maze inside. It made her too stressed out. Most of the time, she left the storeroom up to Charles to manage. She trusted him enough to do so.

Avery waited at the counter for Charles to return. But he took longer than usual. When he returned, she thought it was odd that he had taken so long. His arms were empty, so he wasn't fetching anything from the room. Why had he been in there so long?

"Morning, Charles," she said cheerfully.

She received nothing but silence from him as he put the few bottles he had collected onto the shelves. Avery reached for the visitor's book to see how the customers had been doing lately. She was pleased to see that every entry was positive and that some customers had returned multiple times.

"This looks great! Are you enjoying the tastings?" she asked, looking up at Charles.

Again, he said absolutely nothing and walked back toward the storeroom to disappear for another few minutes. She wasn't sure it was appropriate for him to behave that way, given that she was his boss. The last person she had expected the silent treatment from would be Charles. He was clearly more upset with her than she had initially realized. She didn't quite understand why he was all that upset. She knew she had crossed a line, but they'd already had an argument over it. Why would he just stop talking to her?

She didn't have the time to sit and figure it out, either. She needed to prepare for lunch with the Stammtisch women. She slid her chair out and left it that way, knowing that it was an easy way to irk Charles. *Two can play this game.*

Her home was cheerful when the Stammtisch women arrived. Avery had set out fresh flowers and her best glasses and dinnerware. The shrimp étouffée she had prepared for the ladies was just about ready, and Avery couldn't wait to feed her friends. She was in the mood to enjoy her day for the first time in a week. The women seemed to be matching her energy too.

Within minutes, her home was full of chatter and cheerful conversation, and Avery was able to forget all about the dead man, his wife, the mayor, and Charles' odd behavior.

That is until lunch was done, and it was time to clear the table. Tiffany had stayed behind to help, despite Avery's insistence that she preferred to do it alone.

"What's been up with you lately?" Tiffany asked as they dried the dishes.

"What do you mean?"

"You seem upset. I understand everything with the heron tattooed woman, but I've known you for long enough to know that something else is bothering you."

There was only one person that Avery trusted other than Charles, and that was Tiffany. Avery sighed as she took a seat at the table, motioning for Tiffany to join her.

"I spoke to the mayor the other night at the barbecue," she said. "He said he didn't know the dead guy or Daya."

"Daya?"

"The dead guy's wife," Avery explained. "He said he wasn't there on the first day of the festival, and it made me confused. But then I learned from my dad that he was in the military and the police force. Now, I think he might just be involved with a dangerous woman and not even know about it."

Tiffany stared at Avery for a while. "Okay, yes, I understand why that is upsetting. But how did you get to talking to him about the dead guy in the first place? You don't even know the man."

"I don't know. I just worked it into the conversation somehow," Avery said. "Anyway, Charles is so upset with me that he won't even talk to me anymore."

"That seems like a little overkill," Tiffany said. "But if you need me to talk to him for you, I will."

Avery chuckled. "No, that's alright. I'm a big girl. I can sort this out on my own."

Tiffany seemed pleased with those answers. The two of them finished cleaning up, and she was on her way. Avery was about to get into bed when her phone rang. It was Deb. It was an odd time of night to be calling, but Avery figured she must have just left something behind.

"Hi, Deb," Avery answered. "Did you forget something?"

"No," Deb answered. "I just heard about Charles. Why didn't you say anything?"

For a moment, Avery wondered if Tiffany had already told her about their conversation but knew that it was unlikely. Tiffany had never been much of a gossip.

"I don't understand," Avery said. "What about Charles?"

"Don't you know?" Deb sounded shocked. "I have a friend who has a friend who has been dating one of our police officers. She says that Charles was in trouble with the mayor. Says that he had taken photos of the mayor in a compromising position without any authority to do so."

Avery's stomach dropped. "No, I hadn't heard about that."

"Anyway," Deb continued undisrupted. "Turns out he was let off early, but he can no longer be involved with the police force in any way."

She couldn't stand the thought of it. Charles had taken the fall for her. He had sacrificed something of great importance to him in order to keep her out of trouble. That would certainly explain the way he was behaving. "Are you sure?" Avery asked, nervous about the answer.

"Yes," Deb said. "I think it has something to do with one of their high-profile cases. Why else would Charles be doing such strange things?"

He wouldn't. Avery knew that, and so did Charles, and so did Tiffany. But she had no idea how to put it into words.

"Apparently, he faced quite serious charges, but because of his previous service to the town, the mayor agreed to drop them all if he simply resigned as a consultant to the police force," Deb finished.

Now she understood. She couldn't say anything, and Charles took the fall for her because the charges against her would have been far more severe. Charles had a certain level of protection that Avery would not have been afforded.

"Thanks for letting me know, Deb," Avery said, feeling completely defeated.

"No problem!" Deb sang. "Still, I think we should do something nice for him, you know, to cheer him up. I know how important it all was to him."

Avery ended the call and got out of bed. There was no way she would be able to fall asleep easily that night. She no longer cared at all about the safety of the mayor. She cared only about Charles and how he would be feeling. He had taken a large knock because of her reckless behavior. She absolutely hated the thought of it. She reached for her phone and once again typed out message after message to him, each of which was quickly deleted.

A message simply wouldn't suffice. She needed to make it right, but she needed time to figure out how. At that moment, she feared that she had lost Charles as a friend, and it broke her heart completely.

Chapter Fourteen

When the sun filtered its light through her curtains, Avery knew the best way to make things right with Charles would be to talk to him. He would know what she could do. But in order to talk to him about it, she needed him to talk to her first.

It was no secret that he wasn't on talking terms with her. Nobody had treated her like that in years, and it was working on her nerves. But she couldn't blame him for it, either.

Avery's plan to make that happen was to make sure he couldn't possibly avoid her. And in order to do that, she was going to annoy him into paying attention to her. She had already planned it all out.

Avery snuck into the wine room before Charles showed up for his shift, and made her way through the maze of wine boxes in the storeroom. She took deep breaths to avoid claustrophobia and made herself as small as possible behind some boxes. Then, she waited. It should only have been a few minutes before Charles arrived at work. But as luck would have it, he was late that day.

Despite the boredom of waiting for someone between those boxes, Avery hadn't gone to the bathroom before she hid. So, her eagerness for him to arrive at work was becoming urgent.

She heard the sound of the door being unlocked and opened. Then, she heard him walk over to the keypad to deactivate the alarm. Of course, the alarm would already have been deactivated. Avery chuckled as she heard him mutter under his breath about it. He had never forgotten to activate the alarm.

"Hello?" Charles called through the wine room.

But Avery kept quiet. Her plan was to wait until he came to get the first box of stock, which was routine for Charles to do as soon as he had wiped the counters. Then, Avery would jump out and surprise him. She was certain that he would get a big fright and that it would force him to say at least one word to her, even if it was a curse word. But only as she was already tucked away, silent, and hidden, did it occur to her that he might mistake her for an intruder.

It wasn't going to work, but it was too late to change her plan. She was already there, and Charles would be coming into the storeroom at any moment. She needed to abort the mission somehow. She clearly hadn't thought it through well enough.

Avery got out from her hiding spot and called back to him. "It's me; I'm in here, just looking for something!" She waited to hear if he would respond. But he only let out a little unamused huff and carried on about his business.

Avery needed a different plan. Something that would get his attention without making him afraid or possibly give him a reason to feel that he needed to defend himself.

She popped her head around the corner. "Charles," she called out. "Where do we keep those few boxes of the special red blend?" She knew where they were; she just needed him to say something. "There's no need to stop what you're doing. You can just direct me toward them," she said. *Chicken. Why don't you just tell him you know what happened? There is no need for you to go about it this way at all.* "I can't seem to find it, and I've been searching for some time," she said anyway.

Charles looked up at her with a completely blank stare. He left the wine-tasting counter and made his way toward her. He didn't even need to enter the storeroom. He simply pointed at the stack of boxes right next to the door and left silently again.

Avery could feel her cheeks getting warm with embarrassment. Of course, they would be right next to the door. She should have checked before she continued on with that plan. "Ah," she said sheepishly. "Of course, that was the last place I would have looked."

Just as she thought she had enough confidence to approach the topic of discussion with him, a group of tourists walked in for a wine tasting. She would have to wait.

Charles was a smart man, and he knew that she was waiting for him. So, he took his time with the tourists, giving them what was likely the best wine tasting of their lives. Avery was pleased, despite the amount of time it took, as the tourists left with a large stack of boxes, each filled with six bottles of wine.

When it had finally quieted down again, she took a seat at the counter. Charles was about to leave, but she wouldn't let him. "I know what happened," she said quietly.

Avery saw his shoulders drop as he let out a loud sigh. Still, he remained quiet. She had thought of so many different ways to apologize to him, but at that moment, she had hit a complete blank. "You didn't have to do that. I can take responsibility for what I did," she said.

"It's not that simple," Charles mumbled. "He was ready to take some serious action."

"That's okay. It was my fault, my responsibility," she pressed.

Charles spun around. "Don't you get it?" he snapped. "You could have faced jail time. If I took the blame, I would get no jail time. I still have my job here, so the repercussions were far less severe."

"I'm sorry," she said, knowing that the words alone would never be enough. "I don't know what else to say."

"Why don't you just promise me you'll butt out?" he asked. "I asked you so many times to let it go, and you didn't listen. It was reckless, Avery."

"I know," she complained. "I wish I could take it back, but I can't. I guess I didn't think it would come to this."

"I tried to warn you that it would. If you would just have listened to me!"

She felt terrible. The entire time she had felt as if Charles hadn't been listening to her or taking her seriously. Instead, the truth had been the opposite. She wasn't taking him seriously, and he was the one who paid the price for it.

"I thought the photographs were sent in anonymously," she said.

"Yeah, well, turns out the mayor has some ties in the police force," he mumbled. "And the anonymous tip was still sent from my cell phone."

She had forgotten about that part. He had done it for her. The whole thing was a mess. She had been so worried about what kind of danger the mayor had been in, despite the fact that he was a stranger to her, she had never considered the risk that Charles had taken every time he had helped her.

"It's true. He worked as a police officer for quite some time," Avery said. "I asked my dad about it."

"So you still didn't drop it?" he asked. "After you told me that you would?"

Avery looked down at her hands. "It wasn't like that at all. I was just telling my dad that I had met the mayor, and he told me they were friends. He told me some information about him. I wasn't looking for it, I promise!"

His one eyebrow rose, causing a wrinkle to form across his forehead and Avery knew that he simply didn't believe her. And he didn't have a reason to believe her, either. She had promised him twice that she wouldn't get involved, and each time she had broken that promise.

"I'm sorry," she said again.

"Never mind," Charles said as if Avery still didn't get it. He turned around and carried on with his task at hand. "It doesn't matter now anyway. Just be careful because I cannot help you again. I can't have anything to do with the police."

"It matters to me," she said.

"Is that why you've been hanging out here for hours?" he asked. "How did you hear about it anyway?"

"Deb called last night. She knows someone who knows somebody," she said quietly. "How did the mayor find out about the photographs?"

"They had shown it to Daya during her interrogation. She must have told him about it," he answered. "You can imagine a man like him would do whatever it takes to keep something like that from spreading."

There was a silence between them. "Just promise me you haven't said anything to anyone about the photographs. Because if you did, then I could be in even greater trouble."

Avery swallowed hard. "No, I haven't told anyone. Tiffany knows because she was with me, but she's agreed not to tell a soul."

"Right," he said. "Well, if that's all, then I am going to take my coffee break. It is eleven o'clock now, and I'm desperate for a pick-me-up."

"Eleven?" Avery asked as she dropped the book that was in front of her. "Shoot, I gotta go."

She had completely forgotten that she'd planned to take Sprinkles to obedience training. She had found a course online that was not too far from her, but it started at eleven-thirty and was at least a twenty-five minute-drive away.

First, she had to find Sprinkles. Avery raced through the property, calling for her dog. She didn't even care how many guests she bothered in the process; she needed to hurry up. She had his leash and collar tucked into her back pocket when she found the dog rolling around in a patch of dirt.

"Come, Sprinkles!" she called. "We need to hurry up."

Thankfully for Avery, Sprinkles loved nothing more than to go for a drive. So, the moment she opened the car door, the dog jumped right inside. "Good boy," she said as she raced around to the other side. "Time to get you trained so you can be the good dog you were destined to be."

For the entire drive to the training grounds, she replayed the conversation with Charles in her head. She had never seen him look so down and heartbroken, and she wished she knew what to do about it. She thought about all the ways she could potentially make it up to him.

Avery couldn't understand why he would have gone so out of his way to protect her. She was his boss, and most people would be thrilled to be rid of their bosses. Surely he didn't love his job at the vineyard more than he loved consulting for the police?

Chapter Fifteen

The scene between Brie, the dog trainer, and Sprinkles was like something out of a movie. The trainer behaved as if she was training Sprinkles to go to war. For a short while, it did look a little like a war, with Sprinkles running aimlessly through the field as the trainer tried desperately to get the situation under control.

It had started to look to Avery as if there was little hope that Sprinkles would ever be a well-behaved dog.

"Right now, Sprinkles!" Brie shouted. "Fall in line!"

Avery laughed. There was no way on Earth Sprinkles would understand that command. Still, Brie waited expectantly with her hair slicked back into a tight, neat bun. She even went as far as to consult the watch strapped to her wrist while impatiently tapping her foot against the ground.

By the time they were done, Sprinkles was so exhausted he fell onto his side and took a nap.

"Well, Sprinkles sure is energetic," Brie said with a chuckle.

"Yes," Avery agreed. "Which is why you are so necessary. Thank you."

"Don't worry. I'll get Sprinkles behaving in no time. I've dealt with worse," Brie responded as she wiped the sweat from her face.

"Do you get a lot of difficult students?" Avery asked.

"Not that much, but I was a trainer in the military for a long time. That's where I dealt with the truly difficult students."

Avery looked at Brie and could see it clearly. The slicked-back bun, the neat clothes, and the strict way in which she spoke to the dogs suddenly all made sense. It even looked as if her t-shirt had been crisply ironed, something Avery would never do.

"You were in the military?" Avery asked, trying not to sound too shocked. "How did you wind up being a dog trainer?"

"Well, I trained dogs in the military," Brie responded. "I guess after a while, I wanted to put my work into something that felt a little more rewarding. I lost a lot of students, and it became difficult for me."

"I'm sorry to hear that," Avery said shyly. "How long were you in the military?"

"I served for around ten years, training strictly military dogs. That's where I met most of the people I know today. I even trained the dog that saved our mayor's life!"

Brie smiled widely at her, and Avery couldn't believe how small the world could truly be. Brie seemed friendly and eager to talk. So, Avery decided that she would see how much information she could get on their mayor while she still had the chance.

"You served with the mayor?" she said, surprised. "I only met him for the first time the other day."

"I did." Brie nodded and looked into the distance as if she was searching the field for a distant memory. It seemed a little dramatic to Avery.

"He was an excellent man. He's the reason I decided to keep training dogs. I was willing to give it up entirely!" Brie said.

"If you don't mind me asking...what happened?"

Brie and Avery made themselves comfortable on a nearby bench as Sprinkles lay fast asleep at Avery's feet.

"Well, after I left the military, I had lost so many dogs that I found it difficult to spend any time with them. The dogs, that is," Brie explained. "I had spoken to Oswald about it. Told him that even though I knew what the dogs were doing was important, I cared about them too much."

"That's understandable," Avery interjected.

"Yeah, and he understood it perfectly," Brie continued. "And then I went on to explain to him that I had become so afraid of getting attached to the dogs that even outside of the military, I didn't think I could continue to train them."

Brie took a sip of her water and sighed. "The problem is that the dogs will never outlive us, which bothers me tremendously. Those dogs were sent to be a part of a war they had nothing to do with. I felt incredible guilt for it."

Avery could see the struggle in Brie's eyes as she spoke about it. It was apparent that traces of that guilt were still there. Brie had been perfectly poised the entire time she had conducted the training. But as she spoke about her experience, she suddenly became fidgety. Her fingers trembled as they tugged at anything they could find.

"Well, I couldn't get myself to look at any dog without feeling immense guilt for what I had been a part of," she continued. "I really have loved every single dog I have ever worked with...Sprinkles being next on the list."

Brie looked down at Sprinkles and smiled. "I felt I had done the dogs a great disservice for what I had been preparing them for. And after I left the military, the only job I was offered was to train dogs for the police force, which felt like basically the same thing."

Avery glanced at Sprinkles and tried to imagine him trying to do the work as a police dog or a dog on a battlefield. The mental image was something similar to a circus.

"But when Oswald heard that I had given up my career of dog training, he showed up at my house unannounced with his dog, Smith," Brie said with a smile. "He insisted that I train his dog and refused to let anybody else do it."

"Does everyone, including the dog in that family, have last names for first names?" Avery laughed.

"It would appear so!" Brie chuckled. "Well, I didn't want to do it at first. And in reality, I was upset that he'd even suggested it. But he was so stubborn and insistent that I eventually agreed but swore it would be the last dog I ever trained."

"Is he really that stubborn?" Avery asked, eager to learn more about the man.

"One of the most stubborn men I know," Brie commented. "Anyway, when I trained his dog, I realized quickly that training people's pets is a far more rewarding experience than I had anticipated. The chances of them living long lives and growing old are high. It made me realize I could continue to do this." Brie motioned at the field in front of her. Avery could only assume she was referring to the fact that it was where she did the training and wasn't referring to the actual ground itself. Avery did her best to hide a small smile.

She liked the idea that Mayor Oswald had such a caring nature. She wasn't a fan of anyone quite that stubborn, but she could appreciate his kindness. It had only made her come to the conclusion that he couldn't have known his lover was the dead man's wife. Someone with that amount of kindness could never get involved with a married woman. Avery was certain of it.

"Well, Sprinkles and I are so grateful that you have decided to continue your training," Avery said gently.

Brie packed up the rest of her belongings and gave Sprinkles a big kiss on his head before leaving Avery and Sprinkles in the park. Desperate for a quieter night, Avery decided to see how much more of Sprinkles' energy she could deplete by taking him for a brisk walk before heading home.

She had almost forgotten entirely about her conversation with Charles. The training and the dog trainer had been a brilliant distraction. It had even gotten her to laugh for the first time in a while. She wished that feeling could have carried on.

The closer she got to home, the more guilt crept in for her. She had cost Charles a lot. But she had also learned a lot about the mayor. His behavior regarding the photographs made more sense to her now.

He was a kind but stubborn man. It was more than likely that Daya had led him on and manipulated him. She hated the idea that Daya could potentially ruin the name of such a good man. And she could feel the anger growing inside her. But she could do nothing. She had already done enough harm. She needed to take a step back and keep her promise to Charles.

Sprinkles slept the entire drive home. And when they got home, he drank some water and went to his bed to sleep some more. It meant Avery could have the first restful sleep in a long time, until around five o'clock in the morning when an intrusive thought woke her from her peaceful sleep.

If he's so great, then why is he not married?

She understood not everyone wants to get married and have that kind of life, but he really seemed to her like someone who would be interested in it. Thankfully, he was a public figure, so it wasn't very difficult for Avery to get her hands on the information.

"Mrs. Peters," she said with a satisfied grin as she scrolled the web page with all his information. There she could see the years in which he had served in the military and the police force. She could see some of the details of his campaign to be mayor. And she could see the information about his wife. He'd been married before he had moved to their town. It certainly explained why his father said he hadn't ever been married.

He had married a school teacher. And, if the photographs were anything to go by, they were perfectly happy. So where was she? The page didn't say, but Avery was certain she knew where to look.

It didn't take long for her to find the mayor's wife on social media. In a world so small, and due to the fact that everyone around her seemed to be friends with Mayor Oswald, she figured that there were likely some friends in common.

She had to scroll an absurdly far distance, but she eventually found what she had been looking for. She could read through Mrs. Peters' updates and gather that she and the mayor had separated at one point.

Part of Avery was relieved, knowing that the mayor wasn't having an affair against his wife also. But another part of her thoughts traveled down a new and frustrating path. *If he's so great, then why did they split?*

Chapter Sixteen

Avery pondered the split between the mayor and his wife for most of
the morning. It made her feel foolish, but she couldn't help herself.
It wasn't any of her business, but it had changed the way she had originally felt about the mayor. So, it meant it was important.

She wished she could just ask one of them about it, but how could she
possibly do that without it seeming as if she might be prying? She could
invite the mayor over for some of his favorite chenin blanc and work it
into the conversation. But she was certain that after their last conversation,
he wouldn't be so keen.

Before she could finish that thought, a loud clattering sound came
from the other end of the house. Avery ran toward the sound, bracing
herself for what she might find. But all she found was Sprinkles, standing
in the center of the dining room table.

A bird flew over Sprinkles' head as he tried to snatch it out of the air.
Avery, not wanting to deal with the feathery mess that would be left
behind should Sprinkles have succeeded, ran toward them to come to the
bird's rescue.

She hadn't anticipated, though, that the bird was in no mood to be
rescued. No matter how hard Avery tried to guide the bird in the right

direction, it wouldn't get the hint. It swooped over her head, crashing into and knocking things over.

Eventually, the bird had come to its own defense, swooping down to hit Avery on the head as it passed. Avery rubbed her head and took a step back to assess all the ways she could've handled the situation a little better.

"I'm just going to leave you alone," she finally concluded.

She slumped down on the couch and caught her breath. As with any other moment when she wasn't immediately distracted, she thought about Charles and the mayor. She needed to decide what she was going to do.

Mayor Oswald was a good man who was in potential danger. Everybody seemed to love him and sing his praises, and she didn't want anything to happen to him, knowing that she might have been able to warn him and prevent it all.

Then again, she had known Charles for longer, and she had already done enough harm to him. She had made him a promise to stay out of it, and she felt obliged to keep that promise.

Whatever. He's already mad at me. The damage had already been done with Charles. How could she justify it if the mayor turned up murdered too?

Avery raced through a shower and got ready. She peered into the dining room to conclude that the bird was still creating a large mess, and Sprinkles was still making his best attempt at hunting. Then, knowing they'd both be busy for a while, she left.

She felt increasingly anxious as she raced toward the mayor's house. She was worried that she might already have been too late. *What if she's already murdered him? What if it's my fault for not saying something?* By the time she reached his driveway, she had been driving so fast that her brakes made a screeching sound as she came to a stop. Then, anxious and out of breath, Avery clambered out of her car and sped toward his front door.

She couldn't even ring the bell before the door swung open. The mayor looked completely shocked at her arrival at his front door, and she couldn't blame him.

"Avery, what can I do for you?" he said, trying desperately to keep his composure. He had remembered her name. He really was an excellent man.

"Mayor Oswald," Avery greeted, out of breath. "I'm so happy you're alright." The words had slipped out before she'd given herself a chance to contemplate them better. The mayor gave her a confused look.

"What do you mean?" he asked. He was no fool. He could see the concern on Avery's face. "Would you like a glass of water?" he asked. Avery nodded. Mayor Oswald welcomed her into his home and made her comfortable at the kitchen counter.

She took a look around. His home was neat, as she would expect from a military man. She took a moment to look at his décor and the images he chose to decorate his walls with and made a note that not a single item contained the image of a heron.

"So, what can I do for you?" he asked again, smiling kindly at her.

"I need to warn you about something," Avery said, taking a large sip of water.

"Oh?"

"It's kind of difficult to explain to you how or why I know, and what the full story is. But I really need you to listen to me," she said. Mayor Oswald leaned forward in his chair and focused entirely on her.

"It's about Daya," she eventually said, looking down at her hands.

"I see," the Mayor responded calmly. "What seems to be the problem?"

"I know why your favorite bird is a heron," Avery said, pointing to the back of her neck. "It's because of Daya."

Mayor Oswald clenched his jaw. "I was hoping it hadn't become common knowledge," he said.

"It hasn't," Avery said quickly. "I promise. As I said, it's complicated."

He stared blankly at her for a while then glanced her over as if to try and judge whether or not she was being truthful. "Alright, well, what is this about then?" the mayor continued.

"I suppose by now you know that she was married to the man who had died at the festival," Avery said, looking at him for a response.

"This explains your bizarre conversation with me the other night," the mayor responded. "You already knew."

Avery shrugged the comment off. She didn't want to admit to

anything, and she didn't want to waste any more time. She could see that the mayor was getting concerned, and it was clear she was out of line. But he was patient with her, and she was there and had already said too much. She couldn't stop it now.

"Well, I think she is a dangerous woman," Avery said suddenly.

"You think she's guilty," he said quietly.

"I think it is highly possible," Avery said. "I found some stones on the festival grounds, and I think they were a clue."

"Stones?"

"When her husband was found dead, he had a stone in his hand that had the word Heron on it," she explained. "The only thing that troubles me is where she got the stones. It seems they came from the postman's garden pond? Did you ever take her with you to visit him?"

"Yes, she came with me once to help him in the garden."

The moment she said it, she saw something in his eyes change. She wasn't sure what it was, but it looked like fear. And she knew that she was getting through to him.

"Continue," he said sternly.

"Well, the next night, when I was helping clean the grounds, I found two more stones," she explained. "I took them to the police. They read *Follow* and *The*."

"Follow the heron," Mayor Oswald said as his face paled.

"Yes," Avery agreed. "I took them to the police, but they thought perhaps it had just been a coincidence. You know, some stones that were left behind."

"But you don't think so?" he asked.

"No," Avery said. "See, he bumped into me the night that he died. He was stumbling, and most of us just assumed he was drunk. But he kept repeating himself, and after I found the stones, his words really bothered me."

The mayor wasn't taking his eyes off her anymore, and she knew that he was truly listening to her. For the first time since it had all begun, someone was really listening and believing.

"What was he saying?" the mayor asked sternly.

"She did it," Avery said. "She's the one you're looking for."

The room fell silent, and Avery didn't know what to do. The mayor glanced down, deep in thought, clenching his jaw.

"As I said," Avery continued. "We all thought he just had too much to drink. Of course, now we know he was poisoned."

His head shot up as he looked at her. "How do you know that?"

Avery pinched her eyes closed. She couldn't get anyone in any more trouble. All that mattered was that the mayor remained safe.

"That doesn't matter," she said, brushing off the question. "What matters is that when I spotted the heron tattoo on the back of Daya's neck, it all fell into place for me."

"And what did you decide happened?"

It felt like an odd question, but Avery could understand that the mayor was likely in shock and definitely rather uncomfortable.

"I think she poisoned him," she said. "When I saw her at the coffee shop, she didn't look at all like a woman who had lost her husband. I know what that's like. She was smiling and laughing only days after it had happened."

The mayor sighed. He leaned back in his chair and tapped his hand on the table. He was upset, it was clear, and he had every right to be.

"My reasoning for having a heron as a favorite bird could have meant anything," the mayor said. "Your conversation with me at the barbecue and your conversation with me now leaves me with an important question."

"Yes?" Avery answered, wishing he wouldn't ask it.

"How do you know about Daya and me?"

She knew the question was coming, and she didn't want to answer it. But she would. And she would set things straight for Charles.

"I'm the one who took the photographs," she admitted, keeping her eyes downcast. "I agreed to keep it anonymous, and I never had the intention of telling anyone other than the police."

He remained silent.

"I assure you, I simply got carried away," she continued. "I am aware now of how inappropriate it was, and I promise you, I never intended to overstep such a large boundary."

"Charles took the fall for you," he said as he pieced it together. "And he stopped you at the barbecue, too."

"Yes," Avery said. "He didn't have to, but I guess he is a better friend to me than I had thought. I took it for granted."

"Does anybody else know about any of this?" he asked.

"No, well, I tried to speak to the police and Charles, but they don't believe me. I've been asked to butt out."

"And here you are," he said with a smile.

"Yes," she said sheepishly. "Here I am."

Chapter Seventeen

Avery wasn't sure whether to feel proud or ashamed for how she had intruded on the mayor's evening. She also couldn't quite read his body language as well as she would have liked. It was difficult to know if he was upset or otherwise. She had just dropped a bombshell on him and hadn't considered yet how he might react to the information.

"Thank you for coming to tell me," he said calmly, getting up to pour himself a cup of water. "I am sure it couldn't have been an easy decision to make."

Avery sighed a quiet sigh of relief. "I couldn't sleep. I had to let you know that you were potentially in danger. Please, just know that I won't tell anybody about any of this; you have my word."

"That would be greatly appreciated," he said. "And I won't let anybody know you were here, either."

"Thank you," she answered sheepishly.

Even though she had stepped completely out of line, he was kind and courteous toward her. He really was a brilliant man. She understood what it was that Daya saw in him.

"Well, I guess I'll be on my way then, and I'll let you enjoy the rest of your evening," she said, getting up from her seat.

"I'll try my best," he teased.

As Avery left his house, she felt satisfied with how she had handled the conversation. Without a plan, she had successfully done what she had promised not to do. But it had made her feel better, and that was all that mattered.

Charles would possibly be upset, but he had no reason to find out about it. If the mayor kept his word, the entire conversation would forever remain between the two of them.

Just as her car pulled into her driveway, she remembered the rogue bird that she'd left in her dining room. She pressed the back of her head against her seat and closed her eyes.

What am I going to walk into?

She didn't have much choice but to go in and deal with it. It was only a few hours until the women of the Stammtisch would arrive for dinner. So, she took a deep breath and readied herself for what she was certain would be an awful scene.

When she entered the house, the first thing she noted was that Sprinkles was far too quiet. In fact, he was completely silent. That greatly worried her. She tiptoed through the house and approached the dining room.

When she opened the door and peered inside, she saw something she was not at all expecting. On the ground, next to the dining table, lay Sprinkles, completely asleep and exhausted from chasing the bird all morning.

The bird was walking proudly across the countertop, pecking here and there at something Avery couldn't quite see. She was just grateful Sprinkles wasn't a good enough hunter to have caught the bird. With a clearer mind, Avery got a towel and threw it over the bird, after which she carried it safely outside.

~

It'd been a long time since Avery had grilled up some steak. Le Blanc Cellars had just released a new sangiovese and it would be the perfect pairing to share with her favorite Stammtisch friends.

The night was cheerful as the group of women enjoyed a freshly cooked meal and many decent glasses of wine. The table had erupted into laughter as Avery recounted the dog training event the day before.

"I tell you that Brie is amazing, and she had a ton of energy," Avery said. "She trained the dogs in the military. She said she served with the mayor."

"Oh yeah," Eleanor added. "I remember now about her and the mayor. That was a lot of drama, wasn't it?"

"Drama?" Avery asked.

"Yeah, when the mayor's wife left, everybody suspected it was perhaps because he was having an affair with Brie," Eleanor explained.

"I remember!" piped Deb. "But when it turned out that Brie was, in fact, in the process of marrying somebody else, everyone sort of dropped those suspicions."

"Yep! I guess his wife was the one with the affair, it seems," Eleanor said, shaking her head.

"What makes you think there was ever any kind of affair?" Avery asked. It amused her that the world was still under the impression that a sudden split had to, almost certainly, be caused by an affair.

"Well," Deb said with a shrug. "Why else would you leave suddenly in the middle of the night and never come back?"

"That's what happened?" Tiffany asked, shocked. "I didn't realize it was quite that dramatic!"

"Yeah!" Deb said, raising her glass to her lips. "She barely even took anything with her. She took her clothes, makeup, and her little dog. That sounds like an angry woman to me."

"Or someone who's afraid," Eleanor said.

"Afraid of the mayor?" Deb laughed. "That's like being afraid of a kitten!"

She wasn't wrong. As far as anybody in the town was concerned, the mayor was completely harmless, and incredibly well-loved.

"I mean, there's no doubt he's wonderful," Avery agreed. "But why then would she leave that way?"

"Because she's having an affair!" Deb said. "Isn't it clear? She left to be with another man. She must have been planning it for months!"

It felt wrong to be discussing such a private part of Mayor Oswald's life when nobody there even really knew him. It was town gossip, but Avery figured it was normal. He was, after all, a public figure.

"I have to admit," Avery said. "That does sound as if there was something unsavory going on. Sounds like an affair to me! But I refuse to believe it was on the mayor's side."

"Poor Brie," Camille eventually said. "It tore her friendship with the mayor apart. Even though there was never any proof of the affair, some members of the town had missed the memo and would call her incredibly rude names when they saw her in the street."

Avery shook her head. She couldn't imagine what that would be like. Brie had seemed like a wonderful woman, and she would never call her any cruel names.

"Never mind all this gossip talk," Camille said. "Eleanor, how are things between you and the doctor?"

Eleanor began to blush slightly, and it reminded Avery of when they had spoken months before. Eleanor had told her she would never consider getting into another relationship after her husband had died. Soon after, she met the new town vet, and they had been dating ever since.

They were happy, and it made Avery sometimes wonder whether she would ever move past the death of James enough to spend her life with another person. She and James had shared everything together. They'd loved the same movies and had the same favorite food. It had seemed almost impossible for them to be so similar and get along so well. She was certain she could never find anything like that again.

"Well," Eleanor said quietly. "He asked me to marry him."

There was a loud gasp around the table as everyone waited patiently for Eleanor to continue.

"He said that since we already see each other every day, we might as well," she said. "I mean, if I'm not staying the night at his house, he is staying the night at mine, and we spend every waking moment together."

"So, did you agree?" Deb asked.

Eleanor shook her head. "On one condition," she said. "I don't want to leave my house. I have many memories there that I am not yet ready to leave behind."

"Oh my gosh, I can't believe you've waited this long to say something," Camille laughed.

"It felt terrible making conditions with him, but I couldn't leave that part of my life that easily," Eleanor said. "I told him he should move into my house."

The rest of the group glanced across the table at each other. Nobody was quite sure if she was telling the truth or kidding. It was exactly the kind of joke that Eleanor would tell.

"So, what did he say?" Deb asked cautiously.

"He agreed," Eleanor said with a smile. "Besides, I think it will be great having a vet in the house!"

"When did he ask?" Camille asked, leaning forward with excitement.

Eleanor let out a loud laugh. "Last week!"

Another loud gasp cannoned around the table as some of the women rose to their feet to give Eleanor a congratulatory hug.

"He proposed last week, and this is the first we're hearing about it?!" Deb shouted excitedly. "Why didn't you tell us?"

"I've been a little busy," Eleanor responded with her cheeks turning bright pink.

"I bet you have!" Deb cheered, topping up Eleanor's glass with a bit more wine.

By the time the women left her house, Avery was smiling widely. It had been a successful day. She had done what was necessary to put her own heart and mind at peace, her friends were happy and sharing good news, and it had been a successful year for the business.

All of it had made her feel much better about how things were between her and Charles. Granted, she had a little bit of guilt for everything he'd had to go through, only for her to confess to the crime anyway. But he had acted on his own terms, and so had she.

Avery stepped out onto the porch with a cup of tea to admire the stars. She wasn't really sure why she had done it; it was the first time she had done it in years. It was something that she had often done with her father and then after that with James.

The sky was clear, and the stars were bright. The air was cold, but it only made the warm tea taste so much better. And when Avery finally crawled into bed, it took her no more than a few seconds before she was fast asleep. Not even the sound of Sprinkles snoring loudly at her feet would wake her.

Chapter Eighteen

Although the rain was beautiful, it only made Avery feel sad. She wasn't sure if it was the gray skies or the fact that she couldn't go for a morning walk, but she wasn't as excited about the start of the wet season as the rest of her group of friends.

The one thing that did keep her cheerful was the knowledge that once the rain had passed, beautiful plants would make their appearance. Although it was still morning, she had convinced herself that she deserved a day in bed with her favorite movies.

That was until she received a text from Charles that he wouldn't be at work. He had become ill. Charles had never been out sick, so Avery had never needed to make a plan for when he wasn't there. She had nobody to call, so she knew she'd have to fill in for him.

Avery typed out a quick message to Charles, instructing him to stay in bed and get better as soon as possible, and then dragged herself back out of bed to get ready to work.

By the time she unlocked the wine room, it was already an hour past opening hour. It didn't make much of a difference, though. With the rain, she wasn't expecting too many customers that day. Avery put on some music and started preparing the wine room. She was halfway through her routine when she received another message from Charles.

Just got the news that all charges against me regarding the photographs have been dropped. Apparently, someone confessed, but they won't tell me who. You promised you'd stay out of it.

Avery's stomach sank. She turned off the music and slumped back against the wine bar. Technically, the mayor had kept his promise and hadn't told anybody it was her. But Charles knew that it was her, and he was smart enough to piece it together.

Despite knowing what she had done was right and being happy Charles was no longer blamed for it, she still felt waves of guilt wash over her throughout the day. She had felt so guilty that she didn't even know what to say to him. So, instead, she said nothing at all. Which wasn't a good option either. By the time the work day had ended, and she was loading Sprinkles in the car for his next training session, it was too late. She had gone so long without responding to him, that anything she said to him would have sounded like an afterthought.

Then it occurred to her that perhaps he wasn't ill at all. There was a possibility he was so upset with her that he simply didn't want to see her that day, which was fair. But it made her feel awful. And the fact that she felt so awful about it made her confused. Then, the fact that she felt confused about it made her irritable. *Why are you so concerned? You're his boss, and you're a grown woman. You can do whatever you want.* She needed to run her feelings by somebody else. So, she called Tiffany on her Bluetooth system.

"Hello?" Tiffany's voice crackled through the speakers.

"Can you hear me?" Avery shouted. "Hello? Hello?"

"I can hear you!" Tiffany called back. "Stop shouting! Why are you shouting?"

"Oh," Avery laughed. "I've never used the Bluetooth in my car. I wasn't sure how it worked."

"Welcome to the new age!" Tiffany teased. "Now, what is so urgent that you have to phone me while you're driving? In the rain, might I add?"

Avery gave Tiffany a brief summary of what had happened between the mayor and Charles and her recent conversation with the mayor as well. Tiffany was the only person she could talk to about it because she was the only other person who knew about the photographs.

"You didn't need to take all the blame," Tiffany reprimanded her. "I could have gone with you."

"It was never my intention to clear my name," Avery admitted. "Charles only took the blame because I might have faced jail time."

"Oh, I see," Tiffany said. "And you think he knows you've spoken to the mayor?"

"It's the only conclusion that he could possibly get to!"

"So, what exactly is the problem?" she asked. "I thought it would be good if his name was cleared?"

"I feel guilty, and I'm frustrated that I feel guilty," Avery explained. "Something about it all just gives me a bad feeling, and I can't figure out why."

"I mean, that seems normal to me," Tiffany teased.

"Well, Charles is my friend, and I'm his boss," Avery continued. "And I know I should feel bad, but there's something else. I was really upset with him when he called in sick this morning. How can I be upset if he is ill? It happens! It's normal!"

There was a short bit of silence on the other end of the line, and then she heard Tiffany wheeze with laughter. It took a good few minutes before Tiffany had composed herself again. "I'm sorry that I'm laughing," Tiffany said through sniffs. "It's just that sometimes you can be *so* dumb!"

"I don't understand," Avery said, unimpressed.

"You miss him, you idiot," Tiffany said through more laughter.

Almost immediately, Avery did feel like an idiot. But only because Tiffany had been right. How could she not have figured out that she missed him? The moment Tiffany had spoken the words, Avery knew it was the truth, and all of her emotions fell back into place.

"You're right," Avery said in shock. "How odd."

"It's not odd," Tiffany said. "You guys get along. You're usually joking and laughing together, and now you haven't been. But I'm sure things will come right soon, and you guys will joke together again."

"I hope so because I don't like missing him," Avery said.

"Listen, I have to go," Tiffany said.

In the background, she could hear Tiffany open her front door and greet someone before ending the call. Avery sighed and did her best to swallow her embarrassment. She was sure that Tiffany would be teasing her about that phone call for at least the next few months.

~

There were more dogs in training that day than there had been the previous time. And this time, the owners were expected to join in. Brie seemed a lot less friendly when Avery was on the receiving end of her military-style training.

The wet weather meant they had to do the session in the school gymnasium. Avery had hoped never to find herself back at her old school again, but for the first time ever, it was an enjoyable experience. Sprinkles had been learning fast, and it felt good to do something completely different from her normal routine.

"You guys did well," Brie said as the training ended.

She took a seat next to Avery and patted Sprinkles on the head.

"Thank you," Avery said. "You're a tough coach!"

Brie laughed. "Mayor Oswald said that once too. I used to think I had to be tough on the military dogs because they played such an important role. But I've come to realize that every dog plays an important role. Every single one."

Avery smiled at that thought. "I've been meaning to ask you," she said. "What exactly do military dogs do?" Brie's face dropped at the mention of it, and Avery immediately regretted the question.

"You don't have to answer if you don't want to," Avery said.

"No, that's alright," Brie smiled. "It's an interesting question."

Brie took a large sip from her water bottle. "The dogs are trained to save lives," she answered. "Each mission is different, but sometimes they are sent to detect bombs and that kind of thing. However, when I left, Mayor Oswald was pushing for a new type of training. He felt that the dogs could be used to create distractions, drawing the enemy away from the real threat."

"That's fascinating," Avery said. "I would never have guessed."

"They were pretty successful too!" Brie said. "Especially the dogs that were part of Oswald's missions."

"He led missions with dogs in them?" Avery asked. It felt like every new bit of information she received about the mayor was more fascinating than the last.

"Yes!" Brie said excitedly. "He was an excellent strategist. Hardly any of his missions were unsuccessful. He had a really good way of distracting the enemy in order to get his men through and back alive."

"That sounds really impressive," Avery said softly. "Especially for such a gentle man."

"He is a gentle man now," Brie said with a cheeky smile. "But he could be dangerous when he needed to be."

The conversation came to an end before Avery could ask any more questions. Brie turned her attention to another pet parent who had a list of questions for her.

Avery woke the exhausted Sprinkles and dragged him back into the car. At that moment, she was grateful for the rain on her skin as it cooled her down and washed away the sweat from what felt like a parent-pet boot camp.

As soon as she got home, she thought about Charles again. She had to say something to him. People like to know when they're missed, and she was certain he was no different in that regard. But when she typed out the words, they just felt foolish. And yet, she couldn't just stay quiet completely. If the only other option was to be cheesy, that would have to be it. So, she typed her original message out anyway.

I saw something funny today that I know would have made you laugh. I'm sorry for the trouble I have caused, but I was only doing what I thought was right. I hope that you'll see that one day. I miss you.

She wasn't sure what she expected him to say in response. But when he said nothing, she didn't know what to do. Despite her exhaustion, she could barely sleep. His silence was loud enough to keep her wide awake.

Chapter Nineteen

Avery was unfortunately underdressed as she raced across the lawn in her sleeping shorts and shirt, an excited Sprinkles running ahead of her. One of her dish towels was secured in his jaw, and as far as Sprinkles was concerned, they had just started a fun game.

"Give me that!" she yelled as she raced after the golden retriever.

By the time she had successfully rescued the towel, she was grateful for the cool air and damp grass. She stood a moment to catch her breath before going back inside. Sprinkles, on the other hand, waited a moment to roll around in the dirt before making his way back into the house to lie down on the freshly cleaned sofa.

Avery sighed. "You're lucky you're so darn cute," she mumbled as she chased the dog back outside.

Somewhere in the depths of her home, she could hear her phone vibrating like mad. When she'd finally found it, she saw multiple missed calls from Deb. Avery wasn't sure what had happened, but usually, Deb only phoned when there was some serious town gossip. And she knew it was best to call her back and save herself the string of messages that would arrive if she didn't.

"Hi Deb, what's up?" Avery said when her call was answered.

"Did you hear the news?"

It was a typical conversation starter for Deb.

"You'll have to be a little more specific than that," Avery said with a chuckle.

"The postman, you know, the one with the Velcro shoes?" Deb said.

"I know the one," Avery said as she dried the morning mist from her face. Her hair was damp from chasing Sprinkles.

"Well, he's been diagnosed with arthritis. Apparently, he won't be able to work much longer as the postman!" Deb spoke as if it was the biggest news of the century, and Avery was just amazed she was able to find that kind of information.

"That's terrible news," Avery said blankly, but her mind was running a million miles per hour. His diagnosis and the ending of his long career certainly would have explained why he was behaving strangely the last time that the mayor had spent time with him. He would have been in pain and likely awaiting results from the tests. With his behavior explained, his likelihood of being a suspect began to fade. Still, she couldn't be too certain.

"I just think he should get a second opinion," Deb continued. Avery could tell that Deb was gearing up for a longer conversation than Avery had the energy for. So, she excused herself to get ready for the day and ended the conversation as quickly as she could after twenty minutes.

She was about to leave her phone on the counter when she noticed she had a large number of messages waiting. She was in no mood to read them but knew if she didn't, she would spend the entirety of her shower wondering what they were about.

So, she gave in and checked. There were multiple messages on the Stammtisch group text about the postman's unfortunate diagnosis, a message from her mother about the speed of the Internet, and a message from Tiffany.

Avery responded to the rest of the messages first before opening Tiffany's chat. Tiffany was the kind of friend who only ever messaged if it was something of importance. So, she made sure she was ready for something serious before opening the message.

Just saw the woman with the heron tattoo at the grocery store. Feels weird to walk past her, knowing what I know. Can't believe she isn't in jail.

It came as no surprise to Avery that Daya was seen around town. Charles had explained that they could only detain her for a short time. The fact that she was out of jail meant that the police never did find any evidence to suggest she had been involved.

Avery wondered what the mayor had done after she had been sent home. Had they seen each other? Had he called things off with her? It really wasn't any of her business, but after everything she knew about the mayor, she worried about him.

She had a mind to message Tiffany back and ask if Daya looked sad. That way, she could convince herself it was because the mayor had dumped her. But it really was none of her business, and she had already gotten far too involved with his personal life. So, she resisted the urge and instead showered to get ready for the day. Charles had called in sick again, so Avery was working the tasting room. The rain had stopped, and she was certain the wine tastings would be busier again and looked forward to the distraction.

Charles' message to let her know he wouldn't be in to work had come through in an email. He still hadn't responded to her text, and it left Avery with an unending feeling of emptiness in her stomach and chest. She wasn't a fan of the way it made her feel. She would rather feel nothing than be upset that her employee was missing yet another day of work. Instead, she felt sad and a little bit alone. In reality, she felt completely lost when it came to Charles.

She had no idea exactly how upset he was with her or how to make things right with him. All she could do was accept responsibility for how things were and hope the answers would come to her.

She had her doubts, though. She'd never been good in those situations. In fact, until recently, she had hardly any friends, so situations like that had never been a reality for her. She wondered how silence from Charles could make her feel so alone when she was still surrounded by so many others.

When the workday was over, Avery headed to her home to have a cup of coffee. As she poured the steaming coffee into a bright red mug, she opened the chat box between her and Charles for what she was certain was the hundredth time that day. There was still no response.

The sun was starting to hang low in the atmosphere, and a soft rain had started up again. When she turned to face the window, she saw that the sky had taken on a soft purple color. She knew that the surrounding vineyards would look beautiful in the rain.

She abandoned the cup of coffee and jumped in the car to go for a drive. There had to be something that would cheer her up, and she figured a drive would help clear her head.

Avery envied Deb a little when she felt so consumed by her thoughts and wondered if it was pleasant to be so consumed by the lives of others. Perhaps it would mean that her own life wouldn't cause her so much stress. Maybe that was why Deb liked to gossip so much. Avery could hardly imagine being so focused on the lives of others that her own thoughts were silenced. What bliss.

As Avery's car peaked the top of the hill, she gasped at the beautiful view. The soft purple sky had deep gray clouds rolling in. The vines seemed to be heavy with rain, making the hills look like something out of a movie.

The swallows danced through the sky, creating liquid forms as they enjoyed their last bit of flight for the day. The roads were quiet, and for a moment, so was her mind. In the windows of all the houses, she could see warm glows as everyone prepared themselves for a colder night.

She imagined what she would make for dinner and that perhaps she would make a fire and enjoy a movie and a glass of wine. The drive was doing the trick, and Avery could feel the peace creeping back into her bones.

Small wafts of mist were creeping between the vineyards like a slow smoke machine. Suddenly Avery felt so small compared to the natural world.

Stop worrying. The vines do not worry, and yet they are fruitful. It occurred to her that all of her worrying and sleepless nights had made no difference to the outcome of reality. So what was the point?

The rain poured harder, and Avery knew that her drive would soon have to come to an end. Something about the vineyards and the weather had filled her up again. For the first time in days, she felt as if everything was actually alright.

Just as the rain had washed the dust off the vines so that they could flourish, it had cleansed Avery's own mind of its stagnant thoughts so that she could find relief. It didn't matter how long it took Charles to get back to her, she knew that he would, and all she had to do was wait. It didn't matter how many times she tried to imagine what he might say; in the end, it would be different, and she would find a way to respond.

Avery turned her car around to head home just as the rain started pelting down at its hardest. Visibility was low, and the roads were a little too wet for her preference. So, she dropped all thought of anything and concentrated solely on the road in front of her.

She was only a few blocks from home, waiting at an intersection. The visibility was worse, and she couldn't help but feel that she shouldn't drive just yet. Still, she looked in both directions and saw no headlights heading her way.

The vines don't worry. So, don't worry. Avery relaxed and made her way across the intersection. She was about halfway across when the sound of another car snuck up on her. Just as she glanced to her right, she saw a car with its headlights off, traveling at a speed that was faster than her reaction time. She slammed on the brakes and swerved, but it was no use. The front of her car just clipped the tail end of the speeding car. She saw the rain kick out from under the wheels as the other car came to a quick and dangerous stop.

"You can't be serious," Avery said as she put her hazards on and put her car in park.

Chapter Twenty

"Are you kidding me?" Avery said as she looked out at the car she had just hit. "Now I have to get out and get soaked."

She peered out the window, wishing there was some other way they could go about it. She should have trusted her gut. She should have believed the worry that had brewed in her mind just before her foot had touched the accelerator. "Always trust your gut," she mumbled as she reached for the door handle.

Avery did her best to cover her head with her jacket as she climbed out of her car and into the pouring rain. Even though the situation wasn't the best, the rain actually felt good against her skin. It seemed to cool her frustration.

She walked around her car to inspect the damage. She wasn't sure who she had hit. It was a car she didn't quite recognize, which was better. *At least I didn't hit a friend. Imagine how embarrassing that would be.*

The rain had made it a little hard to see, but she could see a few scratches on her car. Thankfully, it was nothing too serious, but she was sure it would still be pretty expensive. So, she walked over to see what the other car looked like. It had considerably more damage than her own, something she was certain the car's owner wouldn't be too pleased about.

"That's what happens when you're driving like a maniac," she said loudly enough that she was certain the driver could hear her.

Nobody had stepped out of the car yet, which didn't seem fair to her. She was soaking wet, and the other driver stayed nice and dry in their car. Surely they didn't think that the accident was her fault? She trudged over to inspect the damage on the other car and heard two doors slam. "I don't have time for this," a familiar voice said.

Avery knew who it was before she even looked up. She didn't want to believe that it could be him. Of all the people in the town she could have hit with her car, she'd hit the one man whose boundaries she had already crossed far too many times.

"Mayor Oswald, are you alright?" she asked as she walked toward him.

"Avery?" he said, staring at her through the rain. "This rain made it so difficult to see. I am so sorry!"

Avery was smiling at him when Daya walked up and wrapped her arm in his. She stared at the two of them for a moment, quite clearly still a couple. The mayor kept his eyes down as Avery tried to understand why he would stay with a woman who likely murdered her husband.

"Are you okay?" Daya asked, and Avery thought that she would be sick. She simply stared at the woman with such a bad taste in her mouth that she was certain it was showing on her face.

"Is your car alright?" Daya asked again, smiling at Avery.

The mayor shifted uncomfortably on his feet as Daya went to inspect the damage on both cars. Avery simply continued to stare in disbelief as she tried to piece it all together.

Then it occurred to her that perhaps he was in danger. She had seemed like the type of person who would take a man hostage. After all, she seemed perfectly willing to murder a man. Avery's heart started racing. She decided that Daya had to have been driving. It explained the speed of the car and the lack of headlights. She was trying to make a run for it, and she was taking the mayor with her. She must have been driving.

Daya returned to Mayor Oswald's side and tugged on his sleeve.

"It doesn't seem all too bad," she said to him. "Of course, it is unfortunate, but I'm sure it will all be worked out."

"I didn't see you there," the mayor said to Avery.

"You were driving?" she asked, glancing between him and Daya.

"Yes," he admitted with a forced chuckle. "I suppose I wasn't behaving quite as I should in weather like this. I'm willing to admit fault. I was driving way too fast!"

"Oh," Avery said, still uncertain. "Are you in a hurry? Is everything alright?"

"Yes, everything's just fine," he said with a strange, joyful tone to his voice. "We were just not paying attention. I'm just glad nobody got hurt."

"Yes, thank goodness!" Daya added.

He was driving?

She glanced at their car and noticed that there were bags packed in the back seat, along with what looked to be a tent and some blankets.

"Are you going away?" she asked, puzzled.

"Yes," Daya said cheerfully. "We decided we needed a break, and we're going away for the weekend."

"Not too far from here," the mayor added. "We just thought we'd get some space from everything for a day or two."

The mayor chuckled again, and it made Avery feel completely uneasy. Something about the way he was smiling and laughing seemed so odd to her. He seemed nothing like the man she had met at the barbecue or the man she had spoken to at his house.

As the mist began to wrap around their feet, Avery couldn't help but think that he looked as if it suited him. As if he was made for the gray, stormy background against which he stood. The way Daya looked at him seemed to be with comfort and Avery understood that a look like that only came from being incredibly close.

They're way too comfortable.

Then she realized that perhaps it wasn't his behavior at the car crash that she was confused about. Maybe it was his behavior that day at his house that she had misunderstood. He had been calm—a little too calm.

Initially, she was convinced that he was merely shocked. But now that Avery saw him still intertwined with Daya, she felt that perhaps he was a little too unconcerned about her potentially being a murderer.

She thought about everything that she knew about him. The stories about him being in the military, for instance. She had thought it made him a good man, but it might only mean he was strong. She had always understood that being in the military made you an excellent man. But she knew stories of men who were forever changed in a bad way because of it. It had never occurred to her that the mayor might have come out of the military with an innate ability to be unaffected by the good and bad of the world.

That would have been why he was such a good police officer. Who was she kidding? He was a politician. Few politicians were truly good men, and she had led herself to believe that Mayor Oswald was one. But why had his wife left in the middle of the night? And why had the friendship between him and Brie soured?

And she had understood that it just meant that he was good at his job. But being a good strategist in the military is different than being a good strategist in a football game. He was good at coming up with strategies that cost the lives of others, not just their money.

He had planned to use the dogs to create distractions. Strategy was what he had been really good at. He was excellent at creating distractions that could send an entire troop of enemy soldiers searching in the wrong direction.

She thought back to the first conversation she'd had with him and all the reasons why it had initially bothered her. He had lied about not attending the first day of the festival when she was certain she had seen him there.

She looked at him and knew that those were the same glasses that she had seen. In an instant, all of his behavior fell into place. His conversations, his calmness, his eagerness to have the photographs covered up, and why he had been so scarce at the festival. All of it. Avery's feet felt as if they had turned to lead, as if she could never move again.

"Are you sure you're alright?" Daya asked again.

She looked at the woman with the heron tattoo and saw her through a different lens. Why had she been so cheerful that day at the coffee shop? Why could they find no evidence to use against her? Had she done this before? Then it dawned on Avery that they found no evidence against Daya because it never existed.

"I'm alright," Avery answered, forcing a smile. "Just a little cold."

Avery needed to think fast. She needed to decide what she was going to do because every piece of the puzzle had finally fallen into place for her.

Mayor Oswald had murdered the man at the festival. Everything else had simply been a distraction, part of his strategy. And now, he was trying to flee.

Chapter Twenty-One

Avery's head was spinning as she tried to comprehend what she was now certain was the truth. She had been so hell-bent on proving who the murderer was that she hadn't even bothered to look at what had been staring her right in the face.

They were going to get away, and she was the only person who knew about it. She was the only person who knew about any of it. She had to do something to make sure they didn't get away. She couldn't follow them since they would certainly notice. Asking them where they were going wouldn't work either. She had been staring at them for so long that she was certain the mayor could tell she had figured it out. She needed to do something to make it seem like she was just going to carry on with her day. She needed them to believe that they would get away with it and that they would be able to escape. But there was only one person she trusted enough to ask for help in that situation, and he hadn't been speaking to her. Still, it was her best hope and the only plan she could come up with at the time.

"Let me just see if I can take some photographs," she said with a smile. "Then I can leave you to it, and the two of you can enjoy your time away." She pulled out her phone and took some photographs of everything. Then, before slipping the phone back into her pocket, she dialed Charles' number and hoped he would answer. He had no reason to answer her call, but she could still hope that he would.

The rain had let up just enough that it was no longer that difficult to see or hear anything. Just to make sure, she looked at the mayor again, doing her best to assess his body language. He certainly didn't seem like a man that was there against his will.

In fact, he seemed to be impatient. She watched as he checked his watch every few seconds, his foot tapping slightly against the roadside. He wanted to leave and was in a hurry. Daya, on the other hand, didn't seem to behave as if anything was wrong.

The first call went unanswered. So, she pulled her phone out again.

"I see there's an angle that I missed," she said with a nervous laugh. "Let me just get that angle." She snapped the photograph and texted Charles.

Pick up. It's urgent. But don't say anything when you answer. Just listen.

Then, she gave it a few minutes before dialing his number again and holding her phone at waist level with her. She needed to make sure it looked natural. She also needed to see if Charles answered her call.

She was about to give up the notion entirely when she saw the screen change. He had answered. She waited a moment to see the call had been connected for a second or two before she proceeded with the next part of her plan.

She took a step closer to the mayor and Daya. "You know the roads a little better than I do, mayor," she said loudly. "Where would you say it is that we are?"

"We're at the intersection between Jeffrey's Boulevard and Church Street," he said with a puzzled look.

"Oh! Of course, I can never remember the street names!" Avery said cheerfully. "I just want to make sure that I can give the correct information to my insurance."

"That's okay. Let's get it all sorted, and then we can be on our way," he said with a forced smile as he checked his watch again.

"I didn't see you coming!" she said loud enough for Charles to hear. "How unfortunate that we should meet again this way."

The last sentence clearly made the mayor uncomfortable, as the previous time they had been together, Avery had been at his house to warn him about his girlfriend.

"You two know each other?" Daya asked.

"We've met a few times," Avery said calmly. "Only recently."

"I've never met you before," Daya said, taking a step forward.

"No, you haven't," Avery said with a smile, glancing at the mayor. "I'm Avery." Avery took a step toward her to shake her hand. All she could hope was that Charles was able to hear what was being said.

"I'm Daya," she greeted with a friendly smile.

"I'm so sorry about all of this," Avery said and noticed the mayor roll his eyes. "It is tedious, but as soon as we get the details out of the way, then the two of you can continue on to wherever it was that you were in such a hurry to get to."

"Of course!" the mayor said, forcing a smile. "Again, as I said, I was driving way too fast. I really am sorry."

"Nobody's hurt, and that's all that matters," Avery said. "I am sorry that I've interrupted your weekend away. It sure looks like you're packed for more than a weekend, though." Avery laughed to make it seem as if she had simply been teasing them both. She needed to act as if none of it really bothered her. One of the two people in front of her had no problem murdering for their own personal gain. It still wasn't clear to her if they had worked together, though.

"If you don't mind, Avery. I'd like to hurry things up. I need to be checked in before a certain time," Mayor Oswald said, still doing his best to remain friendly.

"Of course not," Avery said. "Let me just make a note of what the damage really is, and you can be on your way. Where is it you're heading?"

The mayor and Daya kept completely quiet.

"I don't mean to pry," Avery said. "It's just that I've been meaning to get away for a while, and I can't seem to find anywhere worth going. I thought that perhaps you could suggest a place for me." The two glanced uneasily at each other.

"It's sort of a surprise for Daya," the mayor said, creating yet another brilliant diversion.

"Yes," Daya said eagerly. "I have no idea where we're going! Isn't that romantic?"

The rain was still falling softly, and Avery would have loved nothing more than to be inside where it was warm. The fingers that gripped her phone were so cold she didn't know if she could move them anymore.

She glanced at her phone and saw Charles was still connected to the call. She could only assume that it meant that he was listening. She didn't know if he would understand what was going on, but she had no choice but to hope it would work.

"Did you hear that the postman has arthritis?" she asked, making conversation in an attempt to stall the events of the day.

All that still bothered her were the stones.

"Which postman?" the mayor asked.

"The one with the Velcro shoes," Avery said, realizing that it was a ridiculous way to identify a man. "You said he was behaving strangely the last time you saw him, maybe that's why."

"Ah," the mayor said as he began to pace slowly. "That would be Evan."

"Evan," Avery laughed. "You know, it's terrible. People like Evan are such a part of my life, yet I never thought to ask his name."

"Yes," the mayor said dryly. "Perhaps you should get to know people a little better around here."

Avery wasn't sure if it was a threat. Had he implied that she should have waited to know him better before rushing to his house to warn him against Daya? Had she scared the mayor off? Had her visit with him been why he was fleeing in the first place?

"You're right," Avery said, making direct eye contact with him.

"You never know," Daya said, joining a conversation she didn't truly understand. "Perhaps you would find that you and Evan get along really well. That happened to me and the mayor."

The mayor cleared his throat and shot Daya a look. She seemed to understand what he meant by it. Clearly, the two of them had been together longer than anyone had originally suspected.

Avery thought about Daya's husband and how he had tried to warn them that she had done it. She thought about the stones and the mayor's lies about his whereabouts. All of it made her angry. It needed to end.

She wasn't sure what she was going to do, but she knew she couldn't let them leave. Still, it was hard to know if she was in any danger. "Right, well," Avery said, pretending to be satisfied with her assessment of the damage. "It seems as if your car has had more damage than mine."

"That's unfortunate," the mayor said. "Thankfully, it is still drivable, so we can still get to our destination in time."

"Wouldn't you like to take note of the damage?" Avery asked. "For insurance purposes? I can send it to you if you like. What's your number?"

"It's really no problem," the mayor said. "Just tell me which insurance company you're with, and I'll make sure to settle all the costs."

"Don't be ridiculous," Avery protested.

The mayor was clearly willing to go to any length to make sure that they didn't waste any more time. "No, really," he continued. "I insist. It was my fault. I was going too fast. Please, don't worry about it."

Avery was playing a losing game and wasn't sure what to do. The call was still connected, but she was ready to call it a night when a message came through from Charles.

I can hear you. Keep going.

Chapter Twenty-Two

S he didn't know what Charles planned on doing about it, but Avery was certain she was staring the real murderer in the face. And she was even more certain that he was about to leave. She had stalled as much as she possibly could but was running out of excuses to keep him there.

"Right, well, as soon as you've done your checks," she said. "I guess we can all carry on with our journeys. Where did you say you were going?"

"It's a surprise," the mayor said, walking toward his driver's side door.

"D-don't you want to take some photographs?" she asked.

Mayor Oswald was growing impatient. She could tell by the way he continuously clenched his jaw. He had the driver's side door already partly open and took a deep breath to calm himself down.

"Why don't you just send me what you have?" he suggested. "We really are in a bit of a hurry. I don't want to miss the check-in."

Avery was beginning to panic. She couldn't let him get away. She needed to do something, anything to make him stay. She was willing to put almost anything on the line, and there was only one thing she could think to do.

She would confront him, and she would confront him well enough that he would react exactly as he should and stay to confront her too. It wasn't a perfect plan, and she wasn't sure it would work, but she knew he was angry, and that could work to her benefit if she played her cards right.

"You killed him, didn't you?" she said as loudly as possible.

The mayor paused and turned to face her, his expression cold and hard. "What did you say?" he said stiffly.

"This whole time, I thought it was her," Avery said, pointing at Daya. "But you killed her husband, didn't you?"

The mayor abandoned his efforts at climbing into his car, and Avery knew that her plan had worked. She just hoped that whatever Charles was doing, he was doing it fast. She could be in danger, and she hadn't thought far enough ahead for that.

"I would suggest that you stop talking," he said through clenched teeth as he approached her.

"What is she talking about?" Daya said, joining them in the rain.

"You said that you weren't there on the first day of the festival," Avery explained. "But I know I saw you there. You were standing behind a building. I thought it was odd. And I couldn't understand why you had lied and said that you weren't there when I saw you."

"Be careful, Avery," the mayor warned again.

"And now you're trying to run, aren't you?" she said. "This is no weekend away. Who leaves for the weekend at this time of day?"

"You said you weren't going to be at the festival that day," Daya said. "You didn't want to make things uncomfortable for Kevin and me."

Finally, Avery learned the victim's name.

"I saw him there," Avery said to Daya. "Just a few hours before your husband was found dead."

"You have no proof," said the mayor. "This is ridiculous."

"No, but I know you're an excellent strategist," she said. "And I know you used to train dogs to create a distraction, isn't that right? And I've just realized that Daya was that distraction."

"What is she talking about?" Daya said, approaching the mayor with caution.

"What was it?" Avery continued. "Did you want to enjoy his insurance money, too? Were the divorce proceedings taking a little too long? Why did you do it?"

"Enough!" the mayor shouted. He was red in the face from rage. "Why couldn't you just butt out like you were instructed to do?"

"And the stones," Avery continued. "They puzzled me at first. But you knew how uncommon they were, and you knew how busy that would keep the police in the investigation. So, you took some that day when you were at Evan's house, when you say he was acting strangely."

"What are you talking about? What did you do?!" Daya shouted through tears of rage.

"I secured a life for us," the mayor said. "He was going to take everything from you. I couldn't stand by and watch it happen."

Avery nearly cheered with excitement when he started talking. But one look at him told her he was angry enough to murder again. She wanted to step away from him, but she needed Charles to hear it all. A glance at her phone told her he was still on the line.

"You placed the stones there as a distraction," Avery said with a coy smile. "Why, though? Why would you frame the very woman you were aiming to protect?"

"Because she's clean, you idiot," he snarled. "You think you're so smart, but you couldn't figure out the simplest part of it all. I knew they would find no evidence on her. She was the only lead they had. It would buy us enough time to get out of town and start our lives together."

Daya stared at him in disbelief. Tears streamed down her cheeks as her legs gave way beneath her, and she collapsed to her knees. "Please tell me it isn't true," she cried.

"You were never supposed to find out about any of this," he said. "If it wasn't for this meddling woman always sticking her nose where it doesn't belong, we'd have been out of here by now, and all of this could have been left behind."

"Why would you do this to me?" Daya cried.

"Because I love you," the mayor said, his shoulders dropping. "I killed innocent soldiers on opposing sides because I love my country. I killed criminals while on duty because I love my citizens. I killed Kevin because I love you."

"Why the stones?" Avery asked. "Wouldn't they have looked into her anyway?"

"It's no secret that our police force isn't the greatest," the mayor laughed. "I just needed to make sure they looked in the wrong direction. But they never even found the stones! It almost hadn't worked. Then, thankfully, you found them!"

"This is insane," Daya sobbed. "This is not what I wanted. They interrogated me for days because of you!"

"But we're free now," the mayor said. "Your name was cleared, just like I knew it would be. And we can leave all of this behind."

"What about her?" Daya asked, pointing in Avery's direction. "She'll talk."

"After everything she's done, nobody will believe her," the mayor laughed.

"I came to you to warn you," Avery said. "I was worried that your girlfriend was a murderer, and I warned you to stay away." Avery glanced over at Daya. "Sorry," she said sheepishly.

"Yes, you did," the mayor smiled. "And it really was very sweet. But it was your meddling that ruined my plan in the first place. They were supposed to accuse her of murder, but our affair was never supposed to come to light."

"Ah," Avery said, wishing Charles would give her some kind of guidance.

"If it weren't for those highly inappropriate photographs of the two of us, my name would have stayed out of this entirely," he shouted.

She couldn't believe his audacity. He blamed her for the failure of his plan, as if she was the bad person in all of this. Meanwhile, he was an actual murderer. Suddenly she wished she had hit them harder with her car.

"And what would have been the reason you disappeared?" Avery asked. "Did you think you could just pack your bags and leave, and it would all be over?"

"Originally, I thought I'd have more time to leave. But, after your photographs, I realized that it would make things more complicated. So, at midnight tonight, those photographs will be leaked. By my own arrangement."

"I don't understand," Avery said.

"Of course you don't," he cried, raising his palms to the sky. "First, the

132

photographs, then the notice of my stepping down as mayor. Nobody will care where I've gone after that."

"You won't get away with this," Avery said.

Despite her fear of being his next victim, she couldn't help but be amused by the irony of the situation. She was using his own strategy of distraction against him. Only, she didn't have a very well-thought-out plan. Hers was being created on the spot.

"What do you think?" he asked. "That anyone would believe you? I've given this town my life. They've always been on my side."

"Not after your scandal comes to light," Avery said. "Do you think they'll still have your back when they see at the photographs of the two of you together?"

"It doesn't matter," he said. "I'll be gone by then. You are nobody to this community. They have no reason to believe a word you say."

She had run out of things to say. The conversation had carried on too long, and she didn't want to risk her safety anymore. So Avery stopped talking and prayed Charles had recorded the phone call.

Chapter Twenty-Three

The rain had started to pour a lot harder as the mayor walked back to his car. And when Avery glanced at her phone again, she saw that Charles was no longer listening. The call had probably been disconnected due to the weather. She had no idea when it had disconnected or how much of the mayor's confession Charles had heard. And it struck her that maybe it had all been for nothing anyway. But as the mayor turned the key in his ignition, the sky lit up with flashing blue lights.

Cars surrounded them with sirens blaring. And Avery just stood and watched, waves of relief crashing through her. Teams of officers ran from their vehicles toward the mayor's car. And when Avery looked again, both the mayor and Daya were being handcuffed and pushed into police vehicles.

"Avery!" she heard Charles call.

She searched for him through the heavy rain and flashing lights. It was hard to make sense of anything anymore. Then she spotted him. He had called to her from a group of officers who seemed to be asking him a stream of questions.

She took a step toward him when a firm hand wrapped around her arm. "Ma'am, you need to come with us for some questioning," an officer said as he led her toward her vehicle.

"Questioning?" she asked. "Have I done something wrong?"

"No, ma'am," the officer laughed. "We just need an official statement from you. We'd like to get all the details of tonight's event. Once we've got that sorted, you'll be free to return home."

She didn't want to go with the officer. She wanted to go to Charles. She wanted to apologize to him for everything and thank him for coming to her rescue despite it all. But another firm tug at her arm told her she had no choice.

The questions seemed to carry on forever. Every question was followed by a series of follow-up questions. She did her best to answer them all as accurately as possible. By the time they were done, Charles was no longer there.

Avery drove home in silence, in complete shock at the events of the day. She still wasn't entirely sure if it was over. Nobody could tell her if she would be required to testify or what would come next. All she knew was that she was desperate to go home and spend a quiet night with Sprinkles. She was certain that she wouldn't get any sleep either. There was too much adrenaline coursing through her system. How could she be expected to wake up the next day and carry on like normal? *Oh, come on. This is not the worst thing you've been through. And yet, you've managed every day since.*

When she finally made it home, she knew that the only way to distract herself would be to cook a meal. It was way too late for it to make any sense. But she expected it to fill enough of her time. And she counted on that.

Thankfully, she remembered that she had some leftover steaks from when the Stammtisch women were over. Time to repurpose those leftovers into some steak sandwiches. Being in the kitchen, chopping away, and getting her hands dirty was Avery's idea of a perfect distraction.

Avery and Sprinkles shared a tasty dinner together as she ran him through some of the new tricks he'd learned from training with Brie. It wasn't the best distraction, but it cleared her mind of thoughts of the mayor and his murderous plans.

However, her thoughts were now occupied with Charles. He had saved her, and she hadn't even had the chance to talk to him. She wasn't even sure if he wanted to talk. He had been so upset with her, and she couldn't expect him to just drop it all.

She would have to find a way to make it up to him, but she had no idea where to begin.

Was he at the police station? Briefly, she considered going there to see if she could find him. Perhaps he was at home, taking it easy just like she was. She could send him a message, but she wouldn't even know how to start it. Everything that she needed to say to him simply wasn't right for a message. She couldn't be that cold. It wouldn't work.

She was elbow-deep in cleaning the dinner dishes when she heard a familiar knock at the door—three knocks, a pause, and then two knocks. She knew immediately who it was. She rushed to the door and pulled it open.

"Something smells delicious," Charles said with a smile as she opened the door. "And I'm starving." She'd never been so relieved to see Charles with a smile on his face.

"Come in; I'll dish some up for you," she said, stepping aside to let him in. "It's the least I can do."

Charles lifted a box in the air. "I have some cake. Bee Sting. That's your favorite, right?"

"My all-time favorite," Avery said with a grin.

At that moment, she understood that no apology was needed from either of them. And they enjoyed a meal together as if nothing had ever happened.

The birds had only just started chirping when Avery opened her eyes. She'd fallen asleep earlier than anticipated. The sun was starting to rise, and Sprinkles was nowhere near awake yet. But when she stepped outside with her cup of coffee, the paper had already arrived.

There was only ever one reason why the paper would arrive earlier than usual. That was if there was some kind of breaking news. Avery glanced at her phone, certain that there would already be several messages from Deb about it.

She lifted the paper and recognized her own photographs splashed against the front page. She had almost forgotten that the mayor had leaked the photographs as a cover. But as she read, she couldn't help but smile.

She had expected the headline to refer to some kind of illicit affair. Instead, it read something entirely different. The police had gotten to the paper first.

MAYOR ARRESTED ON MURDER CHARGES,
LOVE TRIANGLE TURNS DEADLY.

The End.

~

Recipes

Eggs with Smoked Salmon and Mushrooms *(serves 4)*

4 large eggs
16 ounces cremini mushrooms
8 ounces smoked salmon
4 teaspoons butter
1 tablespoon water
salt
chopped green onion

- Clean mushrooms by wiping with dry paper towel.
- Slice mushrooms.
- Heat pan to medium and add 2 tsp butter.
- Add mushrooms and stir into butter.
- Salt and pepper to taste.
- Cook until brown and softened.
- Remove mushrooms from pan and set aside.
- Add remaining 2 tsp butter to pan.
- Crack eggs in hot pan, fry over medium heat.

- Add 1 tbsp water, cover pan.
- Once eggs are set, remove from heat.
- Divide mushrooms on four plates, top with 2 oz smoked salmon each.
- Carefully put egg over mixture and sprinkle with green onions.

Pairing options: Whipped Coffee or Strawberry Thyme Spritzer

Whipped Coffee (serves 4)

4 tablespoons instant coffee
4 tablespoons sugar
4 tablespoons boiling water
32 ounces milk

- In a small bowl, add coffee and sugar.
- Carefully pour in water.
- Whisk to combine (a hand mixer would be a better idea!).
- Coffee is ready once mixture is thick and a much lighter color (about 5-10 minutes).
- Divide milk equally between 4 glasses/mugs (this can be served over ice or hot).
- Divide frothy mixture between glasses or mugs.

Strawberry Thyme Spritzer (serves 4)

12 ounces vermouth, chilled
4 lemon wedges
8 strawberries thinly sliced
4 sprigs of thyme
crushed ice
8 ounces Prosecco

- Divide vermouth equally between 4 glasses.

- Squeeze juice of lemon wedge into each glass.
- Add strawberries and thyme equally between glasses.
- Add ice to each glass.
- Top with Prosecco.

Shrimp Étouffée (serves 6)

1 cup onion, diced
1 cup celery, diced
1 cup green bell pepper, diced
5 tablespoons butter
5 tablespoons flour
4 tablespoons tomato paste
1 pound of shrimp, shelled and deveined
4 cups of shrimp stock
1 cup green onions, sliced
1/2 cup flat leaf parsley, chopped
2 teaspoon salt
1/2 teaspoon black pepper
1 teaspoon cayenne pepper

- Heat pot to medium high, melt butter.
- Add onions, celery, and bell pepper to pot, stir.
- When softened, add flour and combine.
- Stir mixture for 10 minutes.
- Add tomato paste, cook another 10 minutes.
- Add shrimp to pot, cook for 5 minutes.
- Add stock. Cover and simmer for 5 minutes.
- Add green onions, parsley, salt, pepper, and cayenne pepper.
- Simmer 10 minutes.
- Remove pot from stove.
- Rest stew for 20 minutes.
- Plate stew over hot rice.

Shrimp Stock

- Boil shells and heads of shrimp with 6 cups of water for 15 minutes.

Pairing: Chenin blanc or chardonnay

Steak Florentine (serves 6)

2 large garlic cloves, cut in half
3 T-bone steaks (1½ pounds each, about 1½" -1 ¾" thick)
Kosher salt and freshly ground black pepper
1 lemon, cut in half
2 teaspoons olive oil

- Rub garlic cloves all over steaks
- Sprinkle steaks with salt and pepper.
- Refrigerate 1 hour (overnight would be even better!).
- Let steaks come to room temperature (at least 20 minutes).
- Heat grill to medium-high.
- Grill steaks to preferred doneness. Only flip once and don't move after you've flipped them!

Rare: 5 minutes per side
Medium-rare: 7 minutes per side

- Rest steaks 10 minutes.
- Cut the meat away from the bone.
- Slice meat across the grain into 1" slices, squeeze lemon over, and drizzle sliced meat with olive oil.
- Serve with your favorite potatoes and grilled veggies.

Pairing: Sangiovese or syrah

DANI SIMMS

*Bee Sting Cake (serves 8)**

BATTER

4 large eggs
1 cup powdered sugar
½ cup all-purpose flour
1 tablespoon baking powder
½ teaspoon salt

FILLING

2 cups heavy cream
1 package instant vanilla pudding mix
2-3 tablespoons whole milk, if filling is too thick

TOPPING

1 cup sliced almonds
2 tablespoons sugar

GREASING PAN

½ teaspoon butter
1 teaspoon flour

- Preheat the oven to 350°F.
- Grease 9-inch springform pan with butter and sprinkle with flour.
- In a large bowl, beat eggs and powdered sugar with a mixer until creamy (5 minutes or so).
- Add flour, baking powder, and salt.
- Mix until well combined.
- Pour batter into pre-greased pan.
- Sprinkle batter with sugar and almonds.
- Bake cake at 350°F for 30 minutes (test with toothpick).

144

- Remove cake from pan and set aside to cool.
- In a medium bowl, beat pudding mix and heavy cream until thick, creamy, and spreadable (if mixture becomes too thick, add in 1-2 tablespoons of milk).
- Slice cooled cake horizontally in half, forming two layers.
- Spread filling evenly across the bottom layer.
- Place the top layer back.

Pairing: Hot black tea with a splash of milk

*This is kind of a cheater recipe, but I promise you it will taste just as lovely!

Murder at the Vineyard Inn

BOOK 2

Chapter One

Eleanor and Samuel stood proudly at each other's side as they said their vows. The ceremony looked incredible.

In the small chapel were rows of benches decorated with the whitest lilies Avery had ever seen. Soft green accents and a softer dress code made it look truly magical. The light beamed through the chapel's stained-glass windows, painting an ethereal moment for all to enjoy.

Avery hardly recognized the town church as it was full of fresh flowers. She had also never seen Eleanor smile so brightly.

Everyone had pulled together to create a spectacular wedding. And it wasn't only the wedding that had occurred. Many festivities led up to their marriage, each one celebrating something else. There had been bridal showers and kitchen teas, and finally, the day of the ceremony had arrived, and all of them were relieved.

It seemed to Avery that the entire town had been invited. The church was packed full, and everyone watched as the couple pledged the remainder of their lives to each other. It took all her concentration for Avery not to cry.

It seemed not too long ago that Eleanor had told her how she simply wasn't interested in love anymore after her husband had died. And it wasn't long after that when she was introduced to the new town vet, Dr.

Samuel Moses. Now, she stood gleaming, as she prepared to take his last name. It had been love at first sight, and the fact that they had made it to the point where they were married was no surprise to anyone.

Avery wondered if she would ever feel brave enough to look for love again. She'd lost her own husband in a boating accident, and it seemed like an impossible task to her. But it was clear to everyone present that Eleanor and Samuel loved each other deeply. So, Avery thought there might be hope for her to one day feel that kind of love again too.

A loud "AWWWW" traveled through the guests as Sprinkles carried the rings down the aisle. When Avery had first gotten him as a puppy, she wondered if he would ever learn to behave. And for the first few months, it seemed there wasn't much hope.

But after a couple of weeks of military-style dog training, Sprinkles had turned into the perfect golden retriever that she had hoped he would become. They had practiced walking that stretch down the aisle over and over again the days leading up to the wedding. So, naturally, Avery wanted to burst with pride when he did a perfect job of delivering the rings to the happy couple.

Avery waited at the back of the church, crouched low with a treat in her hand, for Sprinkles to return to her. She loved to see him with his white bow tie on and a proud puppy smile that he'd learned to give every time he'd successfully performed a new trick.

Sprinkles made his way back down the aisle toward Avery, soaking up the guests' praise as he passed them. And just as they had practiced, it seemed he would complete his task without any deviation.

That was until he got to the third row from the back. Sprinkles suddenly stopped and turned, pressing his nose against the hand of a man Avery didn't recognize. He was a tall man with thick dark hair. His suit looked as if it was just a little too tight, but purposely so.

He sported a very expensive watch, which he was careful to have on display. Everything about him seemed expensive. But what really bothered Avery was how he seemed to pay Sprinkles no attention at all. His hand rested carefully on his leg as he kept his eyes glued to the proceedings in front of him. There was something about him that seemed completely out of place. He sat upright and still as if he was poised for an audience.

Avery clicked her fingers as quietly as she could to get Sprinkles' attention. And to her surprise, it worked. Sprinkles looked at her and came walking casually down the rest of the aisle toward her, eager to receive his treat.

She looked back at the man, trying desperately to figure out who he was. But she could only see the back of his head. She did notice that he didn't seem to cheer and clap with the rest of the crowd. In fact, he didn't seem all that pleased to be there. The only movements he did make were to check that his watch was straight, his hair was neat, and his suit sat right. He reminded her of many of the businessmen she had seen during her time in the city.

The crowd cheered as the happy couple was finally pronounced Mr. and Mrs. Moses. The cameras flashed, and the crowd erupted once more as Samuel kissed his blushing bride. Soon, they were walking back toward the church doors as white rose petals rained down on them.

The ceremony had been perfect, just as Eleanor had hoped. Sprinkles sat patiently at the doors, accepting every loving pat and scruff the guests had to offer as they left the church. His white bow tie was sitting skew, but his smile remained fixed on his face.

By the time the reception was in full swing, Sprinkles was the life of the party. He spent most of his time waltzing between tables to see who would give him the most love and the most scraps of food from their plates.

Avery wondered if there was money to be made with Sprinkles working as a professional wedding guest for other weddings in town. He seemed to be a hit.

When Sprinkles nuzzled his snout into the hand of one of the guests, it reminded Avery of the man she had seen at the ceremony. So, she looked around the room to see if she could spot him. She knew the color of his suit and figured that perhaps if she saw him from the front, she might recognize him. There were many people in attendance who had scrubbed up well. Perhaps she did know the man and simply didn't recognize him in his finest clothes.

She scanned every table and every person on the dance floor and saw no sign of his tight navy blue suit. She knew that the speeches would soon commence, so she figured she'd find him when everybody stopped moving for a moment.

"What are you looking for?" Camille asked as she took a seat.

Camille was one of the women of the Stammtisch that Avery had joined. It was a group of women that often met on an informal basis, and Avery had come to care for the group quite a bit. It didn't surprise Avery that Camille, being the quietest of the lot, would be found nowhere near the dance floor.

"I'm looking for a man I saw earlier," Avery explained. "I didn't really recognize him from behind, so I figured I'd see if I recognized him from the front."

"That seems reasonable," Camille answered. "What did he look like from behind? Perhaps I can help you find him."

Avery was barely halfway through her description of him when Camille rolled her eyes. "That's Dean Scott," she said. "I saw him in the crowd as well, looking as sour as he usually does."

"You don't seem too pleased," Avery remarked. "I'm assuming you're not a fan of his?"

"Nobody likes him," she explained. "I'm not surprised he left early. He wasn't even really invited."

"And what exactly makes him so unpopular?" Avery asked.

"Well, for one thing, he seems to think he's better than anyone here," Camille explained. "Especially since he moved to the city."

"Oh?"

"Yes, he keeps talking about how he has this big, fancy house there, but nobody's ever been invited to it," Camille answered. "And when he does come to town to visit his mother, he invites everyone over, and then we're basically forced to hear about how fantastic his life is."

"I see. So, he's a little boring?"

"Not boring, no. He's just one of those people whose ideas will always be better than yours. If you have something, his version of it is better...he likes to pretend that he's the most important person in the universe, and the rest of us were simply placed here to remind him of it."

"Sounds terrible," Avery said quietly.

"And he's not all that obvious about it, either," Camille continued. "You don't really notice how bad he makes you feel about yourself until he's left again. He does it all with a smile and a charm that can bamboozle anybody."

"Ah," Avery said. "Sounds like he's a narcissist."

"Well, that's precisely what he is," Camille laughed. "And if you ask him, he'd tell you that it's your fault for seeing him that way."

"I understand why he wasn't invited now," Avery laughed.

Camille stretched her eyes big. "And yet, he still came."

"He would, wouldn't he?" she asked. "You know, if he's a narcissist, it would probably drive him wild that everybody else was invited except him. He probably told himself it was just an admin error or something."

"That does sound like something he would do," Camille answered, taking a sip of her wine.

Le Blanc Cellars had gifted all the wine for the wedding, and Avery was starting to worry it wouldn't be enough. In every direction she looked, she saw another bottle being opened and more wine being poured. She wondered if she'd need to get a few more cases to last them the rest of the night. But then they'd finally reached the part of the night where the music slowed, and she knew most people had likely already had their fill.

"I heard he had his mother bring him as her plus one," Camille said.

"I'm sorry?" Avery asked. She'd been so worried about the wine she'd forgotten what they were talking about.

"Dean Scott," Camille said. "He was only able to come because his mother listed him as her date."

"His mother is Mrs. Scott!" Avery said, piecing it together. "She's the lady with the rose farm not too far from here."

"That's the one! And she's even worse than he is," Camille said.

"In what way?"

Avery didn't really know Mrs. Scott. She'd just caught glimpses of her here and there in town. She was an elderly woman with sleek gray hair. She only ever wore all-white clothes, and Avery was certain she'd never seen her without her red lipstick.

"She thinks she's more important than any of us," Camille said. "She once sold roses to some or other president, and in her mind that practically makes her royalty."

Avery laughed. "How did she find herself with an invitation then?"

"She's old!" Camille cried. "Eleanor felt too bad to tell her she couldn't come, especially since Mrs. Scott insisted on giving Eleanor half-price on her bouquet. So then, Eleanor had to invite her, and then that meant Dean found a way to get himself invited too."

"Do they have a habit of doing that?" Avery asked. "You know, worming their way into other people's affairs?"

"Oh yes, they're experts at it. You've been here long enough now. It's only a matter of time before Mrs. Scott starts poking her nose in your business too."

The way the man had looked and behaved made better sense to Avery now. Everything about him stood out to her, but she understood now that it had been his intention. He had wanted everyone to notice him.

She'd known too many people like that when she lived in the city. And she wondered if he had always been that way and was sculpted by his mother's attitude or if he had adopted that behavior in the city after he moved there.

She wondered what it was about him that had gotten Sprinkles' attention. There had to be something her dog found interesting about him, but she couldn't quite understand what. The more she thought through what Camille had told her, the more she understood the man.

His flashy watch made sense to her, and so did his tight suit. It also explained why he didn't join in the celebration with the rest of the guests. Narcissists are most unhappy when the attention is on someone else, especially if the other person is deserving of the attention they get.

Still, there was something about him that was familiar to her.

Chapter Two

The music had changed and the dance floor was packed. In the center of the crowd danced the happy couple as they clung eagerly to each other. It was the time of the night when the music had become slower, and those dancing together had moved closer to each other.

Couples danced with their arms wrapped around each other, sneaking kisses anywhere they could. Camille had dragged Sprinkles off for a slow dance too. He'd already lost his bow tie at some point in the night.

Every guest that attended the reception seemed to have had an excellent time. It had been a magical evening, and Eleanor and Samuel looked happier than Avery had ever seen them before.

She sat on the sidelines, watching all the other happy couples dance as she contemplated all the ways her life had changed over the last few months. It was a brief moment of peace in which she thought about none of the daily stresses in her life.

But her peace was disrupted when she spotted a slightly tipsy Charles in the center of the dance floor, his arms wrapped around a half-empty bottle of merlot as he swayed his hips to the beat. Avery laughed loudly until she felt she could no longer breathe.

She'd only ever seen Charles tipsy once before, and that was at the launch party for her bed and breakfast, Cellar Vie. That night he had promised Avery he would always take care of her. She'd thought it was nothing but a silly tipsy statement, and although they'd had difficulties in their friendship, he had yet to break that promise.

She wondered what promises he was whispering to that bottle of merlot as they moved slowly from one end to the other, keeping time to the music.

Then, the music stopped. It was abrupt, and Avery worried another string of speeches would ensue. Until she heard the gasps as everybody looked toward the music booth. A group of police officers had stopped the music and were motioning for everyone to gather on the dance floor.

"What's going on?" Avery asked as she walked toward the crowd.

"Can we get everyone's attention, please?" one officer called out to them. "Gather around; it's a serious matter. We need everyone's eyes on us for a moment. We do apologize for the interruption."

Charles had been a police officer before and still worked with them as a consultant. They were good friends, and she wondered if he hadn't perhaps put them up to something as a funny prank on the happy couple. It didn't seem entirely unlike him. But the seconds passed, and nothing funny had happened yet.

It wasn't until she saw the confused look on Charles' face that she realized he also had no idea what was going on. Avery made her way over to stand next to him.

"What is this?" she whispered.

"I have no idea," he answered, placing the bottle of wine on the ground beside him.

At that moment, the door to the venue opened again, and a very concerned chief of police entered with a notebook and haste in his step. He greeted his men who had arrived before him and took his place in front of the crowd.

"Ladies and Gentlemen," he announced loudly. "I'm so sorry for the interruption, but I urgently need to inform you that all the guests who have traveled from out of town are required to stay in town until further notice."

"I don't understand," Eleanor replied. "Have we done something wrong?"

"Regrettably, there's been a murder," he answered.

There was a shocked silence in the room. Avery could feel the fear and tension on her skin. She looked at Charles and knew he had sobered up fast.

"I don't understand," Eleanor said with panic in her voice.

"We have just been to the scene of a crime where a body was found," the police chief announced. "And it would appear that the guests in this wedding are all considered suspects for now. I am sure some of you will be cleared quite quickly. But until we can prove your innocence, you will all be required to stay. Anybody who leaves will have a warrant out for their arrest."

A panicked murmur ran through the guests that still remained at the party. Avery looked to Charles as if he would have answers, but he seemed just as shocked as everybody else. She knew it had to be pretty serious if everybody was expected to stay.

"If we are considered suspects, then shouldn't we know which crime we are accused of?" Samuel asked. His face was red with frustration at the accusations.

"It is with sadness that I inform you of the murder of Dean Scott," the police chief announced. "And we are led to believe that a satchel of money has been stolen from amongst his possessions."

There was a gasp through the crowd. Avery's mouth hung open as she thought about the conversation she'd had with Camille earlier. She looked around the room to read the reactions of everybody else. If one of them could really be the murderer, then perhaps their actions could give them away.

But all she saw were pale faces and mouths that hung open just like hers. It seemed to have come as a shock to everyone, despite Camille's claims that nobody really liked him. The entire situation made her feel uneasy.

"Sorry, sir," Charles said loudly. "But what exactly makes you think that any of us could be a suspect in his murder?"

It was an excellent question, and Avery was grateful Charles had asked it. She wouldn't have had the guts to ask, and she knew it would only keep her up that night thinking about it. Then again, as a retired cop, Charles knew the right questions.

"There was evidence in the man's room at the inn that suggests he was afraid for his life," the police chief answered. "It suggests that perhaps one of the guests at this wedding intended to do him harm."

Avery's head was spinning. She suddenly remembered why the man had looked so familiar. She had seen him before at her guest house. He was one of her guests. She felt sick to her stomach at the thought of someone's murder being carried out in her guest house.

"Sorry, sir," she blurted out. "Was this at my inn?"

"At Cellar Vie, yes," he said, confirming her worst fears.

"Do I need to go there?" she asked in a panic. "Do you need me for anything?" The police chief held up his hand to silence her.

"Your parents have been very accommodating. We'll get your statement in due time," he said. "In the meantime, I suggest you extend the stay of any other guests who have attended this wedding."

Avery nodded, but her mind was completely blank with concern.

"Right," the Police Chief continued. "Now, we ask anybody with any information pertaining to this case to please come forward."

"How could we do that?" Samuel asked, angry at the interruption. "We don't know anything about the case."

"That's true," Deb added. "All we know is that Dean was killed at the inn. We only know as much as you've told us."

"Perhaps if you gave us a little more information," Charles suggested. "If we knew which evidence it was that has made us all suspects, we might be able to help you narrow it down."

The chief of police sighed and signaled to his officers to join him to one side. They discussed it all among themselves. It was only a few seconds, but it felt like minutes that they spoke.

Avery couldn't stop thinking about her inn. She had no information. *Was it messy? Were things broken?* It seemed like silly thoughts to think when a man's life had been lost, but as a business owner she couldn't help herself.

"It's going to be okay," Charles said quietly to her. "Don't worry." And she believed him, but his words did nothing to calm her concern.

"Right," the police chief finally said. "I will share some more information regarding the case with you. Now, as you know, a large sum of money was taken from his room. We know this because he had a list of items that he had brought with him, and we found his safe open."

Avery thought she would be sick.

"It is our belief that whoever did this convinced him to open the safe before taking his life, as the safe seemed to have been opened using the pin."

Avery wanted to hold Charles' hand in case she passed out. But no matter how hard she tried, she couldn't get herself to move a single limb.

"I will read to you, now, a journal entry made by the victim. If this means anything to you with regards to who might have done this, then I insist you come forward immediately to talk to us," he continued. He held up the notebook that he'd had in his hand when he entered and began to read out loud.

I came back here to see the friends and family that I have missed. But I've only been met with unfriendliness and disgust. Threats have been made to my life, and it seems that nobody is on my side anymore.

It is clear to me now that some of the people on the guest list for tonight would love nothing more than to see me dead. But they simply don't understand me. And that is their own loss.

"This diary entry was made last night," the police chief said. "And it is considered to be very important evidence in this case." The crowd stared at him blankly as the bride and groom held each other close, their special night completely ruined. "Well," the police chief said awkwardly. "I'll let you get on with your celebrations then. Congratulations to you both."

If Avery wasn't so shocked, she might have laughed. What a ridiculous notion that any one person present might still be in the mood to celebrate. Instead, the happy couple ended their party and went home.

Avery stayed behind as she spoke to all the guests who were staying at her inn, making arrangements for their lengthened stay. She knew she would have to leave eventually, but she didn't want to know what she would be going back to.

"Wanna share a cab home?" Charles asked as he took a seat next to her. They were the only two people still left at the venue.

"I'm too afraid to go home," Avery said, resting her head in her hands. "Do you think there'll be, like, flashing lights and tape and stuff?"

Charles chuckled. "That is probable. These things take time to clear. You'll likely find there are still a few officers around. I can only hope they've removed the body by now."

Avery groaned and lay her head down on the table. "I can't deal with that right now," she said. "It's too stressful."

Charles put a comforting hand on her shoulder. "They're going to want to ask you some questions," he said. "But I tell you what, I'll wait there with you until everyone has left. How's that?"

"You don't have to do that," she said. "You don't think they think I did it, do you?" she asked, nearly getting lost in her own question.

"It's unlikely," he said. "Besides, I'm your alibi, and I'll be right there for you."

Avery wished she could just run away and come back once it was all over.

"Think of it as character research for your book," Charles said with a smile. "It will be over before you know it."

Chapter Three

When Avery and Charles arrived back at the vineyard, Sprinkles was fast asleep on the floor of the cab. He was so tired that when Avery opened the door, he paid no attention to the flashing lights and crowd of people who had gathered. He walked straight to his bed on the porch and curled up to sleep.

Avery stared at the scene, and she felt sick to her stomach. Her property was littered with police vehicles and news crews. And as the reporters spoke, she kept hearing the name of her beloved Cellar Vie Guest House being used. It had always been intended to be a place of peace and tranquility, and now it was associated with murder.

The officers had already seen her cab arrive, so she knew she couldn't just turn around and leave again, no matter how much she wanted to. She just wished she could wait a few more hours and gather her courage.

"I don't think I can do this, Charles," Avery said, looking at the scene.

"I promise you, it won't be as bad as you think," he said kindly. "You'll be alright. Besides, you don't have a choice. You have to approach them eventually."

There were officers and officials all over the place. Tape closed off the room that Dean had been staying in. Everyone seemed busy, and she hated to see her guest house looking that way. She had no idea what to expect when she approached the officers. But it was her home, and she knew she would have to do it eventually.

"Come on," Charles said, stepping out of the cab. "The sooner you do it, the sooner it will all be over."

She looked despairingly at him. "Can't I just wait here for another five minutes?" she begged.

"Whether you do it now or five minutes from now won't make a difference, Avery," he said with a smile. "I'll stand with you, don't worry."

He was right, and she knew it. She dragged herself out of the cab and walked as slowly as she could toward the group of officers. They had already seen her coming and turned to meet her. As she arrived to speak to them, she saw through the open door to Dean's room as they zipped closed the body bag.

"Avery, we're glad you're finally here," an officer said.

"Sorry it took me so long," she responded. "Needless to say, but I wasn't all that excited to come back to all of this."

"What happened?" Charles asked, keeping his promise as he stood at her side.

"One of the other guests phoned us when she saw that his door was hanging off its hinges," the police officer said. "While she was on the phone with us, she went inside and found him there. It's a terrible thing."

"Was she part of the wedding?" Avery asked.

"No, she's just someone passing through on her way to somewhere else," the officer stated.

"She's been a great help," the other officer said.

"Well, remind me not to charge her for her stay, Charles," Avery said. She looked at Charles and wished she could smile, but she couldn't. The stress of it all had clamped her mouth shut entirely.

"Unfortunately, we will need every copy of the key to his room that you have, and we have to ask that you allow our officers to come and go as they need for the duration of this investigation," the officer continued.

"Of course," Avery said blankly. "I only have one spare set, inside, behind the counter. I'll get it for you in a moment."

"And I'm sure I don't have to tell you," he said. "But nobody may enter that room until the investigation is over or until we officially hand it back to you with the keys."

"Naturally," Avery laughed. "Although, I think it will be a long time before I can convince anybody to go back into that room again."

She glanced back at the door as they prepared to carry his lifeless body out. She wondered what his mother was feeling. She would have heard the news by now. She could just catch a glimpse of the room, and it looked neat, apart from the broken door.

"The other officers said something had been stolen from the room," she said.

"It appears to be the case," the officer responded. "But we're working to confirm that now."

"Right, well, is there anything else I can do for you, officers?" she asked.

"You were one of the guests at the wedding, right?" the officer asked.

"We were both in attendance," Charles answered for her.

"Then you're on our list, and we need to ask you some questions," the officer said.

Avery looked at Charles in panic. She'd never been a suspect before, and it didn't feel good. Despite the fact that she knew she was innocent, there was still something terrifying about having to answer their questions.

She would tell them what they needed to hear in order to clear her name as a suspect, which would be the truth. But she knew that if she said anything even a tiny bit wrong, she would be in trouble.

"It's alright," Charles said with a smile.

"Well, unfortunately, Charles, we have to ask you to step away," the officer said. "You were a guest, and we're under strict instruction to question all the guests."

Charles was led away by the other officer, and Avery stood alone as she did her best not to look too panicked. She didn't want to look guilty.

"When did Mr. Scott first check in?" the officer asked.

"I—I'm not sure, Avery answered. I have someone who does all the checking in for me. But I have a book that should have the date. It's right there on the counter."

Another officer went up to the counter and opened the book. She took some photographs and nodded in their direction, satisfied.

"Did you know Mr. Scott?" the officer asked.

"No," she answered. "I only know of him, but I don't believe we've ever met."

"And do you have someone that can confirm your alibi for the night?" the officer asked.

Avery nodded. "I never left the wedding. I'm sure there are multiple people you can call to confirm that," she said.

"If you'd write some names and numbers down here, please," he said, handing her a notebook.

Avery scribbled down the information about the Stammtisch women and couldn't help but notice the officer cross out Deb's name. "They will have seen me there all night," she said. "I didn't leave once, not even to get some fresh air which is true of most of the guests and I'm sure I will be listed as their alibi."

"Right, well, we'll give some of these names a call in just a moment," the officer said.

"The first time that I saw Mr. Scott was today. My dog, Sprinkles, was the ring bearer, and he stopped to sniff Mr. Scott's hand. I thought it was odd of Sprinkles to do that, but no, I've never met him," she said.

She was aware she was rambling, but that's what she did when she was nervous. The flashing lights and the teams of officers were making her very nervous, and she couldn't seem to stop the words from pouring out of her mouth.

"I see," the officer said.

"But I did ask someone about him, and she explained to me that he wasn't exactly well-liked," she said. The moment she said it, she wished she hadn't. The officer straightened his back and clicked his pen.

"And who was the person you were discussing this with?" he asked. "Who told you that he wasn't well-liked?"

"Camille," she answered. "Her name is on the list I gave you."

She hadn't intended to make Camille look like a possible suspect, and for a moment, she worried they might arrest her. But she knew Camille also had a sound alibi, and it wasn't a crime to speak badly of people.

"Well, I think that's about all we need to ask you," the police said.

"Really?" Avery asked with keen eyes.

"Well, what else can we ask?" he laughed. "Do you have any questions for us?"

"How long will you all still be here tonight?" she asked. "Can I fix you all a cup of tea? A jug of water, perhaps?"

The officer laughed. "That's awfully kind of you, Avery, but no thanks," he said. "Still, you've always had a good eye for these kinds of details. If you think of anything that might be important, will you let us know?"

"She does have a good eye, doesn't she?" Charles said, joining them again. "You know she's decided to write crime novels? I think she'd be great at it."

"Yes," Avery sighed. "I figured I spend so many nights awake, I might as well put that time to good use. And my late husband wrote crime novels. I helped him a bit, so I figured, how hard can it be?"

The officer laughed. "That's excellent," he said. "You should write a story about our town. We've had a few mysteries of late, haven't we? There is enough of fodder for you here in Los Robles, what with the murder at the festival and the sad person that was discovered stuffed in the barrel."

Avery wanted to laugh, but as they carried the body right past her, she worried she might be sick. The officer who had questioned Charles joined them again.

"Well, Charles, your alibi checks out," the officer said.

"Who was it?" Avery asked. "That bottle of merlot that you were hugging on the dance floor?" It was no time for jokes, but all of them burst out laughing at the same time as Charles' cheeks turned slightly red.

"Very funny, Avery, but he's right, you know," Charles said. "This town has had some drama over the last couple of years. It might be a good idea to write about it. I think those stories would be a hit."

"That's a great idea," Avery said. "But honestly, I wouldn't even know where to begin. I only have one perspective on all those stories, and so I run the risk of writing something that is untrue."

"I suppose," Charles said. "But that could also make it interesting."

"Oh, come on, Avery," the officer said. "There are no books about this town. I'd read it if you wrote it."

Avery looked around at the chaos that had occurred on her property and sighed. "Alright," she said. "I'll write a book about this town. But if I'm going to do it, then I'm going to do it properly. Let me write about this story." Avery motioned to the scene around them. There were people with gloves and officers taking notes. There were forensics people searching for fingerprints. It was a perfect scene for the start of a book.

"I don't know," the officer said.

"Let me follow you guys around as you work on this case, and I can use it in my book. I'll just change some of the details slightly. That way, I can call it fiction," she said.

The officers looked at each other.

"She's got a good idea," Charles said. "Don't journalists do that kind of thing all the time? What's the difference?"

"The difference is that she is, technically, still a suspect, and I need to run it by Police Chief Mathers first," the officer said.

"For how long can she still be a suspect?" Charles laughed. "You know her alibi will check out."

The officer scratched his head. "Tell you what," he said. "Because this sounds like so much fun, let me take some time to confirm you were at the wedding all night. Then, I will call Chief Mathers and see if he'll give you permission."

The officers stepped aside as they called the long list of names in their notebooks. And judging by the conversation, some of the names on that list had already been called a few times. That made sense. The guests would all list each other's names for an alibi.

Avery was sure if she checked her phone, she would have a few missed calls too.

It wasn't long before the officers came back to join them.

"Well, you're no longer a suspect," one officer said.

"That's good news, but not surprising," Avery teased.

"And Chief Mathers has agreed to let you follow us on this case for your book," he said with a smirk. "He said he's certain you'll find a way to interfere, as you usually do, and at least this way, he'll know what you're up to at all times." Charles snorted, and Avery laughed.

"That's settled then," Charles said. "Avery, are you ready to write your first book?"

Avery smiled widely in short-lived excitement. And then, the guilt set in as Avery looked at the scene. The man had been alive only hours before.

Chapter Four

It was early the next morning when Avery met the Stammtisch women to help them clean up the mess left behind by the reception. The last of the officers had only left her property well after midnight, and Avery hadn't had very much sleep.

There were bottles and confetti everywhere. The floor was covered in scuff marks from everybody's shoes, and the pile of belongings that people had left behind continued to grow. Everyone looked tired.

"How are things at the guest house?" Camille asked.

"Well, I've had to comp the stay of the poor woman who found his body," Avery said. "And cancel other bookings now that any guests who were invited to the wedding are being forced to stay longer."

"Did they give you any information on what happened?"

"No," Avery answered. "I only know what you know. But it seems that whoever did it broke the door down. I can't go near that room until the investigation is over, and I've had to hand over the keys to the police."

"That sounds like a nightmare," Camille said. "I'm sorry you have to go through all that."

"They're making it up to me by letting me follow them on the case," Avery explained. "I can use it for the book I'm writing."

They cleaned in silence for a short while until Avery found herself on the same side of the room as Tiffany.

"Are you sure you're doing alright?" Tiffany asked.

Tiffany and Avery had been friends since school, so Tiffany always knew when Avery wasn't giving the full truth. It was something that had often driven Avery a little mad.

"I barely knew the guy," Avery said. "So I don't feel too sad about it all. But being questioned like that and seeing that scene on my property was not great, and I'm very tired."

"You must be the only person in town who never knew him then," Tiffany said. "Everybody here has had a run-in with him at least once. You know, he and Deb were in a serious relationship for some time."

Deb was one of the Stammtisch women, and she was known to be the town gossip. As much as Avery loved Deb, she could believe that Deb would be involved with a man like that. He certainly had the look to match her aesthetic.

"He did look like her type," Avery laughed.

"If only he was as good inside as he looked on the outside," Tiffany said.

"Yes, I believe he was a bit of a difficult person to deal with," Avery remarked through a yawn.

"Not only that," Tiffany laughed. "He was absolutely good for nothing. I never understood why she stayed with him for so long."

"I thought he was supposed to be some kind of wealthy businessman-type?" Avery asked.

"Yes, later in life," Tiffany sighed. "But when he was with Deb, she paid for everything while he finished his studies. Only, I don't think he ever really went to class."

"Oh?"

"Deb used to constantly complain that she would come home to find him doing nothing but lounge around on the couch. She would cook and clean and pay all the bills for both of them. She worked herself nearly to death to afford it all."

"That's terrible," Avery said. "Why didn't Deb just kick him out right from the beginning?"

"He's a charmer," she answered with a shrug. "He always seemed to convince her that his studies were more important than anything else, that she was helping him, and that it made her special to do so. I think she thought he would marry her."

"That sounds frustrating," Avery said. "What a terrible situation to be in."

"They had a horrible relationship," Tiffany continued. "They would fight all the time. He never lived with her, but he behaved as if he did. He always wanted to know where she was and what she was doing. She couldn't breathe without informing him of it first."

Avery tried to picture Deb in that situation and found it difficult. Deb was outspoken and fun and had a habit of doing exactly as she pleased all the time. Perhaps that habit only formed after her relationship with Mr. Scott.

"Where is Deb, by the way?" Avery asked. "Wasn't she supposed to help us today?"

Avery looked around the room to make sure she hadn't simply just missed Deb somewhere. But she was nowhere to be found.

"Haven't you heard?" Tiffany asked. "She's down at the police station. They took her in for questioning because of the relationship she had with the victim."

It took Avery by surprise, but she remembered how the officer had crossed Deb's name off the list to confirm Avery's alibi. That made a little more sense to her. They couldn't phone her if she were their stronger suspect.

"Surely they don't think she did this?" Avery asked. "People break up all the time. It's normal."

"It's not because their relationship ended that they've taken her in," Tiffany said. "It's how their relationship ended; that's the problem."

They had been cleaning for hours already, and it seemed as if they had hardly made a dent in the mess. Avery and Tiffany took a break to sit outside and enjoy a cold glass of water. At that rate, they would be there all day cleaning.

"How did their relationship end, then?" Avery said, unable to get it out of her mind.

"Rather suddenly, actually," Tiffany explained. "One day, he was there, and the next, he wasn't. When she heard from him again, he was already living in his new house in the city. She simply never heard from him or saw him again."

"Sometimes it's better for things to end abruptly," Avery said. "It's easier to get over. It's when things are ugly and drawn out that the break up becomes tough."

"I suppose," Tiffany said. "But after he left, things only got worse for her because of him." Tiffany took a long sip of water and shook her head.

"About a week after he left her and moved to the city, she was trying to pay for her groceries when she discovered he had maxed out all her credit cards," Tiffany said. "She checked the statements and learned that he had furnished his new home with her money. And it wasn't cheap stuff, either."

"That's terrible," Avery said. "Surely there was something she could do?"

Tiffany shook her head. "By the time she discovered it, it was too late. And since they had been in a relationship for so long, the bank didn't want to get involved. They said it was impossible to know who was really telling the truth."

"The truth?" Avery asked.

"Yeah, naturally, when the police questioned Dean about the money he'd spent, he just told them she had spent the money on the furniture. He spun some story that they were going to move to the city together, but she dumped him at the last minute, and now she was trying to frame him for a crime he didn't commit."

"Clever," Avery said. "He knew that most banks, officers, and businesses don't want to get involved in that kind of thing."

"Precisely," Tiffany said. "They told her to hire a lawyer. But she had no more money left to do so!"

"So, what did she do in the end?" Avery asked.

"She spent years paying off that debt. It nearly ruined her completely. There was a time when she was considering selling her house to pay it off. I'm so glad she made it through all that," Tiffany said.

Avery felt sorry for Deb. But it made sense now why she would be seen as such a serious suspect. She fit the description of someone who had been seriously wronged by him. And if he knew what was good for him, he should have been concerned about seeing her again.

Avery knew Deb well enough to know that even though she had paid off the debt and made it through, there was no way she would have kept quiet about it if she had seen him. But she also knew that there was no way Deb was a murderer.

"Poor Deb," Avery said. "And now she has to go through all of this also. It's like, even in death, he's made things difficult for her."

"I know," Tiffany said. "But I don't think she did it. She was at the wedding all night with us."

"Still, the police have to do their jobs," Avery said.

Avery and Tiffany headed back inside to continue cleaning up. Avery knew it was likely that they would be there all day, but she wished she could have been present for Deb's questioning. It was exactly the kind of thing she wanted to see for her book. She had promised Eleanor that she would help, and Eleanor was more important than the book. *Besides, I can't promise I won't go storming in there and come to Deb's defense. It might be for the best, after all,* Avery thought.

As she swept, she thought through all that she knew. There weren't many details, but enough to already get her mind wandering. How had he gotten away with treating her that way? How was it that nobody helped Deb get her money back from him?

"How did everybody find out about Deb's debt?" Avery asked. "I mean, I know it is a small town, but you know a lot of details about that relationship."

Tiffany shrugged. "I dunno," she said. "Everybody knew about it. It was the talk of the town for weeks after he had left her."

"That's terrible."

"Of course, everyone felt sorry for her," Tiffany continued. "And we did what we could to help. When she said she would need to sell her house, we held an auction to raise funds to help her with the debt. The whole town came together because everyone knew he was a loser."

Avery liked the thought of that. It made her feel comforted that if she should ever need the town, perhaps they would be there for her too.

"And Mrs. Scott?" Avery asked. "Could she not help?"

Tiffany threw her head back in laughter. "Are you kidding? She's just as bad as he is," she said. "The only thing she did to try to help was to offer to buy Deb's house from her. Can you imagine the audacity of that?"

"No, I can't," Avery said as she raised her eyebrows.

"And what's worse is how angry Mrs. Scott became when Deb refused to sell the house to her. She called Deb ungrateful for not taking her generous offer."

Avery wondered how she would have reacted in that situation. She couldn't imagine it, though. It seemed so unfathomable to her that someone could behave that way. Her son had stolen Deb's money and put Deb in that situation. All she could think to do was take even more from Deb and then pretend she was trying to help?

It was a ridiculous notion, but the more she thought about the descriptions of the personalities of Dean and his mother, the more she could believe it. Avery pitied Deb. It made her see her as an entirely different person, and she understood better why Deb liked to be involved in the lives of all the people in town. They had helped her out of a tough situation. To Deb, they were all her close family and friends.

"I feel sorry for her," Avery said out loud. "I hope they're not being too rough on her at the station."

Tiffany sighed. "I don't know," she said. "I think they're taking a close look at her. I mean, there were many times when Deb said she wished she could just kill him."

Chapter Five

The table was set for two as Charles and Avery tucked into their decadent grilled cheese sandwiches. It was just what she needed after spending the entire morning cleaning up the chaos left behind by the wedding festivities.

They were eating slowly as each took turns talking the other one's ear off. Although Charles worked for Avery in the wine room, he was quickly becoming one of her closest friends, and they shared a weekly meal together.

Avery loved to cook, and Charles loved to eat. So, it was an excellent arrangement. Cooking for one was a tedious task, so Avery was grateful for the weekly opportunity to put her skills to the test.

"Tiffany tells me Deb is a suspect," Avery said, chomping into her sandwich.

Charles nodded. "She's a good one, too," he said. "No, not in that way. I just mean that she'd been very forthcoming and easy to deal with. She's been happy to answer all the police officer's questions and has been very patient with them, which is uncommon in murder suspects."

"I suppose," Avery sighed. "I didn't feel all too good when they were questioning me last night, and I wasn't even a serious suspect!"

"It's just tricky to tell sometimes," Charles said. "Some murderers are excellent liars. That's how they get away with it. And everybody knows how badly he hurt her."

Avery let out a short "mmm" as she took another mouthful of her meal. She nodded in agreement with Charles—not that she agreed with him entirely; she only partially agreed. Still, he wasn't wrong. She knew that all murderers were excellent liars, but Deb had never been able to keep a secret. She was the town gossip. It would be impossible for her to keep her mouth shut about anything.

"I feel sorry for her," Avery said. "I heard what happened. If I were here, I don't know if I'd ever have been able to look him in the eyes again."

"And that's precisely why she's one of the main suspects," Charles said. "I know she's your friend, but when it comes to murder, those things go right out the window."

"I suppose," Avery said. "I just think she wouldn't even waste her time murdering him. She's recovered and moved on. Then again, passion, and especially angry passion, makes people do the stupidest things, doesn't it?"

"Yeah," he chuckled. "By the way, how are you feeling about the prospect of writing your first book?"

"It's funny," Avery said. "I've been talking about doing it and thinking about doing it, but now the opportunity to do it has arrived, and I doubt myself."

"Doubt?"

"Well, I mean, now I actually have to do it," Avery laughed. "I have to put all those words onto paper like I've been threatening to do over the last few weeks."

Charles laughed loudly. "You're going to do great!" he said. "It's not like you don't know anything about writing books."

"That's true," she answered. "James used to think I'd be good at it. And I used to help him a lot. I suppose part of me is afraid that I'll miss him too much."

"Missing someone hurts, but it isn't all bad," Charles said. "It depends on the reminder. Some things are a reminder of the good times, which can be comforting in the tough times. What you're doing is a happy memory you have of your husband. It will be the good kind of missing him."

Avery thought about it for a moment and decided he was right. Perhaps it wouldn't be as bad as her mind would like her to believe.

"Besides," Charles continued. "I think it will be fun to have you following the police around like that. You're going to love it. It's just like gossip but far more interesting."

"I just hope I don't get too carried away," Avery said. "The last thing I want to do is become too interfering and for them to ask me to leave them alone. I don't know if I could motivate myself otherwise."

"That is a risk," Charles said. "You haven't always been on the best terms with them. Just, whatever you do, don't have too much fun."

"Why not?" she laughed.

"I don't want you to sign up to join the force!" he teased. "It's too risky. You're one of my best friends, and I can't lose you. Who will feed me these delicious meals?"

"Oh, the horror!" she said dramatically.

"Precisely!" he joked. "If something were to happen to you, I would live off of takeout and microwave meals, and that is a threat."

"I take that threat very seriously," she answered, gathering their plates.

Avery went to the kitchen to fix them their routine pot of tea after a meal.

"So, do you have any more information on the case?" she asked. "I'd like to get my head thinking about how I might put this book together."

"Actually, yeah," Charles said. "I can tell you how Dean was found. Officer Chase said it looked like a picture in a movie."

"Oh yeah?"

"Yeah, the door was broken, as you know," he explained. "And Dean's body was apparently slumped over onto his desk, his head resting right on the diary that Chief Mathers was reading from at the reception."

"That does sound rather like a movie scene," she agreed.

"But wait, that's not even the really weird part," he said. "Despite the door being broken, there were no signs of a struggle."

"So, let me get this straight. Someone broke down the door, and not only did Dean not fight back, but he unlocked the safe for his murderer?"

"I don't know if we can say for sure what happened until we have some more information, but it looks that way, yes," Charles answered.

Avery poured the tea and wondered how such a bizarre crime could take place. Charles was right in saying it was strange. There would have been an initial force, and then afterward, everything would have seemingly been quite easy for the murderer.

"So, how exactly was he murdered?" she asked.

Charles shrugged. "At the moment, the working theory is that it was suffocation. There are no visible markings on the body that officers would usually look for."

"And how common is it for someone to use suffocation as a murder tactic?" she asked.

"Not that common, but also not uncommon," he said. "It's not easy to do, that's the thing. It requires some strength, and usually, the victim puts up a struggle. But not in this case."

Avery sighed. "This is getting stranger with every word."

"If it wasn't for the broken door and the missing money, we would have just chalked it up to natural causes, most likely," Charles added.

"How can you be certain there was any money in the safe anyway?" she asked.

"Well, there had been a piece of paper in the safe with a record of what had been placed there and how much money it was," Charles explained. "Also, anybody that knew him knew he liked to travel with the same leather satchel. The police searched everywhere and could not find that satchel."

"Okay, so we have suffocation and missing money," Avery said. "That's not a lot to work with."

"Well, we think it was suffocation," Charles said. "There is no official cause of death yet. They're waiting for the autopsy results to come back."

"And you?" she asked. "Have they asked you to consult with them on the case?"

Charles flashed a cheeky smirk. "They have, but I don't think they need me," he said. "I think they want me to keep an eye on you."

Avery rolled her eyes as Charles cackled. It wasn't entirely impossible, given what had happened with previous investigations.

So much time was spent helping James solve pretend mysteries. How could I not get involved in a real one when it comes along?

"So how long until the cause of death is official?" she asked.

"A few days at max," Charles answered. "And it's tricky to investigate too much until then. A cause of death can dramatically change an investigation like this. But we can't exactly sit around and wait, either. People want to go home."

"Yes, I've had a couple of disgruntled guests," Avery said. "It seems, even in death, there are few people who care about Mr. Scott."

"It's a grim thought," Charles said. "But I suppose if you treat people badly as often as he did, these things happen."

"This is nothing like in the books that James wrote," Avery said. "By now, there would have been at least one foot chase and almost a high-speed car chase. Or at least a murder weapon."

"Yes, I suppose you might have to sprinkle those things in here and there in your version of events," he said. "I don't expect either of those things to happen."

Avery poured them another cup of tea, and they sipped in silence for a moment. There weren't many people whom Avery could sit with in silence and still enjoy their company, but Charles was one of those people.

"You know, you didn't have to close the vineyard today," Charles said. "I'm sure it would have been perfectly acceptable to operate."

"It just doesn't feel right," she said. "I don't want to deal with all the people who will be asking questions or gawking through the windows of his room."

"Who's to say anybody would gawk?" he said.

"Wouldn't you?"

Charles thought about it before confirming. "I suppose I might try to take a look, yes."

"You see?" she said. "Besides, it feels a little disrespectful. I know nobody liked him, but he did die last night. It just doesn't feel right to open up the gates and let people come here and drink wine and party up a storm."

"When you put it that way, I suppose I understand," he said. "I'm not complaining, though. I've had a lovely day off from work."

Avery chuckled as she drank her tea. She wondered if she would even have had the energy to run the farm that day. She was so exhausted from the night before and the cleaning she was actually happy to have the day off too.

"You're kind for doing that," Charles complimented her. "Not a lot of business owners would make that kind of sacrifice. It speaks volumes, and

I know the locals will see that kindness, and it will benefit your business in the long run."

Avery smiled kindly at him. He was right. In a town like that, when most of her business relied on tourism, it didn't hurt to think that perhaps her farm would get even more support from the locals during the quiet months.

"Thanks, Charles," she said softly. "You always find the right words to say."

"Well, they're not just there to make you feel better," he said sternly. "They're the truth."

His words silenced her, if only for a moment, before a message on her phone reminded her of something that was bothering her tremendously. Avery frowned. "I'm sorry to change the subject, but I just don't think Deb did this. I know she was angry at him, and I know my word doesn't clear her name, but she just doesn't seem to fit the bill for this kind of murder. When a scorned woman commits murder, it's messy and violent. This doesn't fit that description."

"I agree with you there," Charles said. "It doesn't clear her name, but you're right. This doesn't look like the work of an angry ex-girlfriend."

"So, what kind of person would commit this kind of stranger murder?" she asked.

"You're asking all the right questions," Charles said. "And I am sure we are still going to learn a lot of shocking information about Mr. Scott. But as for now, my main suspect is a lot closer to him. I think it was Mrs. Scott."

Chapter Six

"Do you really think it could have been Mrs. Scott?" Avery asked as she placed her cup down neatly in the saucer. "I just can't imagine any mother murdering their own son."

"And yet, it happens all the time," Charles said. "News reports from all over the world have no shortage of murderous mothers."

"I suppose," Avery said, uncomfortable with the grim reality of it. "I guess I don't know Mrs. Scott at all. I've only ever seen her around in her all-white outfits. She seems like a demanding woman, but I don't know if she seems dangerous at all."

"Well, if you've never known her, you are lucky," he said. "You think Dean had a big ego? His mother's ego is at least twice as inflated. I don't think I've ever had a conversation with her where she hasn't spoken only about herself."

Avery had known someone like that before. It was tedious to have conversations like that, and she could picture Mrs. Scott being that way. It was something in the way she carried herself that made it easy to believe. She was an elderly woman but a fabulous one at that. Avery had never seen her without high heels on, and she knew how to control a room when she entered. It was an admirable trait, to say the least.

"Why do you see her as a suspect, Charles?" she asked. "It can't just be her inflated ego."

"It's a little more than that, yes," Charles said. "She's picked many fights in our community, and most of them she has won. And she's never won them fairly. She's the kind of woman who is quick to get the lawyers involved and will always get what she wants."

"I see," Avery said. "That is a quick way to make enemies, yes."

"Not only that but she's been on bad terms with Dean for months now," he continued. "Of course, she still loved him; I don't doubt that. But there were weeks when they didn't speak at all. She would go around telling everyone what a terrible son he was and how he didn't deserve anything she had ever given him."

"She is wealthy, I assume?" Avery asked.

"Oh, very."

"Then why did Dean steal all that money from Deb?" she asked again.

Charles shrugged. "From what I understand, he did it because he felt he deserved to spend that money. He really did think so highly of himself that he believed Deb owed him for the status he had given her while they were in a relationship."

"Now, that is egotistical," Avery said with wide eyes.

"He comes from generational wealth," Charles said. "And when Deb asked his family to pay off the debts he had created, they refused, saying she had embarrassed their family name by going to the police first."

Avery burst out laughing. "That's absurd! I can't believe what I'm hearing."

"Yes, that rose farm has been in the Scott family going back many generations," Charles explained. "But despite its success, it never gave Mrs. Scott the fame she longed for. Then, one year Mrs. Scott found a small amount of success when she won a beauty pageant. Through that, she was able to advertise the roses."

"She was a beauty queen?" Avery asked.

"Oh yes, and she won a lot of pageants after that, too," he said. "With her publicity, the rose farm boomed. They had always been wealthier than most, but after that, they secured enough money to last them many more generations."

Avery sipped her tea. "That must be nice," she said, thinking about her own farm.

"Yes," Charles said. "But Mrs. Scott soon started to see herself as some kind of small-town celebrity. She claims that she single-handedly put this place on the map."

"Sure," Avery said sarcastically. "It's got nothing to do with the world-renowned wines."

"The problem is that everybody started to treat her like a celebrity," Charles said. "And at first, they were just being polite and celebrating her success. But after a while, she started to expect it."

Avery imagined a young Mrs. Scott walking through the town, demanding free products as her photograph was taken. She wondered if she was ever asked to sign autographs. Avery had always felt fame would be a tedious, tiresome burden. She couldn't stand the thought of people constantly taking her photograph.

"She's a feisty woman, Mrs. Scott," Charles said. "And eventually, people were too afraid not to treat her like royalty. She is known to throw major fits if she doesn't get her way. People treat her well not out of respect but out of fear, and she doesn't seem to understand the difference."

"Surely not everybody is afraid of her?" Avery asked. "There has to be at least one person who is brave enough to stand up to her."

"I suppose she has a few close friends from before she was a pageant queen," Charles said softly. "But once, a coffee shop got her order wrong, and she went to the newspaper asking for them to be boycotted. It was ridiculous, and nobody followed her, of course. But it certainly made people afraid to upset her."

Avery laughed out loud. "Do you think I could get away with that?" she asked. "Do you think I could march through town and just demand that everybody treat me better? Maybe if I'm rude enough, or cause a big enough scene, then I can be treated like a celebrity, too."

Charles sunk his head into his hands. "Please don't ever do that," he begged. "It would be far too embarrassing. And I might change my opinion of you, then."

"I don't want that," Avery teased. "It's alright; I'm perfectly happy being treated like any old ordinary pleb."

"Me too," he agreed. "Being a drama queen sounds like hard work to me."

Avery smiled as she pictured Charles in large sunglasses, marching into the local news agency to report bad service at a nearby coffee shop. Then, she scribbled the thought down to add it to her book. She wouldn't tell Charles about it; she'd simply let him read it and laugh as she watched his face while he did.

The teapot was empty, and Avery carried it to the sink, where she ran a basin of soapy water. She and Charles had formed a routine after their meals. He had been visiting so often that he knew where everything was kept.

So, Avery would wash everything up, and Charles would dry each item and carefully pack it away. Usually, by the time Charles left, there was no evidence of any food having been cooked or consumed in her kitchen. And she liked it that way.

They were about halfway through the dishes when they heard the sound of the candlesticks falling against the wooden table. And a few seconds later, Sprinkles entered the kitchen with the tablecloth hanging from his mouth.

"I guess he just wanted to help with the cleanup," Charles laughed as he took the cloth from the mouth of a very proud Sprinkles.

"I tell you, that dog training is great," Avery said. "But every so often, she teaches him a trick that I could live without."

"I think it's sweet," Charles said. "I'm just glad there weren't any plates left on there."

Charles disappeared to put the tablecloth back on the table as Avery continued to clean the dishes. She thought about everything Charles had told her about Mrs. Scott and pieced together a character description for her book.

"What had Dean and his mother been fighting about?" she asked when Charles returned. "You said they hadn't spoken in weeks."

"It was a major drama," Charles said. "Dean wanted his mother to move to the city and live with him. He said she was getting too old to run the farm, which, as I'm sure you can imagine, is the worst thing a pageant queen like her could hear."

Avery chuckled. "It's not something that any woman wants to hear… pageant queen or not."

"I suppose," Charles said with a laugh. "If I remember correctly, Dean had told his mother he wanted to sell the farm. He wanted the money and told her that if she didn't want to live with him he could put her into the fanciest old age home he could find."

Avery gasped. "No mother wants to hear that from their child. No wonder she was so angry with him."

"Well, it's no secret that Dean always hated the idea of inheriting the farm," Charles explained. "There was a time when he begged his mother to give him a sibling so the sibling could be the one faced with the task of running the farm after her death."

"He didn't want the family business?" Avery asked.

"No, he said that small-town living wasn't for him and nobody could ever make him change his mind. A couple of months ago, she was telling the local butcher he had already received a few offers for the farm, with the business included."

"I've driven past that farm," Avery said. "It's gorgeous. There are roses as far as the eye can see. It looks like something out of a fairytale."

"I know, so you can imagine that when Dean said he wanted to sell it, his mother kicked up a huge fuss," Charles said. "They fought about it for months. In fact, Deb said she heard them fighting at the coffee shop about it on the morning of the wedding, just a few hours before he died."

"That doesn't sound good," Avery said. "I understand why you see her as a suspect. But why would Dean want to sell a business that's been in his family for so long? Why not just keep it and let somebody else do the work for him?"

"You're asking the same question I am," Charles said. "So, I've suggested that one of the officers look into it. I'm not sure how or when they'll get any information on it. But, I suppose we'll have to find out one way or another."

"Why can't someone just ask her about it?"

"She just lost her son," Charles shrugged. "And she's a diva. When the officers did their initial questioning, it took them hours. She kept running out to lock herself in the bathroom to sob loudly. She even threatened to take legal action against the officer if he didn't solve the case by midnight."

"I see," Avery said. "That does seem dramatic."

"All I know is that she refuses to leave her farm and refuses to sell her business," Charles said. "And her inheritance states that she had no choice but to leave the farm to her nearest next of kin when she dies. She can't change it and leave it to someone else. Well...I suppose now that Dean's dead, she can."

"That's a grim thought, isn't it?" Avery quietly said as she washed the last of the dirty dishes.

"I suppose," Charles said. "There was a moment a few months ago where she had even said she would take legal action against her own son. It made me sad to think of it. Could a mother really feel that the land she owned was worth more than her relationship with her own son?"

"Well, they don't seem to respect each other the way a normal family would if you ask me," Avery said. "So, is it really all that surprising?"

Avery and Charles said goodbye to each other, and she watched as Sprinkles chased his car down the dirt road. She looked at the end of her property, where her parents lived in a small cottage, and breathed a sigh of relief, knowing that her family wasn't like Dean's.

She shuddered to imagine treating her parents the way Dean and his mother treated each other. Charles was right to look at Mrs. Scott as a suspect. She was a woman who would stop at nothing to get what she wanted, and women like that could be more volatile than most people.

Avery went back in and sat at the table where her notebook was and wrote countless notes and character traits. It was something she had seen James do at the start of every book. Afterward, she sat back and read through her notes again, making changes where she saw fit. Then she wrote down the description of the murder scene. There was something so interesting about it. It would have been a violent act to break the door down, yet other parts of the scene seemed so peaceful.

From Charles' information, she knew there were no signs of struggle. That meant he had no bruising or scratch marks and that there wasn't any blood. His body would have been in perfect condition, other than his non-beating heart.

Then there was the final detail of his head resting on the very thing that had been the largest clue to his investigation. Avery did her best not to, but before she knew it, she found herself walking softly across the lawn toward his room.

There was yellow police tape across the door, and she knew she could not go inside. Instead, she did the very thing she was worried her customers would do. She peered through the window.

Apart from the fingerprinting dust and the debris from the broken door, the room was in pristine condition. The cupboard door was open, and she could see the safe inside. It was entirely empty. The chair stood at the desk as if he had been sitting in it only moments ago. She wrote down what she needed to remember the scene and made her way back to the house.

Chapter Seven

A very was still full from her lunch with Charles when she arrived at the home of Eleanor and Samuel for tea. The sun would set in an hour or two, and she was already eager to climb into bed. She had enough notes to start creating some ideas for her book, and she wanted to work on them while it was still fresh in her mind.

The newlyweds welcomed her in and guided her through a sea of gift bags and boxes toward the patio. Their entire living room was drowning in wedding gifts, and Avery was certain it would take weeks for them to get through it all.

Every surface had another pile of gifts on it. All of them were still wrapped. Avery wondered what kind of gifts could be inside. It was always tough buying gifts for people who were already so well-established.

"I don't even want to know what's in half of these boxes," Eleanor said. "I'm at an age where I already have everything I want. I can't think what I might do with all of this."

Avery thought about it as if she were in Eleanor's shoes, and her hands became clammy from the stress. Eleanor was right. When you're more established in life, there is little need for that many wedding gifts.

"You'll have to put a shed in the back to store it all," Samuel teased. Eleanor shot him a glare.

It wasn't only the gifts. Samuel had moved in, so everywhere they walked, there was a chair or another item of furniture that hadn't found a home yet. There were still boxes to unpack, and according to Avery, it was a pretty chaotic way to start a marriage.

Outside was a lot calmer, and they couldn't even see the boxes from where they were sitting anymore. There were small cakes, pastries, and biscuits already waiting, and although Avery was full, she knew she could make space for at least some of the treats.

"We've had to postpone our honeymoon because of this murder," Eleanor said. "We should have been sipping sangria in Spain today."

"I'm sorry," Avery said, apologizing for something that was not her fault. "It's a terrible thing to have happened at a wedding. I'm sure the police could have timed it better, but what do I know about being a police officer?"

Avery knew Charles, but there hadn't been too many times that they'd talked about his career as a police officer. They talked about cases, sure, but never the finer details about what the job was actually like.

She hadn't seen Eleanor that upset before and wasn't sure how to react to it. Samuel didn't look too pleased either.

"He wasn't even invited," Samuel said. "Mrs. Scott gifted us with half the flowers for free, then after we accepted, insisted she bring a guest with her. With all those free flowers, we couldn't exactly say no, could we?"

"I suppose not," Avery said. "Did you know it was Dean that she was bringing, though?"

Eleanor shook her head. "She wouldn't tell us. She just said it was a surprise and that we'd all be pleased to see who it was. I had my suspicions, though."

"It seems completely insane to me that she'd do that," Samuel said. "From what I understand, it was common knowledge that nobody wanted to see him. And she knew Deb would be there."

"I see," Avery responded. "I didn't realize she'd sponsored half the flowers. Do you think she did that so you'd have no choice but to allow her to bring a guest?"

"Absolutely," Eleanor said. "I should have known Dean would throw a fit for not being invited. And it's just like him to do something like this, too."

Eleanor folded her arms as Samuel poured them each a cup of tea.

"Something like what?" Avery asked as she tried not to giggle at Eleanor's dramatic behavior.

"Trust Dean to be the center of attention always. He can't stand it when someone else has more eyes than he does," Eleanor said. "So, trust him to go and get himself murdered on the day of my wedding."

Avery had known narcissists before, and most of them had a stubborn determination to survive. The ones she had known had felt so important that the concept of dying seemed to be a detriment that was only a danger to those lesser than them.

"I don't think he arranged his own murder," Avery said. "That's not exactly something one does out of spite."

"No, I suppose you're right," Eleanor said, relaxing her shoulders. "And we're very happy to be married. It's just...that thing he wrote in his diary has me annoyed."

"How so?"

"He makes it seem as if we're all against him, but he put himself in that position," she explained. "If he had just treated everyone with respect, he might have been more accepted in this community."

"As far as I can tell, he was quite the narcissist, so I wouldn't take it too personally if I were you," Avery said with a smile. "What happened with your honeymoon, by the way?"

At that point, Samuel started to show some signs of frustration. "We've had to postpone it, obviously," he said. "The police said we can't go anywhere. It's so ridiculous if you ask me."

"They've insisted they see all the film footage of the day, too," Eleanor added. "We haven't even been able to see a single snippet or photograph yet."

"I'm sorry to hear about that," Avery said, reaching for another treat. "But I'm happy to hear you were able to postpone the honeymoon."

"Only by a few days," Samuel explained. "It's a bit concerning, to be honest. We were only able to push it slightly forward on account of the resort being fully booked. And we've already paid, so we couldn't just find a new resort."

"We're worried that this won't be sorted out in time," Eleanor said. "It's a beautiful honeymoon that we've booked. But the police won't give us any information on how long this might take. It's all too stressful."

Avery felt bad for them. She could see how tense they were about the subject. She could only imagine after months of planning and preparation and a murder at their wedding, they were more than eager to jet off to Spain and leave it all behind for a while.

"Surely you have been cleared as suspects, though?" she asked. "I mean, they can't possibly think that the bride or groom would leave their own wedding to commit this murder."

Samuel sighed. "Of course, they don't see us as suspects. But they have told us to stay behind in case they have further questions for us or need anything more from us. You know, since it was our wedding he was attending and since they think it was one of our guests."

"Even in death, he's managed to ruin the fun for all of us," Eleanor said, biting her nail. "I have half a mind to show up at Mrs. Scott's house and give her a piece of my mind for bringing him along at all."

Samuel placed a comforting hand on Eleanor's leg and smiled. "I'm sure everything will work out fine, my love," he said.

"I know, I know," Eleanor said, taking a deep breath. "It's just that we have so much to lose if we don't make it to this honeymoon."

"Like what?" Avery asked without thinking. She realized after she had asked the question that it was probably none of her business. But the question had sort of just slipped out. Watching the two of them get riled up over the murder was like watching a soap opera. There was drama, emotion, and romance involved. It reminded her of the shows she used to watch when she was much younger.

"Well, our honeymoon is non-refundable," Samuel said. "It was all part of a package. So, if we can't make the new dates that we've arranged, we will lose every last cent we have paid toward it."

Avery had been more involved in the wedding planning than she had liked. The entire Stammtisch had helped Eleanor put it together. It meant that Avery had a vague idea of how much the wedding had cost, and the idea of them losing the honeymoon money made her feel ill. It wasn't her money, and she knew well enough that none of that stress was of her concern. But she cared about Eleanor and Samuel, which meant that inevitably, if they were stressed, then so was she.

190

She wondered if Deb or Camille felt the stress of others, too. Deb knew just about everybody, and Avery shuddered to think of how much stress she would feel if she was like Avery and also took on her friend's stresses.

"Yes," Eleanor said, bringing Avery's attention back to the conversation. "If this doesn't work out, then Dean will have not only managed to ruin my wedding but also our honeymoon. After everything we've had to pay for, it will be a long time before we can afford a holiday again."

"Well, I don't want to think about that," Samuel said. "Because I think it will all work out fine."

"Sorry, Avery," Eleanor said. "You're our first visitor since the wedding, so we're kind of piling it all on you here, aren't we?"

Eleanor dropped her shoulders and looked genuinely upset about the conversation. It made Avery feel a bit better. She felt bad for Eleanor and knew how important it was to talk to others when things that were planned perfectly go completely awry.

Avery laughed. "Don't worry. That's what friends are for. Besides, you guys can keep talking, and I'll just keep eating."

Avery reached for another macaron of a different flavor this time. She didn't have the capacity to eat it, but it looked so delicious that she bit into it anyway. Her desire had overrun her logic, and she knew she would pay for it when her stomach was so full that she could barely move later. But as she bit into it, any potential regret she once felt simply melted away.

"How are you doing?" Samuel asked. "I believe you've closed the farm today."

"Yes," Avery said. "It just didn't feel right to carry on so soon after everything happened. But other than that, I'm alright."

Avery took a sip of tea, washing down the sugary frosting from a piece of cake. "Actually," she continued. "The police have agreed to let me follow them on the case, and then I can write a book inspired by it afterward."

"Oh, that's fun!" Eleanor said. "You must be so excited. I can't wait to read it."

"Yes," Samuel laughed. "And I'm sure this case is bound to take a few turns, given how little information is available at the moment."

"So, do you have some inside information for us?" Eleanor asked.

"Does it look like we'll make it to our honeymoon?" Eleanor looked long-ingly at her, and for the first time since they had sat down, her leg stopped twitching. She dropped her hands into her lap and waited for the answer she was hoping to hear.

But Avery couldn't give it to her. Avery shrugged. "I don't have much, and it is hard to say," she said. "But I promise you they are putting all the energy possible into solving this."

"You see, honey?" Samuel said. "They're going to get this sorted in no time, and we'll fly off to Spain and simply forget about it all."

Eleanor gave him a relieved smile. "I guess you're right, as always," she said.

"By the way," Avery said. "Just out of curiosity...who do you think did it?"

"You mean, who committed the murder?" Samuel asked with wide eyes. Avery nodded as she sipped her tea.

"It's hard to say," Eleanor answered. "A lot of people hated his guts. But I don't know if anyone hated him enough to murder him. Murder just seems like a lot of effort to put into someone you hate."

She had a point. Avery hadn't thought about it that way. Even some crimes of passion weren't born out of hate but out of extreme love. Surely, if anyone hated him that much, they would rather just avoid him.

But the missing money made it seem so planned out and so thought out. "Who would know about the money?" Avery asked. "You know, the bag that was stolen."

Eleanor rolled her eyes. "Anybody that knew him, to be honest. He had a habit of bragging with his cash."

Samuel burst out laughing. "Yes, I only ever met him once, and he even showed it to me. It did strike me as rather odd."

Avery agreed with Samuel. That was an odd thing to do, but the man clearly thought very highly of himself and seemed to have desperately needed to show everyone how important and successful he was.

"And poor Deb," Eleanor added. "They questioned her for hours. And everyone knows it couldn't have been her."

"Yes," Samuel agreed. "She doesn't quite strike me as the murdering type."

The three of them enjoyed their tea as Avery diverted the conversation elsewhere. She could see that it was eating at them and hoped she could create some kind of brief distraction for them. She wondered if that hadn't been why she'd been invited there in the first place.

"Well, let me not keep you two much longer," Avery said, sipping the last of her tea.

The sun was starting to set rapidly, and she knew that after the morning of cleaning and the late night the night before, it wouldn't take her too long to fall asleep. And she was eager for sleep too. Already her eyes burned, and her eyelids felt heavy, and with a belly full of decadent treats, she knew she'd be fast asleep soon enough.

She said goodbye to her friends as she left their driveway. When she glanced back at them, she could see how tired and stressed they were. It showed in the bags underneath their eyes and the slump in their shoulders.

As she drove, Avery thought about the information she already had. She had hoped that the question about the money would narrow down the search. But learning he was the kind of man to show off that type of thing, she felt like it had the opposite effect.

It could have been anyone. The only people Avery knew it certainly couldn't have been were the people who were still present when the police had stopped the music. But by then, many people had already left the party.

Avery knew they needed to move quickly and wondered what she could do to speed things up. She hated the thought of the newlyweds not being able to go on their honeymoon because of a man nobody liked that hadn't even been invited.

Chapter Eight

Avery stood in front of the bookstore and smiled. She had visited that store since she was a child, and it was still her favorite place in the town. It was two stories of secondhand books, and to someone like Avery, it might as well have been a building filled with treasure.

It was an older building with wooden doors and window frames. There were a few steps inside covered in sandstone. A metal spiral staircase led to the upper floor. There were rows of bookshelves against every wall, and in the center of every room, a table with piles of books on top.

She wondered how many hours of her life she had already spent there. It had never changed. The same family had owned the business for as long as she could remember, and even the cash register was still the same.

The bookstore was the only place Avery ever spent her pocket money growing up.

Thankfully, a small coffee shop had opened right next door. So, Avery stopped there and ordered two coffees to go. It was early morning, and the bookstore had only just opened.

Already, there were a fair amount of people inside. The bookstore had made a name for itself and was one of the tourist destinations in the town. Avery was expecting to meet Charles and her father there for some browsing.

She wasn't ready to open the vineyard up to guests yet and was desperate to find new books to read. James had always told her that nobody could ever expect to be a decent writer if they weren't reading decent books. So, Avery planned on stocking up on all the best books she could find. She had a book that she wanted to write, and she intended to write it well. And it was never a bad idea to fill up on inspiration with every opportunity.

Avery stepped inside, coffee in each hand and Sprinkles following closely behind her. She couldn't reach out and take any books yet because of the coffees, but she could at least read the titles and narrow down her potential selection.

She stared at the first shelf for almost five minutes, just reading over the titles and admiring the artwork on the spines. She wondered what her book might look like once it was done and ready to publish.

She imagined that maybe one day she might walk into that bookstore and find her own book on the shelf and hoped that it would have a particularly bent and used spine. The worse the condition was, the more it had been read. She had learned that as a kid. Since then, she'd gravitated to books that looked in bad shape. The more folds and bends it had in the spine, the more times it had been opened. It was a really good book if she opened it and found that some of the pages had been taped back together. A person only goes through that much effort if you intend to read the book again and again. And the best part was that the damaged books were usually cheaper too.

She inhaled and enjoyed the smell of the bookstore, the scent of old pages and wooden bookshelves. She remembered how she used to imagine living in a home that looked just like it one day. And for a while, she did. When she lived with James, they had rows and rows of books. She hadn't had the heart to unpack any of them yet. They lived in boxes.

The thought of all her books living in boxes made her sad, but she was quickly distracted when she noticed Sprinkles was no longer sitting politely at her ankles. Then, she heard a familiar whining sound. She looked over to the cash register and saw Sprinkles whining at the counter. Simon, the current owner of the shop, tried to pat Sprinkles, but he moved away.

"So sorry, Simon," Avery said as she tried to pull Sprinkles away from the counter.

"It's no problem!" Simon said with a friendly smile. "I suppose he's just after one of my snacks." Simon lifted a sandwich out from behind the counter and chuckled. "It's an odd breakfast, I know," he said. "But I do love a decent sandwich."

"There's nothing wrong with a sandwich for breakfast!" Avery laughed as she tried some more to get Sprinkles to leave him alone. However, she much preferred the breakfast of a puffy pancake, like the one she'd had that morning, to a sandwich.

But Sprinkles sat dead still and wouldn't move. He whined some more with his eyes fixated on the counter in front of him. Avery thought it odd. It had been some time since Sprinkles had begged. She wondered what might be on that sandwich that could smell so delicious that Sprinkles would forget his manners entirely. Eventually, she gave up, and Simon assured her that Sprinkles was no bother at all.

At that moment, Charles finally arrived a few minutes late. "Here," she said, shoving the coffee in his hands.

"Oh!" he said with a smile. "How did you know I needed one?"

"It's before noon," Avery laughed. "You need multiple coffees before noon."

"It's true!" he said, eagerly taking a sip.

The two of them walked through the first shelves.

"I hope you don't mind that I've invited my father along," Avery said. "When he heard we were coming to the bookstore, he insisted on joining us. He loves this place just as much as I do."

"It really is no trouble," Charles said. "I thought he'd be coming with you, though?"

Avery laughed. "No, my father's getting old, and so he is determined to prove he is still capable. He refused to let me drive him!" Charles laughed so hard he nearly choked on his coffee. "He offered to give me a lift," Avery giggled. "But I've seen how he drives these days, and I was too terrified. So, I told him I had other errands to run after this."

Charles and Avery shared a chuckle as she reached for a tattered book on the shelf in front of her. But she couldn't concentrate on the blurb on the back because she could still hear Sprinkles whining. She put the book back and reached into her bag for his lead.

"Sorry, Simon," she said again. "Let me get him out of your hair." She clipped the lead onto his harness and gave a soft tug. Sprinkles obliged and left Simon alone.

"I don't even have any sandwich left!" Simon laughed. "And still, he wants a bite!"

Avery let out a weak chuckle and hooked the loop of the lead over her arm. Sprinkles was good with his lead and required little convincing to follow her around. She returned to the book she was looking at and opened it up.

She saw some pencil lines underlining sentences that must have been of some importance to the previous owner. She immediately knew she wanted to read the book and tucked it under her arm.

"Got something so soon?" Charles laughed. "We've hardly even been here."

"I know how to spot a good book," Avery said with a wink. "Besides, I never leave here without a fair stack."

Avery and Sprinkles followed Charles upstairs to the upper floor. There wasn't much room upstairs, but thankfully, they were the only two up there. Avery led Sprinkles to one corner of the room and told him to stay there. And he happily obliged. He lay down comfortably and watched as she and Charles browsed the section with of cookbooks.

"I wonder what will happen to this place now that Dean has died," Charles commented.

"What do you mean?"

"Well, this building belonged to him," Charles said. "It's been in his family some time, and for his thirtieth birthday, his mother officially signed it over to him as a birthday gift."

"That's quite a gift," Avery commented.

"Indeed," Charles chuckled. "The best gift my family ever got me was a bicycle."

Avery ran her fingers along the spines of the books as she waited to find one that was damaged enough for her to inspect. She also kept a close eye on the kinds of books Charles was pulling from the shelves. She was curious to know what occupied his mind when he was spending his nights at home.

"I don't understand," Avery said. "Surely then the building will just go back to his mother? Why would his death affect the bookstore?"

"Didn't you hear?" Charles asked as he pulled a sci-fi book from the shelf. "Dean was going to sell the building to some developer to turn into a hotel."

"A hotel?" Avery laughed. "Instead of the bookstore? I could never imagine such a thing!"

"Yes, I know," Charles sighed. "It does seem ridiculous. Never mind the idea of a full hotel all the way out here. This isn't exactly a hotel kind of place, is it?"

"Well, I have a guest house," Avery reminded him.

"Yes, well, that's different," Charles said. "That still fits in here. A hotel with valets and room service and all that city stuff makes no sense to me out here."

"I suppose," Avery sighed. "Simon must have been devastated when he heard the news."

"That's an understatement," Charles said. "I believe he phoned up a lawyer the moment he heard about it. Not sure what he planned on doing. I mean, the owner of a building can do what he wants with it."

"But this place has always been here," Avery said. "For as long as I can remember. It can't move. It won't be the same."

"Well, a lot of people feel that way," he said. "There was quite an uproar."

"So what do you think will happen to the store?" Avery asked.

"I'm not sure," Charles said. "But I tell you, the timing of his death is pretty good. The sale was meant to go through in a couple of weeks."

"Do you think his mother would go through with the sale?" she asked.

Charles shook his head. "She was against the idea entirely. She's a sentimental woman, you see. It's a family heirloom, this place. She wants it to stay in the family."

"So the bookstore won't close?" Avery said with a forced pout.

"I don't think so," Charles answered. "Not anymore."

Avery breathed a quiet sigh of relief. For as long as she could remember, she would escape to that bookstore any time she needed to find some peace. She didn't know what she would do if it closed. And she thought of Simon and how upset he would have been. She thought of his family and how long they had worked in the building. Without that space, their business would never be the same again.

Then it hit her—what Charles was really saying. She marched up to him and spoke as quietly as she could. "Charles, you don't think Simon is a suspect, do you?"

"He might be," Charles answered quietly. "He was at the wedding, and he has a decent motive. He stands to gain from Dean's death, doesn't he?"

"I suppose," she said as her heart dropped into the soles of her shoes. She thought of all the lengths she might go to in order to protect her own business. She would do just about anything but didn't think she would kill anyone. Then again, she'd never experienced a threat like Simon had.

She knew enough about him to know how badly he needed the business. He had three kids and a wife. He was the sole earner for his family. He told her that once when she had been the only one in the store and they had started talking. He had a lot to lose if the deal had gone through.

"I don't believe it," Avery whispered.

"I hate to break it to you," Charles said. "But when we solve this, I don't think any of us are going to like the truth. Someone at that wedding did it. It's bound to be someone we know personally on some level."

Chapter Nine

Avery recognized her father's voice as he loudly greeted Simon downstairs. Avery and Charles made their way to him. He had reached an age where he refused to believe he was going deaf, so every word out of his mouth was too loud for normal conversation.

"Morning, Dad," she said, giving him a hug. "I hope you don't mind that I didn't get you a coffee."

"That's for the best," he said with a smile. "I can't drink coffee anymore. It goes right through me."

Charles laughed as he said good morning to her father, and they resumed their browsing. But Avery kept glancing at Simon, who seemed to be invested in whichever book he was reading. She looked at him and tried to picture him breaking the door down to murder Dean. It just didn't suit him. He was so friendly and calm. She couldn't imagine that amount of violence or hatred coming from him.

But murderers hardly ever look like murderers.

Sprinkles loved her father, so with his lead in his mouth, he trudged along after him throughout the store. His nose was always pointed up at him, and his eyes glistened like stars whenever her father was around. His tail wagged, kicking up dust from the hardwood floors and making a light knocking sound with every beat. The reason for that was Avery's father had a habit of carrying dog treats in his pocket that he would sneak to Sprinkles when he thought nobody was watching. Of course, in his old age, he wasn't as sneaky as he thought he was, and Avery had caught him almost every time.

Avery glanced up and saw the name *James Parker* printed on a spine in front of her. She almost gasped out loud when she saw it. It had been so long since she'd seen one of her husband's books on a shelf. And there were rows of them, with most of them in bad shape. She smiled a little as she looked at them all. It made her miss him. She hadn't ever seen his book with a bent spine. She had been there when he had written them, so they had always already known the book well enough by the time they were sent to print. All the copies she had were in pristine condition. They had never been opened. They looked better with some wear and tear, though. It was a far more appealing look. Each book used the same font, and the spines were various colors. She remembered how much time he would spend choosing each color to make sure it worked with the story.

She reached for one of the books where her husband had modeled the main character after her. She looked it over and saw it had all the markers she would usually look for in a book. The spine was so bent that it was almost falling apart. There were scuff marks all along the edges. And when she looked inside, she found that some of the pages had been taped back together. She wondered if there was a name for who it had belonged to in the front of the book.

She flipped to the first page and found a handwritten note scribbled in red ink.

> Darling,
> May this be a teaser for an already perfect mind. You can read this on our holiday, with your feet in the warm white sand.
> I love you.
> Your ever-devoted husband.

At that moment, she felt no sadness anymore. Of course, she still missed her husband, but she could see the effect that his life had on others. She knew she was not the only person missing him. He had a following of readers who likely missed him too. And it made her feel a little less alone.

"Come have a look here, Avery," her father called out way too loudly.

He had some arbitrary book about accounting in the middle ages in hand, and she knew that he was simply trying to distract her from the shelf in front of her. Still, she tucked her husband's book under her arm. She would take it home and put it on her shelf so she could remember him the way his readers did. Then she walked with her father as he browsed the military section.

"You know, that Dean was a terrible man," he said.

"What made you think of that?" she asked with a laugh.

"I saw a book about cops, and it made me think of my friend Carl, which made me think of that guy Dean."

"Ah," Avery chuckled.

"My friend Carl lost his job because of Dean. Did you know that?" he asked.

"I didn't even know you had a friend named Carl," Avery said.

"Well, I do," her father snapped. "But I haven't seen him in a while. Thanks to that guy Dean."

Avery quickly looked around the bookstore to see who could hear them, but most of the other customers had left, and Simon didn't seem to be paying attention.

"Carl is a good man," her father explained. "He worked as a cop, and all he wanted to do was help people. And he was good at being a cop."

"So what happened?" Avery asked, motioning for Charles to take a step closer so he could also hear.

"Well, when Dean left Deb with all that debt, Carl felt that their attempts hadn't been good enough to help her," her father explained. "He decided that if Deb had paid for the furniture, it belonged to her."

"I tend to agree with that," Charles said.

"Because you're also a good cop," her father laughed. "So, Carl arrived at Dean's city house one day with the local sheriff there to repossess all the furniture."

Charles became a little uneasy. "Did he have the proper paperwork for that? It can't have been easy to arrange."

"No, but the cops on that side agreed with him, and so they made something happen," her father continued. "But they were barely through the door before Dean's lawyer arrived."

Her father picked out a book that was almost pristine and tucked it under his arm. Avery wanted to stop him and explain that it couldn't possibly be a good book, but he was mid-story and half deaf, so she knew it was no use.

"I don't know exactly how," her father continued as he waved his hands through the air. "But his lawyer knew some other fancy city lawyer."

"That's never good," Charles commented as he reached for a Japanese cooking book.

Avery did her best not to giggle as she envisioned Charles preparing sushi for them one afternoon. He wasn't much of a chef, and perhaps cookbooks weren't a bad idea for him to be buying. But Japanese recipes seemed to be a brave choice.

"No, it wasn't," her father snapped, bringing her attention back to the story. "That fancy lawyer man found some loophole or other and pressed charges against Carl. It was such a story, and the news even got involved."

"That's bound to lose you your job," Charles said, putting the cookbook down again.

"That's precisely what happened," her father explained. "They agreed to drop the charges if he was never employed as a police officer again. It made all of us so angry."

Avery understood why. Dean had done wrong, and Deb had to suffer. Carl was only trying to do the right thing and give Dean what he deserved. Dean, in turn, ruined his life, too.

"And I tell you, Carl never recovered from that," her father said. "He loved being a cop. It was all he ever wanted to do. I grew up with him, and since he was a kid, he was pretending to arrest people in the street with a gun-shaped twig."

"What did he do after losing his job?" Charles asked. Charles was no longer paying any attention to the books at all. He was completely invested in the story, and as a retired cop, Avery could understand why. Charles had left on his own terms, and even then, he continued to consult.

People who become cops have a passion for correcting the wrongs in the world.

"He went down a bad path," her father explained. "He was depressed and couldn't seem to keep a job for very long. It was really sad to see him that way."

"I'm sorry to hear about that," Charles added. "I can't imagine what I would have done in that situation."

"That's not even the worst of it!" her father shouted. "His life only went downhill from there."

Her father reached for another book and took a pause in his story to first read the blurb before shaking his head and placing it back on the shelf.

"His wife couldn't take the stress anymore," her father continued with his story. "She took the kids and went to live with her family in another state. She had lost all faith in him as a husband. He never saw it coming."

"That's terrible," Avery whispered.

The story was worse than she ever could have imagined, and she wondered how Dean could have lived with himself for so many years, knowing how many lives he had ruined and how many lives he intended to ruin. And he did it for money.

"Carl never saw his kids again," her father explained. "He could never afford to go there to see them or to bring them down here for a visit. And with his wife and kids gone, he had nothing to work for. He no longer cared much for himself. So, his health took a turn for the worst."

"Where is he now?" Charles asked.

"Well, he lost his house, of course," her father said with a heavy sigh. "He couldn't afford to pay for it at all."

"Please don't tell me it gets worse than that," Avery said, desperate for the sad story to end.

Only it wasn't a sad story. It was someone's actual life that had been ruined by the victim. Carl wasn't some imaginary character in one of the books on the shelf. He was out there somewhere paying the price for trying to be a better cop.

"He eventually did get back on his feet a little," her father said. "Started to do some odd jobs here and there and found a place to live. But he never did see his kids again. Perhaps he still will one day."

"Carl is still alive?" Charles snapped.

"Of course!" her father answered. "He lives in a small cottage at the end of the Winston's property. They've given him a good deal there. He helps them out on the farm where they need it, and he gets to stay there."

"That's at least a bit of good news," Avery said.

"When I spoke to him last, he said he was saving some money to go see his children," her father said. "I hope he does. He's getting old now, like me, and I'd hate for him to die without ever having seen them again."

Then her father shrugged. "He will never recover from the debt of it all, though," he said. "And he blames it all on that Dean."

"He does?" Charles asked. "Has he said that to you?"

Her father raised his eyebrows. "Of course, he has! He's always telling me how much he hates the entire Scott family for how they treat their neighbors."

Avery looked at Charles and knew exactly what he was thinking. He excused himself and thanked them for the visit. She knew he was going to the police station to list Carl as a possible suspect. He had a decent motive, she knew. What's worse was that he had little to lose at that point in his life. Even to Avery, he seemed like a strong suspect in the murder. Her father had given them a clue without even knowing it.

Avery felt completely overwhelmed by the day, and it was still morning. She had woken up that morning with the intention of finding a new book to read, and instead, she discovered two new suspects in a murder case.

Chapter Ten

The Stammtisch women had gathered at Deb's house for a quick cup of coffee. They were eager to see each other after the wedding. The last few full gatherings of the group largely involved planning and preparation for the wedding, and this time there would be none of that, only some catching up.

"Sorry it couldn't be at my house," Eleanor said. "My home is still piled under unopened gifts. I just can't get myself to open any of them!"

"That's alright!" Deb said happily. "I'm always eager to host you all. You fill my home with laughter and cheer, and that is never a bad thing."

Deb had a fairly large home. It was minimalist and decorated with various shades of light gray. Even the coffee cups were gray, and so was Deb's outfit. The only bit of color Avery could see that wasn't part of their clothing came from the hot coffee in the cups.

The house was so pristine that Avery always had a hard time getting comfortable. She was constantly afraid she might move something out of place and that it might upset Deb. It felt like sitting in a show house.

"Did they treat you alright at the police station?" Eleanor asked with worry.

"Oh yes," Deb answered. "They gave me food and water and coffee, and I was allowed to go outside from time to time to stretch my legs. It's their slow online system that makes it all take so long. But they were friendly, so it wasn't too bad." Deb reached for her cup of coffee and took a sip. "The chairs are awfully uncomfortable, and everything in there is so boring. It was only a few hours, but I missed home."

Avery chuckled quietly at the irony of it. She wondered if the gray inside walls of the police station weren't perhaps similar to the inside of Deb's home.

"Have they cleared your name then?" Avery asked.

Deb rolled her eyes. "No, and I'm apparently not supposed to talk about any of this. But there is no chance I am keeping quiet," she answered. "Despite all of you being able to say you saw me at the wedding all night, they say they can't confidently agree that I didn't do it."

Eleanor shook her head and looked as if she might cry. It did not go unnoticed by Deb.

"At the end of the day, they have no evidence that I actually did do it," Deb continued. "All they have is a motive. But if you ask me, that makes half the town a suspect."

"I'm sorry to hear about that," Avery said quietly.

"Me too," Eleanor said bluntly. "Until they sort this out, there is a high chance I might lose my honeymoon. We still can't get the hotel to budge on our booking."

"That's terrible," Camille piped up with what would likely be her only words for the entire visit.

Deb and Camille had always gotten along very well, and it had always amused the rest of them. Deb could hardly ever stop talking, and Camille barely ever spoke. It seemed like a perfect match.

"Well, I think I might have something to cheer you up," Deb said to Eleanor. "I have a surprise for you!"

Deb leaned forward and grabbed the television remote, which was remarkably gray. She pointed it at her television, which was framed in a pale gray frame, and switched it on. Deb was bouncing in her seat with excitement.

"I have the first batch of footage from the wedding ready to show you," she said with a wide smile.

Deb's wedding gift to Eleanor was to be the videographer for the wedding. Avery had been upset when she heard of it. She wished she had thought about it. Then again, it was Deb that suggested Avery gift all the wine.

Deb pushed the play button, and the screen filled with scenes of all the guests dancing wildly to the music. "Now, I don't have all of it yet," Deb said. "But I do have the dance party, and there are some really great shots here that I wanted to show you."

The entire group burst out laughing when the image of Charles hugging the wine bottle filled the screen. It was even funnier than Avery had remembered, and she had to put her coffee down to avoid spilling all over Deb's light gray sofa.

Then the moment turned sweeter when the camera panned to Camille, her hands holding Sprinkles' front paws as they moved around slowly across the dance floor. And once again, Sprinkles stole the show.

Eleanor was smiling widely as she watched it. It was good to see her looking at her wedding with a smile. There had been nothing but stress for her since the wedding ended, and Avery was happy to know she was being reminded of how great the party had been.

By the time Avery left Deb's house, she felt relaxed. And the coffee had done an excellent job of renewing her energy for Sprinkles' training class. He had already done well, and she had decided to keep doing the training for a while longer.

It was a bright and sunny day at the park where the training was happening, and Sprinkles had become part of a larger class. He no longer needed one-on-one lessons, as he was comfortable around other dogs. And it was good for him to socialize. Already, Avery knew which dogs he preferred to be around, and she even considered making friends with their owners.

That day, Sprinkles performed well in his class. He didn't make a single mistake and followed orders perfectly. She wondered why he had behaved so badly at the bookstore and wanted to know if she had been doing something wrong that day.

Then she thought about the day of the wedding when Sprinkles had sniffed Dean's hand. They had practiced that walk and return many times. Not once had Sprinkles veered from the path or stopped for anything. It was possible that the crowd had made Sprinkles less obedient. He'd always loved to be around people, and she had once or twice before struggled to get him to listen. But that was when he was a very small puppy.

He hadn't misbehaved for months before that day. Then, at the wedding and the bookstore, he suddenly seemed not to listen to her anymore.

But at training, he performed perfectly. He completed every trick without much persuasion needed. He did not beg for food or veer from his path, despite there being a small crowd of other dogs and owners.

It just simply made no sense to her. She couldn't think of anything she might have done differently, but she decided to speak to Brie, the dog trainer, and see what her opinion was.

By the time the training was over, Sprinkles was pretty tired. He collapsed at her feet with a wide smile and his tongue hanging out the side of his mouth. Avery petted him on the head as she refilled his water bowl.

"We'll go home soon enough," she said to Sprinkles. "I just need to ask your teacher something."

She searched for Brie, hoping to catch her and ask her why Sprinkles had not listened to her those two times, but Brie was already in conversation with another woman. Avery waited for a while, but it quickly became apparent that the conversation wouldn't be ending soon.

The woman was much older and had wrapped her hand around Brie's arm in a death grip. Avery knew that grip all too well. It was what elderly women did to stop you from leaving before they were done telling their stories.

Brie looked impatient about it, too. Of course, she was smiling and friendly, but every time she looked up in Avery's direction, her eyes sent out a cry for help. It made Avery laugh a little to see it. She wondered if she would ever be that way when she was older.

By the time Brie looked up for the third time, she thought Brie might be on the verge of crying. Avery wanted to do something to help, but as she glanced down at her watch, she realized that she was completely out of time.

She had promised Charles that she would cook dinner for him. The police had let her know that they no longer needed access to the room and it could be cleaned and reopened for business. Charles had kindly agreed to go in and do the cleaning up for her. He had also arranged for someone to fix the door. It had been am incredibly generous offer, and Avery didn't want to be late for him. So, she mouthed an apology to Brie and loaded Sprinkles in the car to head home. She felt awful leaving Brie in that situation, but she knew it would eventually end.

Sprinkles slept soundly as they drove. His face rested on his front paws, and he breathed loudly enough that Avery could hear it on the front seat. She put on his favorite classical music for him and made the short trip home.

When she arrived home, she looked over at the guest house and felt differently about it. She knew that if she went to Dean's room, it would likely look the way it had before he had ever stayed there. She saw a bin bag filled with yellow tape waiting to be taken away. She breathed a sigh of relief, knowing that the last reminders of what happened there were being removed. It had been tough for the guests who still had to stay in their rooms to walk past the yellow crime scene tape every day, and with that up, there was no chance of her booking out any more rooms.

As she parked the car, she ran through the list of suspects in her head. She wondered which one of them had enough strength to break down the door. Both Simon and Carl had a good enough motive. But did either of them have the strength required?

She didn't know Carl and didn't even know what he looked like. But she did know that he had been a cop once. It wasn't entirely impossible that he had remained in good shape even after he had lost his job.

Her mind was about to be distracted when she, thankfully, found something else to concentrate on. Avery's mind filled with the scent of fragrant herbs as she started preparing dinner for her and Charles. She was excited to cook his favorite childhood recipe of lasagna soup. Avery had been cooking for him regularly for so long that she knew what his favorite meal was, and she prepared it for him that night.

She wondered if other people also had friends who were as good as hers. And as she cooked, all thoughts of the murder filtered out of her mind for a while. She simply moved effortlessly through the kitchen as she reached for ingredients.

Avery knew that cooking could help her process just about anything. It was what she had relied on after her husband had died, and it had given her peace since.

She loved it even more if she was cooking for somebody else. That was when she got really creative, serving up the best that she had to offer that day.

Just before the dinner was ready and Charles was set to arrive, she put on some music and opened a bottle of Le Blanc's aged cabernet sauvignon, leaving it on the table to aerate before their dinner began. It was one of Le Blanc Cellars' best bottles. Avery chuckled, thinking of her pairing this sophisticated cab sauv with Charles' simple but favorite meal. It was the least she could do to thank him; besides, Avery was always eager for a reason to enjoy the good stuff in life.

Chapter Eleven

The table was set outside on the patio. It was a perfect summer night, and soft lights came from the garden around them. Sprinkles slept deeply at their feet as Avery and Charles enjoyed their dinner together.

The food had turned out even better than she had expected. The music was still playing quietly inside, and Sprinkles took deep, calming breaths as he slept. It had been a good day for Avery, and she couldn't think of a better way to end it.

The vineyard was quiet, and the last of the birds chirped happily as they flew by on the way to their homes. The first light of the stars was speckling the sky.

Charles hadn't said a word in a few minutes. He had been too busy finishing his meal. That was normal if he enjoyed his food. It was as if all thoughts of the real world simply evaporated from his mind, and his sole focus became the food that he was eating. He and Sprinkles were oddly similar in that way.

The wine she had opened paired perfectly with their meal, and it was one of the most enjoyable evenings that Avery had had in a long time. So, she ate as slowly as she could, savoring every moment of their dinner together.

It was a special thing to her to have a friendship so lovely that the two of them could be completely comfortable sitting in silence together. She knew the silence wouldn't last long, but still, it didn't make her feel uncomfortable.

When Charles finally ate the last bite of his food, he leaned back in his seat with his glass of wine in his hand. "So, what do we think about the suspects?" he asked. "If this was a book, and you were writing it, which you are...but if it wasn't real life, which one of our suspects would you choose to be the murderer?"

"I have to admit that both Carl and Simon have excellent motives," she answered. "And I was just wondering earlier which one of them might be strong enough to break down the door."

"You're thinking more like a cop every day," Charles said. "But those doors are surprisingly easy to break. It's an old cellar door. I don't think that should be too much of a focus."

"Oh," she answered, almost disappointed at the amount of thought energy she had wasted on that point in particular. "Well, we have one man who was going to lose his entire life's work if Dean wasn't stopped," Avery said. "And then we have another man who did lose his entire life's work and has made an effort to blame Dean for it."

"So different and so similar," Charles said with a chuckle. "And then we have an angry ex-girlfriend who worked for years to pay off the debt he left her in."

Avery had never seen Deb as an actual suspect, and her stomach turned to hear her mentioned in the conversation. She refused to believe Charles actually thought Deb could have done it. "Oh no," Avery said. "Deb is not really a suspect in this, according to me."

"She's your friend," Charles shrugged. "But one thing I've learned is that all of us have the ability to murder."

Avery didn't like that one bit. And she knew how stubborn Charles could be about that kind of thing, but she wouldn't even entertain it in the conversation.

"She can't be the murderer," Avery said. "She's terrible at keeping secrets. She would have told one of us if she had done it. Probably more than one of us! You can't really think she's capable of something like this?" Avery waved in the direction of the guest house, and Charles let out a soft chuckle.

"No, of course, I agree with you," he said. "I don't think she could have done it either. But she is still listed as a suspect, so she is still part of the investigation. Until her name is removed from the official suspect list, she must continue to be treated like one."

Avery hated it when Charles was right. But she thought the fact that Deb was still a suspect was ridiculous. There were two people with even stronger motives. If they were still looking into Deb, they were wasting their time.

"You need to not see her as a friend for a moment," Charles said. "Picture her as just another character in a book. Then look at what Dean did to her and how she suffered because of it. You have to admit that she is a good suspect."

"Absolutely not," Avery said. "Even as a character in my book. Deb is everywhere all the time, and she knows everybody. She has no concept of remaining under the radar with anything. I'm not saying she couldn't be a murderer; I'm just saying that there's no way she would get away with it for this long."

"Do you think she'd break?" Charles asked with an amused smile.

"I heard how she spoke about her time in jail," Avery said. "She was bored. I think she would have broken just to make it more interesting for herself."

Charles burst out laughing at the thought of it. Avery felt terrible for saying it. But Deb had always had a very low tolerance for things that were boring.

"Why is she still a suspect anyway?" Avery asked. "There are multiple people who can confirm having seen her at the wedding all night."

"We're a small town," Charles said. "And nobody liked him. The police can't be certain that her friends wouldn't cover for her. So, even with the confirmed alibis, anybody with a strong enough motive will remain on the suspect list until there is concrete proof that there is absolutely no way they could have done it."

"Our witness statements aren't enough?" she asked as she took another sip of her wine.

"Nope," Charles shook his head. "That kind of crime didn't necessarily take long. And the venue isn't far from here. The police believe it is entirely possible that she could've snuck out of the wedding for fifteen to twenty minutes without anybody noticing."

"You might be right," Avery said. "We were all too busy watching you hug that bottle of merlot."

Charles did his best not to blush, but Avery knew she had embarrassed him. She didn't intend to keep bringing it up. It had just been so funny, and having seen the video footage earlier that day, she was reminded of it. She couldn't let it go just yet.

"At least I was dancing," Charles teased. "You sat on the sideline. How boring of you."

"That's because I know what I look like when I dance," Avery said. "And it is not pretty. It was to the benefit of everyone present that I remained in my seat at all times."

"If you say so," Charles said with a shrug.

Avery frowned. She understood Charles' explanation about why Deb was still a suspect. But she still didn't agree. She thought it was absurd that the police were willing to use any of their resources on Deb.

"Deb couldn't have left the party without us knowing it," Avery said. "She was all over the place and talking to everyone. We would have noticed if the room had suddenly fallen quiet." Charles let out a snort, but Avery wasn't certain she was joking. It had happened before with Deb at other parties.

"Well, unless we can provide concrete proof that there wasn't a single moment when she left the wedding party, then she will remain a suspect until all of this is solved and the real murderer has been caught."

Their dinner was finished, and Charles helped Avery clean up as he always did. Then she carried Sprinkles inside as she waved Charles goodbye.

It was a pleasant night and quiet, and Avery wasn't even nearly sleepy enough to go to bed yet. So, she browsed her stack of movies to see if anything tickled her fancy. There were a few, so she pulled them all out of the shelf and decided to start at the top and see how far she got before she fell asleep. Sprinkles made himself comfortable at her feet, and she poured herself another glass of wine. But she could hardly concentrate on the movie. She kept thinking about what Charles had said. And she started to look at the suspects as if they were book characters and not actual people.

Carl, the police officer, had a good motive. He might have had the strength to break the door down, too. Although Charles felt it wasn't an important point. Still, he was a police officer at heart. Of all the people on the suspect list, he was the one whose entire career had been about protecting people. But Avery knew that cops had killed before, and it wasn't entirely unheard of. She had too little information on him, though. As a character, he was a little empty. She didn't know his age or his description. All she knew was that the victim had cost him his job and ruined his life.

Then, there was Simon, the bookstore owner. Dean had not yet done him wrong but had intended to, according to Simon. His family-run business had been in that building and part of his family going back for generations. They were a tourist attraction for the town. Simon had a large family and a lot of mouths to feed. As the sole breadwinner, he would have lost a lot if Dean had gone through with the sale.

That left Deb for last. She was an angry ex-girlfriend. Dean had stolen from her and gotten away with it. The result of that had cost Carl his job. It wasn't entirely impossible that more than one person was involved, but it seemed unlikely to her.

There had been no witnesses to the murder itself. But she knew that there had been other guests there that night. Some of them had reported hearing the loud sound of the door breaking, but none of them had heard any kind of chatter.

That seemed unusual for a group crime. No, it had to be one single person.

And she knew that it couldn't be Deb. Deb just didn't seem to be the right character for that kind of murder. Ex-girlfriends don't smother their ex-boyfriends. Not after everything he had put her through. Scorned women were brutal. She didn't fit. Avery knew that she had to get Deb's name off the suspect list somehow without interfering too much in the investigation itself. And it all rested on her alibi. It was sound but just not sound enough.

She felt the pressure growing on her shoulders as she thought about her friends. Deb needed her name cleared so she could move on with her life and forget about Dean entirely. And Eleanor needed the murder to be solved so the newlyweds could go on their expensive honeymoon.

The sound of a text on her phone distracted her from her thoughts. It was from Charles.

Thank you for a lovely dinner. If that is my bonus, then I will put in extra work whenever you need it!

Avery chuckled. She stared at the television for a while as her brain numbed itself with thoughts on how to clear Deb's name. It did nothing to ease her stress, but it did an excellent job of lulling her to sleep. Avery and Sprinkles slept deeply on the couch until the sound of the movie title screen startled her awake, and she dragged her feet to her bedroom.

Chapter Twelve

I t was way too early in the morning when Avery started to wake up. The summer sun was beaming in through the gap in the curtain earlier than it usually did. It did a good job of waking Sprinkles up. Avery tried to ignore the sunlight and the hyperactive golden retriever, but she hadn't slept very well at all.

She figured that if she just kept her eyes closed and stayed as still as possible, both the sun and Sprinkles would leave her to sleep for another half an hour. It was a plan she had tried many times before, and it had never worked. But Avery knew that she would try it anyway again and again.

Sprinkles had already been awake for some time, so he was whining for her to open the door to the backyard. She knew that once he had become that awake, there was no way to get him back to sleep again. It was a lost cause.

And even if she could, the gap in the curtains had angled the ray of sun to shine perfectly across her eyes. Her bed was comfortable, but the sun in her eyes took every ounce of comfort that she once had away.

Avery gave up. She rolled out of bed and rubbed her eyes as Sprinkles came to greet her. He hopped up on the bed and snuggled into her neck, and she could feel his wagging tail as it slapped softly against the mattress.

"Okay, okay," she whispered. "I'm up...kinda."

Avery stumbled with blurred vision to the door leading to the backyard and pulled it open. Sprinkles ran out as fast as he could and bounced around. She had fallen asleep earlier than usual the night before, and she wondered why it was that she felt so tired.

It almost felt as if she hadn't had any sleep at all. Her eyes burned, and she could feel how puffy they were every time she blinked.

Oh yes. The dreams. She had dreamed terrible dreams for the majority of the night. Most of them involved the doors to her home being broken down by someone that she couldn't quite see. And then, after that, she had dreams of Deb being dragged away in handcuffs for a crime she hadn't committed. Somewhere in the mix of it, she dreamed of Eleanor and Samuel cooking themselves a very depressed Spanish meal in their home to cheer themselves up after having to completely cancel their honeymoon.

She watched as Sprinkles rolled in the grass without a care in the world. The sky was the perfect blue, and not a single cloud was present. She knew it was going to be a hot day. So, she decided that to clear her head, she would head out for a walk in the vineyard before the sun became too intense for her.

She rushed back in to fix herself a cup of coffee and get dressed for a walk. Then, she called Sprinkles and motioned for him to follow her. The vines were lush and stood proudly in the morning sun. She brushed her hands through the bright green leaves around her. It was time to have them pruned. The vines looked better that year than they had ever looked, and she was expecting a very successful wine season. It made her proud to think of it. But then there was the mark on her pride.

A murder had taken place on her farm just a few days ago. She looked at the ground the vines grew in and thought of the hole at the cemetery where Dean's body would be laid to rest. For the vines, the earth meant life. But for Dean, the earth meant death.

She called for Sprinkles to stay close to her, and he followed her instruction without hesitation. Then, she practiced some of his new tricks with him. He had learned some of them only the day before, and still, he was performing them almost perfectly.

He always had a smile when she was giving him orders. Even when they were out in public, it was as if he enjoyed it. It made her think of his behavior at the bookstore again, and it just didn't sit right with her. He hadn't begged for food the night before when he lay right at the table. She'd eaten a fair share of sandwiches around Sprinkles, and not once had he shown any interest in it at all. She found it hard to believe that Simon's sandwich was so good that it completely made Sprinkles lose his manners. Then again, she didn't have any other explanation for it.

She continued with their practicing as they carried on with their walk through the vineyard. She thought about how many years she'd spent away from the vineyard when she and James lived in the city. As a young woman, she had rejected the idea of running it entirely. But she was grateful her parents insisted that she come back. It was the first time in her life that she felt truly proud of what she was doing.

The breeze was cool and fresh as it washed over them and felt like a comforting embrace across her warm skin. The breeze disturbed some butterflies that had been hidden among the vines, and they fluttered through the sky like confetti.

She looked back toward her home and the guest house, and for the first time, she didn't only think of the crime scene. All of it felt a lot better since Charles had made the room right for her again. She decided that she would reopen the farm for customers the next day. She couldn't leave it any longer. She'd had enough success that the few days they'd been closed hadn't hurt her too badly financially. But she couldn't remain closed for too long. Everything needed to continue as it once had.

Everyone had worked tirelessly to create a successful season, and she didn't want to let them all down. She looked across the vineyard and knew that it deserved to be celebrated.

She reached into her back pocket and pulled out her phone. The screen was tough to see in the bright light, but she navigated her way around quite easily. She opened the chat that included all the staff of the farm and let them know to return to work in the morning. She was certain that not all of them would be as excited about it as she was, but that was the tough part of being somebody's boss.

Before she slipped her phone back into her pocket, a stream of messages came through. They flooded her screen, and they were all coming from the same person. Eleanor had sent her almost forty photographs followed by one sentence.

I've received the first photographs of the wedding!

The photographs just kept coming through, and for a moment, Avery considered just switching her phone off. The buzzing just wouldn't stop, and already some of the other Stammtisch women were commenting on it all. She didn't even know where to begin. But Sprinkles was occupied by a loose branch that had fallen to the ground, and she thought she would let him play for a while.

She started at the top and worked her way down. Most of them were the average wedding photographs. Beautifully dressed people all standing in a line right next to each other, putting on their best smiles. Then there were some photographs from the ceremony. They looked like any other wedding, too. Every wedding that Avery had ever been to had resulted in the same sequence of photographs. Still, she loved to see Samuel and Eleanor so happy.

Avery paused when a photograph of Sprinkles walking proudly down the aisle with the ring pillow in his mouth came past. He had a large smile on his face, and every face that was visible in the background behind him wore an equally big smile.

She immediately made the photograph of Sprinkles her phone wallpaper and sent it on to Charles before looking at the next one. There were photographs of people dancing, making speeches, and enjoying a good meal.

It made her happy to see that every person photographed had a glass of her wine in their hands too. There were too many photographs for her to pay attention to all of them, and she wondered how much more there would be if Eleanor said that these were only the first.

Avery was grateful that the photographer hadn't snapped any photographs of the police intruding on the party. She imagined how Eleanor and Samuel might have reacted to being so frequently reminded of the event.

Then it made her laugh a little as she pictured an album filled with beautifully-dressed people being confronted by the police and all their shocked faces. If it wasn't someone she cared about whom it had happened to, she might have wanted to see something like that.

The sun was beating down on her, and she could feel her skin starting to burn. She looked around for a spot of shade but felt nothing. The earth beneath her feet was also getting warm already, and she had a lot to do if she wanted to reopen the next day.

Sprinkles looked like he was having fun, and she hated to put an end to it. But they couldn't stay out there forever. She could last a few more minutes, though. She watched Sprinkles roll around in the dirt before he got distracted by a passing butterfly. He sat upright and watched as it fluttered daintily past his eyes. Then, the butterfly came to a stop on the tip of his nose. Avery had never seen him stand so still. She opened the camera app on her phone and did her best to approach him as carefully as she could.

She got Sprinkles and the butterfly in the frame and focused, but just as she was about to snap the photograph, the butterfly took off again. Sprinkles sneezed as if he had been holding it in so as not to disturb the butterfly.

Avery raced to check the photographs on her phone to see if she had successfully captured the moment, and as she did so, she realized how she could clear Deb's name and remove her from the suspect list completely.

She urgently motioned for Sprinkles to join her as she walked as fast as possible back toward her home. As she walked, Avery considered all the ways in which her plan could work or not work. It would take her some time, and she needed to make sure that it was guaranteed to work.

As soon as she was through the door and back in the cool shade of her own home, she texted the women of the Stammtisch and summoned them to help her with her plan.

Chapter Thirteen

A very had her laptop on the passenger seat as she drove over to Charles' house. She felt bad calling him so out of the blue. It wasn't her favorite thing to just drop in on people like that. But the women of the Stammtisch had worked hard all day on a way to clear Deb's name.

The directions to Charles' house were scribbled on a small piece of paper which she held in her fingers as she navigated the streets to his house. She felt a little excited at the thought that perhaps by the time she left his house, Deb's name would be cleared.

She hoped it worked, she didn't have any other idea, and she knew Deb was innocent. Avery didn't want the police to spend too much time looking into her as a suspect while the real killer was still somewhere out there.

As usual, because she was in a hurry, it seemed to take her forever to get anywhere. Every car ahead of her was slow, and it seemed like everything was trying to stop her from actually getting to his house. But she took a deep breath. Another twenty minutes won't end the world.

But although her mind was behaving logically, her hands still felt clammy, and her heart still began to race as she did her best to find her patience.

When she eventually pulled into Charles' driveway, it occurred to her for the first time, that she had never seen the inside of his house. She wondered what it would look like inside and tried her best to picture it.

But when he opened the door, it was nothing like she had imagined it would be. His home was filled with antique furniture and smelled of wood polish. One large sofa filled most of the living room, and every surface was piled up with either books or newspapers.

On one wall, there was a bookshelf that covered the entirety of it, and the bookshelf was crammed full of movies. He lived alone, and she knew his family never lived nearby. It had never crossed her mind what he might be doing to pass all that time alone in his home.

His house was clean, but there was stuff all over the place. There seemed to be no true décor style or system of any kind for organization. There was a freedom about it that Avery was almost envious of. But what she was most envious of were the large windows in his kitchen.

His stove had a view of the vineyards that nearly took her breath away. She imagined the meals she might create if she could look out over a view like that every time she cooked.

I should put some more windows in my kitchen.

"You said you have something important to show me that would clear Deb's name?" he said cheerfully, handing her a can of soda.

"Yes," she said with a smile. "Where is the best place for us to sit?"

She tapped the laptop bag that hung over her shoulder to imply that she needed a table, and he ushered her into his dining room, where a large eight-seater table sat covered in more books and stacks of photographs.

At the far end of the dining room was a large wine rack filled with bottles. And she recognized some of the labels. He had an extensive collection—one that she was certain was worth a fair amount of money. It seemed funny to her that, even though she had known him so long, she had learned more about him in the short walk through his home than she had learned in years of conversation with him.

Charles cleared a space on the table for her, and she set up her laptop. Then she opened the folder that they'd put together and paged him through an organized sequence of photographs and video clips. Each of them had a time stamp, and through that, there were only about three minutes of the night where Deb was unaccounted for in the photographs.

It proved that she had never left the wedding. And as Avery showed it to him, she felt quite proud.

Nestled between the stacks of books and newspapers, she noticed that it was a perfect scene for a crime novel detective to find herself in. She made a mental note of what the space looked like. She wanted to add it to her notes later. Charles' home would be the perfect home for her main character.

"This is great," he said, looking quite pleased. "This should do the trick. We should get this down to the station immediately."

"Excellent," Avery said with a small cheer. "We can take my car; I'll drive."

The police looked through it all and then copied every item from her laptop over onto their own drive to take in as evidence.

"This can't have been quick or easy to put together," the officer said to her.

"Of course not," she answered. "But it had to be done. The longer you look into her, the longer it takes to find the real culprit."

"You are correct there," the police officer laughed. "Well, I'll give Deb a call then and let her know that we will no longer be treating her as a suspect, but I'm sure she expects the call."

"Probably," Avery laughed. "She helped us put it all together!"

Avery felt a huge amount of pride as she watched them make the phone call, and Avery noticed a large smile on Charles' face as well. She refused to leave until they had confirmed completely and to her liking that Deb would no longer be questioned as a suspect in the murder. Only when she was entirely satisfied did Charles convince her that it was time to go and leave the officers alone to do their jobs. By the time she and Charles walked out, the sun was already setting, and it would soon be night.

"That leaves only three suspects left, for now," Charles said.

"I don't know if I can handle it if this gets any more complicated," Avery laughed. "I'd like to stick to three suspects, please."

"Unfortunately, that's not how this works," he chuckled. "But for now, we only have three."

"So, that leaves Mrs. Scott, the victim's mother, Simon from the book-store, and the ex-cop that my father was talking about," Avery said.

"Yes, that's it for now," Charles said. "I had a look into that friend of your father's. Carl Brown is his name. I couldn't find much about him, only what your father told us about. Any information after he left the force seems vague."

"Did you ask some of the other officers?" she asked. "Maybe they knew him?"

"I did," he answered. "Nobody really knew him very well; they mostly just knew *of* him, that's all. But we'll find out more somehow. We have to. He's a suspect."

When they arrived back at Charles' house, he invited her to dinner at his place for the first time. And when they walked in, she saw how the setting sun had created a bright, golden glow throughout his kitchen.

She wondered if she could ever just cook one meal there as she watched over the setting sun.

"It'll have to be pizza," he said. "I'm afraid I don't cook much at all."

"You don't cook?!" she asked, shocked. "In here?!" Avery waved through the space with her arms. It was a large kitchen that had clearly been designed by someone who loved to cook. "You're breaking my heart," she teased. "But pizza will be just fine."

Charles ordered the pizza, and when he came back, he had a bottle of wine in his hand. He reached into a cabinet and retrieved two beautiful antique crystal glasses. In between the heaps of papers and old books, Avery enjoyed one of the most luxurious glasses of wine she'd ever had. It was well-balanced, not too heavy on the tannins, and had a slight lingering jamminess on the finish.

"How is it going with the book planning?" he asked her.

Avery sighed. "James used to make it look so easy," she said. "I have all these notes I've made of things I want to include and ideas that I have, and I just have no idea how I'm supposed to stitch them all together."

"I'm sure it will stitch itself together," he said.

"Well, what's worse, is that I have all these pieces of papers with one-liners scribbled down on them," she explained as she took another sip. "I keep waking up at night with what I think are these perfectly sculpted words and descriptions, then I rush to write them down, and when I look at them again, I think they're absolute garbage."

"Even garbage has its place in this world," Charles teased. "Every item in my home was once cast out by another home, I guess."

"I suppose," Avery said. "I mean, I'm not sure anybody ever saw any of it as garbage, but I suppose if someone wanted to keep it, they would have."

"I saw you looking at the collection of your husband's books at the bookstore the other day," he said softly. "He's quite popular in our little town, you know. I have a fair collection of his books myself. In fact, there's a character in one of them that reminds me a lot of you." He pointed to a small bookshelf, and she saw that the entire bottom row was packed with her husband's publications.

"I know you were a part of his process," Charles said plainly. "So, I'm certain you'll be brilliant at it."

Avery wasn't certain what to say, so she sat in brief silence until the doorbell rang to announce that their dinner had arrived. As she waited for Charles to come back with their pizza, she realized that she felt comfortable in his home. Something about being surrounded by books and movies reminded her of how quiet her life had become. There was a time when that scared her, but she had grown to love that silence. And Charles' home was very quiet.

She knew that if he ever did feel the need to occupy his mind with something, he would only need to reach out his arm and grab the nearest thing to him, and it would be filled with words and images to get his mind turning.

"I hope you're hungry," he said. "Because I never eat the leftovers. I always forget I have them."

He placed the pizzas down on the table and filled her glass again, and it seemed just so much like Charles to drink expensive wine while chewing on delivery pizza. And that was the small nuance about him that she liked most.

He was the perfect blend of sophistication and practicality. It made him an excellent friend, and if she were entirely honest, the wine and food paired excellently.

The two of them sat together and spoke about their favorite books and films long after the food had been finished. His home seemed like a treasure chest to her, and she knew that if she opened a cupboard or spent enough time looking at any one shelf or surface, she would find yet another item of interest to her.

When she finally left to go home, she felt as if she had entirely left the world for the few hours that she had been there. She hoped he'd invite her back again and that the next time, she'd feel more comfortable searching through his collection of items. She knew she would find inspiration for her book there, and already she could imagine the scenes that she wanted, and when she finally stepped into her own home again, she found the spaces rather boring.

Chapter Fourteen

Avery had spent most of the previous evening unpacking old boxes full of books and arranging them on her bookshelf. There were books in there she'd forgotten she'd ever read at all, and it made her feel both happy and sad.

Next to her bed lay a pile of books she'd put there with the intention of reading them again. She liked the way it made her home look when it was full of books. It reminded her of the home she'd had with her husband. Not too long ago, she'd been convinced that she would never be able to face it all again. She had been so convinced that it would make her feel sad and cause her to grieve again. But it was better than the room full of closed boxes that she had been living with before. She understood now that there was no point in pretending her life before had never existed.

With her favorite belongings once again decorating the space around her, she had slept through the night without disruption until Sprinkles had woken her up again. And the more the year progressed, the more often that was happening.

But that morning, when she had woken up in her home, filled with the belongings of her old life, she missed her husband. But it wasn't in a bad way. It was a positive desire, she felt, to be reminded of him and all that they had together before. So, she hopped in her car and headed back to the bookstore. She wanted to see if any of her husband's books had more notes in them from those who had owned them before.

She hadn't really considered how his books might have impacted the lives of the people who read them. She'd only ever known how they had impacted hers. And when she walked into the bookstore that day, it didn't remind her of her childhood anymore. Instead, it reminded her of Charles and his home.

She looked around and wondered how many of the books in that store would wind up in his home one day and how many of them she'd be buying for him. She walked to the shelf with her husband's books on it and started taking them off the shelf. Some of them had notes to loved ones on the first page, and others simply just had a name and a year. Avery realized as she paged through them that some books, must have belonged to crime novel lovers, as they had penciled in questions and notes all along the sides of the page.

She remembered an argument between her mother and father that she'd overheard once as a child. Her mother felt it was a sin to write in a book and that the pages should have been kept pristine. However, her father argued that the author of the book wanted the reader to enjoy it in any which way they pleased. He had said that the moment he opened the book, it was ruined. And so, he was free to write in it if he liked. And Avery quite liked the way the pencil notes looked alongside her husband's writing. She hoped that someone would write in her book someday.

"Good morning, Avery," Simon greeted her. "No dog with you today?"

"Unfortunately not," Avery said, somewhat wary of Simon as a suspect. "He's at the groomers today."

"That's a pity!" Simon answered. "I have an especially delicious sandwich here today."

Avery let out an uneasy chuckle as Simon held up the sandwich he had stashed away behind the counter. She thought about asking him what was on it. She wanted to know what was so delicious that it had caused her well-trained Sprinkles to lose all his manners.

But she wasn't too interested in starting a conversation with him. She couldn't be certain that she wouldn't ask him a question related to the case. Avery couldn't risk that, it would only be interfering, and she liked

Simon and his shop. If she started asking questions, she ran the risk of discovering that it was true and that he was not the person she thought he was at all.

But when he held out the sandwich, she noticed an unmissable fragility in his hand. His hand appeared swollen and weak, unlike anything she'd seen before. Her eyes had lingered too long on his impediment, and he had noticed the question burning silently in her mind.

"I have arthritis," he said with a kind smile. "I was diagnosed about a year ago, and I'm afraid it's progressing faster than even I'd like to believe."

"I'm really sorry to hear that, Simon," Avery said.

"It's alright, mostly," he said. "And I like to think the treatments will get better sooner than we think...thankfully, this job doesn't require all that much strength."

"I suppose that's lucky," she said with a nervous laugh. "I've always thought it must be quite pleasant to work in the bookstore."

"It is," Simon said with a wide smile. "And although my health deteriorates, my lovely wife stays as healthy and strong as ever. She has become my hands now, you see. I barely have enough grip left to screw in a lightbulb."

It was such a common, everyday task that the rest of the world took it completely for granted. And at that moment, Avery wondered who would care for her when she could no longer do it. It seemed a paranoid thought, but she'd always assumed she'd be capable and alright on her own.

Nobody expects their strength to fail them. Her parents had each other, and Simon had his wife to screw in the lightbulb for him. If she got arthritis one day, would she be forever doomed to live in the dark?

Another customer, thankfully, took Simon's attention away from her. To avoid getting roped into another conversation with him or completely plunging into the depths about the small possibility that she might not be able to change her own lightbulb someday, she walked up the spiral staircase and disappeared onto the upper floor.

Her eyes caught the row of cookbooks, and immediately, she thought back to Charles' perfect kitchen. It bothered her tremendously that he never used it to cook. In fact, she could see that the stove and oven had barely been touched in years. With that in mind, she set off on a mission to find him the perfect cookbook. At the very least, it would make him laugh. And at best, he could cook a meal for her.

She browsed through all the countries and types of food, and none of them really stood out to her as something Charles might show any kind of interest in. That's when she spotted a cookbook with a spine that was taped together.

There was no longer a name or author on the spine at all, and the pages seemed stained by food and wine. She pulled it from the shelf, and it fell open on a specific page. It must have been the original owner's favorite recipe.

It didn't take her long to realize it was a pizza recipe book. And it was perfect for him. She looked over the pages, growing hungrier by the second as she gazed over all the delicious recipes.

She tucked the book under her arm and made the decision that it would be the perfect gift for Charles. But she'd have to go downstairs and speak to Simon again. Avery thought about his shaking hand and how he had no strength left and made a note to research how one got the disease as soon as she got home. If there was some way that she could avoid it, she intended to do just that. But when she heard the sound of the door creaking from another customer entering the store, it dawned on her. If he wasn't strong enough to screw in a lightbulb, then there was no way that he could have broken down the door to Dean's room. Neither would he have had the strength to smother Dean.

She breathed a sigh of relief, knowing that it dramatically cut down their suspect list to only two people, which meant they could solve the crime, and her two newlywed friends could make it on time for their honeymoon.

She happily made her way back down the spiral staircase to pay for the book. She said goodbye to Simon, wishing him the best of luck with the disease, and within a few minutes, she was pulling into the driveway at her own home.

But a nagging voice in her mind said she needed more proof that Simon couldn't have done it. She looked at the entrance to the guest house. It was an old cellar that they no longer used, and it had become a rather popular guest house. But there were still some empty rooms, and she decided that she would test the door to see how easy it was to break it down. She risked doing damage to the property, but if they were easy enough for her to break, then she had bigger problems on her hands. Avery wanted to know her guests were safe. She never wanted to learn that a murder had occurred on her property ever again. So, she went in and checked which room was empty. She picked one all the way at the end to avoid bothering any of the existing customers that were there.

Staring at the door, Avery realized she had no idea where to begin if she wanted to break a door down. She remembered the movies she'd seen, so she moved back and tried to ram it down with her shoulder. But that only resulted in a sharp-shooting pain, and the door barely budged. She kicked it, tried running up to it, and still, the door didn't budge. She was pleased that her guest house was safer than she thought, but she was also certain she had bruised herself in a few places. Out of breath and out of ideas, she concluded that Simon could certainly not have broken down the door and decided to let Charles know of the new information she had received.

Simon couldn't have done it. He has arthritis and no strength left. That leaves only Mrs. Scott and Carl. Let me know when I can call to tell you what I know.

P.S. I have a new book for your collection.

She read through the message twice until she was satisfied that it was good enough and then sent it along. And it wasn't long before he responded with a time for her to call him. She paged through the pizza recipe book she had bought him and wrote down some of the ones that she also wanted to keep.

When she decided it was time for a glass of wine, she felt oddly disappointed to see a shocking lack of antique crystal in her cabinets. *That'll have to change.* But she settled for her average wine glass and poured herself a chilled glass of chenin blanc before making herself as comfortable as possible on the sofa.

She spent the rest of her evening paging through the recipe book while her favorite movie played on the television, only getting up to refill her wine from time to time. Sprinkles sniffed the books on her shelf eagerly, his tail wagging as he enjoyed the new décor.

It was a perfectly pleasant evening as the warm summer air wafted in through the windows, creating the perfect atmosphere after a hot summer's day.

When she finally rested her head on her pillow, she stared at the light-bulb that was nested neatly in her ceiling lamp and sighed. *Who will change you when I no longer can?*

Chapter Fifteen

A very looked through the notes she'd made for her book and saw that two suspects had been crossed off the list. The ex-girlfriend and the bookstore owner had red lines through them. Something about it was incredibly satisfying to her, and already her story didn't seem so all over the place anymore.

There were two more names on the suspect list, and she was eager to find out which one of them would do it. It felt strange to look at a case that was currently unfurling and see it as a story that she was piecing together; it gave her an odd perspective on the entire thing.

She flipped through the stack of pages, going over all the ideas she had already accumulated, wondering if, somewhere in there, the answer was already obvious. All they needed to do was narrow it down to one of the two people left on the page and hope that another suspect didn't make themselves known.

How hard could it be?

She scoffed at that thought when she remembered all the manuscripts James had thrown into the trash because there were too many questions with impossible answers or too many issues with continuity. He had always told her that even the perfect story had the potential to fall apart completely. The difference, though, was that her story was happening on her own doorstep, and she could watch it and learn. The questions would eventually answer themselves, and anything that happened would be completely possible because hers was based on something true.

Her phone buzzed, and instinctively, she reached to check who the text was from.

The police just phoned. We're free to go on our honeymoon, provided we answer if they call. We'll see you all in two weeks!

Attached was a photograph from Eleanor of their two suitcases, packed and waiting at the door. The Stammtisch group chat exploded with excited responses, and Avery was pleased they could make it after all. They deserved a happy honeymoon after everything they had been through.

A cold, wet nose was pressed against her ankle as Sprinkles came to ask her to open the door for him. She checked her watch, and saw there was still some time before she was expected to call Charles and tell him what she'd learned about Simon.

So, she took her time to sip a cup of coffee out in the backyard as Sprinkles played with anything he could find lying on the lawn. The sun had already warmed the ground, and the birds were chirping merrily in the trees above her.

She looked out over the sunny lawn and wished she could make herself comfortable there all day with a good book and some good food. It would be the perfect day—just her and Sprinkles, the sun, and the birds. The only thing that would have made it better was if a cool breeze arrived to cool them down.

The sound of her phone ringing canceled out her daydream, and she rushed inside to see that she'd been late to phone Charles, and he was phoning her instead.

"Charles, sorry," she answered. "I was outside with Sprinkles."

"It's a beautiful day outside," he said cheerfully.

She walked with her phone and sat down on one of her patio chairs, watching as Sprinkles attempted to herd the birds back into their tree.

"So, tell me about Simon," Charles said.

She told him about the tremor in his hand and his weakness. And

Charles agreed that someone that weak couldn't possibly have broken the door down or suffocated the victim, as both things required some strength.

"And that should be easy enough to verify; we just need to speak to his wife and get some proof...a pharmacy receipt for his medication or something," he said.

She scribbled it down to add to her ever-growing pile of notes. "That's a good idea. And that leaves us with only two more suspects on the list."

"You are correct," Charles said. "We've got the victim's mother and your father's friend, Carl."

"I think they should bring Carl in for questioning next," she said.

"They are reluctant to do so for two reasons," he explained. "Carl is the only one on the suspect list that actually wasn't a guest at the wedding, and they have no evidence to arrest him. Apparently, when they phoned to speak to him the other day, he refused to answer any of their questions."

"That seems a little unfriendly," Avery said.

"Well, he knows his rights, and I don't think he's been fond of the police ever since he was forced out of his job," Charles answered.

"And what about Mrs. Scott?" Avery asked.

"She's a grieving mother," Charles said. "So, they're approaching her carefully. She has enough money to sue the department into bankruptcy if she were so inclined."

"I might have an idea to get some information regarding Carl's involvement in this; let me see what I can do," Avery said as she swallowed the last sip of her coffee.

"Just don't do anything that could get us into trouble," Charles said. "He's smarter than you think about all of this, and I don't want to scare him away."

"Of course," Avery said. "I wouldn't do such a thing. I'll leave the heavy work to the police. We just need enough information to warrant an arrest, right?"

"That's right," Charles said. "And it has to be obtained legally. So, we either need a statement from him or a witness who is willing to testify."

She understood perfectly. So when she ended the call, she got dressed as quickly as she could and made the pleasant walk to the end of the property to visit her parents. But it wasn't so easy to stick to the topic at hand.

"What's with all those empty boxes in the trash?" her mother asked as she handed Avery a cup of coffee.

"I unpacked some of my old books," Avery answered. "Why are you taking note of what's in the trash?"

"Your mother can't help herself," her father said, entering the kitchen without greeting. "She doesn't miss a thing, I tell you. I've never gotten away with anything in my life."

"It just seems odd, is all," her mother continued. "You've had those boxes in storage for so long. Why unpack them now?"

Avery stared blankly at her mother as she took a sip of coffee. "That's not important. I've actually come here to ask Dad a favor."

Despite it having little to do with her mother, the elderly lady sat down at the table and paid full attention. Her father didn't seem to mind or care—he'd gotten used to it after so many years of marriage.

"I'll do anything for you, dear, you know that," he said with a kind smile. "Do I need to get my toolbox?"

"No, it's not that kind of favor," Avery asked.

Without hesitation, her father reached for his wallet, and Avery put out her hand to stop him. "And it's nothing like that either, Dad. I haven't needed money from you for almost twenty years now."

"Well, if it's not handy work, and it's not money, what is it then?" he said, looking completely lost.

"Your friend, Carl, that you told us about the other day at the bookstore. Do you remember?" she asked.

"Yes, of course," he answered with a shrug.

"Well, because of what you told us about how his life was ruined by Dean Scott and how he always blamed Dean for everything that had gone wrong with him...he's made it to the suspect list in the murder case," Avery explained.

"They're accusing him of murder?!" he said, raising his voice.

Her father frowned so deeply that the wrinkles of his face almost completely covered his eyes, and all Avery could see were the folds of skin and gray eyebrows.

"They're not accusing him of murder yet," Avery said calmly. "But they do suspect him of it, given the way he feels about the victim."

"That is an outrage," her father said, slamming his hand on the counter.

"Oh, calm down, love," her mother interrupted him. "It can't come as such a surprise to you. I think he's a good suspect."

"You barely know the man," her father argued.

"Perhaps that's better," her mother said. "Who wants to be friends with a murderer?"

"He's not a murderer," her father insisted. "And I don't understand what it is you expect me to do about any of this."

"Well, he's not being easy with the police," Avery explained. "I was hoping that you could go and visit him and just find out one small bit of information somehow."

"And what might that be?" her father asked as he crossed his arms. "Do you want me to walk into my friend's house and ask him if he murdered someone on my property?"

"No," Avery said. "And I certainly don't want you to be so direct about any of this either. I simply want you to find out where he was on the night of the wedding. And work it into the conversation...don't be so obvious."

"Oh, please," her mother laughed. "Your father is the most obvious man on Earth. He knows nothing about being discreet. I knew about the engagement ring weeks before he proposed. I kept seeing the box in his pocket!"

"That doesn't matter anyway," her father argued. "Because I won't do it. He is my friend, and I won't insult him like that."

"Don't think of it as trying to prove his guilt, Dad," Avery said. "Think of it as trying to prove his innocence. If we can prove his whereabouts were nowhere near the guest house on the night of the murder, then you have saved him from a great deal of trouble."

There was a pause in the conversation as her father thought it through. He was a stubborn man, and she knew he might need a little more convincing than that, but that was her best argument.

"He'll do it," her mother said.

"You can't decide that for me," her father snapped.

"Yes, I can, and I have," her mother said. "You are going to visit him; you've been meaning to do so for some time, and you are going to help him clear his name of this. It's what a good friend would do."

In the end, Avery didn't have to argue any further. As it had been her entire life, her mother was the deciding voice, and her father agreed to set up a visit with Carl.

"Right, then, that's settled," her mother said. "So tell me about the books. Why have you unpacked them now?"

Avery's jaw dropped. After everything they had just discussed, her mother was still more interested in her personal life.

"I just missed them, that's all," Avery eventually answered. She didn't want to give more detail than that, so she swallowed what was left of her coffee and said her farewells before heading to the wine room to let Charles know of her plan.

It was a busy day at the vineyard that day, and Avery hardly had any more time to look at her book or piece together what little amount of her story she already had. And by the time the sun started to set, she and Sprinkles walked slowly together through the vines, enjoying the silence as she sipped on some velvety merlot.

The bright orange of the sun cast rays up from behind the green vines, creating what was easily one of the most spectacular sunsets that Avery had seen in a long time. She wondered if the sunsets in Spain would be just as beautiful and how much longer Eleanor and Samuel had to wait before they reached their destination.

Even Sprinkles had stopped to admire the sunset, his ears perked and tail wagging as Avery went to stand beside him.

Chapter Sixteen

Although it was completely dark outside, the air was still warm. Avery washed the dishes after cooking dinner and dreamed about one day having a view to look at while she did so. She thought about Charles' kitchen again and wondered how much it would cost to demolish hers and build one exactly like his.

With each passing day, her home was filling up a little more. She'd promised herself that she wouldn't let it get too cluttered. It was Deb that had first suggested she tried minimalism. She'd said it would clear her mind. But the more she unpacked her favorite belongings and put them out on display, the quieter her home seemed to her and the cozier. Suddenly, the color of her sofa didn't bother her so much anymore, and she'd lost the urge to paint and repaint every available wall.

Feeling more at home than ever, Avery made herself comfortable at the dining room table, next to her a list of admin that she needed to catch up with for the vineyard. She was only a little bit behind, but it was a tedious job, and she'd never liked doing it.

Avery had only just gotten started when a knock at the door startled her. With her reading glasses still resting on her nose, she answered and was surprised to see her mother standing alone in the dark with a worried look on her face.

"Where's Dad?" Avery asked, peering behind her mother.

"He's at Carl's house, of course," her mother said, annoyed.

Her mother pushed past her, and she noticed what appeared to be an empty shopping bag hanging over her shoulder. She followed her mother into the living room, where she was already looking through all the freshly unpacked books, checking them for dust.

"Where's your flashlight? You didn't walk in the dark, did you?" Avery asked.

"Pfft," her mother scoffed. "I've been walking that path for so many years now. I could do it blindly."

"You have osteoporosis, Mom," Avery said as she rubbed her eyes. "How many times do we have to go through this? You can't walk in the dark without your flashlight. If you trip over a root, you'll break your hip."

Her mother turned to face her and tapped her hip impatiently. "My hip's fine," she said. "I see you haven't painted this wall yet."

"No, I've decided I will leave it that color," Avery said. "Is there a reason you've dropped by, Mom?"

"Can I not visit my daughter?" her mother asked.

It was clear that something was bothering her mother, and she knew that her mother would come out with it soon enough. But she hadn't bargained on an argument that night and wasn't sure where she'd find the energy to fight it.

Avery sighed. "Alright, well, can I make you some tea or something?"

"Chamomile," her mother answered shortly.

Avery turned to put the kettle on, and as she walked through the entryway into her kitchen, her mother decided that it was the perfect moment to talk about why she had really walked all the way over there in the dark.

"You shouldn't have asked your father to go see Carl," her mother said.

"Mom, *you* encouraged him to do it," Avery said, exasperated. "What made you change your mind? I thought you agreed with me."

She watched as her mother walked along the shelf of books, picking out the ones she found interesting and placing them in the empty bag on her shoulder. And Avery wondered if she'd ever see those books again.

"Well, I did think it was a good idea at the time," her mother said with a shrug. "But that was before I knew how stressed out it would make your father. He's been pacing up and down all day, worrying about what he might say to start the conversation."

"You have got to be kidding," Avery said.

"It's no joke," her mother responded. "You should have seen him. He barely even watched the television today. I've never seen him like that before. It's not fair on him. You know he has a weak heart."

"And you have a weak hip," Avery mumbled.

"I heard that," her mother snapped as she added another book to her collection. "Now, how far are you with that tea?"

Avery made two cups of tea, one for her mother and one for herself. She hoped the tea would calm her down. She didn't want to argue with her mother, but she was being particularly stubborn, and she knew it would be hard.

Thankfully for Avery, the kettle took a while to boil, so she had plenty of time to breathe and compose herself. And by the time she made it back into the living room with the tea, her mother was paging through the notes she had made for her book.

The cups clinked as she placed them on the table, taking the papers from her mother's hand and placing them aside.

"If that was so stressful, he could have just told me," Avery said. "I would have been fine with it if he changed his mind. I was only asking him a favor. He had every right to say no."

"You know your father is too stubborn to do that," her mother answered. "Once he's committed to something, he has to do it. Otherwise, he doesn't sleep at night, and he tosses and turns. It drives me mad!"

You're driving me mad.

Avery felt terrible knowing she had caused her father so much stress. She wished he had told her; she would have stopped him. It was a terrible thing to imagine him pacing through the house, feeling as if he was being forced into something he didn't want to do.

"I'm sorry, Mom," Avery said softly.

Avery's mother looked through the room, her eyes resting on all the items that Avery had recently put out on display. They were items that Avery had brought with her from the city, and although her mother had visited her often there, she looked at them as if she'd never seen them before.

She lifted the photography book that was placed on the center of the table and paged through the first two pages before also adding it to her bag of books. But she noticed that there was something else bothering her mother, and it wasn't anger. Her mother looked really concerned. There was a crease in her brow that Avery had only ever seen when something truly frightened her.

"Is something else bothering you, Mom?" Avery asked, reaching out to place a hand on her mother's nervously twitching leg.

"I told you that you stressed your father out," her mother said, avoiding eye contact.

"I can see something's wrong, Mom," Avery said softly. "Please, will you tell me about it? You think Dad is the stubborn one?"

Her mother's lips pursed as if she was physically struggling to keep the words in her mouth. She sipped on her tea and pretended to be interested in a decorative ashtray on the side table.

"Mom," Avery said, losing her patience. "What's wrong?"

At last, her mother relaxed her shoulders and put her teacup back on the coffee table.

"I'm worried," her mother said. "Your father left hours ago to see Carl, and he hasn't been answering his phone. He should have been back by now. He completely missed dinner."

"How many times have you phoned him?" Avery asked.

"About five," her mother said. "I keep phoning, and it goes straight to his voicemail message. His phone is off, I think."

Avery didn't like the sound of that one bit. Not only did her father never stay out later than dinner, but on the rare occasion that he did, he was pretty strict about answering his phone. And it wasn't often that he left the house without her mother.

"He told me he was just going for some coffee," her mother said. "I thought he'd be back hours ago already. And he usually lets me know if he's going to be later than expected."

"That is odd," Avery said quietly.

"What if he said something wrong?" her mother broke, tears threatening to spill. "That man could be a murderer for all we know! What if your father said something wrong and met the same fate as that idiot Dean?"

"I don't understand," Avery said as she rubbed her fingers against her temples in an attempt to stop the inevitable headache. "You were both so certain he was innocent, and now you think it could be him?"

"Your father thought he was innocent," her mother corrected her. "I think he is a very suitable suspect."

"Then why did you say Dad should do it?" Avery said. "Why did you take my side earlier?"

"Because your father said he was innocent, and your father knows him better than me," her mother said. "But the more I think about it, the more I remember that your father has made some terrible judgment calls about people before. Do you remember that man he hired to paint our ceiling? He made off with my pearl earrings!"

"Do you think Dad is in danger?" Avery asked.

"I think it isn't impossible," her mother answered unhelpfully. "It just isn't like him not to answer his phone." Her mother looked like she would burst into tears at any second. Her hands fiddled nervously with the cushion she had pulled onto her lap.

"Why didn't you phone me earlier?" Avery asked.

"I didn't want you to worry," her mother answered.

Avery closed her eyes and turned her head to the heavens, asking for the strength and patience she needed not to lose her temper with her own mother. Then she got up and went to get her phone from where it was placed to charge.

"Alright, well, I'm going to phone him now," she said.

Avery dialed his number, and it didn't even ring. Immediately she heard her father's voice asking for the caller to leave a message after the beep. Her chest tightened as her stomach sank.

"His phone is off," she said.

"I know," her mother answered dryly. "I told you so."

Avery was trying hard not to panic, but it wasn't easy. She could feel a lump in her throat, and already she imagined how her heart would break if her mother's suspicions had been true. She could never live with herself if she had asked her father to visit the man who turned out to be the murderer, and it had gotten him killed.

"Do you know where he went?" Avery asked. "I mean, I know Dad said he's on a nearby farm, but do you have an address for Carl? Did Dad tell you which farm?" Avery was struggling to find the right words to formulate her questions as her stress levels peaked, and her concern for her father's safety caused her brain to scramble.

Her mother reached her shaking hand into her pocket and pulled out a small piece of paper with a vague address written on it. It had no house number, only a street name. But it was a good enough place to start.

"Alright, let's go and get him then," Avery said. "But let me phone Charles. Maybe he can meet us there or arrange for the police to get there before we do."

Her mother lifted the bag of books over her shoulder as Avery dialed Charles' number.

"Leave the books, Mom—Charles, hi," Avery greeted him. "Listen, I'm texting you an address for Carl. Well, it's a street name. We're worried about my father; his phone is off, and he was expected home hours ago."

As Avery talked, she gathered her car keys and unlocked the front door.

"Yes, we have the same concerns that you do," she continued. "Do you think you could—"

As Avery pulled the front door open, she saw her father standing there with his arm raised in the air, about to knock on her door. She felt dizzy with relief when she saw that he looked absolutely fine.

"Don't worry, Charles, my apologies; he's just arrived home. False alarm," she said before ending the call.

"Where were you off to?" her father asked. "I figured your mother would be here when I found the house empty."

"Dad, why aren't you answering your phone?" Avery snapped. "Mom's been worried sick about you. She thought you'd be home ages ago, and we were about to send the police to look for you!"

Her father shrugged. "My battery died, dear," he said. "I did send your mother a text to let her know that I'd be eating dinner at his house."

Avery turned to look at her mother, whose mouth was hanging slightly open.

"Well, I never received any message," her mother said.

Avery held out her hand. "Let me see your phone, Mom," she said.

There, as clear as day, was the notification that a message had come through a few hours before. She opened it, and it was from her father explaining that his battery was dying, that he'd be home late, and all was well.

She showed the message to her mother.

"Well, I didn't see it," her mother said plainly as if that made all their panic alright.

"Are you having tea?" her father asked between cheerful whistles. "Any chance I could get a cup?"

Chapter Seventeen

Her father walked right past them and made himself comfortable on the sofa. He had a wide smile on his face as he looked at the new décor in Avery's house.

"The books look lovely, dear," he said proudly. "I always forget how many of them there are."

"Thanks, Dad," Avery said, still dizzy from the stress that was leaving her body. "Tell me about your visit with Carl."

"Oh, it was just lovely to see him again," her father said. "He's doing so well, and we had so much to catch up on. That's the trick, isn't it? You avoid your friends for a few years, and then when you see them again, you actually have something new to talk about!"

Her father let out a child-like chuckle before leaning across the coffee table and taking Avery's cup of tea.

"Not at our age," her mother laughed. "If you wait too many years, your friends die, and it was all for nothing!"

"Everything was fine in the end!" her father said happily. "We spoke easily, and he was just as funny as I remember him to be."

"I told you everything would be fine," her mother said to him.

Avery couldn't believe it. Her mother had been the one who had started all the stress in the first place! She stared at her mother in disbelief, but she avoided complete eye contact with Avery. She sat down, her legs almost shaking from the brief panic she had just been through and leaned against the back of the armchair.

"What's even better is that I now know he is completely innocent!" her father said. "Just as I expected him to be."

"Oh, that's wonderful, dear!" her mother said, clasping her hands together with excitement.

Her mother carried on as if she hadn't just been on the verge of tears, convinced that her husband had been killed by a murderous lunatic. The entire thing had made Avery extremely tired, and she hoped her parents would finish their cups of tea soon so she could get into bed and forget that any of it had ever happened.

"Where was he then on the night of the wedding?" Avery asked, unamused by either of her parents.

Her father took a long sip of his tea as he lifted the ashtray on the side table, inspecting it.

"This was in your city house, wasn't it?" he asked. "I remember it used to sit on the table outside on the patio."

"That's right," Avery said, doing her best not to roll her eyes.

"He wasn't even in town," her father eventually explained. "In fact, he only returned to town yesterday. You should see his tan! He looks like he's just spent a month on a tropical island. He's been in Florida, enjoying the sun and the food if I looked at the size of his gut!"

Her mother gasped as if news of Carl's growing belly had been the most shocking part of the entire evening.

"Was he visiting someone there?" Avery asked. "Anyone that could provide an alibi?"

"That's the best part of all!" her father cheered. "He has just gone to see his children for the first time since they moved away. He hasn't seen them since they were young children."

"Isn't that wonderful?" her mother asked. "It must have been such a special moment. And I'm glad that his ex-wife finally let it happen."

"That's just the thing," her father explained. "His ex-wife wasn't too pleased about it, apparently. But his daughters are both adults now and live on their own, so they invited him to come and visit. And there was nothing that his ex-wife could do to stop it."

"It's a terrible thing to keep a father from seeing his children like that," her mother said. "I'm sure it must have meant the world to him to see them again."

Avery made a note of Carl's visit to Florida on one of the pieces of paper she had confiscated from her mother only a few minutes before. But she wasn't quite ready to drag a red pen line through his name yet.

"Apparently, those two daughters of his are quite the clever girls!" her father said. "One of them is an attorney of law, and the other just started her own business. He says he barely had to pay for a single thing while he was there."

"Do you think he could go live there with them?" her mother asked. "It's the least they could do for him after how he was treated by their mother."

"I wouldn't think so," her father explained. "Not so soon, anyway. He hasn't seen them in so long that he probably needs to get to know them all over again."

"I suppose that makes some sense," her mother agreed. "What a shame."

Her mother shook her head and tutted as she thought about it. Avery looked at the clock and saw that it was well past ten and wondered how long it would take before her parents were too tired and agreed to go back home.

"I tell you what, though," her father continued at full steam ahead. "He's certainly improved his cooking skills since I last saw him. I had a really delicious meal!"

"Now I'm jealous that I didn't go along with you!" her mother teased.

"Not to worry," he answered. "I've taken the liberty of inviting him over for coffee next week. He said he remembers you fondly and was eager at the thought of seeing you again."

Avery was happy her father was so certain he was innocent because that narrowed their list of suspects down to one person. But she knew her father's claim regarding a conversation that nobody else had heard was not enough.

If they were going to convince the police that he wasn't involved, they would need a concrete alibi, something that proved his innocence without a shadow of a doubt.

"That's all lovely, Dad," Avery said with a somewhat forced smile. "You didn't perhaps get a contact number for one of his daughters or a photograph of the two of them together so that we can confirm his alibi?"

"How do you propose I could have worked that into the conversation?" her father asked with a frown.

"You never said anything about that when you asked your father to do it," her mother immediately joined in. "You just said that he had to make some light conversation."

"If you needed me to get those things for you, then you should have told me so," her father continued. "I didn't know that was necessary! I don't know how all these police things work!" Her father was waving his hands through the air, and Avery watched as a small drop of tea splashed out of his cup, landing all over his pants and the sofa beneath him. She had asked one question, and it had instantly upset both her parents.

"How, precisely, do you suppose it would seem normal for your father to ask his friend for a photograph to keep?" her mother continued. "You said he mustn't make himself suspicious! That would have sounded awfully suspicious to me!"

"Did you at least get a name for one of his daughters?" Avery asked.

"He mentioned their names a couple of times, but I wasn't paying enough attention. I'm an old man; I don't remember new names, only the old ones," her father answered.

"I'm sorry I asked," she said softly. "Just forget it. Thanks for going to see him, Dad. It was more helpful than you know."

Her parents finished their tea and with Avery's flashlight in their possession, they made the walk back to their home. Her mother's shoulder sagged under the weight of the books that she'd shopped for from Avery's bookshelf. Avery watched them until she couldn't see them anymore and then waited for the text from her mother to say they'd made it back in one piece.

Avery collapsed back into the armchair and reached for her notes. She stared at Carl's name with the red pen in her hand. But as much as she wanted to cross out his name, she couldn't yet. Her father had gotten some useful information, but there was no evidence to prove his claims.

Still, in her mind, Carl was no longer a suspect. So she wouldn't focus any more attention on pinning the crime on him. Beside his name she wrote the story her father had told her about how he hadn't seen his kids since his wife had left with them all those years ago. It was a good back-story, and she included a brief description of a large man with tanned skin and a love for cooking. And with that, one of the main characters of her book came to life. She wondered how many of James' characters had been modeled by people they had known personally.

Avery reached for the phone and dialed Charles' number.

"I'm really sorry about that; it was all a big miscommunication," Avery said when he answered.

"That's no problem," Charles said cheerfully. "It's always good news when a crisis turns out not to be a crisis at all."

"My father had been to dinner with Carl," Avery explained. "He was pretty casual about his choice of conversation, but he learned that Carl had been out of town in Florida. And if his story is true, then he only returned yesterday."

"How long was he gone?" Charles asked. Avery could hear him reach for a paper in the background.

"A few weeks at least, from what I can tell," Avery said. "He was staying with one of his daughters. My father didn't get any names or contact details, naturally."

"Oh, that's not a problem," Charles said. "I'm sure it won't be too hard for the officers at the station to get some information on his daughters. There should be contact information for them somewhere in the database. Or, at the very least, their mother could tell us."

"That's excellent," Avery said. "Will you let me know if you hear anything at all?"

"Tell you what," Charles said. "Why don't I pick you up tomorrow? We can go to the station and be there when they make the call."

"That sounds like a great idea," Avery said. "I can take some notes for my book. The more accurate, the better!"

"Great, I'll see you at ten then," he answered. "Now get some sleep."

"Don't mind if I do," Avery chuckled.

Avery took the entire stack of notes with her as she climbed into bed. She stared at the last remaining name on her list of suspects...Mrs. Scott. If the information they had was complete, then that made Mrs. Scott the murderer. She imagined the woman beating down the door and suffocating her own son. It just didn't seem to fit the appearance that Mrs. Scott liked to convey at all. She didn't seem right for the scene in any way. Or did she seem so wrong for it that it, in turn, made her perfect for it?

Avery wasn't sure she liked Mrs. Scott as the murderer, but she had a feeling that there would still be a lot that would come to light as the rest of the investigation continued. Her view of Mrs. Scott could still change completely, and she hoped it would.

She thought back to all of the books that James had written and tried to remember if, in any of them, the mother had been the murderer. There wasn't a single one. It had simply seemed too great a sin to write about, even in a crime novel.

Then again, few mothers were like Mrs. Scott, and few sons treated their mothers quite as badly as Dean had.

But there was one thing that didn't fit that potential storyline at all. Mrs. Scott would have no reason to break into her son's room. She was his mother, and if she had knocked, he would simply have let her in. Unless she had not done that on purpose to convince the police that the person who had done it had not been that close and friendly to him...

Chapter Eighteen

I t was a warm morning when Charles picked her up. Avery was tired; she'd been up late working on some admin work for the vineyard. Everything at the vineyard was going smoothly, despite the fact that she was spending so much time away from it. It made her feel good to know it.

She was glad to see the cup of coffee waiting for her as she made herself comfortable in his passenger seat. She accepted it gladly and took a large gulp. She'd slept well the night before, but it had been so well that it had made her tired.

Avery had slept right through all of her alarms, including Sprinkles. And by the time she did wake up, she had to rush to be ready in time for Charles' arrival.

She had been in his car before and wondered why his car wasn't as cluttered as his home. If one had to judge him purely on the experience of his car, one might assume that his house was filled with clean lines and minimal furniture. There wasn't a speck of dust or dirt in his car, ever. In fact, Avery knew he had a habit of having it cleaned every week.

"Here," she said, handing Charles the beat-up cookbook from the bookstore. "I saw it, and it made me think of you."

The book landed heavily in his hand, some pages threatening to slip out and land softly on his lap. He pulled it closer and inspected the damage to the spine and cover and smiled. "Must be a good one, I guess," he teased. He paged through it and laughed. "Surely the pizza wasn't so terrible the other evening?"

"Not at all," she chuckled. "But your kitchen looked so sad and unused and lonely...just promise me you'll try at least one recipe out of the book?"

Charles leaned back and placed the book on the back seat. It was the ugliest item in his car, and the look of it kind of made Avery laugh.

"I'll make one," Charles agreed. "But you're going to have to come and taste it. I'll need an honest critique."

"Deal," she agreed. "I'll be as brutal as you need me to be."

At the station, Avery watched for what felt like hours as the officers made phone call after phone call. Eventually, they found someone who had been friends with Carl's daughter in school, and she had an old number for Carl's ex-wife. That number led them to one of her old friends, who had a forwarding address. Once they had that address, they could get his ex-wife's landline number. It took a few tries before she answered, but eventually, she was able to give them the contact numbers for both of his daughters.

She wondered how often they needed to go through such a lengthy process just to get the information that they needed. Carl knew his alibi would check out, and still, he refused to speak to the police when they had tried before.

That was a level of stubbornness that outmatched both her parents combined. And in a way, she respected it. She wondered if it had made him a better cop and if that was why he had decided to continue to pursue the case against Dean, even when he was told he needed to stop.

She wondered if his stubbornness had been what had caused his wife to take their children and move all the way to Florida without him. Perhaps her mother had once contemplated the same.

It was finally time to phone his daughters. Everyone present gathered around the phone as it was placed on speaker. One officer was elected to speak, while everyone else was instructed to keep as quiet as possible and warned that the phone call was being recorded. They dialed the number for his eldest daughter, and it rang for what felt like minutes before the call ended without any answer. Then, they tried the number for his youngest daughter. Again, the phone rang and rang, and just when it looked as if that call would cut out too, there was a sound of a receiver on the other end as it clicked.

"Hello?"

"Hi, Miss Brown?" the officer answered.

"Speaking."

The officer went through all the formalities, explaining which precinct he was phoning from and even went as far as to give her his badge number for security purposes.

"Right," she said, sounding unamused. "I need to leave the house for a very important meeting. Is everything alright with my father?" She sounded nervous as if she was worried that she was about to receive some bad news.

"There's been a murder here, unfortunately. Your father is alright, but he is currently a suspect in the case. We're hoping you can confirm his alibi for us. Is it true that your father has been with you for the past few weeks?"

"That is correct," she answered hesitantly. "He spent two weeks here with me and two weeks with my sister, who I am certain would be happy to confirm."

"That's alright," the officer said. "Do you think you could both send us some photographs confirming the trip? Anything with a date stamp and a landmark in it should suffice."

His daughter happily agreed, and within minutes, an email had come through with photographs that proved his trip to Florida. They were happy photographs of a man in the sun, enjoying the day with his daughters. It was clear in the pictures how pleased Carl had been to reconnect with them.

Avery drew a red line through his name on her notes and then used the same red pen to circle the name of the remaining suspect.

"Our list of suspects is getting rather short now," Charles said out loud.

It wasn't her place to join in on the conversation. She was only a visitor in their investigation, and she'd been extra careful not to get too involved or to step on any toes while she had been there.

But she wished she could and knew that if she didn't concentrate hard on not talking, that the words would come falling out of her mouth and they wouldn't stop until she had said too much. She didn't want to do that. She wanted to keep the opportunity to follow them around. Avery wanted to write her book, and she wanted it to succeed. And for now, that meant biting her tongue and watching without interference.

"Yes," the officer agreed. "Mrs. Scott is the only name left up on the board. And I really thought it would be Carl, I tell you."

Avery wondered what they would do next. Time was of the essence, and there was a town full of people who needed answers. The talk in all the coffee shops was that people were afraid. One of the people among them was a murderer, and the reality of that was causing paranoia in the community. That was a dangerous place to be as a small town.

"I guess it is time we should bring her in," the officer said. "There's only so long we can wait out of courtesy. She is our only remaining suspect, and courtesy no longer matters."

The police officers in the room decided on their best approach. It was decided that the best option was to go and collect her and bring her in for questioning. It was the consensus that she was the kind of woman who would simply refuse to come in without her lawyer present. They hoped to speak with her for a while without his presence. Everybody knew who her family lawyer was, and he was a fierce practitioner of the law. He knew every loophole and had no problem suing anybody and any business on her behalf. And as long as there was money involved, she was happy to go forward with any suggestion he had to make.

Avery had met a few lawyers like that one when she lived in the city. She could spot them from a mile away. They always sported the finest watches and shoes. They walked in a certain way and spoke to everyone as if they were the smartest person on Earth. She tended to stay away from people like that for as long as she possibly could. And she knew well enough that if Mrs. Scott asked for her lawyer, it could mean trouble for the precinct.

The officers prepared themselves. Each one was given a different role to play. They had one chance to get her without her lawyer present, and they weren't prepared to miss that chance.

"Should we follow them?" Charles asked quietly, with a wide smile.

"Are we allowed?" Avery responded. "Won't they be upset with us if we do?"

"As long as we don't get in the way, and as long as we don't interfere, we are allowed to go wherever we please," he answered. "Provided we're not trespassing on private property, of course."

Avery knew most of Mrs. Scott's farm was open to the public. It meant they could drive onto her property, and legally, they were allowed to be there as long as they stayed off her private driveway.

She had nothing better to do at that moment, and she had been curious about Mrs. Scott and what she was like ever since Charles had added her name to their list of suspects. Avery wasn't going to pass up this opportunity.

"In that case," Avery said. "Of course, I want to follow them."

They followed as closely as they could in Charles' car, and Avery took note of every small detail. While she was in the car, she made a brief summary of the events of the day so she could use them accurately in her book.

Scott Rose Farm was titled proudly in brushed steel on the large gate as they entered the property. Every wall was white, and white roses stood proudly at the sides of the road. Avery looked out of her window and gasped quietly. It looked like something out of a book or a princess movie.

As far as the eye could see, there were roses of every color and every shape. On a different day, she would have loved to go out and touch them and smell them. She wondered if Mrs. Scott ever got tired of the scent of the roses around her.

I never get tired of the smell of wine.

When they finally came to a stop, there was already a police officer telling Mrs. Scott that she needed to go with him. Her house, painted bright white, was tucked away between the roses, almost invisible from a distance. And Avery had to squint to see her.

One thing was for certain; it was one of the most impressive farms Avery had ever seen. She wondered why Dean would ever have considered selling it. Who wouldn't want a place that beautiful?

"What is this about?" Mrs. Scott asked sternly.

As usual, she was dressed in all white. Her lips were red, and her hair was done up the way it always was. She looked as if the farm had sculpted her, and she had been born from its very foundations. The white of her clothes was the exact white of the walls and the surrounding roses.

"Some new information has come about regarding your son's case," the officer said. "We'd like you to come to the station so that we can discuss it."

Mrs. Scott looked skeptical, and Avery couldn't help but think that her skepticism made her seem guilty. But the officer just remained as calm as he could be, and he remained friendly with her, and eventually, she was convinced.

"Good job," Charles said quietly.

They watched as Mrs. Scott climbed into the back of one of the police cars, her lips pursed and her arms folded. One thing was for certain—she wasn't happy. Surely a mother would be happy to hear that there was some movement on the investigation into her own son's death?

To Mrs. Scott, the entire thing just seemed like one great inconvenience.

"Where will they take her?" Avery asked. "To a cell?"

"No, she has to be under arrest for that," Charles answered. "She'll be taken to a room for questioning. There'll be cameras and microphones. I expect she will lawyer up as soon as she sees the room."

Charles was right. When they made it back to the station, Mrs. Scott had been placed into one of their interrogation rooms. She looked entirely out of place against the gray concrete walls and the gray table and chairs in the room with her. The room was small, but the emptiness made it seem as if it loomed over her head.

They watched on a sea of television screens as she checked her watch and rolled her eyes. She tapped her foot impatiently as if there was perhaps somewhere more important she needed to be at that moment.

"Odd behavior," Avery said. "If it had been family of mine, I'd be willing to wait as long as necessary to know how the case was going."

"You're absolutely right," Charles said. "And these moments are precisely why we make them wait. It's important to see how a suspect behaves without an officer present. She looks calm, frustrated, and impatient even."

"So what does that mean?" Avery asked.

"That means that should they ask her a question, and she suddenly bursts into tears and becomes distraught, that all of that is likely an act."

"I see."

"If she were going to cry and grieve, she would be doing it now in this brief moment of silence that she has to herself," he continued. "People who have lost loved ones to murder find it hard to maintain their composure in a room like that. The police station is a horrible reminder to them of the truth."

"What if they're just trying to be brave?" she asked.

"Nobody puts on a brave face when they think they're alone," he said, pointing at the screen. "If this were normal, she'd be a lot more heartbroken than she appears to be right now."

An officer that Avery didn't recognize joined them as they watched the screens closely for signs and clues in her body language.

"Are you sure these are all recording?" Charles asked. "This is great body language to use in your case against her."

"Yeah," the officer answered. "And we're just preparing to start the questioning. We won't let her stew for too long, and we don't want her getting nervous and calling a lawyer."

"That sounds smart."

"Do you think I would be allowed to watch the questioning?" Avery asked, her eyes glued on the screen as she scribbled down notes.

The officer looked at Charles. "Is she a consultant like you?" he asked.

"She's writing a book," Charles explained. "Chief Mathers agreed to let her follow the case for some inspiration and research."

"I see, well, I'd have to run it past Chief Mathers, and I don't want to waste too much time," the officer said.

"Not to worry," Chief Mathers' voice answered from behind them. He stood beside them and faced the screen. "She can watch," he said. "Take her to the viewing room. I'll be there in a minute too. I'd like to see this one myself."

"Thank you," Avery said with a curt nod.

"Just don't cause any trouble for me," Chief Mathers said. "Women like that will take any reason to make my life hell. I can't afford that; my health is bad enough as it is already."

"You have my word."

Avery followed the officer down a few narrow passageways until he opened a door for her. And there she was, just on the other side of the glass. Mrs. Scott was staring at her own appearance in what she thought was a mirror.

But to Avery, it looked as if she was staring directly at her.

Chapter Nineteen

Chief Mathers joined Avery and Charles in the small viewing room. "Right," he said, clasping his hands together. "A few rules for you, Avery."

"I'm listening," she said, her eyes still fixated on Mrs. Scott.

The light hanging above her had made her look even paler, and all her white clothes seemed to glow. She looked ethereal, and she sat dead still, staring straight ahead. Avery wondered how she managed to remain so calm through all of this.

She looked particularly at peace for a woman who had just lost her son and had just been taken from her home to sit in a cold room and wait for ages for anyone to even explain to her what she was doing there. If Avery had been in her shoes, she might not have been able to sit so still. Even as she watched, she felt so excited that she was shifting uncomfortably on the spot.

"You can take notes, but you cannot use actual quotes," he said. "And you certainly can't use anybody's real names. I am doing this to help you with your book. I ask that you are respectful of my rules. None of what is said inside here can leave this room. The police force can face some serious consequences."

"I understand," Avery said with a kind smile.

She knew that Mrs. Scott had enough money to open a lawsuit against the department, just as her son had done when he ended Carl's career. Avery reached for her notebook and pencil and waited eagerly for the questioning to start.

Chief Mathers eventually left them, and Avery waited a few seconds before the door opened into the little gray room, and he stepped inside. He was colder than she expected him to be. He greeted her with a short "Mrs. Scott" and a polite nod.

He sat at the table across from her. Avery watched as he moved in his seat over and over again, as if he was finding it impossible to get comfortable. The chair creaked and squeaked, and eventually, he sat still and sighed. Then, he opened the folder in front of him and arranged and rearranged the pages inside over and over. From where Avery was standing, it seemed to be entirely without purpose. He sprawled the pages out in front of him before stacking them up again.

After that, he took his pen and pretended to read through some of the sentences here and there on the pages. Avery kept her eyes on Mrs. Scott, whose pout was becoming more and more pronounced. At that point, Chief Mathers took out a clean piece of paper and tested his pen on every corner, even though it wrote perfectly fine. Charles let out a short chuckle next to her as she watched what she felt was a ridiculous way to start any kind of interview.

Finally, Chief Mathers seemed ready to start questioning, and he leaned forward on his elbows, looking up at Mrs. Scott for the first time since he had entered the room. What he met was a death stare that could end the world.

"Ah," he said, getting up from his seat. "I forgot my coffee."

After all of that shuffling and fiddling, he walked right out of the room with the folder under his arm, leaving Mrs. Scott alone in there again. Mrs. Scott rubbed her temples and let out an exasperated sigh. At that point, the door opened again to the viewing room, and Chief Mathers walked in and stood next to Avery.

"What was all that about?" Avery asked.

"I'm just trying to frustrate her a little," Chief Mathers explained. "I do think I'm getting somewhere, don't you, Charles?"

Charles snorted. "I think so, yes."

"Why are you trying to frustrate her if you want her to work with you?" Avery asked. "You need her to be forthcoming, not furious!"

"Well, in my experience, people who are calm keep a level head and lie better," Chief Mathers said. "But people who are angry and stressed will snap. And what follows that is usually some kind of rage-fueled confession."

"He's right," Charles said. "I used to use this method all the time when I was still on the force."

Avery wondered what a woman like Mrs. Scott would be like if she was pushed to the point of explosion. *Is that what happened when she killed her own son?*

"I'd like to get to the bottom of this, and she is a tough lady," Chief Mathers said. "So, hopefully, this helps."

Chief Mathers then left the room again, and what felt like minutes later, the door opened, and he rejoined Mrs. Scott without any coffee in hand. "I got all the way there and realized I don't actually want any coffee right now," he said with a casual chuckle.

"Excellent," Mrs. Scott deadpanned.

Avery made a note of Chief Mathers' tactic to get her to snap. It was an interesting one that Avery was certain would work on her. But at that point, it was clear that Chief Mathers couldn't waste any more time.

"Your full name and surname, please," Chief Mathers said with a pen in hand.

"Please tell me you're kidding," Mrs. Scott said. "You've known me for years, Adrian."

"It's a formality," Chief Mathers answered. "Your full name and surname, please."

Avery found it almost comical as Chief Mathers asked her a string of questions that he almost certainly had all the answers to already. With each answer that Mrs. Scott was expected to give, the less patience she had with him.

"I think it's working," Avery said quietly.

"I have to admit," Charles chuckled. "He sure knows how to frustrate a woman, doesn't he?"

Although Mrs. Scott's face seemed unchanged and stern, from where Avery and Charles were standing, they could see her fiddling with her hands beneath the table. Avery made sure to note everything about her body language, slowly creating a new character for her book.

"I'm sorry, Adrian," Mrs. Scott eventually interrupted him. "What exactly is it that I'm doing here? If this is all you need from me, we really could have done this from the comfort of my own home."

Mrs. Scott trailed the gray walls with her eyes, giving every inch of the room a disapproving look.

"Well," Chief Mathers sighed. "I should probably tell you that you're a suspect in this case, Mrs. Scott." Her mouth fell open as he finished his sentence. She looked as if she had seen a ghost, and unbelievably, her face became even paler. Mrs. Scott swallowed hard.

"That's preposterous," she said softly. "I thought you had brought me here to tell me that you'd finally caught the person who has done this."

"We've brought you in for questioning," Chief Mathers confessed.

"Why is he telling her?" Avery asked. "He shouldn't have told her yet. He was really getting somewhere earlier."

"He has to tell her," Charles explained. "She asked him, and he cannot take her from her home and bring her here without reason."

Avery scribbled that down in her notebook and turned her attention back to Mrs. Scott and Chief Mathers.

"How dare you," Mrs. Scott said through gritted teeth.

"Well, she snapped," Avery deduced loudly. "Perhaps we'll get a confession out of her after all."

"We have reason to believe you might be the murderer here," Chief Mathers continued. "We know you've been angry at him. He wanted to move you and sell some of the heirloom buildings. We know he wanted to sell the farm."

It looked as if a fire had ignited in her eyes at the mention of her farm being sold. And for the first time since they had put her in that room, she showed some kind of emotion. But it wasn't remorse or grief. It was pure anger.

"We might not have been on good terms. That is no secret," she said. "But that does not mean that I have murdered him."

"Look, I know this is tough because my mother is your friend," Chief Mathers said kindly. "But I need to solve this case, and if you're a suspect, then you will be treated just like every other suspect."

"It's those other suspects you should be talking to right now," she barked.

"They've all been cleared, I'm afraid," Chief Mathers said, leaning back with his hands comfortably behind his head. "You're the only suspect left on our list."

"I might have joked about killing him or threatened to do so while we were fighting," she said with a massive frown. "But that doesn't mean I'd actually do it. It's insane for you to believe that!"

Mrs. Scott's foot was tapping impatiently against the concrete floor. She looked as if she wanted to reach out and slap the chief of police right across the face.

"You're supposed to be protecting our citizens," she snarled. "Not wasting taxpayers' money on this kind of nonsense."

"Questioning a suspect is not nonsense, in my opinion," Chief Mathers said. "And I am sure the rest of the town would agree."

"Well, get on with it, then, so you can see that I am innocent and take me back home," she said impatiently. "Then you can get back to work trying to catch the real murderer."

"She's awfully defensive," Avery said quietly.

"Mrs. Scott, where were you on the night of the murder at around ten o'clock?" Chief Mathers asked.

"I had dropped Dean off at his guest house, and then I drove home," she answered. "I offered for him to stay with me, but he said he'd rather die than do that. I suppose he sealed his own fate, then."

Avery was appalled at her lack of emotion toward the death of her own son. She understood how the other people in town might not have liked him. But it really takes a lot to get a mother to not like her own child.

"Was there someone with you?" Chief Mathers asked. "Or someone who saw you arrive home and can confirm that time for us?"

"You mean someone that can confirm my alibi?" Mrs. Scott mockingly asked. "No, I drove home alone that night and walked into my house alone. It's one of the many symptoms of being a widow."

"Well, we can't just take your word for it," Chief Mathers said. "Without evidence that those were your actual whereabouts, you will have to remain a suspect in this case."

The questioning was nothing like it was in the movies. They didn't throw images of the crime scene across the table at her, and there was no spotlight shining in her eyes. The police chief wasn't smoking heavily. It was clean, cold, and to the point.

Mrs. Scott was a small, petite woman who somehow had the ability to make herself seem like a giant with just the tilt of her head. She peered at Chief Mathers down the length of her nose and stared at him for a while.

"If I am your only suspect at the moment, then I fear for the safety of our town," she said. "Because that means that our police force is truly incapable."

"I don't think that's accurate," Chief Mathers argued. "This might not have gone the way you would have liked, but we have followed procedure, and we have taken someone we believe to be potentially dangerous off the street." He paused for a moment and shrugged. "And today, that person is you."

Mrs. Scott gasped. "I've never been more insulted in my life," she said. "Just wait until the news hears about this."

"I'm not here to flatter you, Mrs. Scott," Chief Mathers said. "I am here to catch a murderer. And right now, that murderer might be you."

At that point, Mrs. Scott shut off entirely. She closed her mouth, and it quickly became clear that she had no intention of opening it again any time soon.

Chapter Twenty

C hief Mathers dropped his shoulders. From where Avery was standing, it looked as if he knew he had pushed her too far. Her lips were sealed, and that was the end of it. Mrs. Scott folded her arms and turned her eyes away from him.

Chief Mathers folded his arms, too, mirroring Mrs. Scott's every change in demeanor.

"When she moves, so does he," Avery whispered. "Why?"

"It's a technique that Chief Mathers always uses," Charles explained. "He mimics her. It's in an effort to relate to her. It's a complicated theory, but it works...puts them at ease, and eventually, they talk more."

But Mrs. Scott wasn't saying a single word.

Avery still couldn't understand it. All of this should have devastated her. She should have cried, pleaded, and had angry outbursts. She was angry, yes, but it wasn't exactly an outburst. As far as it was all concerned, she seemed too calm for what would have made sense to Avery.

It looked like a dismal scene. The overhead lights had started to flicker, and there was a prolonged silence. It carried on so long that Mrs. Scott eventually started to check on the condition of her nails.

"I'm giving you a chance to come clean before this goes too far," Chief Mathers said, his confidence breaking slightly.

In the darkness of the viewing room, Avery held her breath. She felt so tense about the situation; it felt as if they had been moments away from the entire murder being solved, but they missed it.

"We've lost her," Charles said quietly. "She's closed up and won't talk again, that's for sure."

"How can she be so calm?" Avery asked.

"I don't think she is," Charles chuckled. "She might look calm, but I think she is holding back and maintaining her façade."

"Her son was murdered, and they're accusing her of doing it. How can she keep this up?"

Chief Mathers sighed and shuffled some of the pages around as loudly as he could. He was still trying to get her to snap.

"You know I wouldn't have brought you here if I didn't think there was some gravity to this," Chief Mathers said sternly.

Mrs. Scott barely blinked. She didn't even turn her head.

"In that case, I won't speak again until my lawyer is present," she said coldly.

A coded knock at the door got Chief Mather's attention. He looked toward it as if he was waiting to hear another knock, and that knock would come. He clenched his jaw, frustrated immensely by the interruption.

"If you'll excuse me, it seems that my attention is needed elsewhere for a moment," he said as he gathered his papers together. "I assure you, I will be back here as soon as I possibly can."

"And I hope that my lawyer will be with you when you get back," Mrs. Scott responded.

Chief Mathers scratched his head in defeat and exited the room. Avery expected him to step back into the room with the suspect within a matter of moments, but that never happened. Instead, the door to the viewing room opened, and in walked Chief Mathers along with another police officer she didn't recognize.

"This better have been a good interruption," Chief Mathers barked.

The officer reached into his bag and pulled out a file. "I have the results of the autopsy of Dean Scott."

Chief Mathers paled and took the folder from him, flipping open the cover of it. His hands paged through it all as he read the information before him. He nodded and sighed as he paged through each page, paying careful attention to each detail.

"What does any of this even mean?" he eventually grumbled.

The officer took the folder back from him and tried his hardest not to roll his eyes. He pulled out a single page with some information listed on it.

"This is the only page that really matters," the officer said. He pointed to a line on the page. "It seems that the alcohol levels in his system were ridiculously high."

Chief Mathers looked back toward Mrs. Scott. "She said she drove him home but never mentioned he was intoxicated. When we'd questioned her initially, on the night of the murder, she said he seemed to be rather tired. She didn't say that he was drunk."

"And that would be because of this," the officer said, pointing to another piece of information on the page. "It shows that he had a lethal dose of Alprazolam in him."

"Alprazolam? And what might that be?" Chief Mathers pressed.

"It's a medication prescribed to handle high stress and anxiety," the officer answered. "It appears that this is the cause of death."

"Not suffocation?" Chief Mathers asked.

"There seems to be no evidence of suffocation on his body," the officer said.

Chief Mathers closed his eyes and ran his fingers through his hair. The tension levels in the room were so high that Avery felt the hair on the back of her neck stand up. She knew this information would change everything. It was the perfect plot twist.

"We have to rethink everything now," Chief Mathers said, looking toward Mrs. Scott. "When the method changes, so does how we look at our suspects."

"That medication could have been given to him at any time. It means that the suspect wouldn't even have had to leave the wedding to murder him," Charles said. "They'd have to be there to steal the money but not to administer the medication."

Avery couldn't even make any more notes for her book. She watched as each person in the room started to show signs of nervousness.

"Go in there and ask her if her son was on any kind of medication for stress," Charles suggested.

And they watched as Chief Mathers did just that. But he got no response at all. She remained silent, with her lips sealed shut as tight as they could be.

"I guess we're really not getting anything more out of her, are we?" Chief Mathers said when he returned.

"These things happen, Chief," Charles said calmly. "Just gotta keep pressing on. At some point, the evidence will point in the right direction. Until then, keep asking questions and keep finding answers."

But the chief of police was in no mood for any kind of advice.

"Thank you for reminding me how to do my job," he answered sarcastically.

Avery didn't care about the sarcasm and the tension in the air at all. In fact, she had practically stopped listening. Her mind was flooded with thoughts and questions. She went over everything she knew about Dean in her mind as she tried to piece together the events of that night.

Then, she reached for her copy of the diary entry that the police had read out loud that night. She read it again for what felt like the hundredth time.

I came back here to see the friends and family that I have missed. But I've only been met with unfriendliness and disgust. Threats have been made to my life, and it seems that nobody is on my side anymore.

It is clear to me now that some of the people on the guest list for tonight would love nothing more than to see me dead. But they simply don't understand me. And that is their own loss.

This time, as she read it, it seemed entirely different to her. The voice in her mind that spoke as she read the words sounded different. His diary was such a personal thing to him. Could it be possible that it was the only place in his life where he showed any sincerity?

If that was the case, then the diary entry meant something entirely different from what any of them had initially thought.

Avery tugged on Charles' shirt and motioned for him to follow her outside.

"What's up; are you okay?" he asked with concern.

"I'm alright. It's just...read this note again, with the information that we have now," Avery said.

Charles took the page from her and read it silently. But she saw the look in his eyes and knew that he saw it differently, too. He read it again and gazed upward, his eyes fixed on the wall behind her.

"What are you thinking?" he asked.

"I don't think he wrote this in the way we initially thought," she explained. "I don't think this points the finger at the guests of the wedding, or anybody else, for that matter."

Charles thought about it for a moment. "Does it then hold no significance at all?" he asked.

"Knowing what we know now about the Alprazolam, I think he took all those pills himself," she said.

"That's an interesting thing to say. What makes you think that?" he asked.

"He was a narcissist," she explained. "And although it is unlikely for narcissists to take their own lives, they might do it with the sole purpose of hurting someone."

"That's a bit of a stretch," he said, but she knew he was thinking it over a little more.

"If he really had been under severe stress, enough to need medication...who knows how that might have affected his ability to think straight after all that alcohol?" she asked. "Perhaps it was just a bad cocktail, and his mind got the better of him."

"What about the missing satchel of money?" he asked.

Avery shrugged. "It's missing," she said. "But we don't have proof that it was stolen. He was drunk and highly medicated. He could have done anything with that money, for all we know."

"You might be onto something," Charles said. "I mean, nobody at the wedding wanted him there, and he would have known that. Alcohol and medication might have blown the situation well out of proportion in his mind."

"He's so narcissistic that he might have done it out of spite," Avery said.

"And in that state, with all of that in his bloodstream, it is entirely possible that he broke his own door down," Charles continued. "He might not have intended to do it. If the door was already loose and he lost his footing, it might have been easy enough."

"He would have opened his own safe," Avery added. "And who knows what he did with the money in that deluded state?"

Charles read through the diary entry again and raised his eyebrows. "This isn't the whole thing. This is only the part that they felt fit for the public to see. Wait here."

He disappeared down the hallway for a bit and returned with a paper in hand. "Here's the rest of it," he said.

I came back here to see the friends and family that I have missed. But I've only been met with unfriendliness and disgust. Threats have been made to my life, and it seems that nobody is on my side anymore.

It is clear to me now that some of the people on the guest list for tonight would love nothing more than to see me dead. But they simply don't understand me. And that is their own loss.

My mother doesn't want to move. And they don't want me to sell the building. The bookshop wants to stay where it is. Multiple people tonight have told me to pay back the money to Deb. I can't think straight anymore.

Perhaps it is time to give them all what they want.

"Why didn't they want us to see this?" Avery asked. "Why was this not part of what they read?"

"They didn't want people to automatically point fingers at the people mentioned. And they figured he had just decided to do what was right. Nobody thought that the last line referred to his death," Charles explained.

Avery stared at the diary entry and noticed that the rest of what was written was barely legible. She ran her fingers over the badly scribbled words.

"This must have been once the medication and alcohol had taken full effect," she said.

"Maybe he took all the Alprazolam on purpose," Charles said. "We need to tell Chief Mathers."

Avery and Charles entered the viewing room, where the discussion was still ongoing. Chief Mathers was asking the officer with the autopsy report a string of questions about the medication and some details about the autopsy.

"Excuse me, Chief," Charles said. "But we have something we'd like to run by you."

"Are you sure it's important?" Chief Mathers said, unimpressed. "I'm kind of in the middle of something right now."

Charles looked him dead in the eyes. "We think he killed himself."

Chapter Twenty-One

C hief Mathers and the other officer stared at them with their mouths hanging open. It took them a few seconds before either of them could find something to say.

"That's a rather bold statement," Chief Mathers said bluntly. "What makes you so convinced?"

"This is really Avery's theory, so I'll let her talk you through it," Charles said, stepping aside.

Her stomach sank to the bottom of her feet, and she swallowed hard. She felt like a girl in school, expected to give her presentation to the class. Avery had never been comfortable with that kind of thing, and immediately her fingers started toying nervously with the seam of her shirt.

"It's the rest of the letter," she said, holding it out to Chief Mathers. "I think he medicated himself and overdosed. And as Charles has theorized, he might have broken the door down himself in his intoxicated state."

She stepped further into the room so she could speak more directly to Chief Mathers. "I know there is missing money," she said. "And that does seem odd. But there really is no evidence that it had been stolen."

A vein appeared across Chief Mathers' head, and it was as if Avery could witness the headache forming beyond his skull. A frown broke across his face as he sighed.

"Well, you make a compelling argument. Thank you," he said, sounding rather ungrateful if Avery was honest.

"It's a lot more work for us to look into," he continued. "But I'd like to make sure that we're positive suicide isn't an option before we continue looking at it as a murder."

"Are you sure?" the other officer asked.

"Unfortunately, yes," Chief Mathers answered. "Looking at the note now, it is entirely possible that he did this to himself. I don't want to waste our time any further if that's the truth."

Avery wasn't sure if she should be proud or apologetic. She was pleased that she had pieced it all together but had completely disrupted their process. And none of the officers involved seemed pleased about it.

"I want you to go through all of his belongings again," Chief Mathers instructed the officer. "Look for prescriptions, receipts, or bottles... anything that can prove the medication was his. In the meantime, I'll try to find out who his doctors were."

The officer glanced over at the interrogation room. "What will we do about her?" he asked.

Chief Mathers sighed and looked at her for a while. "Well, we can't really question her anymore," he said. "We'll have to let her come in with her lawyer. I think I've pushed her too much already. We can't face another lawsuit from the Scotts."

Avery didn't like that. She had hoped to see some more drama from Mrs. Scott. What she had seen wasn't nearly enough for her book. She had hardly anything to work with yet. But what she did get was an idea of the process, and that was better than nothing.

Chief Mathers exited the viewing room, and a few moments later, he appeared in the interrogation room. His shoulders were hardly as squared as they were when he had first entered, and his hands were empty of any folders.

"Mrs. Scott, you are free to leave whenever you please...unless you'd like to talk," he said.

She didn't say another word. She stood up, fixed her hair, and walked toward the door. But Chief Mathers stopped her before she left.

"I will need you to be back here next week, and you can bring your lawyer. We still have a lot of questions for you," he said.

"A week?" she scoffed. "I won't be dealing with this for a week. I'll be back here tomorrow. Don't waste my time again."

The sound of Mrs. Scott's footsteps echoed past them as she walked through the halls and toward the exit. She kept her head up, proud, but the slight twitch in her lip was a faint sign that she had been embarrassed.

"I assume someone will be driving me home?" she called loudly.

A nearby officer jumped up to be of assistance, and she dumped her white bag into his hands. He followed her as if he was her personal chauffeur. Avery had never seen such an impressive display of confidence and wondered if it would work for her, too, or if she first needed a couple million dollars.

"Right," Chief Mathers said. "I have a lot of paperwork to do after all of that, and my officers have some evidence to comb through. Avery and Charles, you two are welcome to stay, but who knows how you'll keep yourselves busy here. That's it for now." With that, he spun on his feet and left them behind. The other officer walked calmly in the direction of the evidence room.

"So, now what?" Avery asked.

Charles shrugged. "A few steps back in this investigation, unfortunately. But for now, I'll wait to hear more, and I'll let you know."

"Do you think they'll let me come back tomorrow for the questioning with Mrs. Scott?" she asked.

"It's tough to say," he answered. "Everything is a little different when the lawyers get involved. But let me see what I can arrange."

Charles and Avery walked through the police station, and around them, officers worked tediously at heaps of paperwork. Phones rang constantly, and the faint smell of coffee lingered permanently in the air.

They'd spent so much time in the viewing room that when they finally stepped outside, the bright sun blinded them. The day was already in full swing in town. Coffee shops were full, and people filled the streets. The weather was good, and everyone seemed happy.

But all Avery wanted was another cup of coffee.

"Shall we get back?" Charles asked, holding the door open for her.

It seemed like a foolish question. They had nowhere else to be, and if he had been asking her to go somewhere else, he had a funny way of doing it.

"I guess," Avery chuckled.

Avery enjoyed driving with Charles. It was nice not to be in control for a while, and she easily trusted him with her life.

"How do you know all that stuff about narcissists?" he asked.

"James wrote a book once where the main character was a narcissist," she explained. "I know it seems crazy to base all my theories on a book character, but there was extensive research done."

"Is that so?" he asked. "Well, it's paying off."

"Yeah, James and I went to talks and read books about narcissists in order for him to craft the perfect character. It's amazing how clear they become once you know what to look for," she said.

"Yeah?" Charles asked. "I didn't realize there was a blueprint for people like Dean."

"Well, there is one book that came close to being just that," Avery said. "Sydney Koh wrote a book called *Dealing with the Unavoidable Narcissist in Your Life*. That book alone shaped the entire character that James had written."

"It sounds like you were pretty involved in those books," Charles said. "More than you like to let on."

"Well, one thing you don't understand about writers is that their work becomes their life," she said. "And not in a bad way. They're creative people, and they can't help it. And I wanted to spend as much time with him as possible. Thankfully for me, it was kind of fun."

Charles laughed. "And you learned a lot too! I'm sure it was an interesting way to live. It paid off. I've read his books. All that work was certainly worth it."

"Thanks," she said bashfully.

"So, how did that book end?"

Charles looked at her, and he had a childlike smile on his face. He seemed completely interested, and Avery wasn't used to it. Most people tried not to talk to her about her husband too often or for too long. It made them worry that she might be sad or it would ruin her day.

But Charles didn't mind it so much. He seemed adamant that Avery remembered the good times that she used to have with her husband. And she appreciated him for that. In the process, he got to know her better.

"Well," she chuckled. "The narcissist had taken some medication in an effort to get some attention. She only wanted to be hospitalized. But it went wrong."

Charles raised his eyebrows.

"She took too much and died accidentally," Avery continued. "In the end, there was no murderer."

"I see now how you pieced everything together back there, then," he said. "Do you think Dean Scott could have done the same?"

"I don't know," she said. "But his diary entry does seem a little odd. And there were people making his life difficult. It had crossed my mind that he hid his money to make it look like a robbery."

"It seems like a silly way to go," Charles said. "Accidentally killing oneself. And it seems like a lot of work just to get back at someone."

"Not when you're a narcissist," Avery explained. "People like that are always thinking of themselves. They are the center of the universe, and they refuse to believe that their idea might be a bad one. Some of them might truly believe that they are above the laws of nature. And those who are unfortunate enough to get close to them rarely make it out undamaged."

They pulled back into the driveway at Charles' house. Just seeing his house made Avery smile as she remembered the pleasant experience she'd had there when they enjoyed pizza and wine.

"Thank you for your help," he said as he opened her door for her. "And I am glad we were able to clear Carl's name. None of that could have been done without your help."

"It's really no problem at all," Avery said. "My father had a great time talking with his friend. I believe he will be going back to visit soon. It's just a pity we didn't get more out of Mrs. Scott."

"Well, how about we have some lunch and talk more about this suicide possibility?" he offered.

Avery looked back at his house. She thought about his antique glasses and the endless heaps of books. She wanted so badly to go inside and have a look at his treasure chest of a house. She thought about the good wine that she had there the last time and how he had made her laugh. She wished she could accept his offer. But she couldn't.

"I'm expected at a wine tasting with the girls," she said, a little disappointed.

"Ah," he said. "Stammtisch?"

He acted casual, but Avery noticed a slightly disappointed slump in his shoulders. He tucked his hands into his pants and swayed slightly, looking out over the mountains in the distance.

"As always," Avery laughed. "But perhaps we can have lunch here soon? I need a new book to read, and you have an impressive collection."

"Alright," Charles agreed. "But how about next time you come, I make you one of those pizzas? I can't promise that it will be edible, but I can promise that I will put my best effort into it."

"That sounds like a great idea," Avery laughed. "I'll bring the wine."

Charles gave her a hug. They didn't hug often, but this time felt a little different. Charles wrapped his arms tightly around her and lingered just a little longer than she was used to. It felt good to be comforted—it was a feeling that Avery hadn't felt in quite some time. Charles was warm and comfortable, and he was familiar to her. And when she left, she felt sad to be leaving him behind. They'd spent the entire morning together, and she still wanted to spend more time with him.

She enjoyed his company, his conversation, and she felt warmer after she had been with him. She watched him grow smaller in her rearview mirror as she gave him one final wave goodbye. And he watched her leave until she was out of his sight.

Chapter Twenty-Two

The wine-tasting room was large, with glass walls and ceilings. Avery felt small inside the giant glasshouse as she sipped on the wine. The views surrounding the farm were some of the most beautiful that Avery had ever seen. Outside, Sprinkles enjoyed the fountain along with some other dogs who had accompanied their owners for the day.

Rolling hills were on display in every direction, and large trees cast shade under which families held picnics and fed the birds. Inside the glass house were easily a hundred plants, creating a wild, tropical paradise for those eager to sample some of the vineyard's best wines.

All the women of the Stammtisch, excluding Eleanor, sipped happily at their wine. And the more they sipped, the more they laughed. Glasses clinked, and chatter filled the air as they caught up on everything they had missed since they had last seen each other.

They usually saw each other often enough that there wasn't all that much to catch up on. And Avery had become grateful for their gatherings. They'd been a healthy distraction from her busy work life and a pleasant change from her quiet personal life. They made her feel less lonely. Without them and Charles, all she would have was her work at the vineyard and Sprinkles.

So, even if she had heard the same story thousands of times, she listened happily, eager for them to fill some of the quieter moments in her life.

When they'd sampled a little too much of what the vineyard had to offer, they went for a walk to cool their cheeks and work through some of the alcohol. It was a pleasant day, and it was a beautiful place for a walk.

Small footpaths circled various gardens on the property, showing them only the prettiest views and spaces that the vineyard had to offer, and for a brief period, the women could pretend that they were far away from their town and somewhere new entirely.

"Thank you for all your help getting me removed as a suspect," Deb said cheerfully. "It really means a lot to me."

Avery wasn't entirely sure how to respond. With the new information on how Dean had really died, she couldn't be certain that they wouldn't put her back on the suspect list. After all, it was entirely plausible that Deb had placed the medication in his drink while they were at the wedding.

Deb did seem to Avery like the type of person who might take such medication. She had been through a lot of stress and behaved like someone who experienced a fair amount of anxiety. But that was merely speculation, and Avery didn't want to linger too long on that thought.

"It's really no problem," Avery said. "We had to do something...it was getting ridiculous! And the rest of the bunch helped a great deal. They provided so many photographs and videos."

"It was your idea, though," Deb said, nudging her. "And it was a genius one! What did their faces look like when you showed the pictures to them? I hope they were irritated like they had irritated me."

Sprinkles barked playfully at a passing butterfly and bounced after it, stumbling over a nearby twig. But he was barely on the ground before he was up and running cheerfully back to Avery's side.

Avery wasn't entirely sure what to say to Deb. In the end, the officers had moved on so quickly after removing Deb from the suspect list it was hard to believe they ever cared about it at all. So, she had no answer for Deb's question.

Instead, she just said, "I'm really sorry you ever had to go through any of that...the whole suspect-in-a-murder-thing but also everything Dean put you through. It's rather pathetic if you ask me."

Deb shrugged. "I should have known that it wouldn't end well. There were so many signs that should have told me how unimportant I was to Dean."

It was a terrible thing to say, and Avery felt bad just hearing it from her.

"I guess not entirely unimportant," Deb chuckled. "I gave him a place to live—not that he needed it."

"It's easy to see those things once you're through it. When we reflect, it all seems so much clearer than when it was staring us in the face," Avery commented.

"It should have been more obvious to me, though," Deb said. "Our relationship was all about him. And there were days when I was so aware of it. But if he bought me even one bunch of flowers, I would just forget it all and convince myself somehow that I was happy."

"We can convince ourselves of many strange truths if they have a pretty enough face," Avery said. "You can hang artwork over a hole and, in a matter of seconds, forget that the hole had ever been there, to begin with."

Deb nodded. "He had this way of making me feel as though he cared about me and what I was doing," she said. "He always told me how he wanted me to be successful and wanted to see me at my full potential."

She sighed and stopped to inspect a leaf of a nearby tree. "But he actually wanted my success for himself. He knew that the more I made, the bigger our house could be. None of it was because he cared. He had an image to maintain, and he wanted to make sure that I could fit the description."

"Well, I am sure that, in reality, you were too good for him, anyway," Avery said, placing a comforting hand on Deb's shoulder.

"And in the end, there had never been anyone that was good enough for him," Deb continued. "If my information is correct, I was the longest relationship he ever had, and no girlfriends after me ever really stuck."

"Can you blame them?" Avery laughed as she took a stick from Sprinkles' mouth, tossing it for him to run after.

"It made me feel foolish in the first few years after we split," Deb said. "How had it been so clear to the women who had followed, and yet I had been so blind to it all?"

"Don't beat yourself up about that," Avery advised. "There's no point to it anymore. You've moved on just fine after him, and that's all that matters."

"He left me and went to the city when he felt that I hadn't been successful enough for him," Deb explained. "That's what it said in his notes. He said he was going out to find someone who really understood him and what he needed from life."

Avery had never heard of anything so hurtful. She imagined how she might have felt if someone had said or done those things to her. And even in her imagination, it stung more than a hot blade through her chest.

"That's terrible," Avery whispered.

Deb nodded. "And he felt that I owed him for all of his wasted time. He said it was because he was putting so much work into me that he hadn't had the time to collect the furniture he needed for his own home in the city."

"It seems like an absurd notion," Avery said. "But to a man like that, it must have made perfect sense. Men like Dean believe the entire world owes them something...gratitude for their very existence. They show up and believe their presence has changed the world. It's ridiculous."

"Well, he certainly changed my world when the bill arrived for my credit card," Deb said. "I'd never been so heartbroken in my life before."

Avery could see the heartbreak on Deb's face and knew that it still hurt her.

"He set me back by years," Deb said. "By the time he left, I had worked hard for everything that I owned, and I had to sell almost all of it. I had no money to spend on anything other than my bills for years. And in the meantime, he lived happily in the city, carefree and in his own world."

"It's hard to believe that there was nothing that could be done about it," Avery said.

"Well, I gave him my credit card with permission once to go and buy some groceries for me. It was one stupid mistake. Because of that one time, he was able to spend my money and get away with it," she said. "And by the time I learned about it, it was way too late."

"I can't imagine how devastating that must have been," Avery said. She wasn't entirely sure what Deb wanted or expected her to say. It was a terrible story, but Avery realized Deb simply wanted to get it all off her chest. Dean's death would have been a painful reminder to her of what he had done.

"He had the money to buy those items," Deb said. "He was rich, and so was his family. But that didn't matter to him. According to him, the energy that he supposedly put into me was worth something. He had billed me for his time."

"Did you really never get back any of the money?" Avery asked.

Deb shook her head. "No, he never sent me back a cent. In fact, he never spoke to me directly again. Every correspondence I received from him after he left was in the form of a formal letter from his attorney."

"Was he really that much of a chicken?" Avery asked. "Too afraid to speak to you?"

"I don't entirely blame him," Deb chuckled. "After I had first received the bill for my credit card, I kind of went off the rails a little. I said some terribly hurtful things to him and about him. After that, he refused to ever speak to me again."

"Did he speak to you at the wedding?" Avery asked.

"Of course not," Deb said. "He stayed as far away from me as possible. Everybody there knew what he had done to me. He was probably concerned about what they might say if we were seen standing so near to each other."

"Why do you think he went to the wedding at all?" Avery asked. "You heard what he wrote in his diary. He knew nobody wanted him there and that everybody hated him, and still he went."

"Attention," Deb said with a scoff. "It had to have been for the attention. It didn't matter to him if everyone hated him. Even if the attention he was getting was bad, he was eager for it. As long as his name was on everyone's lips, he didn't really mind what they were saying."

"Well, he might have slowed you down a little, but he certainly didn't hold you back," Avery said. "Look at you now. You are more successful than he ever was, and you got there with honesty. And everybody loves you. You were better off without him."

"That's for sure," Deb agreed. "I hate to think of what my life might have been like if he had stayed. If I had married Dean, I don't think I would ever have truly been happy."

Deb reached for a flower and plucked it, tugging lightly at the petals as she inspected them closely. "It took me many years to trust anybody again after Dean left," Deb said. "I really had never expected it from him, and it shattered me. Still, I am careful with new people. But after all this time, nobody has ever hurt me like that again. So, I suppose it's time to let it go."

Avery wondered if she would ever feel comfortable enough to move on from James. She wasn't entirely certain she had the courage to do it. It was not easy to put trust in another person like that, and she had spent so much of her life with James that she wouldn't even know where to begin with someone new.

She missed her husband. There was a space that he had always occupied, and a silence that he had always filled. But the thought of him no longer pained her. Avery knew she would never stop missing him or grieving for him. But she was grateful that the hurt she felt after his death had finally started to subside.

Chapter Twenty-Three

When Avery woke up the next morning, she knew Sprinkles was too restless for his own good. He got so excited to see her that he bounced around on the lawn with his ears flapping around, slapping him in the face. She needed to get rid of some of his energy, so she called him to join her for a walk. It was time for her to take a look at some of the vines at the edge of the property, and she figured that this was a perfect opportunity. He walked eagerly at her side as she picked a different route for that day. She walked all the way to the end of the property, past her parents' house, and along the perimeter fence.

There were some trees there that provided some much-needed shade for them as they walked in the morning sun. The bugs and the birds were coming to life as they moved, and bees buzzed past her, happily going about their daily business.

The vines looked healthy, and it made Avery feel proud. She wondered if Mrs. Scott got the same feeling when she walked through the endless rows of roses on her farm.

Sprinkles stopped to admire every bird that sang and nipped happily at the butterflies that flew past. He was growing into his ears and his paws, and that only made him quicker and more agile as he playfully chased the beetles that zoomed past him.

Avery's eyes were still puffy as she tried to wake up, and her cup of coffee warmed the palm of her hand, creating a soft cloud of steam as she walked in the crisp morning air. The only thing she was missing was her sunglasses which sat waiting for her on a table right by the front door, with the plan that she would never forget them again.

She was deep in thought about the nature around her when she heard footsteps approaching. A small amount of city instinct kicked in, and she spun around, anticipating an unfriendly figure sneaking up on her.

Instead, she was met with the friendly face of her mother, who was out of breath from walking fast enough to catch up with them.

"I thought it was you that walked past earlier," her mother said.

"You thought?" Avery answered. "But you weren't sure. What would you have done if you marched all the way up here and I was somebody else?"

Her mother shrugged. "I would have wished them good morning and gone back to bed." She smiled. "Good morning."

Her mother attempted to give a sleepy smile back, her eyes puffy. One thing that Avery and her mother had in common was that neither of them were morning people at all.

"I forgot my sunglasses," her mother said, squinting into the sun as she approached Avery's side.

They walked together for a short distance, but Avery knew something was on her mother's mind. The only time her mother was that quiet was when she was trying to find the right words to say, which meant that she hadn't come out there just to make casual conversation.

"Everything alright, Mom?" Avery asked as she sipped her coffee. "You're awfully quiet this morning."

Her mother glanced back at the cottage she shared with Avery's father. "Your father has sent me to apologize," she said bluntly.

Avery chuckled. "What does he want you to apologize for?"

"For the other night," her mother said. "I shouldn't have walked without my flashlight, and I caused you stress. I'm sorry. I just—I can't get the hang of these silly cellphone things. I missed his text, and it caused a fair amount of upset, and I feel terrible about it." Avery had already forgotten all about that ordeal, and the thought that it had bothered her parents so much was all that worried her now.

"It's alright, Mom," Avery said. "You did the right thing. You thought he was in trouble, and you came to me. You'll know better to check your texts next time," Avery said.

Her mother shrugged. "We'll see," she said ominously.

"I'm sorry too," Avery said softly. "I didn't mean for Dad to be so stressed before meeting with Carl. I hadn't considered that it might make him so anxious. I never wanted him to feel that way."

"We know that," her mother said. "I shouldn't have gotten so upset with you about it. He's a grown man; if he didn't want to go, he should have just canceled."

"When has Dad ever canceled plans?" Avery joked. "He's got commitment issues, but not the usual kind. He commits too seriously and then never goes back on his word, even if it means trouble for him."

"You're right!" her mother laughed. "Like that time he nearly got his nose pierced because of a dare. Thank goodness the piercing place was closed that day, and I had a little extra time to talk some sense into him."

Avery laughed at the memory and the mental image of her elderly father walking around with a pierced nose.

"Still," her mother continued. "As we get older, your father and I feel more and more foolish. We get so worked up about things that are really not such a big deal. We forget that everything is easier these days."

"It's okay, Mom," Avery said. "I understand that well enough. I am sorry I argued with you the other night about everything. I was just worried about Dad, that's all."

"Well, I put you there, so if you argued with me, I deserved it," her mother commented. "Maybe you should just come and show me how to do the stuff on the cellphone again." Avery shuddered at the thought. She'd spent countless hours with her mother, talking through every step of the process. If it were going to work, it would have.

"I tell you what," Avery said. "Why don't you and Dad just agree to stick to phone calls only? No more texting."

"That does sound a little simpler," her mother said. "That's the part I know how to do. It works just like the old phones. Punch in the number and dial 'em up! I don't understand why we ever needed to change that system."

Avery considered how significantly more complicated her life would be if she never had a cell phone to do her daily tasks. Although she had a memory of a time before cell phones, it seemed so distant and foreign to her. She no longer remembered what it felt like not to be so connected to the outside world.

"Hello, little one," her mother greeted Sprinkles.

Sprinkles had come to sniff her mother's shoes and legs and licked her hand to wish her good morning. He had a wide smile on his face as her mother ruffled the fur on his head, his ears swinging at the sides of his face.

He'd always liked Avery's mother. She had a tendency to sneak him treats when he wasn't allowed, and Avery wondered if she didn't perhaps have some in her pockets. Her suspicions were confirmed when her mother stuck her fingers into her pockets and retrieved a small dog biscuit, happily giving it to Sprinkles to enjoy.

"You can't keep doing that, Mom," Avery said. "How many times do I have to tell you? He is going to training lessons. If you give him a treat now, you are teaching him bad manners. I can't allow that." She had told her mother that countless times and her mother had never verbally responded. That silence was her mother's way of letting her know that she wouldn't listen and would continue to give the dog treats if she so pleased.

"How is it going with his training, anyway?" her mother asked.

Avery held out her hand, and her mother retrieved the rest of the dog treats, handing them over to her. Then, she called Sprinkles over to perform a demonstration.

Sprinkles performed flawlessly. He rolled, sat, and shook Avery's hand. Then, she showed how she could walk and keep him at her side, showing him when to change sides. Sprinkles showed Avery's mother how he could come to a complete stop or break out into a full sprint at the mention of a single word.

"Impressive!" her mother said with a wide smile.

"Yeah, we've been working really hard," Avery said. "So quit it with sneaking him treats."

"He's such a sweet dog! I can't help it," her mother said. "And so well-behaved—that training is really paying off."

"Not all the time," Avery said. "He did something so odd at the bookstore the other day."

"With Simon?" her mother asked, as if there could be any other bookstore that Avery was talking about.

"Yes," Avery sighed. "He begged Simon for his sandwich; can you believe it?"

"Sounds perfectly normal for a dog if you ask me," her mother said.

"Not for Sprinkles," Avery said. "I've been very strict in teaching him not to beg. And he hasn't begged for food in months, and then not again since that day. And none of my attempts to get him to leave Simon alone worked either."

"I'm sure it was just a moment of weakness," her mother said. "I wouldn't think about it too much."

"I wanted to ask the trainer about it the other day, but she was busy with another pet mom," Avery said. "Hopefully, I can catch her next time, and she can tell me what to do if that happens again. He needs to behave when we're in public."

"What kind of trainer is she?" her mother asked. "Is she one of those friendly folk who always speaks in a high-pitched voice the moment an animal comes near?"

Avery shook her head. "Nope, she used to train dogs in the military. She's strict, rigid, and ruthless when it comes to her training."

"Military?" her mother said. "That seems rather rough, doesn't it? Why would you need to train a dog that way?"

"Sprinkles loves it," Avery said with a smile. "He runs around smiling when he's there. She's strict, but she's still friendly. He's learning a lot that I think he wouldn't learn at any other training school."

"I've never heard of such a thing in my life," her mother said.

"Have you ever had a dog?"

"No," her mother laughed. "But I always wanted one. Your father wouldn't let me. He said I'd wind up loving the dog more and kick him out!"

"Well, Sprinkles does occupy most of the other half of my bed," Avery chuckled.

"So, is he learning anything in this special military training that he can't learn at any other training school?" her mother asked.

Avery nodded, swallowing the last sip of her coffee. "A few things, definitely. I've enrolled him in the advanced class," she explained. "I don't know if it will be entirely necessary, but he loves the classes, and it's a good release of energy for him."

"I see, so you take him there to tire him out a couple of days a week?"

"Mhmm," Avery answered. "And it's been great fun. Whenever he's done with training, he sleeps right through the night. I wish she would have a class on a Friday so I can sleep in a little on Saturday morning," she joked.

"So what kind of things has he learned in this special class?" her mother asked.

They watched as Sprinkles gleefully picked up a stick and brought it to Avery to throw. Naturally, she obliged and threw it as far as she could. Sprinkles raced after it, kicking up clouds of dust behind him as he ran.

"It's been pretty interesting," Avery said. "He has learned how to recognize and track smells, just like the police dogs do."

"Now, that is impressive," her mother said.

"It gets even better than that," Avery said. "He's learned how to be alert when someone nearby is showing signs of extreme distress. I'm not really sure how he knows, but Brie taught it to him, and I think it is pretty fascinating."

The sun was dappling through the leaves of the trees, creating a confetti effect on the ground as they walked. Her mother went quiet for a while as if the concept of a support dog had been completely foreign to her.

Avery wondered how her father would feel if she bought them a dog now. Would he still think it was a bad idea? Did her parents even have the energy left to care for another soul?

Her mother seemed to like Sprinkles a lot. And perhaps it would be a good incentive to get them out of the house to go for walks every day. Then again, it could backfire, and Avery would wind up caring for the dog for most of the time.

"So, what's the sign if someone is in distress?" her mother asked.

"Sprinkles will automatically try to comfort that person and stand at the person's side," Avery said. "It can be easy to miss, but it's meant to be subtle. If you know what you're looking for, it is easy enough to spot."

Suddenly, it dawned on Avery why Sprinkles had gone to Dean that day at the wedding.

Chapter Twenty-Four

A very stopped dead in her tracks as she spoke the words. She had described what Sprinkles was doing when he stopped near Dean on the day of the wedding. He had been signaling that Dean was in distress, and Avery hadn't noticed. It made so much sense to her now. Sprinkles had pressed his nose into Dean's hand in an attempt to comfort him. But when Avery called him away, he happily answered. Avery felt dizzy as the realization hit her, and she immediately instructed her mother to turn around.

They walked as briskly as they could without risking her mother tumbling to the ground and breaking a limb. But Avery felt in a hurry to confirm her new theory. When they got back to her parent's cottage, her mother did her best to lure Avery in for a cup of coffee, but Avery managed to decline. It only took a few minutes of negotiation. And as Avery raced back to her own home to get ready for the day, she phoned Deb.

Deb had the footage from the wedding video, and Avery knew that there was no way the videographer missed the shot of Sprinkles walking down the aisle. She just had to get the right moment and watch it again to make sure she was right about it all. By the time she stepped out of the shower, Deb had sent the video.

Avery threw on some clothes, poured another cup of coffee, and played through the footage, waiting for the moment when Sprinkles stopped at Dean's side. When she watched it, she knew that she was absolutely correct.

"Clever dog," she whispered in Sprinkles' direction.

On the video, she could clearly see Sprinkles stop dead at Dean's side. He attempted to nuzzle into Dean's hand and get Dean to stroke him, but Dean wasn't interested at all. In fact, his hand seemed bizarrely unfeeling.

Avery messaged Charles to meet her at the police station and piled into her car. The traffic moved slower than she would have liked as people tried to get to work and drop their children off at school. Avery's finger tapped nervously against the steering wheel. By the time she got there, Charles was already waiting for her, and he had a cup of coffee in his hand.

"You're a blessing, do you know that?" she said as she gratefully accepted the coffee.

"You're welcome," he laughed. "Now, what's the hurry?"

"You'll see," she said as she rushed inside.

Chief Mathers watched through the footage as Avery pointed out what it was they were looking at. "I'm certain this is his signal to say that this person is in distress," Avery said. "I think Sprinkles stopped there because he could see that something was wrong with Dean."

There was silence as Chief Mathers scrubbed backward to watch the footage a few more times. "Is there someone that can confirm this?" he asked. "Who is the trainer for Sprinkles?"

"Brie," Avery said, pulling her phone out of her pocket to make the phone call.

Brie was confused when she arrived but no stranger to that kind of event. After all, she had trained dogs for the military and the police force. She just hadn't expected that kind of call to come from Avery.

Brie greeted everybody by name as she walked through the crowd of officers, and all the service dogs in the area came to greet her too. She knew the dogs all by name as well.

"What's this all about then?" she asked as she joined them in Chief Mathers' office.

Avery showed her the footage. "You trained Sprinkles to alert signs of distress in people, right?" she asked.

Brie nodded. "We've done a couple of classes like that, yes," Brie answered.

Avery pointed to the screen where the footage played. "What is Sprinkles doing here?"

Brie watched it once and smiled. "He's alerting to distress! I can't believe he picked it up so quickly! What a good boy! —Wait...isn't that the guy who was murdered?"

Brie looked up at Chief Mathers. "Yes," he answered. "This was taken just a few hours before he overdosed on Alprazolam."

"Well, he was in distress at the time that this video was taken," Brie said. "That is without a doubt."

"That means probably one of two things," Chief Mathers said with a sigh. "Either he was already contemplating the overdose, or he was already feeling the effects of it."

Brie raised her hands. "This is more than I should know," she said. "Is there anything else that you need me for?"

Chief Mathers smiled. "If you could just file an official statement before you leave to say that you've seen the footage and what your opinion is, that would be helpful."

"Of course," she agreed before leaving the office.

The doors to the police station flew open, and in marched Mrs. Scott. At her side was a tall, lanky man with a briefcase. He was most likely her lawyer. He wore a large, expensive watch and crocodile skin shoes.

The two of them together looked like the type of people one would see on the front page, accompanied by a headline announcing their latest corporate scandal. She didn't stop to greet anyone. Mrs. Scott simply walked directly in the direction of the interrogation room that she'd been in the day before and waited impatiently at the door.

"I guess that's my cue," Chief Mathers said, rising from his seat. "Avery, you can watch if you like. Same rules as last time."

Avery waited for them to be in the interrogation room with the door closed before she stepped into the viewing room. Charles joined her again, and this time she knew that what she would learn would be of real importance.

"He's going to have to rethink his entire questioning strategy now, thanks to the new information," Charles said. "Good catch, by the way."

Avery smiled as she sipped her coffee which, at that point, had already gone cold.

"Mrs. Scott, there is something I would like to show you," Chief Mathers said, reaching for his phone.

He opened the video and played it for her a few times. It was the first time Avery had seen Mrs. Scott show any emotion. The footage of her son, taken just a few hours before his death, caused a slight wrinkle around her lips as the corners of her mouth became downturned. Finally, Avery thought she saw some signs of sadness in the stone-cold woman. There was something that made her human.

"That dog is alerting to signs of distress in your son," Chief Mathers explained, this time with a much kinder approach to the day before. "This footage has only recently been provided to me, and the woman who trained that dog has agreed this is his signal for distress."

Mrs. Scott watched the footage a few more times, her façade breaking more and more with each replay. Eventually, Chief Mathers put it away just as Avery thought she might see a tear from the victim's mother.

"We have reason to believe that Dean might have been struggling with his mental health," Chief Mathers said. "Do you know anything about that?"

Mrs. Scott looked toward her lawyer, who nodded to say that she could answer the question.

"Of course, he struggled with his mental health," she snapped. "How could he not after everything he has been through?"

Chief Mathers made himself comfortable in his chair. "I'm afraid I'm not entirely sure what you are referring to."

"Of course, you don't," Mrs. Scott answered. "Dean had a way of only ever showing the world what he wanted everyone to see. Behind closed doors, his life was completely different."

"Will you tell me what happened?" Chief Mathers asked.

Mrs. Scott again turned to her lawyer to get his approval before speaking. He nodded, and she turned her attention back to Chief Mathers.

"His business went under," she said plainly. "Just as I warned him it would. That's why he suddenly became so dead set on selling everything. He was drowning in debt and didn't want anybody to know about it."

Charles let out a disgruntled scoff. "I wonder if any of the money from those sales would have gone back to Deb."

"And I assume that he wasn't coping well with any of this?" Chief Mathers asked.

"Of course not," Mrs. Scott replied. "Everybody just assumed he was a monster, eager to ruin lives. In reality, he needed to sell the buildings to pay off his debt and attempt to save his business. And he was willing to do so at the expense of others."

"As far as the rest of us are concerned, his business has been thriving. He had made a point to tell us all that when we saw him just before the wedding," Chief Mathers said.

"Well, I suppose he was just trying to keep his reputation," Mrs. Scott said. "He stopped doing well after I cut him off financially."

Chief Mathers leaned back in his seat and seemed completely stunned. "I had no idea that he had no more access to your money," he said.

"That's because it isn't anybody else's business, now is it?" she retorted.

"She's got a point there," Avery mumbled.

"May I ask why you decided to cut him off?" the chief asked. "Even when he was struggling so badly financially?"

Mrs. Scott looked to her lawyer, again and again, he nodded. Avery wondered what his purpose was there that day. He seemed to be alright with every one of Chief Mather's questions.

"If you must know," she said, "I cut him off because he was blowing all my money on his gambling habit. I couldn't do it anymore. It was too risky. So, I cut him off. All he had was his business and the buildings that were in his name. Of course, at that time, I didn't know he'd already run his business into the ground."

Chief Mathers wrote it all down, making markings on the parts that were of particular importance to him.

"Had he ever mentioned to you about going on any medications to help with stress or anxiety?" Chief Mathers asked.

"No, he didn't," she answered. "We didn't talk much anymore after I stopped him from losing my money. There has been little love between us over the last few years."

It seemed like an absolutely absurd thing for a mother to say about her son. But they were no ordinary family. It was quickly becoming apparent to Avery that the Scotts revolved their entire lives around money, and to them, money mattered more than anything else. Even family.

"When we spoke to you the night of the murder, you stated that there was nothing out of the ordinary when it came to Dean's behavior," Chief Mathers said. "But our autopsy results show he had a very high alcohol level. Why did you not mention to us that he had been drunk?"

Her lawyer opened his mouth to stop her from talking, but she ignored him. A frown broke across her face as if the question had insulted her.

"It has been a long time since I've seen my son sober," she said. "If he was drunk, then he wasn't acting out of the ordinary. That's been normal for him for the longest time now, so I doubt I would even have noticed." She paused for a moment and blinked away some tears. "If he'd been sober, I might have thought he was acting strange. Now, that would have been something worth mentioning."

Finally, Mrs. Scott showed signs of mourning. But she didn't mourn for the son who had died a few days before. She mourned for the son that she'd had years ago—the one that she'd lost to gambling and alcohol.

By the time it was all over, Avery felt completely defeated by it all. She slumped into her car and pulled the door closed. She had no idea how to feel about any of it. She certainly hadn't expected to become quite so invested in it all. By the time she left, they were no longer getting any information from Mrs. Scott. Her lawyer had finally intervened and put an end to it.

There was still a lot that the police needed to learn before the case was solved. They had spoken about finding out which medications Dean had been on if any. And they wanted to conduct a search of his private home in the city.

It was looking more and more as if there had been no murder at all. It left Avery feeling conflicted. She wanted to go home, but her hands rested calmly on her lap, not reaching for the steering wheel. She stared ahead as she tried to imagine Dean's last moments and piece them together.

With this new theory, she had no book. There was no murder and no strong enough story. Something about Dean's truth didn't really seem like something she wanted to sell. Avery sighed, and in her mind, she attempted to close that chapter and tried to convince herself it was time to move on.

She drove home in silence, her heart feeling conflicted about the conclusion of the case. It wasn't closed yet, but it seemed as concluded as it could be. She thought about Mrs. Scott and her strange behavior about her son's death.

Avery didn't have children, but she couldn't imagine acting that calm if anybody close to her had died. Let alone a child. She had Sprinkles, and she couldn't even imagine how she would react if he had died. Then again, Sprinkles wasn't going to move her out of her home and try to sell her business.

When she got home, a cheerful-looking Sprinkles awaited her. Avery knelt down to greet him, and he ran into her arms. She held him close, hoping that he'd simply live forever. It had been an intense day, so Avery was desperate to do something else and clear her head.

Chapter Twenty-Five

Avery waited outside her beloved bookstore for Charles and her father to join her. The sun was warm, and the town was bustling. As she waited, she watched the people around her and let her mind drift. When Charles finally greeted her, she jumped in surprise.

"Didn't mean to startle you," he said with a chuckle.

"That's alright; I wasn't paying attention," she said sheepishly. "I was too busy watching the world go by."

Sprinkles wagged his tail in excitement as Charles bent down to greet him but quickly abandoned him when Avery's father arrived. And as usual, Sprinkles went right to his pocket, and her father retrieved the treat.

"Dad," Avery sighed. "Please, I have asked you so many times not to do that!"

Her father signed to Sprinkles to keep quiet, winked, and didn't respond to Avery at all. Within a few moments, the group was inside and browsing the books. But Sprinkles was ill-behaved, just as before. He tugged at his leash, whining at the feet of Simon, who was trying desperately to mind his own business.

"See, Dad?" Avery said. "You're teaching him to beg for treats. All those hours at training are for nothing if you keep doing that."

"Nonsense," her father said. "He's not begging. He's on the hunt!"

"I'm afraid you might be right," Simon laughed as he produced a handful of treats.

She was about to argue with them both when Charles motioned to her to step to one side with him. She knew him well enough to know that the look in his eyes was one of concern. Avery handed the leash to her father and followed Charles to the other side of the store.

"He's not begging," Charles said quietly.

"He's not on the hunt either," Avery said, frustrated that nobody seemed to care.

"No," Charles said urgently. "Look at him carefully. It's like in the footage from the wedding. He's alerting."

Avery looked up, and from a distance, she saw it. Sprinkles wasn't whining at Simon; he was alerting to something else entirely. His tail wasn't wagging, and he was focused on only one spot below the counter. "What if that's just where the treats are?" Avery asked, but she knew it was a foolish question.

She knew that Sprinkles didn't beg. And as she looked at her puppy now, she knew that he was alerting to something—it just wasn't clear what, or why.

She tugged on Charles' sleeve, and he followed her back to where Sprinkles and her dad were. "Thanks, Dad," she said as she took the leash back from her father. "Simon, are you feeling alright?"

Simon looked uneasily at her and smiled. "Better than ever," he answered. "Today isn't as bad as it could be."

"Are you sure?" she asked.

"Are you okay?" Simon asked hesitantly.

The three of them had been looking at him. Avery and Charles were watching him closely for signs of distress, and her father had no idea what was going on. But he was eager to be part of the conversation anyway.

"Of course," Avery said.

Avery let go of the leash. She wanted to see where Sprinkles would go. And when he ran behind the counter, she and Charles took a step closer. Sprinkles had his nose pressed against a wooden box that was tucked away beneath the counter.

In an instant, Simon's demeanor changed.

"Hey, get your dog out from behind here!" he shouted. "If you're going to bring him in here, you better keep him well-behaved."

"What's in the box?" Charles asked.

"His treats, obviously," Simon answered.

"No," Avery said calmly. "You have treats in your hand. If he were after the treats, then he would have gone for the ones in your hand."

"Just out of interest sake," Charles said, acting casually, "show us what's in the box."

"This is getting ridiculous," Simon said, getting to his feet. "And it is a massive invasion of my privacy."

It had seemed that they were at a loss, and they really had no way of forcing him to open the box. But Sprinkles wasn't confined to the same rules that humans were. He bumped the box with his nose and let out a short bark to get their attention.

The box crashed to the ground and burst open. Dean's satchel came tumbling out, and the money fluttered to the ground, spreading all around Simon's feet. Before Avery and Charles could react appropriately, Simon had run for the door. But he was met by Avery's father, who stood in front of the closed door.

"Get out of my way," Simon growled. "Or I'll make you move."

"I don't think you will," her father said calmly, gesturing at Simon's shaking hand.

Simon looked around and knew that he was outnumbered. From where he had stood moments before, Sprinkles smiled proudly.

Within minutes, Chief Mathers was there, and Simon was being led away in handcuffs. It felt strange to see him that way. But the man he had become when they had questioned him about the box was not the friendly store owner she had known for so many years.

Avery's father was sent home with Sprinkles as Avery and Charles followed the police back to the station. Their statements would be necessary. And there was no way that Avery was going to miss the questioning.

It took longer than she would have liked to answer the police's questions about what had happened at the bookstore, and once she made it into the viewing room, the process was already well underway. But to her surprise, Simon was leaning casually back in his chair with his shaking hands resting on his knees.

He seemed friendly and unafraid, and once again, the reaction of the suspect made no sense to her. Had James had it wrong in all his books? Had they portrayed murderers in the entirely wrong way for all those years? She was looking at a criminal investigation for real now, and she saw no nervous jitters or angry outbursts. All she had seen were confident suspects that were unconcerned about their futures.

Simon smiled as he answered the questions and cracked jokes with the police officer.

"I tell you, Chief," he laughed. "I was just as surprised to see that money there as the rest of them were!"

"Then why'd you try to run?" Chief Mathers asked, unamused.

"I was coming to get you!" Simon explained. "The moment I saw that cash settling around my feet, I knew I had been set up."

"If that's the case, then why did you refuse to open the box?" Chief Mathers asked.

Simon shrugged. "It wasn't mine to open," he explained. "I didn't know whose it was, so I couldn't go and open it, now could I?"

Chief Mathers sighed. "This doesn't look good, Simon, and it doesn't make any sense either."

"Look at me!" Simon argued, holding his shaking hands out in front of him. "I can barely hold a cup of water! How am I supposed to murder anyone?"

Avery was holding her breath and hadn't realized it until she felt a wave of dizziness wash over her. She leaned on Charles to keep herself upright, and he didn't seem to mind.

"You alright?" he asked quietly.

"Yeah," she said. "Just a bit nervous."

"I'm afraid this might not go the way you think," Charles said. "They might have a motive, but they have no evidence that he actually killed the man. All they have is possible theft. And, I hate to say it, but he could be telling the truth."

"He ran," Avery said shortly.

"I know," Charles said. "But without proof that he had the means to do the murder, we can't pin it on him."

Avery's mind was swimming with frustrated thoughts and unanswered questions, and she didn't want to deal with it for a moment longer.

She had an idea, but she just needed help from someone she could trust who wouldn't ask any questions.

"Wait here," she instructed Charles. "I'll be back. Don't leave until I'm back."

"Avery?" she heard him ask as she closed the door behind her.

Chapter Twenty-Six

"I'm here," Tiffany said, out of breath. "I came as soon as I could. I told everyone at work I had an upset stomach. What's so important?"

"I knew I could trust you," Avery said with a smile.

To Avery's surprise, the bookstore was still open. Behind the counter, she spotted a man that looked like a younger version of Simon. It had to be his son. It occurred to Avery that times must have been really tough for his family if they couldn't even close the shop for one afternoon while his father was being arrested.

It almost made her rethink the entire idea. But then she remembered Dean and how he had died. She turned to Tiffany and walked her through the plan, and just as Avery had anticipated, Tiffany happily agreed.

Tiffany walked into the building first. Her only task was to distract Simon's son long enough to get him up the stairs. Avery waited outside and peered through the window, waiting to see their two pairs of feet as they moved up the spiral staircase.

But Tiffany played her role even better than Avery could have ever expected.

A high-pitched scream came from the upstairs floor of the bookstore.

"A rat!" Tiffany screamed. "There's a great big rat!"

Simon's son went hurtling up the stairs to tend to the damsel in distress, and Avery took her shot. She moved in as fast as she could, going straight behind the counter and into the room where the kitchen was. She searched through the shelves as quickly as she could. She was looking for something specific.

Her hands fumbled at every bottle and jar that she could find, but she didn't find it. Then, she searched behind the counter, beneath the cash register. There she mostly found notebooks, stamps, and pens. She could hear Simon's son's voice getting louder.

"I don't see anything, ma'am," he said. "I suppose you'll have to let me know if you spot it again."

Then she heard the first of his steps at the top of the staircase. Avery was running out of time, and she knew it. But as she glanced up, her eyes caught sight of a small zipped-up bag on top of a pile of books to the side of the counter. On it was a label with the word medicine printed on it. She reached for it and stuffed it under her shirt, making it out of the door just in time to not be spotted. It wasn't clear yet if she had found what she was looking for, but she had done the best that she could.

Tiffany followed her act through to the end. "Well, thanks," she said as she walked toward the door of the bookstore. "I'll be back again once you've dealt with all the rats in here." Tiffany beamed with pride as she walked back onto the street. She looked as if she'd had way too much fun.

"Did you get it?" she asked eagerly.

"I hope so," Avery said. "You did a great job, by the way."

"Thanks," Tiffany said proudly. "We should do that more often."

Avery had no time to waste. She drove back to the police station, and as soon as she arrived there, she asked for a pair of gloves. With the gloves secured over her hands, she searched through the contents of the bag, looking for what she was certain she would find. When she did find it, it took every ounce of her self-control not to jump up and down and cheer. But her excitement was short-lived. Because on the bottle of pills was the name Simon Simmons. The officer behind her went deadly silent, and there was a soft exhale.

"He's going to want to see this," he said.

He pulled on some gloves and reached out his hand. Avery placed the bottle in his hands and followed him down the hall and back into the viewing room.

"What did I miss?" Avery asked as she joined Charles at his side again.

"Not that much," he said. "He says he didn't do it, but they still think he might have. I really don't know what to think. Where'd you go?"

"You'll see," she said with a small smile.

The door to the interrogation room opened, breaking the solid gray of the wall only momentarily. The officer who had just been with Avery stepped inside, and it was clear to everyone by the look on his face that his interruption was important.

The officer leaned down to whisper in Chief Mather's ear before handing him the bottle of pills. Avery watched Simon's face closely, and as he watched the handover happen, he lost all the color in his face. His casual demeanor changed, and his eyes darkened.

He looked to Avery like someone who knew he'd been caught.

"Simon," Chief Mathers sighed. "I really think it would be best if you just came clean."

Chief Mathers slid the bottle of pills across the table. In large blue letters, it was labeled, Alprazolam.

"Where did that come from?" Charles said seriously.

"From a little bag on the bookshelf of his shop," Avery said.

"How did you get it?" he asked, turning to her in disbelief.

"I'll tell you about it later," she said hurriedly. "Do you think he'll confess?"

Simon looked at the bottle, which clearly had his name on it, and shrugged. "Not entirely sure what this is supposed to mean," he said, doing a terrible job of pretending that he didn't care.

"This," Chief Mathers said, tapping the top of the bottle, "is the medication that we know murdered Dean Scott."

"That's ridiculous," Simon said. "Do you know how many people take that medication? Me and anybody else with stress and anxiety. It's not that rare."

"Well, piece it together with the discovery of the missing satchel in your possession," Chief Mathers explained, "and I can't help but think you're the one who murdered him."

"I have no reason to have murdered him," Simon said. His arguments were only becoming more and more feeble. His shirt was slowly darkening with sweat, and the shaking in his hands was getting worse.

"Of course you do," Chief Mathers said. "You stood to lose your business if he sold that building, and that reality was only weeks away."

Simon remained quiet. He took a deep breath and stared at Chief Mathers with angry eyes. Avery wondered what his plan was. Did he think he could intimidate Chief Mathers into dropping the accusation?

"Oh, come on," Simon said. "Everybody in this town knows me. They'll all tell you that I could never do this."

"That doesn't matter if we have the evidence," Chief Mathers said.

With the adjustment of his shoulders, Avery knew that Chief Mathers was done arguing with Simon.

And his stare was enough to make Simon break. Simon's eyes filled with tears, and his shoulders dropped.

"I spoke to him at the wedding," he explained. "I wanted to know what he was going to do about the sale of the building."

"Go on," Chief Mathers said, writing it all down.

"I didn't want to do it, but I would lose everything if he sold that building," Simon continued. His eyes were downcast at his swollen hands, and Avery could see the shame that loomed over his head.

"I had hoped that he was going to say that he decided not to sell the building after all," Simon said. "If he'd just gone with that decision, I would never have slipped the Alprazolam into his drink."

"But that's not what he said, is it?" Chief Mathers asked.

Simon shook his head. "No," he said softly. "He said that the sale was due to go through any day now. I hated him for that so much. And in that moment, there was nothing I wouldn't do to change that reality."

"How did you get it into his drink?" Chief Mathers asked.

"I had it ready, just in case," Simon explained. "I had it crushed up and in a small pouch tucked into the cuff of my sleeve. I just pointed at a beautiful woman, and while he looked away, I slipped it into his wine."

Avery watched as he was read his rights and charged with the murder of Dean Scott. It was a crime that he very nearly got away with.

"Well done, Sprinkles," Charles said. "Remind me to get him some treats."

Simon was taken away in handcuffs as he requested his lawyer to be contacted, and Avery wondered if he thought it was worth it. Granted, his family could continue on with the business, but they would lose their father to prison.

Perhaps he really wasn't the man that the community had believed him to be.

Chapter Twenty-Seven

Three months later...

Every paper and news program was filled with the news of Simon's sentencing. All the evidence had pointed against him, and in the end, it was easy for a jury to find him guilty. Avery had attended every one of his court dates, and she'd learned more than she could ever have imagined.

Simon would spend the rest of his life in jail and still awaited trial for many other crimes that had been uncovered during the investigation. Avery wasn't sure yet if the bookstore would survive it, but she had high hopes. There was no reason that a place so magical needed to suffer for the actions of one selfish man.

It had been a long trial. Simon had used his health to delay the court dates as much as he possibly could, making it a tedious and drawn-out experience.

Avery sipped her coffee victoriously as she saw the image of him behind bars on her television screen.

But by the time the sun was at its highest point in the sky, she had forgotten all about Simon. She joined the women of the Stammtisch as they gathered in the backyard, along with Avery's parents. Chief Mathers had promised he would make an appearance at some point as well. She wished Charles would be there, but he still needed to work in the wine room.

There had been a party tent set up, and there were treats and wine enough for the entire town, it seemed. The music was flowing, and it was the perfect day. Summer was coming to an end, but the sun was warm enough that day as if it had put on one final show for Avery and her celebration.

There were fresh flowers on the table, and the women had all color-coordinated their outfits. Bright colors made them look more festive than ever as they celebrated the release of Avery's first novel.

In the center of the table was a single copy on display. "The Bookshop Butcher" stood proudly for all to admire. And within a few days, copies would be available for purchase in almost every bookstore. It seemed unreal to Avery, but nobody else seemed quite as surprised.

"I've already read the book twice!" Deb bragged as she slid her chair nearer to Avery.

"Well, I started reading it, but I got too stressed out!" Camille commented.

Eleanor reached for the book at the center of the table and looked at it as if it was the first time she'd ever seen it. She admired the cover and read the description on the back, despite the fact that each person in attendance at the party had received a personalized copy in the mail weeks before.

They celebrated until the last bit of daylight disappeared behind the horizon. Avery enjoyed the celebration very much. It only made her want to do more things that were worthy of a celebration.

When Avery finally put on her pajamas and got ready to collapse onto the couch, the party décor was still outside. She was too tired to tidy it up yet and knew that it wasn't going anywhere. *I can do it tomorrow.*

She picked out a movie to watch and was about to press play when she heard a familiar knock at the door. Avery chuckled as she realized she had come to know Charles so well that she could recognize him by the way he always rapped three times against her door paused for a moment and then knocked one last time.

"You had to wait until I was in my pajamas, didn't you?" she said as she opened the door with a smile.

But Charles' face was obscured by a badly put-together cardboard box.

"I promised you I'd try it," he said as he handed it to her. "Besides, there was no way I was going to miss celebrating with you today."

Avery opened it, and inside was one of the worst-looking pizzas she had ever seen. She stared at it a moment, doing her best to keep a straight face, but it wasn't working.

"Oh," she said, flustered. "Well, you did your best, and that's all that matters."

Charles burst out laughing. "Luckily, I brought these along too!"

He revealed his other hand, and in it was a pizza box from the pizzeria down the road from him. And on top of the box sat two antique wine glasses with a ribbon tied around them.

"I saw these and thought of you," he said with a smile. "I know you've got the wine to fill them if you're interested?"

Avery and Charles celebrated on their own with pizza, wine, antique wine glasses, and a movie that neither of them had really seen before and neither of them really enjoyed, either. Thankfully, they had more than enough to talk about to drown it out.

The End.

Recipes

Puffy Pancake (serves 4)

4 tablespoons salted butter
4 large eggs
¼ teaspoon salt
1 cup all-purpose flour
1 cup whole or low fat milk
½ lemon, cut into wedges
Powdered sugar for dusting
Maple syrup, if desired

- Preheat oven to 425°F.
- Put butter in a 9x13 inch pan and into the oven as it is preheating (to melt).
- Combine the eggs, salt, flour, and milk in a medium-sized mixing bowl.
- Whisk the mixture to make a smooth batter.
- Pour the contents of the mixing bowl into the pan directly over melted butter.

- Bake for 15-20 minutes until the mixture puffs up and the top is slightly browned.
- Serve immediately, dusted with powdered sugar and lemon wedges (juiced over the pancake, to taste) on the side.

Excellent with fresh fruit, whipped cream, and sausages!

Pairing options: Earl Gray tea or Eiswein (ice wine)

Killer Grilled Cheese Sandwiches (serves 4)

2 tablespoons butter
8 tablespoons grated parmesan cheese
4 tablespoons fig jam
8 slices sourdough bread
16 slices of Swiss or gruyere cheese

- Heat pan to medium.
- Melt ½ tablespoon butter in pan.
- Spread 1 tablespoon of fig jam on the inside piece of sandwich bread.
- Sprinkle 2 tablespoons of parmesan cheese over butter in pan.
- Place two slices of bread open-face in the pan over parmesan (this will form the crusty goodness).
- Divide four slices of cheese over bread.
- Once the cheeses start to melt, assemble the sandwich.
- If the cheeses aren't melting fast enough as the crust browns, microwave sandwich for 30 seconds and finish on pan.
- Repeat with remaining ingredients.
- Serve with potato chips or tomato soup.

Pairing options: Sparkling white wine or ice-cold pale ale

Lasagna Soup (serves 6)

2 tablespoons olive oil, divided
1 pound ground beef (90% lean or higher)
1 large yellow onion, diced
4 garlic cloves, diced fine
4 cups chicken broth
1 can (14.5 ounces) crushed tomatoes
1 can (14.5 ounces) diced tomatoes
3 tablespoons tomato paste
2 teaspoons dried basil
1 teaspoon dried oregano
½ teaspoon dried rosemary
½ teaspoon dried thyme
Salt and freshly ground black pepper to taste
8 lasagna noodles
1 ½ cups mozzarella cheese, shredded
½ cup parmesan cheese, shredded fine
8 ounces ricotta cheese
2 tablespoons fresh parsley, chopped

- In a large pot over medium-high heat, add 1 tablespoon of oil.
- Brown ground beef and season with salt and pepper. Drain and set aside.
- In the same pot, add remaining oil and onion. Sauté until softened (3-4 minutes).
- Add garlic, sauté additional 30 seconds.
- Carefully pour in broth, tomatoes (both crushed and diced), tomato paste, dried herbs, and beef.
- Salt and pepper to taste.
- When the mixture starts to boil, reduce to medium-low heat.
- Cover and simmer for 25 minutes.
- Cook lasagna noodles per package instructions. Once cooked, cut into bite-sized pieces.
- In a medium bowl, prepare cheese mixtures by mixing mozzarella, parmesan, and ricotta cheeses.

- Add lasagna pieces to the pot of soup.
- Add chopped parsley.
- To serve, spoon soup into bowls and top with cheese mixture.

Pairing options: Cabernet sauvignon or amarone

A Different Kind of Lemon Bar (serves 6)

Bar ingredients
1 cup butter, softened
1 ¼ cups sugar
2 tablespoons lemon zest
4 eggs
2 tablespoons fresh lemon juice
1 ½ cups all-purpose flour
1 teaspoon baking powder
Lemon glaze ingredients
1 ¼ cups powdered sugar
4 tablespoons fresh lemon juice
5 tablespoons lemon zest

- Preheat the oven to 350°F.
- Prepare a 9×13 baking pan by lining with parchment paper.
- Whisk flour and baking powder together in a large mixing bowl.
- Beat together the butter, sugar, lemon juice, and zest with a hand or stand mixer until the mixture is light and fluffy.
- Add eggs one at a time and mix until combined.
- Slowly add flour and baking powder until combined.
- Pour batter into the baking pan
- Bake in the oven for 25-30 minutes. Test with a toothpick (should come out with few crumbs).
- Cool completely in the pan.
- To make the glaze, whisk powdered sugar, lemon juice, and zest in a large bowl until smooth.
- Spread glaze over warm lemon bars.

It'll be tempting, but be sure to allow the glaze to set up overnight!

Pairing options: Oaked chardonnay or limoncello

Murder at the Cheese Shop

BOOK 3

To GJS...

I love you more than you love cheese.

Chapter One

The cold morning air stung the tip of Avery's nose as she waited outside Cheesy Does It. She needed to buy some cheese for that evening's gathering of the Stammtisch. They were a group of women from Los Robles who got together informally to enjoy each other's company. And in that small, central region of California, the gatherings were becoming more and more frequent and that group of ladies was quickly becoming best friends.

But she was too early for the cheese shop that morning. She had been in such a rush to get there so she could buy cheese and get back to her vineyard to start the daily work that she didn't realize she had left way earlier than any of the shops on that stretch opened. Thankfully, there had been a coffee shop nearby that was serving.

So, she sipped the coffee, allowing the steam to defrost the tip of her nose while her golden retriever, Sprinkles, slept at her feet. It had been an earlier-than-usual morning for him too. That part of Los Robles was so quiet that morning that it felt as if she was the only person on the street.

When she answered a call from Charles, she felt as if her voice was the only thing that could be heard for miles, and she wondered if she'd be responsible for waking up everyone within walking distance of where she was standing.

She had gotten used to the small town. It had been a while since she'd moved from the city after her husband had died in a boating accident. She had been convinced that she would never recover from it. Yet, she had survived.

To her surprise, since she left the bustling city and moved to a smaller town, she had been busier than ever before. Apart from running her parents' vineyard, she had written and published many crime novels, a skill she had learned from her late husband.

She hadn't written nearly as many as he had in his career, but she had certainly adopted his passion for it. It filled her late, sleepless nights and gave her a creative outlet that she never knew she needed. With friends in the Stammtisch, a rewarding job, and a newfound creative passion, she was feeling more at home than she ever had before.

"Charles, it's way too cold out here," she said. "This cold has come earlier than I expected; I worry about the vines."

"What are you talking about?" Charles laughed on the other end of the call. "You've had a great few seasons! A bit of cold weather shouldn't scare you. Besides, there's always eiswein!"

"Oh, I don't know if those good seasons came because of me, or because of luck," she teased. "Honestly, there are some days where it feels like I have no idea what I'm doing."

"Well, you have a good way of hiding it," Charles answered. "You always look completely in control if you ask me. I think you're just tired, and it's making you feel worried about everything that didn't worry you before."

"If that's the case, then the good news is that I've run out of books to write."

Charles burst out laughing on the other end of the line. "What do you mean?" he asked. "How can you run out of books to write? You only just got started."

"I don't know where James found all the inspiration," she said. "The first few I wrote were inspired by some of the old case files here in Los Robles. The police were kind enough to let me go through them."

"So, go through some more," Charles eagerly suggested.

"I've tried!" Avery argued. "There's nothing interesting anymore! There are only boring murders left. If there is such a thing."

"Boring?" Charles asked. "They're murders!"

"I know, I know, but you know what I mean," she said with a chuckle. "They're all the standard ones. You know, an angry wife catches her husband cheating... There's not much of a story there. Not one that I can work with, anyway."

"I can't believe you'd think any kind of murder is boring," Charles said.

"You were a police officer," Avery argued. "You see these things differently. I need a story to tell. I need something with twists and turns and drama. Most of the murderers here seem to turn themselves in. I can't work with that."

"I see," Charles said. "I get it, but it doesn't sound right when you say it was boring," he teased.

Sprinkles had startled awake after the first cyclist for the morning came zooming past them. Thanks to his training, Avery could keep him still with just the motion of her hand, which was difficult to do that morning considering her hands were currently full.

She was starting to understand why some of the younger people around her opted for headphones and earbuds to talk to their friends. She quite liked the idea of hands-free calling. Especially when she was talking to Charles, as their conversations tended to go on for quite some time.

"Tell you what," he said. "When you come over to my house tomorrow, we can go through some of those so-called boring case files, and we can think of ways to make them more interesting. You just need a little inspiration, that's all."

"No kidding," she said sarcastically. "I need a LOT of inspiration. I have publishers asking me when I'll start the next one, and not a single thought in my brain about what I could possibly write about."

"Well, we'll just have to fix that, won't we?" he laughed. "I'm sure you'll find a story. As I said, you're just worrying too much about everything because you need some rest. It's been a busy time at the vineyard, and with all your work and the books, you've barely had time to slow down."

"Oh, no, no, no," she said. "No slowing down for me. That's what my parents did and look at them now. They decided to slow down once, and they just got slower and slower and slower. Now, they both move at a snail's pace and drive us all nuts!"

"Here's an idea," Charles said sarcastically. "If you aren't finding what you're looking for in the old case files, then why don't you just make one up? Create a whole story from scratch. You can have as many twists and turns as your heart desires."

Avery sighed. "I tried, Charles. It didn't work. My imagination has become stagnant, I tell you."

"That's just not possible," Charles argued. "How can you say you have no imagination?"

"I sat for hours the other night trying to think of a new murder plot, and all I could think of were the cases I had just read through that morning in the old case files," she explained. "I could think of nothing new! Eventually, I got so frustrated I went to bed."

"You're tough to please, aren't you?" he teased.

Avery had a chuckle as she sipped her warm coffee. She looked down the street and saw that some of the shop workers were waiting to enter their shops, but still, the doors were all shut.

"Hey, listen, while I've got you on the line," Charles said. "See if you can't convince the cheese shop to stock some of your wine. What better place to sell wine than alongside cheese?"

"I'm way ahead of you," she said. "I've got a bottle in my bag for the owner to take home and taste. You don't know who owns this shop, do you?"

"No, sorry," Charles said. "I haven't been to that side of town in years. I go to the same three shops each week. That's how I've always done it, and that is probably how I will continue to do it until I die."

"Now you, my friend, are easy to please," Avery joked.

Charles and Avery had become friends since she'd taken over the vineyard. He worked in her wine room and did all the tastings. He was excellent at his job, but he was an even more excellent friend to her.

In general, he was somebody she could rely on. Having worked as a police officer in his life, Charles also had great respect for his work, which was a quality that she didn't always see in the other members of her staff. She had quickly learned that she could teach a new employee just about anything except work ethic. Contrary to popular belief, this was not a learnable skill. And thankfully for her, Charles had undeniable integrity to ensure a job well done. He sold so much wine each week that Avery genuinely worried about what would happen to her business if anything ever happened to him.

"Did you take the shiraz?" he asked. "We're selling that one like crazy lately. It must be the weather, but everybody wants a case of it. I'm almost tempted to fill it out on the order sheets in advance!"

"I'll be honest with you. I was in such a rush to leave the house this morning that I'm not sure which bottle I took. But I know it is some kind of a red," she said through laughter. "And it turns out that I didn't need to rush at all. None of these shops are even open yet!" she said.

"Are you sure?" Charles asked. "It seems like the time for them to have opened."

"Well, I'm looking down the street, and every door is still locked," Avery said. "I guess this side of Los Robles starts later in the day."

"Did you see that the bookstore is for sale?" Charles asked. "I'm considering buying the business. It's been around for so long, and it's pretty well-established. Then when I buy it, I can have an entire shelf just for your books."

"You can't buy the bookstore!" Avery argued. "I need you at the vineyard. You're the best employee I have there. If you leave me, I will never forgive you."

Charles laughed. "I was just going to buy it. Do you think I'm interested in selling books all day?"

"You sell wine all day," Avery said blankly.

"Yes, but wine is fun!" Charles said. "People come in here and sip and talk, and I learn about them. It's a social thing. Bookstores are always quiet, serious places. No, I'd hire people to run it for me, but it would be mine."

"I don't know...it seems like—"

She didn't have the chance to finish her sentence. Sprinkles had started tugging on his leash, and no matter how many times she gave him the signal to calm down, he refused. So she turned to see what had him so interested and saw that he was pushing open the door to the cheese shop with his nose.

"It's open!" she said to Charles. "I must have been so distracted with our conversation that I missed them unlocking it."

She had noticed that all the other shops in the street still remained shut and that the employees of those shops who waited outside seemed equally as confused about it as she was.

"Let me know what he says about the wine sales," Charles said excitedly.

Avery walked inside and came to a complete halt. It was so sudden that even on the other end of the line, Charles could tell that something was wrong.

"Avery?" he asked. "Is everything alright?"

"I don't think we're going to be selling wine here," Avery said with a shaky voice.

"What? Did you ask him already? What are you talking about?" Charles asked.

Avery swallowed hard. "I can't ask him anything," she said. "Because I'm looking at his dead body."

Chapter Two

S ince Charles had still been on the phone with her when she found the body, he alerted the police to meet her there as quickly as possible. Avery knew that no amount of sleep or distraction could ever erase the memory of what she had stumbled on that day.

When she walked in, she was faced with the blued body of Mr. Cederic Davis, the cheese shop owner. He had been placed in the display cabinet so that he could easily be found. His entire body had been wrapped up to his neck in cheesecloth.

It was reminiscent of the ancient mummies of Egypt. Only, his head was unwrapped, and the end of a red ribbon stuck out of his mouth. The police had taped off the shop, and outside, a large crowd had gathered. They were already preparing their rumors and stories for their neighbors and friends. And Avery knew that it was only a matter of moments before Deb, the biggest gossip in the Stammtisch, would send her a message to tell her all about it.

What remained of Avery's coffee had gone cold, and yet, she still clung to the cup as hard as she could.

The police moved around her in the chaos. They picked up every cheese knife and every piece of cheese that had been strewn across the floor and bagged it for evidence. One of them had been asking her a string of questions.

Some of them were the same questions, just with different wording.

"So, is this the first place that you stopped this morning?" the officer asked.

"No, I was here before the shop opened, so I made a quick stop at Javatini. You know, the coffee shop? I've just been waiting outside for a while," she answered. "I was talking on the phone to my friend, Charles."

"So, you didn't stop anywhere else before you came here?"

"Just Javatini," Avery repeated. "I left home, grabbed some coffee, and came directly here."

"And how did you notice that the door was unlocked?" he asked, clicking his pen constantly.

"My dog, Sprinkles, pushed it open with his nose," she explained. "He was whining and tugging on the leash like he wanted to show me something."

"Like he wanted to show you something?" the officer asked with a skeptical frown.

"He's had some training," she said. "Military training. So, he learned to alert in different ways. When he opened the door, he was telling me that he wanted to show me something."

"I see," the officer said, writing it all down. "And what did you do when you found the body?"

"I froze for a moment," she answered. "As I'm sure you can imagine, I was in a bit of shock. Thankfully, I was on the phone with my friend, Charles, and he called you guys to come here."

The officer wrote down something that seemed to take longer than it should have, and Avery lifted her head to see if she could peer at his notepad.

"And you didn't see anybody enter or leave the shop before you walked inside?" he asked.

"No, I was distracted," she answered.

At that moment, Chief Mathers entered the scene. Avery knew him. He had been helping her with the old case files to inspire her books. But he didn't give her the warm welcome that he usually did. Instead, he barged right in and started talking to the officers. He gathered a few of them, and they spoke in hushed tones. Every few moments, they would look up in her direction, all of them unsmiling and stern. It made Avery feel a little more unsettled than she'd have liked.

He then picked out one of the detectives and appeared to give him some kind of instruction. Avery wished that she could read his lips so she could know what was going on.

"So what was your intention at the shop today?" the officer asked.

It was an annoying question, and Avery was certain that her annoyance was evident on her face. "I was here to buy some cheese. I have some friends coming over later today."

"So, you weren't here to see Mr. Davis personally?" he asked.

"No," Avery answered. "I was here to shop and to offer him a free bottle of wine to take home and taste."

"Why would you do that if you didn't know him?" The officer acted as if he'd just caught her out in a lie.

"I own a local vineyard and I was hoping to convince him to sell some of my wines," she answered.

The officer stretched his eyes wide. "So, you must be new to town then."

"Relatively," she said, confused by his reaction. "But not all that new, either."

At that point, the officer who had taken instruction from Chief Mathers interrupted them. He stopped the officer who was questioning her and took his notepad from him.

"Right, Avery, is it?" he asked.

Avery nodded with a forced smile.

"You can go," he said. "But the chief has asked that you make yourself available for some more questioning at some stage."

"Oh," she said, eagerly jumping to her feet. "Great! Yes, of course. He knows where to find me and has my number."

She was happy to be out of there and driving away from the scene as fast as the legal limit would allow. She had no cheese for the Stammtisch gathering, but she was certain they would understand that.

Avery was grateful to be headed back to the vineyard. There, she could work hard all day until her friends arrived, and it would distract her from the morning that she'd had. One thing was for sure, she wouldn't be getting any sleep that night.

Every time she blinked, she caught a glimpse of Mr. Davis' cold, dead eyes as he lay in the display cabinet. There was something wrong about the entire scene, apart from the obvious issue of the dead body.

It felt to Avery that too much effort had been put into his display. But then again, she was a crime writer, and perhaps her imagination had finally been jolted.

~

"Sorry, I have no cheese," Avery said jokingly as she placed the platter in front of the women of the Stammtisch.

"You have the murderer of Mr. Davis to thank for that one," Eleanor remarked.

Eleanor was a chatty woman who always had a new insight or fresh information on whatever topic was being discussed. Avery got along with her very well, and she valued her advice from time to time. Eleanor had recently been married and had only just reached the point where she was no longer making every story somehow about her new husband and their relationship.

The women were gathered around Avery's dining table as the wind blew outside. It wasn't the most pleasant day, and she desperately missed their backyard gatherings.

"I don't know if I'd be willing to thank the murderer for anything," Avery said. "I might be scarred for life after today."

"I'm sorry, Avery," Eleanor said sheepishly. "I suppose it's too early to joke about it?"

"Not at all," Avery remarked. "In fact, please make jokes about it. Perhaps if we can make it a little more lighthearted, then I might get some sleep tonight."

"So, will you write about this one?" Eleanor asked. "I mean, this is bound to be a good story if you found him all wrapped up like that!"

"I haven't really thought about it," Avery said. "I don't really know if I should. I know I was complaining that the old case files are boring. But this just seems a little too nuts, if that makes sense?"

"Well, if you're worried about feeling sorry for the victim, don't," Eleanor said. "He's exactly the kind of man who would capitalize off of another person's death."

"He owns all the shops on that street, you know?" Deb said. "So, none of them opened for business today."

It didn't surprise Avery that Deb seemed annoyed by it. Deb was always around if there was a story to be heard. She loved to gossip, so it made sense that if Mr. Davis owned all the businesses on that one street, she would go to one of his other shops to get some information.

"Yes," Eleanor said. "Every single one of them except for the yogurt place. And he owns a couple of shops on Morton Street, too."

"I've always wondered how he manages to have so many businesses," Deb added. "Especially since everybody else knows not to do any business with him."

The entire group of women hummed in agreement with Deb, except for Avery. And it became apparent that there was something she had missed. But her glass was empty, and that was more important than any information after the day that she'd had.

She leaned forward and grabbed the bottle.

"Why is that?" she asked as she poured another glass of wine. "Why should other businesses have stayed away from him?"

"He's just a shady businessman," Eleanor said with a shrug. "It's not uncommon for him to take months to pay for his stock orders. And when he eventually does, he makes the payment so complicated that it takes ages for the receiver to actually get their hands on it."

"Oh, I know!" Deb cried. "You know, last week, he paid for his eggs with a check. Like, an actual check, like they used to do in the fifties! Thankfully, the man who sells the eggs is about seventy years old, so he knew what to do with it."

"Yes," Eleanor said. "That's why none of the vineyards stock their bottles there anymore. One even tried to do it on consignment. The bottles would fly off the shelves. It took him half a year before he saw any money for it. He had to pay to get lawyers involved."

"Ah," Avery said.

She had wondered, when she tucked the bottle into her bag for him to taste, why his shelves had been devoid of any wine. It seemed uncommon for a cheese shop like his. Now she knew.

"And the McClarens of Petit Cellars," Deb added. "They took some bottles for his shop once, only to learn that they never even hit the shelves. Mr. Davis used them all for one of his lavish, private parties."

"Oh, I got invited to one of those once," Eleanor said. "It was awful. Incredibly pretentious. He literally had his nose pointed upward the entire time. And I'm pretty sure the wine we had that night had been cheap wine decanted into an expensive bottle."

"Never mind the tampering with the stock thing," Tiffany added as she scoffed.

Tiffany had been Avery's best friend since school. She was a smart woman and the newest member of the Stammtisch. She seemed to fit right in, not that there was any doubt that she would.

"Tampering?" Avery questioned.

"He would break the items and then refuse to pay, saying that the stock was broken and unusable," Camille explained.

Camille was the quietest of the group. She kept her personal life pretty private, but she always showed up and had a good time. She only spoke once or twice at each gathering, but she laughed easily, and on the days when she couldn't attend, her calming presence was always missed.

"Surely, he didn't get away with it," Avery said. "Not multiple times?"

"He would wait until someone new came into town," Eleanor explained. "Or he would buy stock from businesses outside of town and advertise them as the next best, fancy thing here. Once I saw a chopping board that he'd had for sale when I was visiting the city. It was from a mass-production factory shop! Mr. Davis had sold it as hand-made and put a massive markup on it."

"He really sours his relationship with any business that approaches him," Deb added. "As I said, it's amazing he was able to keep so many businesses open here, given the kind of businessman that he was."

"He never even once attended the charity event," Camille added, fulfilling her quota of conversation for the day.

Chapter Three

It was a gloomy morning when Avery opened her eyes. The gray weather didn't make her feel as down anymore as it once did. She knew the importance that it had for the grapes. So, she welcomed it that morning.

When she sat up in bed, she found the piece of paper on which she'd scribbled a new character description the night before. It was based on the way that the women of the Stammtisch had described Mr. Davis. Avery found the most unsavory characters the most interesting. She couldn't understand them, and that's precisely what fascinated her. The people that she couldn't relate to were the ones who made the better main characters in her books.

She needed an unsavory character if she was going to write an unsavory story. She got up and checked her calendar. She had a full day of work ahead of her on the vineyard that day. There was plenty to do, and she looked forward to it.

As she walked toward the kitchen to get the pot of coffee flowing, she heard the sound of Sprinkles' paws against the floor as he slumped out of bed. He walked up to her with sleepy eyes to greet her for the morning.

He wasn't as thrilled about the gray skies as Avery had been. Sprinkles knew if it rained, he would likely miss out on his daily walk. There'd been a few days like that already, and he had spent most of those days sulking at the windows.

Avery got dressed for the day. She was eager to get started in the hopes that she would finish early enough to enjoy the sunset with a glass of red wine. As she put on the last of her makeup, she heard the sound of the coffee dripping its last drops in the kitchen.

Her duck boots squeaked against the floorboards as she eagerly approached the pot of coffee. By that time, Sprinkles had woken up a little more and was waiting patiently for his bowl of kibble. He had become so large that he could no longer sleep on the bed with her.

Avery checked her watch and realized she had just enough time to make a quick breakfast before she started her day. With all that she hoped to accomplish that day, she knew she needed to attack her tasks with a full belly. She swung the fridge doors wide open, grabbed a few eggs, and made her mom's creamy scrambled eggs.

Avery spent a few moments in front of her laptop with her cup of coffee and eggs as she went through the list of emails that awaited her. It wasn't long before she was through them all and ready to leave the house.

She drained the last few sips of coffee as she headed for the front door, her umbrella awaiting her there. But as she was about to pull the door open, there was a knock. It startled her, and she needed to take a moment to breathe before she answered. The people standing on the other side of the door were the last ones she expected a visit from that early in the morning.

Two officers greeted her with friendly smiles. They weren't officers that she recognized, but they greeted her by name.

"Sorry to bother you so early in the morning, Ms. Parker," one of them said with a smile. "But Chief Mathers has asked us to bring you in for some questioning."

"Oh," she said, her brow furrowed. "I knew you needed to ask me some more questions, but I kind of expected a call or something. I didn't expect you to come and pick me up."

The officers looked at each other with a small amount of unease. "Well, we're here to take you back to the station."

She nodded and reached for her coat and bag, and a few moments later, she was in the back of a police car on her way to the station. She reached for her phone to let Charles know.

Police are taking me in for some more questioning about yesterday. Totally unexpected. I will probably be late today. Hopefully, it doesn't take too long.

She knew it would be a little while before Charles saw the message. He didn't wake up quite as early as she did, and he was only expected at work later in the morning. From the back seat of the police car, Avery enjoyed the view and the small talk with the officers seated in front.

Things only became more confusing for her when she got to the station. As soon as she walked in, she was expected to hand over all of her personal belongings. She had some suspicions that it wasn't normal, but she figured perhaps she simply didn't know the processes all that well.

Then, she was led through the station and into a small interrogation room. The room was entirely gray, and in the middle of the room stood a single table. There were a few chairs around, and she was placed in one of them.

Something about the room made her feel colder, and something about the way she had been treated made her feel uncomfortable. It took Avery longer than it should have, but she eventually came to realize that she was in the interrogation room because she hadn't been requested for any ordinary questioning.

Avery knew well enough that if she was in the interrogation room, she was there so every answer she gave would be recorded and kept on the record. She also knew the interrogation room was largely used for suspects.

Given the fact that she'd had all her personal possessions taken from her, she understood that she was a suspect. And her heart dropped. Despite her innocence, her hands became clammy, and she started to bite at her nails.

Her leg bounced in a nervous twitch. She had no idea what was going on, and she hadn't had nearly enough coffee for that kind of morning. And all she could do was wait. And that was the worst of it. In a moment like that, minutes would feel like hours.

Eventually, the door opened, and the familiar face of Chief Mathers entered.

"You can't be serious," Avery said. "Chief, please tell me you're not looking at me as a suspect."

Chief Mathers sat down silently and spread the files in front of him. Then he took a deep breath. This wasn't going to be easy for either of them.

"Avery, we have a few questions for you," he said as calmly as he could.

The way he spoke to her, it would be hard for anyone to believe that they actually knew each other. He was cold and professional, and it made Avery feel small.

"How is this even possible?" Avery mumbled as she leaned forward with her face in her hands.

"We've got the autopsy results back, Avery," Chief Mathers explained. "We suspect the victim was murdered by being hit in the head with a large wheel of cheese. Blunt force trauma."

Avery suddenly understood why she had been taken in as a suspect. She lifted her head and pushed her hair out of her face.

"It's kind of like James' book," she said. "So, you think I had something to do with it?"

Chief Mathers moved some of the files around seemingly aimlessly. He did a fairly good job of hiding it, but he was as uncomfortable with it as she was.

"You have to admit, it's a little odd," he said. "It's not a common form of murder."

Avery laughed. "Yeah, it's a really weird way to kill someone. So, what makes you think that I would do it?"

Despite her laughter, she didn't find it funny at all. It was entirely absurd to her. It was a stretch, to say the least, to think that she would not only murder someone but would do it in a way that had a direct link back to her.

"There is no motive for me to have committed the murder, and you know it," she said.

"Well," Chief Mathers said between clearing his throat. "There is a theory that we have currently."

"A theory?" Avery scoffed. "I'd love to hear this."

"We believe it isn't entirely impossible that you might do something like this to sell more books," he answered.

She refused to believe that he didn't find it as ridiculous as she did.

"And how would that work, exactly?" she asked.

"Everyone at the station knows you use our cases to write your books," Chief Mathers explained. "And, it's not hard to learn that the books based on true events in our small town sell better. You might have created an elaborate murder so you have a new story to write. One that will sell better than all the rest."

Avery stared at him wordlessly. Her lips parted with the intention of speaking, but she found herself entirely devoid of anything logical to say in response to such an outrageous accusation. And it was clear to her that Chief Mathers was having a hard time with it as well.

"Were there any other similarities to the book?" she asked.

"Well," Chief Mathers muttered as he consulted his notes. "Not that we can tell at this moment, but we will only be learning more about this murder as the investigation continues."

"There are so many people who have read that book," Avery said. "It could be anyone."

"You're the only one with a motive," Chief Mathers said.

"Now you're reaching," Avery argued. "Such an elaborate scheme just to sell some books? Do you understand how crazy that sounds?"

She knew she was crossing the line by speaking to him that way. But the idea that her husband's book had inspired an actual murder was upsetting enough, never mind the idea that she had been the one to carry it out.

"We're just doing our jobs," Chief Mathers said.

Avery dropped her shoulders and stared at him. It felt like some kind of sick joke. She thought back to how she had found the body. The entire situation was making her sick to her stomach.

"Well, do it better," she snapped. "No offense, Chief, but while you're looking into me, the real murderer is getting away."

"You're who we've got at this moment," the chief said sternly.

Avery crossed her arms and leaned back in her chair. She had pushed too far with Chief Mathers, and she could tell by the clench in his jaw that he was getting tired of it.

"Question away then," she said, gesturing to the space around her.

"Let's get my name cleared so you can get back to work catching the real murderer."

Chief Mathers nodded and cleared his throat as he pulled a page closer. "Did you know the victim, Mr. Davis?"

"Like I told the officer yesterday, no, I did not," she said defiantly.

"Alright, and why were you at the cheese shop yesterday morning?" he asked.

"They asked me this yesterday!" she whined.

"Avery, please, just answer the questions," Chief Mathers said with a look of frustration.

Avery sighed. "I was there to buy some cheese, which is generally what one does at the cheese shop. But I was early, so I waited outside."

"Thank you," the chief said. "And how did you discover that the door was open?"

"Sprinkles showed me," she answered. "I was on the phone with Charles at the time, and Sprinkles pushed the door open and alerted me that there was something he needed to show me."

"He alerted you?"

"Yes, as he learned in his training," Avery answered. "It should be in your notes."

It didn't feel good to be treated like a criminal. She knew there was likely someone on the other side of the glass watching too. She felt embarrassed and frustrated. And all she could do was answer the same questions she'd already answered the day before and hope that it would make a difference.

Chapter Four

Avery and Chief Mathers were in the small, gray room, and things between them were uncomfortable, to say the least. Avery hadn't intended to have such a bad attitude toward him, but she didn't like what she was being accused of and found herself more defensive than even she had anticipated.

Chief Mathers' pen scribbled across the page, and with the tension in her body, to Avery, it seemed as if it was the loudest sound in the world.

"And how long were you waiting outside the shop?" Chief Mathers asked.

"I don't know," she shrugged. "About as long as I was on the phone with Charles. Maybe twenty minutes? If I had my phone, I could check."

Again, he made a note of what she said and seemed to be cross-referencing it with some other information that she could not quite see.

"Why were you so early yesterday morning?" he asked.

"I guess you could say I was a little too eager," she explained. "I wanted to get there as the shop opened so I could get back to work as quickly as possible. But in my rush, I wound up arriving earlier than I had anticipated."

"And did you go anywhere else on your way there?" Chief Mathers asked.

"I stopped at the coffee shop nearby. They were open, and I was desperate for a cup," she said. "I was there for three minutes while they poured it and just a short walks away from the cheese shop."

A note was made, and Chief Mathers let out a frustrated sigh. From what Avery could see, there were still a few pages worth of questions that they had prepared for her. It was gearing up to be a long conversation.

"Okay, and...where were you the night before the murder?" Chief Mathers asked.

Avery thought about it for a moment. In order to answer that question, she needed to know what day it was that day. Then, she could count back and figure out where she had been the night before. But she worried that her silence was suspicious.

"I was at Charles' house," she answered. "We had dinner, and I was there until around eleven o'clock at night."

"And after that?" he asked.

"After that, I went home and got into bed," she said.

"Is there someone who can verify this?" he asked.

"Not a person," she said. "But I suppose the alarm company could send you the logs of when I arrived and disarmed the house?"

"Alright," Chief Mathers said.

Avery was so frustrated with it all that suddenly every item of her clothing felt as if it didn't fit right. Her hair felt too heavy on her neck, her shoes were uncomfortable, and no matter how many times she adjusted herself, the back of the chair still pressed against all the wrong parts of her spine.

Chief Mathers shifted some more pages around. "We'll arrange to speak with Charles and confirm that alibi," he said, but Avery suspected it was an instruction for whoever was on the other side of the glass.

She peered at what looked like a mirror on her end, knowing that there was a room on the other side of it. And she wondered if the person on the other side felt that she was looking at them. She wondered how many people were there, watching and hoping she would confess.

"Do you intend to question every person who has ever read the book that my late husband wrote?" she asked. "You know, the book that you claim was the inspiration for this murder?"

"That would be impossible to do, Avery," Chief Mathers said, unimpressed. "There are probably millions of people that I would have to question then."

"Oh, come on," she said. "Just like it's impossible for me to have committed this murder!"

She knew she needed to dial it back on her attitude, but she was having a hard time doing so. Avery knew they would find her innocent soon enough and so all the questioning felt like a massive waste of time.

"And why do you say it is impossible?" he asked. "From where I sit, it still might be possible."

"Think about it," Avery said. "How much did the victim weigh?"

Chief Mathers inspected his notes. "According to his autopsy, he weighed about two-hundred pounds."

"And how exactly do you think I lifted that entire two-hundred-pound body into the display cabinet?" she asked.

Chief Mathers studied her. Avery was a petite woman in her late forties. She was fit but certainly not fit enough to carry such a large weight.

"And how do you think I would easily lift a wheel of cheese over my head and bring it down on him hard enough to kill him?" she asked. "And what did he do while I was struggling with the cheese? Do you think he just stood there and waited for it to happen?"

"The scene does show signs of a struggle," Chief Mathers commented.

Avery pulled her sleeves up. "Do you see any signs of a struggle here?" she asked. "I saw what that shop looked like. If it was me, I'd have bruises."

Avery crossed her arms again. "This just really doesn't seem plausible to me," she said. "I don't have the physical strength to have pulled it off."

"Very few people do," Chief Mathers said. "Alone, anyway."

"What are you implying?" she asked.

"Currently, we are of the belief that more than one person was involved," Chief Mathers explained. "The murder is simply too difficult for one person to pull off, as you said."

Avery felt quite pleased that she'd figured that part out, even if she was being looked at as a suspect. It made her feel as if she was finally wrapping her head around the way things like that were looked at through the eyes of a detective.

But her excitement was short lived when she remembered that she was a suspect in the murder.

"Have you read the book?" she asked.

"Yes," Chief Mathers explained. "That's how I made the connection."

"Then, how do I know that you didn't do it?" she asked.

Chief Mathers stared blankly at her for a moment before pulling his files closer again. He was searching for something, and she wasn't sure what. She searched the walls for a clock or something that could tell her how much time had passed, but there was nothing.

To Avery, it felt as if she had been there for most of the morning already. In reality, she hadn't even been there an hour.

"Do you really think I have it in me to commit a murder like this?" she asked.

This time, she had no more attitude when she spoke to him. She was tired and worried about her safety. She had no idea if she would be arrested or how serious things were looking for her. She didn't know if her answers to his questions were working in her favor or against her.

"We need to look at anyone with a connection to the crime," he explained.

She didn't know what that meant, and it certainly didn't actually answer her question. She understood he could give her nothing. And she also knew that things would certainly go much better if she calmed down first. As Chief Mathers wrote his notes and checked his files, she closed her eyes and took a deep breath.

"When you found the body, what were your steps immediately after?" he asked.

"I was still on the phone with Charles," she explained seriously. "And he was able to alert the police. He walked me through it and told me not to touch anything else and to wait outside for the police to arrive."

At that moment, there was a knock at the door, and one of the officers that had collected her from her home stepped in.

"Sorry to interrupt," he said. "But there is a man here, Charles, and he is pretty insistent that he speaks to you, Chief. He refuses to speak to anybody else."

Chief Mathers looked back at Avery and let out a sigh. "I'll be back in a few minutes," he said, pushing his chair away from the table.

And just like that, Avery was alone in the room again. But she knew someone was still watching her and likely paying attention to every small detail of her body language. So, she sat as calmly as possible and focused only on keeping calm.

She wondered what her late husband, James, would have thought about one of the murders in his books coming to fruition like that. Would it fascinate him? Or would it horrify him? Avery thought about her own involvement in his books.

And she couldn't help but feel a small amount of guilt. She wondered if Mr. Davis would still be alive if the person who'd done it hadn't read her husband's book. Her books were inspired by murders. But this murder had been inspired by a book. It was backward and wrong.

She didn't like the way she felt about it.

Without a clock, it wasn't clear how much time had passed, but Avery had been so caught up in her own thoughts that when the door opened again, it startled her. Chief Mathers came in, but this time, he didn't sit down.

"Charles has come to clear your name," he said. "Your alibi checks out, and I've confirmed with your alarm company what time you got home."

Avery let out a loud sigh of relief.

"We're pretty much done here, and I'm all out of murderers," Chief Mathers said in a feeble attempt at lightening the situation with a joke.

"Thank you," Avery said. "I'm sorry about my bad attitude."

"It's perfectly understandable in moments like this," he responded. "You're not the first person I've had in here who's had a bit of an attitude." Chief Mathers smiled and flashed her a wink. "I'll be honest," he continued. "I'm rather happy I don't have to put you in jail. This wasn't at all easy on me."

He held the door open for her as she stepped out into the hallway. "I'll walk with you," he said.

Avery wondered if she'd get any work done that day. She was so shaken by it all that, even though it was still morning, she felt like she needed a nap. And she certainly needed to reward Charles for all his help in clearing her name.

"I'm sorry I had to treat you that way," Chief Mathers said. "It wasn't easy, but I had no choice. I hope you understand."

"I understand," she said. And she wasn't lying. She did understand.

He treated her like a murderer because, at that moment, he thought she was one.

"Are you alright?" he asked.

Avery smiled. "I'm a little taken aback if I'm honest," she said. "But I think I'm alright. I'm not in jail. Things might have been a lot worse there."

"Only if you were guilty," Chief Mathers said kindly. "Why don't I buy you a coffee to make up for it sometime?"

"No need," Charles said cheerfully. "I'm already a step ahead."

Avery greeted Charles, who held a cup of coffee in his hand for her.

"Another time then," Chief Mathers said. "It's the least I can do."

"Thank you," she said. "That sounds pleasant."

She wasn't sure what it was, but something in Charles' face soured slightly. She chalked it up to his annoyance at how they had treated her like a murderer. But she couldn't be entirely sure. She did notice that when Chief Mathers left the room, his face straightened again.

She gratefully took the cup of coffee from him and let the comforting liquid fill her mouth. She could feel the warmth of it move all the way down into her belly when she swallowed the first gulp.

"Let's get you out of here," Charles said.

Chapter Five

Charles was holding the door open for her, and Avery had never been so happy to be leaving the police station. But she barely had her foot out of the door when they were stopped in their tracks.

"Avery?" Chief Mathers interrupted them.

"Yeah?" she answered. "Do you need anything else from me?"

"Not exactly," Chief Mathers said as he fixed his jacket. "I had a proposition for you."

"I'm listening," she said with a smile.

Chief Mathers smiled. "Would you like to follow the case?" he asked. "I just know that this will make an interesting story. You could watch the case and take notes and stuff."

Avery wasn't expecting that kind of invitation. In fact, until that moment, she had intended to stay as far away from the case as possible. But, she thought about the paper with the character description sprawled on it that waited next to her bed.

"I'll think about it," she said.

"You'd be crazy not to do it," Chief Mathers said. "I've read one of your books. You're a great writer. I think this would certainly make for an excellent story. If you don't write it, I just know that somebody else will."

Charles was next to her, and his body language changed. He had suddenly become stiff and stood upright. It became apparent to her that something about Chief Mathers was annoying him. She made a mental note to ask him about it later.

"Are you sure it's alright if I do that?" she asked.

"Of course," he said. "With your alibi in place, there's no way you could be involved. Besides, with your knowledge of the book that inspired the murder, perhaps you could serve as a consultant on the case."

The idea was becoming more and more enticing with every passing second. She needed a new story, and she needed something good. The murder of Mr. Davis met both of those requirements. Still, she felt a little uncomfortable.

"Wouldn't the book just be too similar to my husband's book, then?" she asked.

"Perhaps," Chief Mathers said. "But you never know where this murder might go. Maybe it turns out to be entirely different. Let it be an inspiration, at least."

"Alright," she said. "I'll do it. Thank you."

"It's the least I can do," Chief Mathers said. "See you soon, then."

Avery and Charles left the building and piled into his car.

"Thank you for saving me," she said again. "I don't know how long I was in there, but it was too long."

"Of course," Charles said. "As soon as I read your message that they had come to pick you up from home, I knew something wasn't right. I rushed right to the station to see what was going on."

"It was a little nuts," she said. "They treated me like a criminal. And it made me feel like one too!"

"Why did they think you were a suspect in the first place?" he asked.

"The way the victim was murdered," she explained. "He was hit on the head with a wheel of cheese. James had written a book just like that, so they figured I did it."

"I still don't understand," Charles said. "He was killed by...a wheel of cheese?"

"Yeah!" Avery said. "Blunt force trauma. They had some story that I was doing it so that I could sell more books."

"I know it sounds nuts to you," Charles said. "But police officers see so many wild and crazy things that it actually sounds pretty plausible."

"It's insane, Charles," Avery sighed. "Anyway, we all know I'm innocent, and that's all that matters."

"So what about that book?" Charles asked. "Is there any relation to the murder?"

Avery shrugged. "Kind of. But not that much. The only similarity is the murder weapon. Everything else is different."

"I see," Charles said.

"It was kind of weird to see Chief Mathers that way," Avery said. "He was so serious and stern, and I almost thought he was convinced I had done it."

"Well, he's good at interrogations for that very reason," Charles said. "If the suspect thinks the detective is already convinced, they're more likely to confess."

"That makes sense," Avery said. "Awfully sweet of him to offer to buy me coffee, though. And to let me follow the case."

Charles didn't say much about it. He just let out an unimpressed "Mmm."

Avery wasn't sure what Charles' problem was with Chief Mathers, and she had half a mind to ask him about it, but she decided against it. She'd had enough drama for one day. She would ask him another time.

"I'm sorry you had to go through that," Charles said.

"It was frustrating," Avery said. "And for a few moments, it was a little bit scary. But in the end, it wasn't all that bad."

"It could have been," Charles said.

"I know," Avery said.

She sipped her coffee and enjoyed the views of the misty vineyards. The birds had all woken up and were fluttering about. The town had come to life while she had been in the interrogation room. It was always a good life.

By the time they arrived back at her vineyard, she could feel the last little bit of tension falling away from her shoulders. Avery hopped out of the car, and Sprinkles ran eagerly to greet her. When she opened the door, Avery found the cup she'd had in her hand when she answered the door, still waiting for her on the entrance table.

"Thank you again," she said to Charles. "I don't know how to thank you."

Charles smiled sheepishly. "Perhaps you can make me a character in one of your books," he said. "But a nice character. Don't make me the murderer."

Avery laughed. "Deal!" she said. "Coffee?"

"A third cup?" Charles laughed. "Sure, why not?"

He stepped inside and hooked his jacket onto the coat rack. And, in the end, he made coffee for both of them. They were good enough friends that he knew his way around her kitchen. They sat out on the patio to drink their coffee as they watched the morning mist rise.

The rays of the sun lit up the vineyard, creating a golden glow across the fields.

"It is a beautiful sight, isn't it?" Charles said.

"It really is," Avery said. "And to think that not too long ago, I had a view from my balcony that I thought was just great."

"What kind of view was it?"

"Just a bunch of buildings," she laughed. "Occasionally, when the wind blew the pollution out of the city, I could see the mall in the distance."

Charles laughed loudly. "Sounds great!"

"You never lived in the city?" Avery asked.

"Never," Charles said. "I visited a city once as a child, and since then, I've known that I am not cut out for city life."

"Why's that?"

"All those cars zooming around," Charles said as he waved his hand through the air. "And there are so many people around, and it just never seems to be quiet."

"That's a pretty accurate description of the city," Avery laughed.

They sipped their coffee, and before Avery knew it, it was time for Charles to start his job in the wine room. Avery saw the sun shining on the vineyards, and she knew she needed to capitalize on it, despite the amount of work she needed to do that day.

She called for Sprinkles, and the two of them went for a walk. Sprinkles walked easily at her side. His tail wagged through the air as he sniffed the path that he had walked hundreds of times already. But still, he behaved as if he'd never seen it before.

They walked until they got to the middle of the vineyard. There, she crossed off one of the items on her to-do list. She inspected the new hole that she'd ordered to be dug there.

They were in the process of building a large pond. Her plan was to place some tables and chairs around it so there could be parties and weddings, and occasionally when the weather was good, they could do their wine tasting out in the center of the vines.

The pond was going to be bigger than she had ever planned, but she was excited to see it in full swing. She had already ordered the koi fish, and they were just waiting for their new home to be ready for them. Later that day, she expected the first delivery of the new lawn furniture to arrive. She stood for a moment and pictured what it might look like when it was done and filled with people who were all laughing and having a good time.

She breathed as she tried to release the tension from the day. As she exhaled, she wondered what might have happened if Sprinkles had never alerted her to the unlocked door of the cheese shop. Somebody else would have found Mr. Davis, and she might have been spared the trauma.

As if he could sense her tension, Sprinkles came bounding toward her and nudged his nose into her hand. She scratched his ear, and he smiled up at her. It made her feel that much worse about letting him know that it was time for them to go back home.

Avery led Sprinkles back toward her house. By the time she got back, she was starving. She opened the fridge to look for a snack.

Her eyes fell on the brie that she had kept on the top shelf. She could barely stand to look at it. So, she pulled it from the fridge and threw it into the trash. Needless to say, she would be done with cheese for a while.

She spent the rest of the day working through her to-do list. It took most of the day, and she worked well into the night. Avery was so tired when she crawled into bed that she barely closed her eyes before she fell asleep.

That night, she had a really strange dream. She dreamed of the man that she had found dead in the display cabinet. Only, she dreamed of him as if he was alive. In her dreams, she saw how he had done shady business deals and how he fought with other business owners over owed money. She saw him laughing on a large heap of money that he actually owed to somebody else.

Then her dream changed to something else entirely. She dreamed she held a wheel of cheese right over her head. It was heavy, but somehow she had the strength to lift it and bring it down on his head. Despite the panic that the dream brought on, her mind seemed entirely blank. She couldn't stop herself from swinging the wheel of cheese down, and she woke up just as she felt the thud.

Avery was breaking out in a sweat when she woke up. It was terrifying to have dreamed of herself as the murderer but not unexpected. She quickly wrote down all that she could remember about the dream as she had learned to follow the leads to success, something that had proven fruitful in the past.

For the rest of the night, she got little rest. All the stress of the day trickled into her dreams, and at one point, she even dreamed Charles and Chief Mathers had gotten into a physical fight. Finally, after the fourth nightmare, she gave up on getting sleep and got out of bed to watch a movie instead.

Chapter Six

Avery was working in the wine room, and to say that she was bored was an understatement. Charles couldn't be there as he was attending the funeral of Mr. Davis. He never knew the man personally, but his mother did. She had somehow twisted his arm into going with her.

Most of the town was at the funeral. Which meant it was a particularly quiet day in the wine room. Avery had already caught up on all her paperwork, and she had already searched for something to clean. But Charles was such a good employee that everything was spotless.

So, she resorted to doing an unnecessary stock take. It was a pity about the funeral as it was a bright and sunny day, and the wine room would otherwise have been packed full. As Avery counted, her mind wandered. She thought about Chief Mathers' offer to buy her a cup of coffee and the weekly dinner that she would have with Charles. She thought about the pond that was in progress and wondered how different it might be that evening when she walked to take a look at it again. And before she knew it, she had lost count and needed to start again.

She counted only a few before giving up. She had no doubt that Charles' stock take from the week before was accurate, and it wasn't working well enough to keep her busy or entertained. She was about to close the wine room for the day when the doors opened, and the bell rang to signal someone's arrival.

A woman walked into the room, dressed from head to toe in black. The rhythmic sound of her high heels echoed through the room as she walked. She was a fabulous woman. Her brunette hair was tucked back with curls and braids.

She sat down and smiled at Avery. Her makeup was done perfectly, and her lips were painted with a deep red, the color of a perfect pinot noir.

"I'd love to taste everything that you have available here," she said calmly.

The woman pushed the menu aside and waited patiently for Avery to pour the wines. As she poured, Avery noticed the woman looking at all the details of the wine room.

"It's quiet here today," the woman said.

Avery nodded. "It's not exactly tourist season and the locals are at the funeral of a local businessman," she explained.

"Ah," the woman said. "Yes, the funeral was rather full and rather dull. I left early and came here instead."

"You knew Mr. Davis?" Avery asked.

"Knew him?" the woman chuckled. "I was married to him for years."

"You're his wife?" Avery asked.

"Ex-wife," the woman corrected her. "I haven't been married to Cederic for quite some time, thankfully."

The woman sipped the first wine but didn't really seem to be doing much actual tasting. She seemed pensive and calm for a woman who had just attended her ex-husband's funeral. But Avery didn't want to ask too many questions. It didn't seem right.

"Do you live in Los Robles?" she asked instead.

The woman nodded. "I live right on the edge, though," she answered. "It's a beautiful house, and it's far away from everyone, which I love."

The lady finished the first wine and moved on to the next, placing the empty glass to one side.

"I didn't really want to go to the funeral," she said. "I mean, it's not as if Cederic and I loved each other. But our son wanted me to go, so I did. It got a little tedious, though, so I left early." The woman let out a chuckle, and Avery couldn't tell if she thought it was funny or just a little ridiculous. It was hard to tell. The woman's demeanor was hard as stone, and her shoulders relaxed.

"Did you know him?" the woman asked.

Avery shook her head. "No, I didn't."

She didn't know how to tell the woman that she had been the one to discover her dead ex-husband's body. They might not have gotten along, but he was the father of her child. And they had spent ten years together; the woman might have seemed unbothered, but Avery thought it was impossible that she didn't feel some kind of emotion about it. Especially considering the way he had been killed.

It wasn't long before all the glasses in front of her were empty. She seemed satisfied enough with it all.

"Those were all lovely," the woman said. "I'd love to taste them all again."

She was Avery's only customer. So, she happily poured another tasting for the woman. She had obviously been going through a lot, and Avery figured she needed it.

"Thank you," the woman said.

She sipped the wines as she stared into the distance. Avery wondered what she was thinking about, if her son was alright, and all the worries that were not Avery's to bear. But somehow, she could not help herself.

"It's a beautiful day, isn't it?" the woman asked, turning to look out the window.

"Yes," Avery said with a smile. "On any other day, we would have been packed!"

"I should imagine so," the woman answered. "It's a beautiful place, and the wine is excellent."

Avery thanked her and pretended to be busy with something else, but she quickly ran out of things to fiddle with.

"What is your name?" the woman asked.

"Avery," she introduced herself. "And this is my vineyard."

The woman sat upright. "Yours?" she asked. "Then we certainly must get acquainted. My name is Audrina."

The woman reached out her hand, and Avery shook it. She didn't seem like the kind of woman that Avery would normally be friends with, but Audrina had suddenly become very interested in them getting to know each other.

She asked Avery a string of questions about her life, all of which Avery tried to answer as vaguely as possible. And the more the woman spoke, the more she drank, and it wasn't long until Audrina was tipsy.

"When did you last see Cederic?" Avery asked, taking her own turn to ask personal questions.

"I haven't spoken to him in years!" Audrina said with laughter. "And to think, he thought he had it so much better with the new Mrs. Davis!"

Audrina packed out with laughter. "At least when he was with me, he was alive the entire time!"

Avery didn't find it quite as funny, but she forced a chuckle in an odd attempt to be polite.

"He thought he was going to find himself an easier wife to deal with," Audrina said. "But he picked out the most expensive and high-maintenance woman in all of Los Robles!"

"Is that so?"

"Yes!" Audrina said, reaching for the next glass. "She spends more money than any other person I know. All she ever does is shop." Audrina flashed Avery a pleased smile. "Let's just say that Cederic had a taste for glamorous women."

"Clearly," Avery said, gesturing at Audrina, who took it as a compliment.

"But he never really understood that looking like this costs a lot of money," Audrina said. "And it takes a lot of time. Especially when you need as much work as Collette."

"Collette?" Avery asked.

Audrina gulped down a large sip of wine. "His new wife, Collette," she answered. "I shudder to think what she might look like after a shower."

Clearly, there was some animosity between the two wives. Avery didn't want to pry enough to know why. She was already learning way too much about their personal lives. But she would listen to whatever Audrina told her, as she knew it would help for her book.

"You know, the last I heard, Collette had created a fair amount of debt for them," Audrina said, leaning forward as if she was telling a secret.

Avery wondered if Deb and Audrina knew each other. They would be good friends, as each of them seemed equally eager to gossip.

"Yeah," Audrina said. "That's what my son told me a few months ago. He had heard them arguing over it. Apparently, she refused to stop shopping and insisted that he simply wasn't earning enough to keep up with her." Audrina burst out laughing. "Cederic threatened to take away her credit cards. I wish I could have seen her face when he said it!"

Avery couldn't relate to a single thing that Audrina was saying. She wasn't much of a shopper. She kept herself neat, but she wasn't particularly glamorous, and she couldn't ever imagine shopping so much that she landed her own family into debt. These were certainly not Avery's kind of people.

"I bet she did this," Audrina said as she narrowed her eyes. "I bet she is going to run off with his life insurance money and never be seen again. I won't be surprised if she remarries next week! She never cared about Cederic, only about his money."

"Is that so?" Avery asked.

She didn't want to take part in the gossip, but it occurred to her that Audrina might have some information that was valuable to the case.

"Yeah," Audrina scoffed. "A few weeks ago, when my son went to visit there, he found the insurance paperwork on his father's desk. Apparently, he has a massive insurance payout in the case of his death. Collette will get every last cent of his money from him."

"You don't really think she did it?" Avery asked. "You're just joking, right?"

"I wish I was," Audrina said. "It's not impossible that she was behind this. She had a serious shopping addiction, and it's no secret what kind of things people might do to feed their addictions. If his life insurance was really worth what my son had told me, I am sure she wouldn't have hesitated."

Avery stood there in shocked silence. Everything about their conversation was entirely inappropriate. And Audrina didn't seem to care at all.

"That's just my opinion," Audrina said as she drank the last sip from the final glass. "I suppose that's for the police to figure out, isn't it?"

"I suppose so," Avery said casually.

Satisfied and relatively tipsy, Audrina called herself a cab to take her to the next vineyard. After that, Avery closed the wine room. She wasn't sure that anybody else would come, and she felt completely overwhelmed by her conversation with Audrina. As soon as she got a moment, she phoned Chief Mathers to tell him what Audrina had said.

"I'll look into the life insurance policy," Chief Mathers said. "And the debt. Thank you for letting me know, Avery."

"You're welcome," Avery said. "Happy to help."

Chief Mathers cleared his throat. "Have you given some more thought about that cup of coffee?" he asked.

"I have, actually," Avery said cheerfully. "I have a spot next week if you'd like to meet somewhere?"

"Great!" Chief Mathers said cheerfully. "I'll text you to set up a day and time if that's alright?"

"Sure," she answered. "See you then. And let me know if you're bringing in Collette Davis. I'd like to see the questioning, if that's alright?"

"Of course," Chief Mathers said. "Happy to do anything that helps you write another unputdownable book."

Avery sat down on the patio with a cup of coffee as she pondered everything that Audrina had said. She wondered if she could ever find the time to be that glamorous. She tried to imagine a captivating woman committing the kind of murder that Mr. Davis had experienced, and it just didn't seem right to her at all.

Then again, there was nothing about the murder that seemed normal. Everything from the murder weapon to the way the body was displayed was entirely strange. And there was one detail that stuck out to Avery the most.

She thought of the small bit of red ribbon that she had seen hanging out of his mouth.

Chapter Seven

Avery waited at the station for them to bring in Collette Davis. When they arrived with her, it was no quiet affair. Collette marched in with officers at her side. Her sleek blonde hair waved softly in the breeze as she stepped through the door.

Her heels were even taller than Audrina's had been, and she was much younger than Audrina. She wore flashy clothes, and there were large diamond rings on her fingers. Earrings that were large enough to be small chandeliers rested on her shoulders.

"What is this all about?" she questioned. "Can't you leave me to grieve? My husband just died!"

"We just have a few questions for you, Mrs. Davis," the officer said. "It shouldn't take too long. If you could drop your bag and phone in this bin, then I can take you through to wait for Chief Mathers."

"My phone?" she gasped. "I have to leave it here? What if somebody needs me?"

"I suggest you let somebody know where you are," the officer said, unamused. "That way, if it's urgent, they can phone here, and we can relay the message to you."

Collette pursed her lips and dropped her phone into the bin. "This is ridiculous," she muttered.

Avery followed closely as they led her to the interrogation room. She slipped into the viewing room on the other side of the mirror and watched as they led Collette in and invited her to take a seat. She inspected the seat before wiping it down for any dust. Then she collapsed onto the chair and folded her arms. She still had not removed her sunglasses, and she twirled her hair impatiently as she checked her appearance in what she thought was nothing more than a mirror.

Collette had long, dazzling nails that tapped against everything as she moved, and her jewelry made a constant jingling sound. Right at that moment, Charles stepped into the viewing room and stood at Avery's side.

"Here," he said, handing her a cup of coffee, which she happily accepted.

"Here," she said, handing him the cup that she had bought for him.

It meant that they each had two cups of coffee. They stood, with both hands holding their coffees, and chuckled.

"We should plan this better," Avery chuckled.

They turned their attention back to Collette.

"Look at her nails," Avery said. "How is she supposed to do anything with those? There's no way she could kill someone. She can barely reach for anything in her pocket."

The door to the interrogation room opened, and Chief Mathers stepped inside. Collette laid her eyes on him, and her demeanor immediately changed. Her eyes lit up, and she put herself on display for him, leaning forward on the table.

"Well, hello," she said. "Aren't you a sight for sore eyes?"

"Hello, Collette," he answered. "I'm Chief Mathers."

"Ooh, a chief!" she said as she flashed him a flirty smile.

Chief Mathers ignored her sudden excitement at his job title and spread his files in front of him, a movement that was quickly becoming one of his key character traits. He paged through the first few documents in silence, and Avery noticed the nervous tap of one of Mrs. Davis' fingers.

"How long have you and Mr. Davis lived in Los Robles?" Chief Mathers asked.

"Together?" she asked. Without giving him a chance to answer, she said, "Well, Cederic has always lived in Los Robles, and I moved here just after my first job. I must have been about...twenty or twenty-one years old."

"That's awfully young to move to a small place like Los Robles," Chief Mathers said. "What was your reason for moving out here?"

Mrs. Davis chuckled. "It does seem odd, doesn't it?" she said. "I guess I was just tired of the city pressure. There's too much going on in the city. I prefer a quieter life."

Chief Mathers glanced at her expensive jewelry and clothes and moved on to the next part of his questioning. He cut right to the chase. He reached for a specific paper, turned it to face her, and slid it across the table.

"Mrs. Davis, after speaking to some people, we've heard that you're in quite a bit of debt," he explained. "We've contacted your bank, and we've learned that the debt is pretty substantial."

Mrs. Davis rolled her eyes and slumped back in her seat, the way a teenage girl would behave toward her least favorite teacher.

"Cederic and I were fighting about it constantly," she said. "He never told me that the money coming in wasn't enough for my spending. Not until it was too late, anyway."

"You didn't know you were spending too much money?" Chief Mathers asked. "How could you not know?"

"He promised he could provide for me!" she whined. "He gave me the credit card and told me to go out and buy whatever I liked. And I took that literally, I guess. By the time I learned that his businesses weren't doing so well, it was too late."

"I see," Chief Mathers said. "Were the businesses failing?"

"Not in the slightest," she explained. "There just isn't enough money for how much I like to spend."

"Alright."

Chief Mathers took the bank statement back and placed it in the file. Then he reached for another document and slid it across the table to her.

"This is the document that shows the amount of your husband's life insurance," he said. "It's a fairly substantial amount, enough to settle your debt and live comfortably for a few years."

Mrs. Davis pursed her lips into a pout. Her eyelids fluttered, and her once rosy pink cheeks had paled completely.

"If you're accusing me of murdering him for his life insurance, you're barking up the wrong tree," she said blandly.

"We're just trying to get a clear picture here, Mrs. Davis," Chief Mathers said.

"You are so typical, aren't you?" she snapped. "Man winds up dead... accuse his wife. It's absurd. We had a payment plan to pay back the debt. I don't need his life insurance money."

Avery watched her body language change in an instant. She no longer behaved like a frustrated teenager. Instead, she behaved defensively, and her manner of speaking had become rude.

"Mrs. Davis, where were you on the night that your husband was murdered?" Chief Mathers asked.

"I was at home, waiting for Cederic to get back from working late," she explained. "Except he never did, and I simply assumed he was having an affair and that perhaps he was with another woman."

"Did he have affairs?" Chief Mathers asked.

"I've never caught him," she said, shaking her head. "But he was out so late and so often, I am certain there was someone else in his life. Perhaps she did this."

"Well, we'll have to see if there is any evidence of an affair before we look into that," Chief Mathers said as he wrote it all down on the page.

"So you just stayed at home that night?" he asked. "You didn't go to a store or go to get some food or anything like that?"

"No," she sighed. "I was at home. I was watching movies and drinking wine. A little too much, probably, because I fell asleep on the couch."

"Is there someone who can confirm this?" he asked. "Someone we can call who was with you at home that night? Did you make any phone calls that we can check on the records?"

Mrs. Davis shook her head and shrugged. "I'm afraid that neither of the children were there that night. Cederic's son was out at a friend's house, and my daughter was staying at my sister's house that night."

Chief Mathers scribbled all the information down as Mrs. Davis stretched her neck in an attempt to see what he was writing.

"Unless my cat learns to talk," she joked. "I stayed in the house the entire day. I hadn't left since breakfast. I was trying to spend less money, I guess."

Chief Mathers continued to take notes. In his hand was a wooden pen that had been stained red. Mrs. Davis kept her eyes on it for some time and smiled. When Chief Mathers looked up at her, she pointed to the pen.

"I like that color," she said. "I had a ribbon almost exactly that color in my hair when Cederic and I got married."

"Is that so?" Chief Mathers said, and he wrote that down too.

"And you were happily married?" he asked.

"I dunno," Mrs. Davis said. "I was, but I wasn't always certain that he was, you know?"

Chief Mathers nodded as he continued to scribble it all down. He seemed to be writing more than what Mrs. Davis was saying.

Avery nudged Charles in the ribs. "Why did he write that down?"

"Nobody knows about the red ribbon," Charles said. "And we can't figure out why it's there yet. So, the red is symbolic of something, no doubt. Perhaps it's the ribbon she wore in her hair on their wedding day?"

"What do you mean nobody knows about it?" she asked. "The murder is all over the papers and the news."

"The police decided not to mention it," he shrugged. "That way, should one of the suspects say something about the red ribbon, then they'd have to have been there. How else would they know?"

Avery scribbled that tactic down in her notebook. She'd heard of the police doing that before, and she was excited to see how it would play out in this particular case.

"So, she's mentioned a red ribbon now, but not in relation to the case," she said.

"Yes," Charles answered. "And it does seem odd that she's thinking of that red ribbon right now, doesn't it?"

"I'd say."

She looked up at the woman and couldn't understand her behavior. She was talking about the day she had married her husband while being accused of murdering the same man. And her eyes barely watered. She showed no signs of grieving.

Mrs. Davis fixed her hair, and her bracelets tinkled loudly, filling the room with sound. Then, she straightened her shirt, and again, the tinkling cut through the silence. She was quiet for only a moment before she sighed loudly.

"Look, if you want to know who did this, then I think I can help you," she said.

Chief Mathers dropped his pen softly and paid attention. "If you have any information regarding this case, then I suggest you tell me now."

Mrs. Davis smiled. "It's the ex-wife, Audrina, obviously."

"And why is that obvious?" Chief Mathers asked.

"Well, because of all their fighting recently. Cedric was fighting for custody of their son, and Audrina was not happy about it."

Something about Audrina's unhappiness gave Mrs. Davis so much joy that the laughter bubbled up right from the depths of her stomach.

"You should have heard the voice messages she left us!" she laughed. "The woman is insane!"

"Did she make any threats?" Chief Mathers asked.

Mrs. Davis nodded with wide eyes. "Oh, yeah," she said. "She once said that she would do *whatever it took* to make sure she kept custody of their son. It doesn't sound like much when I say it now, but I could hear in her voice that she sounded very serious and scary."

"Do you still have the voice message?" Chief Mathers asked. "This is very serious, Mrs. Davis. I hope you understand that."

"Well, I would hope you're taking this seriously!" she said. "I want this murder solved. This is my husband we're talking about!"

She took a moment to breathe and calm down. "And no, I don't have the voice message anymore. I deleted it."

"I'll find out from the phone company if we can get that recording from their records," he said.

"She's the one who did this," Mrs. Davis said sternly. "I am certain of it."

Chapter Eight

I t was barely an hour after Mrs. Davis had been questioned when Audrina was brought into the station to be questioned. Contrary to the current wife of the victim, Audrina wore darker colors. Her dress was black, and her red shoes matched her red lipstick.

She sat entirely still at the table in the interrogation room, just as she had sat in the wine room. Her hair was pulled back neatly, and her makeup was done to perfection. Chief Mathers entered just as he had done with Mrs. Davis.

"Audrina, my name is Chief Mathers," he introduced himself.

Just as Mrs. Davis had, Audrina perked up and flashed him a dazzling smile.

"Well, isn't it a pleasure to meet you, Chief Mathers?" she said.

Avery snorted. "These two ladies clearly have the same taste in men," she teased.

Charles chuckled too. "You're right there," he said. "If only they weren't both murder suspects, Chief Mathers could have his pick. It would be good for him to find someone else."

"Someone else?" Avery asked. "Chief Mathers is in a relationship?"

"No, he isn't," Charles said with a frown. "Never mind."

Avery brushed it off. She had no idea what Charles was referring to, but she had other things to concentrate on. She watched as Audrina pulled at her dress so just a little more of her bosom was exposed.

"Now, what did you want to talk to me about, Chief?" she asked.

"We just have a few questions for you, ma'am," Chief Mathers said.

"Well, I'll be happy to answer all of them and be out of your hair," she said. "I assume this has to do with the murder of my ex-husband?"

"Yes," Chief Mathers said. "Now, first, how long were the two of you married?"

Audrina counted on her fingers. "About seven years. We split when my son was five years old."

"Was it a difficult divorce?" he asked.

"Are there easy divorces?" she asked. "It was tough. It's always tough when there is a child involved. I had to take him away from his father. It was one of the most difficult decisions of my life."

"And where is your son now?" he asked.

"He's with his grandparents," she answered. "He's been there for a few days. I'm afraid I couldn't get many days off work, and he needs some comfort right now."

"May I ask why did the two of you divorce?" Chief Mathers asked.

"He was always working," she answered. "I became convinced that he was having affairs. But I didn't have any proof."

"And you took full custody of your son?" Chief Mathers asked.

"Yes," she answered. "He worked too many late nights. He had no time to care for our child. Cederic had a certain number of visitation days each month, a lot of which he missed in the early years."

"Audrina, how often was he seeing his son recently?" he asked.

"Please," she said, placing a hand on the table right next to his hand. "Call me Red. All my friends call me Red."

Chief Mathers looked up in interest. "And why is that?" he asked.

"Because I never go anywhere without my red lips," she said with a wide smile. "It was actually Cederic who called me Red first."

Avery made a note in her book. "There's the mention of red," she said.

"It is interesting, isn't it?" Charles said.

"She left the funeral early," Avery said. "She told me it was boring. And she said the only reason she went to the funeral in the first place was that her son had asked her to."

Chief Mathers cleared his throat. "Well, Red," he said. "How is your relationship with his current wife?"

Audrina shrugged. "I don't know her very well, and as I am sure you can understand, we don't talk often. The only time we really talk is when I'm phoning to speak to Cederic and she answers the phone."

"And how was your relationship with Cederic the last couple of months?" Chief Mathers asked. "You said he was seeing your son more often. Does that mean that the two of you were on better terms?"

"No," Audrina chuckled. "We've never been on good terms. There might have been two or three years when we enjoyed each other's company, but after my son was born, we fought a lot. The last few years of our marriage were very troubled."

"Is that why you left the funeral early?" Chief Mathers asked.

"You've done your homework," she teased. "I left the funeral early because of the looks I was getting and because I was a little bored."

"Looks?"

"Yes," Audrina sighed. "As I am sure you can imagine, Cederic's family members aren't fond of me. They were there, and so was Collette and her entire family. I am sure you can imagine that none of them were all that thrilled to see me."

"No, I suppose not," Chief Mathers said. "So, why did you go to the funeral at all, then?"

"Will this really help you solve the murder?" she asked.

"Any bit of information might help," he said. "We're just trying to get a clear picture here of where everybody fits in. I'm sure you understand."

"I went to the funeral for my son," Audrina said. "He asked me to go and said that it was important for me to be there. So I went."

"It's amazing what we'll do for children," Chief Mathers said.

"Do you have children?" she asked as she peered at him.

"I have a son, too," he said. "It's tough to watch them grieve."

"Are you married?" she asked. "Sorry to pry, but I just want to ask a few questions, too, and make this a little less one-sided, you know?"

Chief Mathers clenched his jaw. "I was married, but unfortunately, my wife passed away a few years ago."

"I never knew that," Avery said as she turned to face Charles. "How did I not know that?"

"How well do the two of you really know each other?" Charles asked.

"I know; not that well," she answered. "But we spend so much time together, and it feels like I should know these things. I suppose all we talk about are old cases."

"Perhaps it's better that way," Charles mumbled.

Avery ignored Charles' odd response because Chief Mathers had corrected his posture and had taken out the next page on which he was going to take his notes. To Avery, it meant that an important question was coming.

"Where were you the night that Mr. Davis was murdered?" he asked.

"I was sleeping," she said. "My son was at a friend's party, so I took a sleeping pill and allowed myself to get some rest. And it was a great rest, I might say. The best sleep I've had in years."

Chief Mathers wrote it down. "I don't suppose there was someone else with you who could confirm this alibi?"

"No," Audrina answered. "Unfortunately, I've been getting into bed alone for far too many years now."

Audrina created a perfect pout and raised her eyebrows to make herself look sadder. Then she fluttered her eyelids. It took everything in Avery's power not to laugh. Although she marveled at Audrina's confidence, she couldn't think of a worse time to attempt flirting with someone.

Charles did a worse job of keeping his composure, and a chuckle escaped him. "I wonder how uncomfortable that made him," he said.

Chief Mathers adjusted himself in his seat as Audrina cast her gaze down the length of his body. He cleared his throat and averted his eyes from her in an attempt to make sure she didn't think he was interested.

Then, he pulled out another document.

"Audrina," he said.

"Red," she corrected him.

"Alright, Red," he said with a pained voice. "I have some evidence here that suggests Mr. Davis was attempting to get full custody of your son, Jason."

Audrina's demeanor changed entirely. A scowl crossed her face, and she clenched her jaw. "That's right," she said, folding her arms. "After all those years, he suddenly decided he wanted to get involved in Jason's life."

"I believe that this caused quite a problem between the two of you," he continued.

"A problem?" Audrina scoffed. "That's an understatement. Not only was he coming for my son but for my reputation."

"Would you tell us what happened?" Chief Mathers asked.

Audrina rolled her eyes in a similar fashion to Mrs. Davis. It occurred to Avery that not only did both Audrina and Collette have the same taste in men, but Cederic had married two women who were pretty identical in behavior.

"I left my son at home for a weekend by himself," Audrina said. "I had to be somewhere, and Cederic had made it clear to me that he wasn't available. So, what choice did I have?"

"And that upset Cederic?" Chief Mathers asked.

"Yes," she snapped. "He tried to say that I was an unfit mother for leaving our son at home alone without any care and no guardian. But it's not as if Jason is a young child. He's a teenager, and he is perfectly capable of taking care of himself."

"So, it got pretty ugly, huh?" Chief Mathers asked as he took notes.

"Uglier than it should have," Audrina said. "He was just trying to hurt me. But it wouldn't have worked. I'm sure he knew that."

"You seem pretty certain of that," Chief Mathers remarked.

"Because I am," she responded. "Jason has made it clear that he would never actually choose to live with his father full-time. And he had a great time without me around. He played video games and ordered takeout."

"But Mr. Davis felt there was cause for concern?" Chief Mathers asked.

"He became convinced that Jason had a party while I was gone," Audrina said. "He claims a bunch of his friends came over and got into my booze. But I tried to tell him that there was no booze missing. I had drunk all that was missing from those bottles."

"Jason is a good kid?"

"An amazing kid!" Audrina said. "I really don't know how I got so lucky. Jason really is a mother's dream child."

"Well, we have reason to believe that you left threatening messages on the Davis' answering machine. Is that true?" Chief Mathers asked.

"I have nothing to hide," Audrina said with a shrug. "I left him some threatening messages, sure, but I never threatened to murder him. I just threatened some cheap shots, like suing him for defamation and things like that. And I would never have followed through with it. That's way too much paperwork."

"What was the purpose of those threats, then?" Chief Mathers asked.

"I wanted to upset him," Audrina said with a smirk. "And it worked. He had upset me greatly, and I just wanted to make sure he also felt some of it."

Chief Mathers quietly wrote it all down, cross-referencing parts to other notes that he had taken. And something about how much he was writing was making Audrina uncomfortable. She nibbled nervously at her nails.

"I can get a little crazy sometimes when I'm angry," she admitted. "I can admit that some of those messages were unnecessary and cruel. But I would never actually hurt the father of my child. I had no reason to. The custody battle would not have gone his way, anyway."

"We'll look into that, too," Chief Mathers said calmly. "But for now, I think we have enough here. As with all our suspects, I have to ask you not to leave town until the investigation is complete."

Audrina released a deep, pent-up breath. "Of course," she said. "Whatever I can do to help. You have my number, right?"

"We do indeed," he answered.

"Well, feel free to call me anytime, for any reason," she said with a wink.

And with that, the questioning came to an end, and she was sent home.

Chapter Nine

The coffee was flowing and steaming from their cups as they joined each other in the boardroom to discuss the interrogations that had occurred that day. Chief Mathers looked exhausted, and Charles was scratching his head in thought.

There were a few other officers there too, and they waited patiently for somebody else to start talking first.

"We have two suspects," Chief Mathers started. "Both with motives, and neither of them has a provable alibi. So, where do we go from here?"

"I suppose we need to look into their lives and relationships, and perhaps ask their friends and loved ones some questions too?" an officer said.

"That's our best option right now," Chief Mathers said. "Gather some officers and make sure you get on that. I want a report as soon as possible, and let me know immediately if you learn anything interesting." The officer nodded and left the room.

"I can't get a good read on either of them, to be honest," Chief Mathers said. "Normally, I have a gut feeling when I'm in the room with the murderer, but here I feel completely torn between the two."

Avery thought about each of them, and in her mind, she tried to choose which one was her pick of the day. However, just like Chief Mathers, she couldn't decide. It felt like an odd thing to contemplate, and Avery quickly spiraled into a thought of how anyone could make the choice whether another person gets to live or die when she couldn't even decide in secret who she thought should go to prison.

But that, she understood, was the only difference between normal humans and murderers.

"They're both blaming each other, too," Charles said. "Which means either both of them are wrong or one of them is lying."

Chief Mathers let out an agreeable, "Mmm."

"I think it's a little telling that Audrina left the funeral so early," Avery added. "And when she spoke to me in the wine room, she showed no grief for Mr. Davis at all. That's why I decided to tell you about our conversation. It just seemed odd."

"I don't think it's that odd," Charles said. "I think there are many divorced men and women who would feel the same way."

"I agree with Charles," Chief Mathers said. "I don't think it's strange. She clearly had hard feelings toward him, and as she said, she didn't want to attend at all. She did it for her son and left when she got uncomfortable."

"I think the strangeness is how eager both women seem to be to pin this murder on each other," Charles said. "They clearly have bad blood, despite being rather similar in nature."

"Yes," Chief Mathers said. "But I don't think it's that odd for them to point fingers at each other. It's a normal thing to see the current wife and ex-wife behave that way about each other."

It occurred to Avery at that moment that, despite her life's complications, her life really hadn't been that complicated at all. Her husband had died in a boating accident. There were no interrogations or investigations. She only needed to grieve, and for the first time, she felt almost fortunate that it had been that simple.

"I think I have something interesting," Charles said, pulling Avery from her thoughts. "I found it while I was looking into Mr. Davis' life."

Chief Mathers put his empty cup down on the table. "Well, I'm eager to hear anything that might be of help."

Charles reached into his briefcase and pulled out a newspaper from a few weeks ago.

"For the first time in my life, I was grateful for the stack of old newspapers that I keep at my back door," he said with a chuckle. "Take a look at this article."

He placed a copy of the local newspaper on the table, and on the front page was the news that Cederic Davis had won the local cycling race. There was a photograph of the victor smiling widely with his gold medal around his neck.

Avery scanned the article and learned he had won by quite a fair distance and had broken a record in the meantime as well. Chief Mathers glanced through the article, too, and didn't seem too impressed with anything that he had read.

"I don't understand what this has to do with the case," Chief Mathers said.

"Take a look at the photograph," Charles said. "Look at the others and tell me what you see."

Avery peered over the table and spotted what Charles had been referring to.

"The red ribbon," Avery said, pointing at the man in second place.

Charles smiled widely. "You're getting good at this," he said.

Chief Mathers reached for the paper and lifted it off the table. His brow furrowed as he searched for his reading glasses so he could get a better look.

"I see the red ribbon," he said. "But that can't possibly mean that he has committed this murder. That's a bit of a stretch."

Charles took the paper and turned a few pages. "Well, this is where it gets a little more interesting."

On the fifth page of the newspaper was another article about the race, in which Cederic Davis was being accused of cheating. It was a small-town race. It wasn't monitored as well as the larger races in the city, and other racers claimed that Cederic had veered off course and taken a shortcut while nobody was looking.

It was an old-fashioned way of cheating in a race, but life in small towns could largely be old-fashioned at times. There seemed to be multiple people who claimed they had seen him cheating at the race, but the organizers had stated they had no way of proving that he had.

Some were calling for his medal to be taken from him, and the largest spokesperson for that was Gregory Marsh, who had come in second.

"Gregory Marsh," Charles said, "stated in this article that he wanted to see Cederic pay for what he had done."

Chief Mathers scratched his head. "It's unfortunate, and they're likely right that he did cheat. It is rather unusual for anyone to beat a record by so much. But that isn't really a motive, is it? Murder seems a little excessive for Gregory."

Charles shrugged. "There are many stories of his short temper," he explained. "I looked into Gregory and learned that several of his ex-girl-friends have said he has a very short temper. Apparently, he can lose his patience in a heartbeat. There are even rumors going around that Gregory is using performance-enhancement drugs."

"Can that be proven as fact?" Chief Mathers asked.

"Well, I spoke to one girlfriend who is willing to sign a formal state-ment to say that she saw him administer the drugs into his system before a race. Apparently, he is aiming for the big leagues and wants to win at all costs."

"Well, I'd like to have a word with her if you'd invite her here?" Chief Mathers said. "And in the meantime, why don't we go get Gregory and bring him back here for questioning?"

"Sounds like a good idea to me," Charles said.

Avery gulped down the last of her coffee. If she was going to watch a third interrogation for that day, then she needed all the coffee she could get. She and Charles got into his car and followed the police over to Gregory's house.

His house was a large, brick-face home. But there wasn't all that much to look at. Unlike the other lush yards in the town, Gregory's home was devoid of all bright colors. All she saw were bricks and one perfectly mani-cured patch of lawn.

Chief Mathers walked up the driveway and toward the front door, and behind him were two officers. They knocked on the door and waited. But there was no answer. So, they knocked again and again, there was no answer.

Avery was so focused on waiting for the front door to open that she hadn't noticed a neighbor approach the window on the passenger side of

Charles' car. When the woman knocked, Avery's heart leaped out of her chest, and she had to cover her mouth not to scream from fright.

When Avery had regained her composure, she opened the window, and the elderly lady all but stuck her face right into the car.

"What are the police doing here?" the woman asked.

"We're just looking for Mr. Marsh," Charles answered with a smile.

The elderly lady shrugged. "I haven't seen him around here in a few days," she answered. "We were wondering where he went. Thought maybe he went on a vacation."

Charles sighed. "You really haven't seen him?"

The woman shook her head. "Not his car or his bike, and no lights on at night. Is he in some kind of trouble?"

"We're just trying to get hold of him, that's all," Charles answered.

The woman nodded and smiled, and with a short wave, she left the car. Avery caught her breath.

"She came out of nowhere," she said with wide eyes.

Charles chuckled. "I got a fright too," he said. "Mine just wasn't quite as obvious. Let's go tell the chief that he isn't here."

Avery and Charles got out of the car and walked up to the front door. Some of the officers had gone around to peer through some of the windows.

"He's not here," Charles said. "The neighbor just told us that nobody has seen him for a few days."

Chief Mathers called the officers back. "We need to get through this door and search the house," he said. "We need to make sure that he isn't in here."

"I found an open window," one of the officers said, pointing to one side of the house. "We can get through there."

Chief Mathers nodded, and Avery watched as two officers disappeared into the house. They returned a few minutes later with the news that Gregory wasn't there, but all of his furniture and belongings still were.

"It looks as if he might have packed a few items of clothing, but that's about it," one of the officers said.

"Do you think he made a run for it?" Chief Mathers asked nobody in particular.

"It's possible," Charles said. "If he's been taking performance-enhancement drugs, then some level of erratic behavior isn't hard to believe."

"We need to find him," Chief Mathers instructed.

~

When Avery got home, she had a fair amount of work to catch up on, but she found it hard to do. Her mind was filled with the idea of a murderous man on the run.

There were three suspects, all with a motive and all with a connection to the red ribbon in the victim's mouth. When she got into bed that night, she struggled to sleep. Gregory could have been anywhere, and any sound that she heard sounded to her like a murderer had been hiding out on her property.

By the time the sun came out, she was exhausted and wished she could take just one day off. But as her business grew, her free time became less and less. Most days, she loved the hustle and bustle of her life, but some days she wanted nothing more than to stay in bed and sip hot chocolate all day.

Chapter Ten

By the next morning, there was a team of officers out looking for Gregory Marsh, the cyclist they suspected had gone on the run. And despite the increasing workload that Avery needed to attend to, she was at the police station again.

Charles had let her know early that Kendall Griffin, one of Gregory's friends, had agreed to speak about him to Chief Mathers. Charles couldn't be there. He needed to work in the tasting room, but Avery didn't want to miss it. She needed to know about Gregory's character. Questions about it had been keeping her up all night.

Chief Mathers handed Avery a cup of coffee as they entered the boardroom.

"I don't know how you take it," Chief Mathers said as he handed the coffee over to Avery. "But I brought some sugar and some cream on the side."

Avery reached for one sugar and stirred it in with some cream while Chief Mathers paid close attention. "I'll remember that for our coffee appointment in a few days' time," he said with a smile.

"Thank you for the coffee," Avery said softly as she took her first sip.

Chief Mathers gave her a friendly smile. It was a kind smile that she hadn't seen on him before, and for a moment, he looked like a totally different person.

"Thank you for agreeing to come and talk to us about Gregory," Chief Mathers greeted Kendall as an officer led her into the room.

"Of course," she said. "I'm just not sure what all of this is about."

"We just want to know a little more about him; he is a person of interest in a case that we're working on," Chief Mathers said.

Kendall didn't say it out loud, but Avery could see in her expression that she had already pieced it together.

"Were the two of you close friends?" Chief Mathers asked.

Kendall tucked her hair behind her ear and laughed nervously. "Yes, but Greg and I also dated for a short while, unfortunately," she said.

"It wasn't a good relationship?"

"It was alright for the most part, but he would have these intense mood swings," she explained. "One moment he would be sweet and romantic and understanding, and the next minute, he would lose his mind over the smallest thing."

"In that case, I am glad you got out of the relationship," Chief Mathers said calmly.

"His mood swings were why we split," she continued. "He asked me to move in with him, and I told him that I wasn't quite ready yet. He started screaming and shouting at me, accusing me of seeing other men and being unfaithful. It was too much for me. So, I ended things."

"Was he ever physically violent?" Chief Mathers asked.

Kendall shrugged. "He never hurt me or anyone that I know of," she said. "But he would break plates and throw things around sometimes. Projectile anger, if you will."

Chief Mathers and Avery both took extensive notes.

"Were the two of you dating at the time of the cycle race?" Chief Mathers asked.

Kendall nodded. "Yes, I was there on the sidelines, cheering him on."

"What do you remember about that time with Mr. Marsh regarding the race?" he questioned.

The woman swallowed, and her eyelids fluttered slightly. "I had never seen Greg that angry. When it turned out that Cederic had cheated, he lost his temper completely. He wound up breaking one of his great grandmother's teacups that day."

"And is it your belief that Mr. Davis cheated during that race?" he asked.

"Oh, yeah," she laughed with an exaggerated nod. "I mean, everybody knows that. There's just no way he won that race and broke a record. At the time, he'd only been seriously cycling for a couple of months."

"Hmmm," Chief Mathers commented.

He sat quietly for a moment as Kendall took a sip of her coffee, and Avery followed her lead. The heat of the coffee warmed Avery's belly and made her forget completely about any of her stresses of that day.

"There are rumors that Mr. Marsh used performance-enhancing drugs. Do you know anything about that?" Chief Mathers asked.

Kendall glanced nervously around the room, her eyes catching Avery's for only a second as she put her coffee cup down.

"It's alright," Chief Mathers said. "Everything you say to me stays in this room. You have our full confidence."

"Um," Kendall said nervously. "He was definitely using something like that."

"Is there some way you can confirm this?" he asked.

"Well, other than saying I saw him do it once, not really," she answered. "I caught him with the injection once when I got to his house early. I asked him about it, and he said he needed it to get ahead. He wanted to do this big international race and felt like he needed the extra help." Her voice quivered slightly as she spoke. "We had a huge argument about it," she said. "But it puts his mood swings into perspective. I didn't feel comfortable confronting him about it again."

"So, Mr. Marsh wasn't good with confrontation?" Chief Mathers asked.

"Not at being confronted, no," she answered. "But he had no problem confronting others."

"Mr. Marsh was pretty vocal about how he felt toward Mr. Davis when the rumors began about him cheating," Chief Mathers said. "Do you think it's possible that he confronted Mr. Davis?"

"Oh, absolutely," Kendall said without hesitation. "He was furious at him. I am certain he would have made an effort to talk to him about it."

And it wouldn't surprise me if Greg got entirely worked up in the process."

"You don't perhaps know if Mr. Marsh has gone away or anything like that?" Chief Mathers asked.

"No," she answered. "I stopped talking to Greg a few weeks ago. But he's not much of a traveler. He prefers to stay home."

"Thank you," Chief Mathers said as he put his pen down. "I think that's all we need from you today. Why don't I walk you out?"

Kendall happily accepted his offer, and Avery followed the two of them out of the boardroom. She was eager to go home and get started on the huge stack of paperwork that urgently needed her attention. But before any of them could make it to the front door of the station, an elderly lady stood up and greeted Chief Mathers by his first name.

"Mrs. Sutton, what are you doing here?" he asked.

"I've been waiting for you," she said with a shaky voice. "I need to speak with you about something."

Chief Mathers saw Kendall out and turned his attention back to Mrs. Sutton. She wore a floral skirt and pressure socks. Her bony hands clutched her walker as she smiled widely at Chief Mathers.

"I hope I am not bothering you," she said.

"Not at all," he answered kindly. "You're my mother's best friend. I'll always have time for you. Could I get you a cup of tea, perhaps?"

Mrs. Sutton shook her head. "No, thank you," she said. "I won't stay that long. There was just something I thought I should mention to you about this mess at the cheese shop."

Chief Mathers glanced up at Avery. She had thought about leaving the two of them there, but now she couldn't. She wanted to know if there was any more information.

"Anything you have, Mrs. Sutton, I'd love to hear it," Chief Mathers said.

"Well, I was at the shop recently," she said, placing a hand on his arm. "And there was a big argument going on between Cederic and one of the boys who works in his shop."

"Do you know what the argument was about?" he asked.

Mrs. Sutton nodded and cleared her throat. "Yes," she said shakily. "The boy was being fired by the sounds of it. From what I could gather, he had come in late too many times. I remember seeing that boy behind the counter for years. I can imagine it must have been awfully disappointing for him."

"Was it an intense argument?" Chief Mathers asked.

"Oh, yes," she answered with wide eyes. "That young boy was shouting all sorts of profanities at Cederic. It was so terrible to see a young man behaving so badly."

"Do you know his name?" Chief Mathers asked.

Mrs. Sutton shook her head. "No," she said. "But I can tell you he was tall, with blonde hair and brown eyes. Blonde curly hair—so gorgeous! I've only ever seen him in his uniform, though... that red apron which he always tied in a perfect red bow behind his back. It looked like a ribbon on a present!"

Mrs. Sutton chuckled, but both Avery and Chief Mathers understood the red ribbon reference that she had unknowingly made. Avery was making notes when Chief Mathers couldn't. She made sure not to leave out a single detail.

"But what a terrible boy," Mrs. Sutton continued. "The next day, when I'd come back, I saw Cederic cleaning some spray paint off the windows. He said that the boy had spray-painted something awfully rude on the windows. I thought it better not to ask and minded my own business."

"I see," Chief Mathers said calmly.

"I just thought I'd tell you about it, you know, with the murder and all. I thought you might find it interesting," she continued.

"That really is very helpful, Mrs. Sutton," he said.

"Well, I'll leave you to it, then," she said.

The two said goodbye, and Mrs. Sutton returned to her daughter who was waiting to take her back home. Avery tore the page from her notebook and handed it to Chief Mathers.

"Thanks," he said with a sigh. "Why don't I make a copy, and then we can both use these notes?"

"Sounds good," Avery answered.

She was about to leave when Chief Mathers checked his watch.

"Avery," he said, stopping her. "I have some time. Would you like to move our coffee appointment and go get a cup with me right now?"

Avery checked the time. There would be no difference if she lost a little more time, so she agreed, and the two headed across the street to the coffee shop.

She had anticipated talking about the case or about the book. That's all they had spoken about before. Instead, they spoke about everything else. She learned about Chief Mather's son, and he learned about her life the way it was in the city.

Chief Mathers laughed easily at her jokes and smiled widely the entire time. It was unusual for Avery to see him that way. She had only ever seen him as the chief and not as someone who could potentially be a friend.

"Thank you for the cup of coffee and the interesting conversation, Chief," Avery said as they exited the coffee shop.

"Adrian," he said kindly. "You can call me Adrian; I think we know each other well enough by now."

"I suppose so," Avery said happily. "Well, I'll see you soon, I guess, Adrian."

He smiled, and before she could stop him, he wrapped his arms around her for a hug. Avery didn't get many hugs, and she certainly hadn't expected to get one from the chief of police, but she happily accepted it.

"Well, I better get running," she said. "I have so much to do, and I am expecting the Stammtisch at my home for lunch later."

"I hope you enjoy it," he said. "Charles has said only great things about your cooking. Perhaps one day I'll be fortunate to enjoy it myself."

"Maybe I'll have a great big dinner party!" she said excitedly.

The two bid each other farewell, and Avery went home and dove into her paperwork. But she struggled to concentrate. The case had made so much progress, and yet they were nowhere near capturing the murderer.

Chapter Eleven

B usy in the kitchen, Avery chopped all the ingredients she would need for her famous "nacho regular nachos" she was making for the Stammtisch ladies. She'd been looking forward to this casual and nontraditional lunch all week.

Avery was still preparing for lunch when Charles knocked on her door. He had finished his work day and was eager to hear about the talk with Gregory's friend. Avery caught him up on it all, and he listened carefully.

Charles wore a frown that Avery recognized; it meant that he was thinking so hard that any moment he would ask her for a coffee so he could focus his thoughts again.

"Any chance of a coffee?" he asked on cue.

Avery smiled and nodded as she reached for a coffee cup.

"The food smells sooo good, by the way," he said. "Can't I stay?"

"No," Avery teased. "It's for the Stammtisch."

"Then let me join the Stammtisch!" Charles argued.

"I can't," she argued back. "It's for women."

Charles smiled cheekily. "I could pull off a wig, don't you think?"

Avery laughed loudly. "Speaking of coffee," she said. "I went for that coffee with Adrian today."

"Adrian?" Charles asked blandly. "Since when do you call him Adrian?"

"Since today," she said with a smile. "What a friendly man outside of work, don't you think? It was so pleasant to talk to him and get to know more about him. I think he and I could be good friends."

Charles cleared his throat and glanced down. "On second thought, Avery, cancel that coffee. I forgot I have someplace to be."

His mood had changed instantly, and Avery wasn't entirely sure why. But it seemed to be a repeating pattern any time that she mentioned Chief Mathers in conversation. Before she could argue, Charles was out the door, and she stood there with an empty coffee cup in hand.

But a few hours later, it had all been forgotten as Avery and the women of the Stammtisch enjoyed a glass of port with their strawberry cheesecake—a perfectly refreshing dessert post-nachos.

"How is everything going with the vineyard and the books and everything?" Deb asked. It was a question that was impossible to answer as simply as it had been asked.

"It's going alright," Avery said. "It's a lot of work, but it gives purpose to my day."

"I see there has been some construction," Eleanor added. "I'd recognize those tire tracks anywhere!"

"Yes," Avery said. "I'm building a large pond. It's still very much a work in progress, but would you like to see it?"

Eleanor beamed. "Oooh, yes!"

"Who fancies a walk?" Avery offered the rest of the group.

With their glasses in hand and Sprinkles cheerfully trotting alongside, they walked the path to the center of the vineyard to behold the construction still underway. Avery wasn't kidding. There wasn't much more than a hole in the ground at that moment. But she could see what it was eventually supposed to be.

"What's the purpose of it?" Eleanor asked.

"I want to have some wine-tasting tables around the water," Avery explained. "Don't you think it will be so pretty and romantic?"

"Definitely," Deb sighed. "But you already have your hands so full; where are you going to find time for this as well?"

Avery shrugged. "I'll make it happen. You sound like Charles now.

He's always worried about how much I work. I told him last week that he's beginning to sound like my father."

The four other women of the Stammtisch all glanced at each other knowingly. Then Eleanor began to chuckle. "Be careful of that," she said.

Avery frowned. "Of what?"

"Well, one minute they're concerned about your well-being, and the next minute you're tying the knot!" she cried.

"Oh, please, don't be ridiculous," Avery said with a scoff.

"I'm not being ridiculous," Eleanor said. "I'm talking from experience. That's how it started with me and Samuel. One day he was worried about my stress levels, and before I knew it, we were engaged and soon after happily married."

Avery didn't like where the conversation was going, not one bit. She hadn't seen Charles in that light, as someone who cared for her in that way, and she wasn't sure she wanted to.

"I really don't think there's anything like that to be worried about," Avery said.

"Eleanor's right," Camille said in a rare event of her speaking. "That happened to my mother, too. She met this guy down at the post office, and he helped her with her shopping bags. She walks with a walker, and he didn't want her to struggle. They were married a year later."

"Oh, dear," Tiffany said. "I don't think I'm ready for another wedding yet."

"There isn't going to be another wedding," Avery whined. "Never mind. My point was that I have enough staff who I trust in other parts of the vineyard to take over and run those areas. I will have more than enough time for the pond."

The women all giggled among themselves. But Avery continued with the tour, nonetheless, showing them all the places where she intended to make pathways and hang lights. She even had plans for a small stage in the future where local musicians could come and serenade those who were enjoying Le Blanc Cellars' latest offerings.

"Looks to me like you're building quite an empire for yourself here," Eleanor said.

"I guess you could put it that way," Avery said. "There's just so much here that I want to share with everyone."

Tiffany smiled. "This pond is going to do well," she said. "I can tell. Will there be ducks?"

"Of course!" Avery said. "What is a pond without ducks?"

"Maybe you should put a table out in the center of the pond," Deb suggested. "Or somewhere where people can get married out in the middle of the water. You know...speaking of weddings and all that."

There was another giggle amongst the women. But, to Avery, it wasn't a bad idea. She imagined elaborate weddings where the bride and groom stood in the center of a well-lit pond as they tied the knot. It would certainly put Le Blanc Cellars on the map.

"I'll definitely give that some consideration," Avery said cheerfully as she continued her walk around the pond.

Sprinkles weaved between their feet as they walked, threatening to bring them all down to the ground. And before Avery could stop him, he ran into the dirt pit and rolled around in the recently loosened dirt. By the time Sprinkles stood back up, the once golden retriever was now a muddy brown retriever.

Avery sighed as she watched him happily dirty himself even more. She was torn. She loved Sprinkles and wanted him to have as much fun in his short life as he possibly could. But she wasn't particularly in the mood to bathe him when she got back home.

It didn't really matter, though. It was too late. He was already filthy. He might as well get dirtier. And as she watched Sprinkles enjoy himself in the pit, she thought of what the women had said about her and Charles and decided to laugh it off.

The notion that she needed anyone in her life other than Sprinkles just seemed completely absurd to her. Still, she couldn't quite get it out of her mind. She worried that Charles might actually feel that way about her. It would certainly change things.

She had no idea how to go about finding out what his true feelings were. And at that moment, she decided to leave the entire thought alone. She didn't need to listen to the women of the Stammtisch. Although they made many valid points, they didn't know everything.

She just couldn't imagine moving on from James. He had been there for so much of her life, and she had only just gotten used to not having him around. And when they had been together, she'd never dreamed of a life when he wouldn't be there. All their future milestones dashed in an instant.

Even when he drove her absolutely mad, it was the kind of mad that she enjoyed because she knew that she only felt so angry at him because of the immense amount of love that lurked behind her frustration.

Avery accidentally sighed out loud.

"What's that about?" Tiffany asked quietly.

"Oh, nothing," Avery said, trying to think of something to say. "Just thinking about having to bathe Sprinkles. Look at him! He's filthy!"

Despite feeling as if she had done a good enough job, Tiffany gave her a look that would lead her to believe otherwise. They'd been friends for most of Avery's life, so it was only expected that she'd know when Avery was lying.

"Oh, I can just picture it all!" Deb said excitedly. "I can see soft lights in the darkness, and I can hear the water of the pond and the clinking of the glasses. This is really going to be something special, Avery."

"Thank you, Deb," Avery said with a smile. "I think I should have a party to help celebrate its opening. You know I love a good party. I expect all of you to be there."

"Of course!" Eleanor said as Camille nodded silently.

And at that point, most of the women decided it was time for them to go. The walk had successfully quelled the effects of the wine, and they were starting to yawn.

"I think I better get going," Eleanor said. "There's a movie that I'd like to see tonight. But it's starting to feel like I might fall asleep halfway through it."

"Me too," said Deb. "I need to phone my parents. They're on vacation, and the time difference is just a nightmare. Two days ago, my mother phoned me at three o'clock in the morning!"

Avery looked out over the horizon and saw a familiar cloud pattern. She knew that it meant there would be an impressive sunset. She also knew that she didn't really want to miss it.

"Are you sure you don't want to stay and watch the sunset?" Avery asked. "We could get a top-up and find a place to sit here."

"Oh, no," Eleanor said. "If I have another glass, then I am going to fall asleep out here. I better get going."

"Me too," said Deb. "I don't want to miss this phone call; otherwise it will happen again at some insane hour of the night."

"I'm also going to get going," Camille said quietly without any explanation.

"Alright then," Avery laughed.

They walked back to her house. Once they walked through the door, Tiffany finally piped up. "I'll stay for the sunset."

"Awesome!" Avery said. "I was beginning to think it would only be me."

"I wasn't going to," Tiffany said. "But I think it's going to be impressive. I'll fill our glasses, and we better be quick if we still want to see it."

Avery and Tiffany eagerly bade their friends farewell and took their filled wine glasses back out toward the pond. And as they waited for the sunset, Sprinkles chased the last few butterflies of the season as they fluttered about tiredly.

"You know it's alright if you and Charles care about each other in that way," Tiffany said kindly. "Nobody really cares."

Avery rolled her eyes. "It's nothing like that, Tiff," she said. "He's probably just being grouchy like he can get from time to time."

"What I mean is, it's alright for you to move on from James," Tiffany said. "I know it can be tough, but nobody would think anything of it."

"I would," Avery said. "And besides, Charles just isn't that kind of person for me. Anyway, he's been acting so strangely lately."

"Strange how?" Tiffany asked.

"Every time I bring up Adrian, he gets kind of sour about it. There's something not so right between the two of them, I think," she said.

Tiffany laughed. "I agree, and I think I can tell you what it is," she said. Tiffany's eyes lit up like a child who had just spotted their favorite candy on the shelf. And her cheeks turned red from laughter.

"Oh?"

Tiffany nudged Avery in the ribs lightly. "He's jealous," she said.

"Oh, don't be ridiculous," Avery snapped.

Chapter Twelve

"It's the furthest thing from ridiculous," Tiffany said. "Even you have to see it, Avery."

"I just don't think you're right," Avery argued.

"Oh, come on," Tiffany laughed. "You told me the other day how weirdly he behaved when Chief Mathers offered to buy you a coffee. It started there."

"Well, what's there to be jealous of anyway?" Avery asked.

Tiffany took a sip of her wine. "Tell me about the coffee that you had with Chief Mathers. How did it go?"

Avery thought back to it as she sipped her wine too. "We just had a pleasant time," she shrugged. "Adrian and I got to know each other a little more outside of just working through old case files. I learned a bit about him as the man without the badge."

"Precisely," Tiffany said.

But Avery still didn't quite understand.

"You can't be that blind, Avery," Tiffany said. "Charles thinks the two of you went on a date! And I wouldn't be surprised if Chief Mathers thinks the same way!"

"It was *not* a date!" Avery argued.

"When was the last time you even went on a first date?" Tiffany teased. "Would you even still be able to identify one?"

Avery gasped in shock. She hadn't been on a first date since the one that she and her husband had gone on. And that was a very long time ago. Tiffany might have been right in saying that Avery wouldn't even know she was on one. It had been that long.

She was about to argue back again when Sprinkles started barking incessantly at the fence that bordered the vineyard. He made such noise that Avery got up to inspect what it was that was bothering him so.

Avery walked toward the fence, and in the background, Tiffany was still laughing at her. She did feel a little embarrassed at the thought that she might have unknowingly accepted a date with Chief Mathers and that it might have been the reason why Charles was behaving so strangely about it.

She approached Sprinkles who was clearly barking at something on the other end of the fence line. She looked out over the neighboring property to see if there was some kind of animal there that Sprinkles might have been barking at, but the sunset was so bright that all she could see was a silhouette of the horizon. But as the sun lowered even further, she noticed an unusual shape on the ground. It took her eyes a moment to focus, but when they did, she spotted what seemed to be a makeshift tent on the neighboring land.

There was some material propped up on some poles and sticks. Outside were signs of a fire and an old burned-out pot. There was even some laundry hanging on a nearby tree to dry. She hadn't seen it before, not that she often peered out over the fence like that. But it seemed to have been there quite some time. She motioned with her hand for Tiffany to come and take a look and signaled to her to move quietly. Tiffany got up from her seat, and with both her wine and Avery's wine in hand, she tiptoed carefully so as not to spill a drop.

She pointed at the tent, and Tiffany stared at it with big eyes. "Who do you think is staying there?" Tiffany whispered.

"I don't know, but it's private property. Whoever it is, they shouldn't be there," Avery said.

"Maybe the owner of that property knows about it?" Tiffany whispered back.

Avery shook her head. "He's been abroad for a few months," she answered.

"We need to find out who it is," Tiffany said.

Avery didn't have the chance to stop her. Within moments, Tiffany had raised her voice as loud as she could.

"We've found your tent!" she yelled as Avery tried desperately to shush her. "Hello?! Helloooooo! Is there anybody home?" Tiffany struggled to get the last sentence out without laughing. And Avery wanted to run away.

"Maybe they're not there anymore," Avery said with a hint of relief when the tent remained quiet.

"No way they left their laundry behind," Tiffany said. Avery watched as Tiffany filled her lungs in preparation to shout again. "If you're in there, just come out. We won't report you or anything!"

Avery nudged her. "Why are you saying that?" she whispered. "Of course, we're going to report them."

"Okay, never mind!" Tiffany shouted through stifled laughs. "Come out! We're definitely going to report you!"

Avery covered her eyes with her hand and sighed. But then the tent started to rustle and shuffle, and out stepped a man with a beard and some dirt on his face. He seemed entirely sunburned and as if he hadn't eaten well in quite some time.

But there was something familiar in his eyes. Avery gasped. "Gregory Marsh," she said, recognizing him from the newspaper article.

"Do I know you?" he responded.

"No," Avery said. "But I recognize you from a picture in the news... about the cycle race."

"Greg?" Tiffany asked as she squinted into the sun. "Is that you?"

"Hi, Tiffany," he said cheerfully.

"You two know each other?" Avery asked.

"Kind of," Tiffany answered with a shrug.

"We met once at a copywriting class," he added.

Tiffany snorted. "The girls are going to be so mad that they missed all of this," she said as she reached for her phone.

Tiffany immediately began typing to the Stammtisch group about what had happened after they left. But she obviously didn't understand the true gravity of the situation. Avery stared at Gregory in disbelief. He looked like half the man he was on the front of that newspaper. And what was he doing all the way out there?

There were so many questions that she had for him, but she knew Chief Mathers needed to be the one to ask them. And now Gregory knew that she knew where he was. Avery didn't know what to do but decided that the simplest option was best.

"What are you doing all the way out here?" Avery asked, trying to seem as friendly as possible.

Gregory brushed his unruly hair out of his face. "I've been living here for a short while," he answered, looking somewhat embarrassed. "It's been rather peaceful, actually."

"Out here?" Tiffany asked. "Surely you don't have to come all the way out here and live in a tent to find peace?"

Gregory shrugged.

"Mr. Marsh," Avery said, getting his attention. "Are you aware that the police are looking for you?"

He stretched his eyes wide. "The police?" he asked. "What for?"

It had occurred to Avery at that moment that perhaps Gregory wasn't all that well in his mind. And for that, she decided to simply tell him the truth. Somehow, she felt that it would all work out better that way.

"They want to talk to you," she said. "It's about the murder of Cederic Davis."

Gregory looked as if he was going to fall over from shock. He held onto one of the poles that held up his tent and threatened to bring his home crashing to the ground.

"He-he's been murdered?" he asked.

Either he had no knowledge of it, or he was a gifted liar because Avery thought she saw genuine fear in his eyes.

"Unfortunately, yes," Avery said. "The police were at your house to look for you, and you weren't there. They think you're on the run."

"On the run?" he asked. "Oh no, no, no. I'm just out here. I'm not hiding from anybody but myself out here."

The more he spoke, the more nuts he sounded.

Avery could feel the buzzing in her pocket as Tiffany continued to text the sequence of events to the Stammtisch group. And the buzzing didn't seem to stop, either.

"Well, a neighbor said she hadn't seen you in a while," Avery explained. "And all your stuff was still at your house. It looked as if you had left rather quickly."

Gregory shook his head. "No, I had planned this for quite some time... to come out here. But when you live like this, you simply don't need much. That's all."

Avery was quite certain now that he was off his rocker. She looked at his tent and his clothes that hung to dry in a tree and wondered exactly how much planning really had gone into it and what kind of a person would actively choose to live like that.

She had seen his house in town. It was perfectly comfortable looking. His tent looked hardly big enough to fit him sleeping stretched out inside. His skin looked dry and sunburned, and his hair looked dirty and matted.

"Well, would you mind coming with us to the station then?" she asked kindly. "I'm sure it won't take long, and then you can return...home."

She looked over his shoulder at the tent again and wondered if he really would return home or if Chief Mathers would make him seek some kind of medical help.

"Of course!" he said. "I'll do anything to sort all this mess out."

"Right, well, I'll call us a cab then," she said. "We've been drinking, and we can't drive."

Gregory hopped the fence, and they made their way back to Avery's driveway just in time for the cab to arrive and take them to the police station. Avery offered to get a separate cab to take Tiffany home, but she refused. She wanted to see what was going to happen.

"Besides, maybe they need my statement, too," she said.

As soon as they were headed in the right direction, Avery picked up the phone and called Chief Mathers.

"Adrian," she said, which Tiffany immediately mimicked in a teasing manner. "I am on my way to the station, and I need you to meet me there."

"What's wrong?" he asked. "What's happened?"

"We're all fine," she said. "But we've found Gregory."

"What do you mean you've found him?" he asked in shock. "And who's we?"

"Tiffany and I," she explained. "It's a long story, but he was camping out on a neighbor's property. We're in a cab with him now and on the way to the station."

"You're in a cab with him?" Chief Mathers exclaimed. And it was so loud that Avery was sure Gregory could hear it. "You're in a cab with a man that we suspect of murder?"

When he put it that way, it didn't really sound like a good idea. But it was too late to change any of it, and she just needed to make sure they all remained calm.

"Yes," she said confidently. "Can you meet us there? He says he had no idea about the murder or the search party or anything."

"I'm already putting on my jacket," he answered. "I'll see you in a few."

Avery hung up the phone and did her best to inch a little further away from Gregory without being too obvious. Chief Mathers was right. She was seated next to someone who might have brutally taken another man's life not too long ago. She should have thought about that before she offered to escort him, though.

But Gregory was calm the entire drive to the station. And as he stared out the windows at the streets, Avery picked up her phone to call Charles.

"I'm already on my way," he grumbled.

"What?" Avery asked. "How did you even know?"

"Tiffany sent me a message," he said. "I suppose I don't have to tell you that it's a terrible idea to lock yourself in a car with a potential murderer, do I?"

The sarcasm in his voice was a clear indication that he was still grumpy from earlier that day. Avery felt a knot in her stomach. She just wanted everyone to get along. But for now, she just needed to make sure everyone in the car made it safely to the police station without winding up the same way that Cederic Davis did.

And for some reason, the drive seemed to be taking way longer than usual.

Chapter Thirteen

Chief Mathers had a hard time not letting his jaw drop when he saw Gregory Marsh walk through the front door of the police station. One thing became clear by the look on his face—he wasn't expecting the disheveled man that had been brought before him.

Within moments, Gregory was easily led into the interrogation room. Once again, Avery and Charles stood side by side as they watched the event unfold.

"They should put some chairs down here for us at this point," Avery teased.

But Charles only returned the joke with a disgruntled, "Mmm."

"Mr. Marsh," Chief Mathers began. "I have to ask. What are you doing all the way out there in that tent?"

Gregory brushed over his beard with his hand. All that was really visible about his expression was his eyes that stuck out between the hair on his head and the hair on his face.

He blinked a couple of times. "I suppose you could say I was trying to escape the world for a little while."

"Or possibly escape being arrested for murder," Charles mumbled.

One thing was clear to Avery—Gregory Marsh was not a healthy man. Whether that was in his body or in his mind, it wasn't yet clear. But he no longer looked anything like the fit man she'd seen photographed on the front of the newspaper.

He looked concerned but sat in a relaxed position. It was a confident stance, and it had Avery questioning whether or not he was really responsible for the murder.

"And what were you escaping from?" Chief Mathers asked.

Gregory took a deep breath. "I suppose you could say I had a breakdown. It was a mental, no, nervous, no...whatever they call it. I had one of those breakdowns."

"And so you ran away?" Chief Mathers didn't really sound very convinced.

"Well, at the point of the breakdown, I flew into a rage so terrible that I actually scared myself. I'd gotten angry before, you know, but I had never scared myself like that, and it had me questioning everything about myself. So, I decided to go camping."

"Well, there's a difference between going camping, Mr. Marsh, and escaping for days on end. So, which one were you doing?" Chief Mathers asked.

"It started out as a camping trip," he answered. "I only intended to go for two or three days to clear my head. But when those days came to an end, I found it difficult to convince myself to come back. I had gotten so used to the quiet and the peace out there. I wasn't ready to leave it yet."

"And what happened that scared you so much that you decided to run away?" Chief Mathers asked.

Gregory's leg started to bounce, and he was quickly becoming uncomfortable.

"I got angry at my mother," he answered. "And I left her a stream of threatening voice messages on her phone. I have never spoken to my mother like that, and I'm really embarrassed that I did."

"And that's the reason you went out camping?" Chief Mathers asked, unconvinced.

"The problem is not so much what I said or how I said it," Gregory answered. "Although, that was wrong too. The problem was that I had no recollection of ever having left those messages."

"You didn't remember doing it?" Chief Mathers asked.

"No," Gregory answered. "I went to visit my parents the next morning

CHAPTER THIRTEEN

as if nothing had happened. And when she played the messages to me, I couldn't believe I had said those things. It really scared me. What if I had acted out on one of those threats?" Gregory was getting emotional as he spoke about it. His eyes teared up, and there was a cracking sound in his voice.

"Do you think he could have murdered Mr. Davis and not remember it?" Avery asked.

"I think it's highly possible, but how do we prove that he doesn't remember?" Charles answered. "He could be lying about it right now in order to set himself up for what is to come."

"You think this is all an act?" she asked.

"I think it's entirely possible," he answered. "But it's too early to tell."

That possibility only made it all the more interesting to Avery, and she took a step closer to the glass. Gregory had turned his eyes down to his lap, where his fingers fiddled nervously with the hem of his shirt.

"It really scared me," he said, barely above a whisper.

"Do you understand that you are trespassing by camping out there where you were found?" Chief Mathers asked.

Gregory shook his head. "No," he said. "I know Robert, the owner of that property. He's away for a while, but I called him up and asked, and he said I was welcome to set up camp there on his property."

"I see," Chief Mathers said. "We'll have to call him and check that story."

"You're welcome to," Gregory said. "I'll leave his number with you."

"There's no need," Chief Mathers said. "I've known Robert for years. I'll give him a call after this."

"Oh, that's good," Gregory said.

Chief Mathers kept a close eye on Gregory and didn't take notes quite as often as with the other interrogations. Instead, on this occasion, he had a tape recorder on the table to record every one of Gregory's answers.

"Why does he have a tape recorder this time?" Avery asked.

"He must feel that Gregory is a strong suspect," Charles said. "He's keeping a close eye on his body language and wants to be able to listen back to this word-for-word."

"Gregory seems to be very comfortable answering questions," Avery said. "Isn't that unusual for a murderer being questioned?"

405

"Not necessarily," Charles said. "He might think it makes him look less suspicious. I've seen it done countless times before. Murderers think that if they're forthcoming and helpful in the case, then they'll seem less capable of the crime."

"I see," Avery said.

"And you still have access to your home?" Chief Mathers asked him.

"Absolutely," Gregory nodded.

"Well, Mr. Marsh, I'm going to ask you not to return to your tent," Chief Mathers said. "We need you to stay at home until all this is over. And I'm going to ask you not to leave town either."

"I understand," Gregory said with a nod. "Besides, when I passed that coffee pot in the hall, I suddenly realized that there's a lot I miss about being at home."

"Now, Mr. Marsh, I am going to ask you something rather personal," Chief Mathers said. "And I won't necessarily prosecute you for it."

"I'll answer any question you have for me, Chief," he answered.

"There are rumors that you have been using performance-enhancing drugs in order to be better at your sport," Chief Mathers said. "Is there truth to this statement?"

Gregory slumped his shoulders. "Yes," he said shamefully. "I was using it, and I think that's where the trouble began with all my rage. I suppose I thought I was the exception to the rule."

"And what do you mean by that?" Chief Mathers asked.

"I knew the risks when I started doping," he answered. "But I thought that it wouldn't happen to me. Or that I had a smarter way of doing it that wouldn't have the same effects. I suppose I was desperate and naïve."

"You thought it would be different for you?" Chief Mathers asked, confused.

"I just wanted to win so badly," Gregory said, tearing up again.

"And when was the last time that you spoke with Cederic Davis?" Chief Mathers asked.

Gregory sniffed back some tears. "I last spoke with him on the day of the race," he said. "I wasn't exactly nice to him, and he wasn't nice to me either. We exchanged some cruel words, and that was it."

"I have some people saying you threatened to teach him a lesson and that you were really angry at him for cheating at that race," Chief Mathers asked.

"Of course, I was angry!" Gregory answered. "He cheated me out of a win that was rightfully mine. I had put my body through so much to get there, and it was taken away by a cheat."

"Some would say your doping is cheating, too," Chief Mathers reminded him.

"I know," Gregory said, glancing down. "But as angry as I was at him, I never wanted to approach him about it again. I knew that I would likely hit him, and that might disqualify me from competing in the future. The risk was too great."

"And you didn't speak to him again?" Chief Mathers asked.

"No, but not for lack of trying," Gregory said. "I wanted to talk to him and convince him to confess. But he wouldn't answer or respond to my calls and messages. He just never got back to me again. So, eventually, I gave up."

"I see," Chief Mathers said, looking through his paperwork.

"I guess I just have one more thing I need to clarify with you then, Mr. Marsh," Chief Mathers said.

"Go ahead."

"Where were you on the night that he was murdered?" he asked. Chief Mathers slipped a photograph of the crime scene across the table and pointed at the date printed in the corner. Gregory's face went pale, and Avery thought he might be sick when he looked at it.

"Why didn't Chief Mathers just tell him the date?" she asked.

"He wants to see how Gregory reacts to the image of the crime scene," Charles answered. "You can tell a lot by that."

Gregory started to sweat slightly and looked away from the photograph.

"I, um, I was already camping at that point," Gregory answered. "I had been in the tent for about two days by then."

"And I am assuming there hasn't been anyone there with you who can confirm that?" Chief Mathers asked.

"Unfortunately not," Gregory answered. "I'm really sorry; I wish I could be of more help."

"Well, Mr. Marsh," Chief Mathers said. "You are currently a suspect in this murder, and because of that, we will be keeping a close eye on you. Is that understood?"

"Understood."

"And if, over the coming days, there is anything you can think of that might be helpful in proving your whereabouts on the night of the murder, do not hesitate to let us know."

"You have my word," Gregory said. "You'll be the first person I contact."

"Right, well, why don't you go home and get cleaned up, and we'll be in contact should we need you again," Chief Mathers said.

Gregory seemed to take the hint and left the police station quietly. As soon as he was out of earshot, Chief Mathers instructed two police officers to follow him home and make sure that was where he went. He then instructed another officer to put together a team to keep an eye on Gregory.

"Do you have officers watching Audrina and Collette too?" Avery asked.

"Of course," Chief Mathers said. "It's an odd situation we find ourselves in here."

Avery tilted her head and frowned. "How so?"

"There are three suspects, and none of them have a sound alibi," Charles answered on Chief Mathers' behalf. "It means that all three of them are viable."

"Yes," Chief Mathers said. "We can't rule any of them out, and each of them has a vastly different motive."

"Then there's the guy that got fired from the shop," Avery said. "He seemed like a possibility to me."

"Yes," the two men answered simultaneously.

Avery looked at them both and thought about what Tiffany had said. Could Charles really have been jealous of Chief Mathers? And had she accidentally gone on a date with the Chief of Police without really understanding what it was meant to be? She shook the thought from her head. It was ridiculous, anyway. And none of it mattered. She wasn't ready to move on.

Chapter Fourteen

I t was a particularly busy morning for Avery at the vineyard. Her
attention was required in various areas of the land, and she could feel
the exhaustion in her bones. But everything seemed to be going smoothly,
which only made her feel more confident in her business' future.

She had made the vineyard the most important thing in her life,
second only to Sprinkles. She was prepared to put everything she had into
it while she was still young enough to do so. Her parents had always
decided to wait for a better time to make changes in the business, and they
had gotten too old for it before they ever got the chance. Avery was terrified of that happening to her.

It was a gorgeous time of year in Los Robles. Rolling clouds and spots
of sunshine created a moody scene suitable for a magazine cover, and
Avery found herself getting lost in the views more and more often. She
had just arrived at the site for the future pond, and they were already
preparing to fill it with water when she received a text from Chief
Mathers.

> *We've got the employee from the cheese shop here for interrogation.*
> *Questioning begins in about forty minutes. You're welcome to watch*
> *it if you like.*

She thought about it for a moment. She had little time for anything extra in her day and was expecting Tiffany for a glass of wine later that afternoon. But she had become massively invested in the case and needed more substance for her book.

So, she let Chief Mathers know that she would be there. Forty minutes was too short notice, but she would do her best. With that, she left the pond behind and headed to the wine room to find Charles. He greeted her with a warm smile when she walked inside.

"How are things going here?" she asked as she motioned toward his new trainee assistant.

"Beth is catching on really quickly," Charles said proudly. "She's already done two perfect tastings and one almost perfect pairing today."

Avery smiled. That's exactly what she wanted to hear. She anticipated an increase in tasting visitors and needed to train more staff members in preparation for the pond's opening day. So, she had started hiring some trainees and placing them in Charles' care.

"And how is business here today?" she asked.

"A little on the quieter side, but I suppose this weather keeps threatening some rain. It is to be expected, isn't it?" Charles answered.

"Well, then, in that case, how does Beth feel about taking over here for a few hours?" Avery asked.

Charles shrugged. "Do you need me for something?"

"There's another interrogation happening, and I'd like to go. I've come to see if you'd like to go with me," she said. Charles didn't hesitate. He nodded, wished Beth good luck, and stepped out from behind the counter.

"She's going to be just fine," he said. "She's a smart girl and enjoys wine about as much as the rest of us do."

"That's good news for me!" Avery cheered as they hopped in her car.

Charles seemed cheerful about going with her to the interrogation, and on the way there, they briefly discussed how they thought it might go. Each prediction was vastly different and highly impossible.

"I think he'll confess if he's guilty," Charles said. "He's young and in over his head. Young people like that give in to pressure very easily. Chief Mathers just has to stare at him in an angry way, and he'll break."

"I don't know," Avery said. "If he was the one who did it, I'd be very surprised. I was thinking about it, and I'm not sure it was him."

"Just yesterday, you said he was a good suspect...why the change of heart?" Charles asked.

"It's the way Cederic was murdered," Avery said. "The guy who got fired was angry, and this doesn't strike me as an angry crime if that makes sense."

"I suppose," Charles said. "And you're right. When angry people murder, they make a mess of it. They stab multiple times or beat somebody worse than Cederic was."

"Exactly," Avery continued. "Cederic was hit once on the head, and that was the killer blow. Then, the murderer stopped hitting him."

"So, if it wasn't out of anger, then what emotion do you think was behind it?" Charles asked.

"It seems...vindictive to me," Avery said. "It feels like somebody simply had enough of him and decided to take him out of the world."

"If it's not anger, then would it be the cyclist?" Charles asked.

"His motive would have been anger and jealousy, I suppose," Avery said. "But he already experienced rage amnesia once. Who's to say that's not what happened here? Perhaps he wanted to humiliate Cederic the way he felt he'd been humiliated at the race?"

"That's not a bad point," Charles said, impressed. "Hey, if you don't already have plans with the chief later this week, would you like to have some dinner at my house? It's been a while since we've had one of our dinners."

"Of course," Avery said with a smile as they pulled into the station.

For a moment, it seemed as if Charles let out a sigh of relief at Avery's positive response. Avery decided not to think about it too much, and she and Charles walked into the station together, where they were immediately ushered into the viewing room at the side of the interrogation room.

They had missed the first few minutes of the questioning, but Avery didn't mind. It meant they had missed the boring bits where Chief Mathers put the suspect at ease. They had arrived just as the man was complaining about his old boss.

The young man sat with his legs as wide as he possibly could, taking up the space of at least three people. He had his arms crossed, and his cap

411

rested backward on his head. He chewed on gum, and each sentence he started was prompted with a casual shrug of his shoulders.

"I just hated my job there, man," he said with yet another shrug.

"And why is that?" Chief Mathers asked.

"Cederic was an unreasonable boss," he answered. "He would get worked up over the tiniest things and then disappear for days on end when we actually needed his help. Some days it felt as if the workers there actually owned the place. Only, he earned all of the money while we worked for minimum wage."

"Where were you on the night that he was murdered?" Chief Mathers asked, jumping right to the point.

"Do you guys think I did it?" he asked.

"We are looking at you as a suspect at the moment, yes," Chief Mathers said.

The young man rubbed his temples as if it was the most annoying thing he had ever heard and then readjusted his cap.

"I was at my grandma's house," he said. "I had to move in there because I couldn't pay the rent anymore because I got fired."

"I see, and what were you doing on the night of the murder?" Chief Mathers asked.

"I was watching movies, probably," he said. "That's what I do most nights now that I don't have the money to go out with my friends. My grandma will tell you that I was there all night."

Chief Mathers made a note of that, and one of the officers in the viewing room understood that it meant he needed to get the grandmother's contact details ready to make a call.

The man adjusted his posture slightly and sat a little more upright. "Look, Cederic and I never got along—that's no lie," he said. "But I would never have killed him. I'm not that stupid. I don't want to spend the rest of my life in prison."

"Mr. Stratton, there's just one more thing I still need to discuss with you, and then you may go. But I must ask that you do not leave town. If you do, we will have a manhunt for you, and you will be taken into jail, understand?" Chief Mathers said.

"I ain't going anywhere," the man answered.

"Good, now, tell me about your uniform," Chief Mathers said.

"Why do you want to know about that?" the young man asked.

Chief Mathers didn't answer that question. He followed it with a different question instead.

"I believe your uniform included a red apron?" he asked. "Where is that apron now?"

"I lost it," the man answered. "That's why I got fired in the first place. Cederic said it was a symbol of my commitment."

"Were you an uncommitted worker?" Chief Mathers asked.

The young man scoffed. "The furthest thing from it!" he said. "I used to work overtime and come in early. Sure, it wasn't the first time I had lost my apron. But I had never missed a day of work. So, you can understand why I was so angry."

"Yes, that must be frustrating."

"That's why we fought all the time," the man answered. "Cederic would constantly question my work ethic. And not only mine...he would question the ability of every person who worked for him, and I never stood for it."

"So, you were a difficult employee?" Chief Mathers asked.

"I wouldn't say difficult," he answered. "But I did stand up for us all when I thought he was being unreasonable, and he might have seen that as troublemaking."

"I see," Chief Mathers said.

"He was not an easy man to work for," the man explained. "I know a few of the people that work in his various shops. All of them have room-mates, and all of them are overworked. We work all the time and barely earn enough to pay the bills. Nobody will be happy that way."

"I have to agree with you there," Chief Mathers said.

Then, he gathered all his paperwork and smiled at the young man. "Thank you, that's it for today. As I said, stick around in case we have any more questions."

"Of course," the man said before getting up to leave.

The man shook Chief Mathers' hand and walked out of the interrogation room. Chief Mathers sighed before joining Avery and Charles in the viewing room.

"I don't think he did it," Chief Mathers said. "He seems far too relaxed about it all. But why don't we make sure and call his grandma? What do you say?"

Avery and Charles nodded in agreement and followed Chief Mathers to his desk, where the number for the man's grandmother was already waiting. In one phone call, his alibi was confirmed, and he was removed from the suspect list.

"Chief Mathers, this might seem a bit odd, but what are the chances I could get his number?" she asked.

"What do you want to do with it?" he asked with a quizzical look on his face.

Avery smiled. "I'm hiring people to train them as sommeliers for my new wine-tasting area in the making," she said. "He needs work and seems to understand what's important about a job. I'd like to give him a chance."

Chief Mathers smiled and scribbled down the number. "Here you go," he said eagerly. "Perhaps just make sure to stock up on a few uniforms in his size, considering how often he loses his."

Charles and Avery left the police station to discover that all the over-cast clouds had gone, and it had turned into a beautifully sunny day.

"That's really kind of you to offer to employ that guy," Charles said. "But are you sure? He fought a lot with Cederic."

Avery chuckled. "That won't be my problem," she said. "Don't forget —I've made you manager for the tastings. If he fights a lot, that's going to be with you, not me."

Charles sighed and widened his eyes. "You're right," he said. "He's going to be my problem."

"Yes," she said with an amused smile. "But I have a good feeling about him. What was his name again?"

"Justin," Charles answered. "And I have to admit that I like the idea that he stood up for his colleagues. It's an endearing quality. Cederic was not an easy man, and he did it anyway."

"Precisely," Avery said. "I'll give Justin a call tomorrow."

Chapter Fifteen

The weather had held up, and Avery and Tiffany enjoyed a glass of merlot on the patio as they waited for the sun to set. Out on the lawn, Sprinkles happily chased butterflies and bugs as they headed to their safe spaces before dark.

It was Avery's favorite time of the day. Sprinkles was playing, and the work day had come to an end. The vineyard was quieting down, and the world around them seemed to be settling.

It was a beautiful autumn evening, and Avery was happy to spend it with her friend. Tiffany had been working harder than ever, and she hadn't had the chance to see her as often as she usually did. So, she was eager to catch up with her.

"How's work been?" Avery asked.

Avery was tired and happy for the distraction from all of her work and from the case at hand. It felt to her as if every minute of her day was either going into the vineyard or spent in the viewing room of the police station.

It was nice to sit for a while and enjoy some good company. And the wine seemed to pair perfectly with the weather.

"Work has been so dull lately," Tiffany said. "I mean, I'm working harder than ever. We're massively understaffed. It just feels like the same thing every day."

"You're a tax consultant," Avery laughed. "What do you expect?"

"I dunno," Tiffany shrugged. "Your life seems so exciting. You're building ponds and following criminal cases. I just stare at numbers all day and do more filing than any sane human should ever have to do. And what's worse, it seems we're losing clients. That's never a good sign."

"You never know, maybe you'll find some tax fraud soon while doing your work, and you'll get to enjoy a criminal case too!" Avery teased.

"That's not funny," Tiffany said. But she laughed anyway.

"You do not want more excitement," Avery said. "Take it from me. I'm exhausted. I'm just happy to be sitting for a while. I wouldn't mind a couple of dull days."

"I'll swap with you," Tiffany joked.

Avery sighed and took another sip, enjoying every aspect of the flavor. This particular merlot was easy drinking. Sprinkles had rolled over the lawn, creating green streaks on his light fur. But he seemed happy enough.

"I tell you, one of the most terrifying moments of my life was when I realized that the police thought I was a suspect in the murder," Avery said. "I don't envy the people who are currently still suspected of this murder."

"Did they treat you like one?" Tiffany asked. "I mean...like was Chief Mathers all strict and scary and stuff?"

"He had to be," Avery said. "He treated me like he treats every other murder suspect, I suppose. It's not a good feeling. I keep thinking how scary it must be for the actual murderer to be there."

"I suppose if you're brave enough to commit murder, then Chief Mathers isn't so scary," Tiffany said casually.

"Do you think bravery is required to commit murder?" Avery asked.

"Of course!" Tiffany said. "You're potentially throwing your entire life away. I don't think it's an easy decision to make to follow through with it. I think it takes a lot of courage. But like, in a bad way."

"I suppose," Avery said. "Still, it was terrible. I didn't even do it, and I am having nightmares about what it would have been like if I did do it."

"Nightmares?" Tiffany asked.

"Yeah, since the questioning at the start of the case," Avery said. "I keep dreaming that I'm somehow able to lift this big wheel of cheese and bring it down on the head of this man that I never even knew. And let me tell you, the stress I feel when I wake up from it is intense."

"It sounds like you need a vacation," Tiffany said.

"Yes, definitely somewhere with yummy food," Avery suggested. "Speaking of, would you like to stay for dinner?"

"You're cooking?" Tiffany said. "Of course. I'd be a fool to pass on that."

"Would you mind if I invite Charles?" Avery said. "I promised I'd make plans with him this week, and it might be nice to have an impromptu dinner party."

"Go ahead," Tiffany said with a smile. "But we're going to need a lot more wine."

"That can be arranged," Avery joked as she motioned in the direction of the vines.

Avery called Charles, who happily agreed to join them for dinner, and she wasted no time getting a third glass and filling it in advance for him. When he got there, he greeted Avery and Tiffany cheerfully. Avery was happy to see him, too.

"So, how do you feel about one of James' books potentially inspiring a murder?" Tiffany asked as Avery prepared her recipe of decadent mac and cheese.

"It's not something I ever thought I would have to face," Avery said. "I don't really like the thought of it all that much, if I'm honest. And I don't think James would have been too happy about it either."

"But how much similarity was there really?" Tiffany asked.

"Only the method of murder, really," Avery said. "But when we were writing those books, they were meant to be strange and unusual methods of murder. Never in our right minds would we have expected anybody to actually murder someone in those ways."

"I suppose a wheel of cheese is a pretty odd murder weapon," Tiffany said.

Avery was only slightly concerned at how casually the three of them seemed to talk about the death of another person. But she couldn't get hung up on it. They needed to be casual about it. If they weren't, the whole thing would take too big a toll on Avery.

As terrible as it seemed, she needed to remove as much emotion from the scenario as possible. Otherwise, she would feel too much stress about the entire ordeal. And she didn't want that. She wanted to learn, and she wanted to write a well-thought-out book.

"I don't allow myself to think of it as a murder from James' book," she said. "There's too much risk of feeling a massive amount of guilt that way."

"That makes sense," Tiffany said. "I'd feel guilty too."

"There's no reason to feel guilty," Charles said. "There are countless crime novels that the murderer could have modeled it after IF that's even what they've done. It just so happens that it is similar to one of James'."

"I suppose you're right," Avery said with some relief. "Thank you, Charles."

Charles came around and topped up her wine while she stirred away at the stove.

"It smells amazing," he said with a smile. "I can't wait to taste it."

"I guess it isn't really connected to his book anyway," she said. "The rest of the murder is so vastly different. It's nothing like the book at all."

Avery was done cooking and served them a warm meal which they carried out to the patio to eat as the sun began to set. Then, they spoke about something else, to Avery's relief. That was until Charles brought the conversation back around.

"What are the main differences?" Charles asked out of the blue.

"The main differences of what?" Avery asked.

"Between the book and the actual murder," Charles said. "I know we've discussed it before, but that was pretty brief. And it's actually really interesting to me."

"Well, James' murders were clever, intriguing, and carefully plotted out," she answered. "And for the most part, they were classier."

"Classier?" Tiffany asked with a frown. "How is one crime classier than another?"

"Well, in the books, there was little blood and mess. And that's what made the crime so interesting. There'd be little to work with, you know, for the police and such," Avery said. "But this crime scene was just a mess."

"It really was," Charles agreed.

"Yeah, there was stuff all over the place, and Mr. Davis was so blatantly displayed. It was kind of grotesque, really," Avery continued. "It had a shock factor worthy of headlines."

Charles nodded in agreement and refilled all three of their glasses.

"This crime seems so over-the-top," Avery said. "It's a little extravagant, don't you think?"

"I suppose it is a little theatrical," Charles said.

Tiffany sipped on her wine as she listened to the two of them.

"Why would someone do that?" she asked.

"What? Murder?" Charles asked with a chuckle.

"No," Tiffany said. "Why would someone make such a big scene out of it?"

Charles raised his eyebrows as he pondered it. "I'd like to hear what you think of that, actually, Avery," he said. "If this was a book that James wrote or a story that you were working on... Why would you have the murderer make it so over the top?"

Avery thought about it a moment as she sipped at her wine. The sun had halfway set, and the sky had lit up bright orange. It was a perfect sunset, and she stared into it as she thought it through. She imagined the scene as words on paper and thought about the motive behind those words.

"I would write it to serve as some kind of distraction," she said.

"A distraction?" Tiffany asked. "All of that effort for a distraction?"

"Yeah," Avery shrugged. "The only reason I would write such an extravagant crime was if I wanted the police to waste their time on other aspects of the crime."

"Distract them from what?" Charles asked.

"The truth," Avery said. "It's like adding a few more unmatched pieces to a puzzle. You could build the puzzle, thinking that those pieces are meant to fit somewhere, and they just don't."

"That's interesting," Charles said. "Like decoy evidence?"

"Yeah," Avery said. "Only, it isn't a puzzle. It's a murder. And that means that no matter how supposedly random the decoy evidence is, it would still be a clue. Because somebody had to put it there, and it would always have a link to that person."

Charles raised his eyebrows. "Now, that is an impressive thought, Avery."

Avery smiled. "Thanks," she said. "I learned a lot from James in the years that we were married."

"Yeah, you're really good at this," Tiffany said.

Avery wasn't sure if that was a good thing. Her connection to crime novels and understanding crimes in that way had already made her a suspect in one murder. It was getting a little too close to home. And still, she found herself eager to know what would happen next.

The three of them finished off the bottle of wine. And when the last glasses were poured, Avery lifted hers to the air.

"I want to propose a toast to a gorgeous sunset and to a wonderful dinner with my two closest friends," she said.

Charles and Tiffany toasted along with her. Avery couldn't help but notice a new kind of smile on Charles' face. He seemed pleased to be referred to as a close friend, and Avery was glad to have cleared it up.

It occurred to her that perhaps she had misunderstood her time with Chief Mathers when Charles had understood it clearly. Charles had always been there for her, and he was an important friend to her. She wanted him to know that.

Within an hour, Tiffany had left, and Charles was helping her clean up as he always did. He was more joyful than he had been in some time and brought a happy energy to the home.

"Thank you for dinner," he said as he prepared to leave. "But I'm still going to invite you to my place for dinner like you promised."

"Will you be the one cooking?" she asked in a joking manner.

"If you're brave enough to eat the food," he said. "I found another cookbook in my collection. It was my mother's. One of my favorite meals of hers is in there. I thought I'd try to recreate it. But I might need your help."

"I'll be there," Avery said. "I'll wait on the sidelines with the fire extinguisher."

Charles laughed loudly. "That might be necessary. But who knows? Maybe I'll surprise us both!"

Avery said goodbye to Charles and got ready for bed. Her head had hardly hit the pillow, and she was fast asleep. That night, she had pleasant dreams and slept through the night. It was as if she had found some relaxation and some peace in the few hours that she had spent with her friends.

Chapter Sixteen

I t was late morning when Avery took her seat at the boardroom table at the police station. Coffee, treats, and snacks filled the center of the table. Up on the far wall were photographs of the crime scene. It certainly made the table of snacks seem a little less inviting.

It looked like something out of a crime movie. All the suspects' photographs had been pinned up onto the board, and there were lists beneath each name and photograph. She scanned through it for any information that she didn't know yet.

To the side stood an officer with a marker in hand. He was ready and prepared to add and adjust the list as the discussion went on. Avery took a deep breath and helped herself to some of the hot coffee. Charles did the same, but he also helped himself to some of the snacks. He didn't seem bothered by the gruesome crime scene photographs. Of course, he'd been a cop, so Avery figured it didn't bother him.

Chief Mathers and a few officers also sat around the table, and Charles had just made himself comfortable in his chair. Nobody in uniform looked well-rested, and it occurred to Avery that they had been working long hours.

The case had become rather prominent in the news, and every day the police department was being bombarded with questions from the press.

And each day, they had to report that there was no new information. It was taking its toll on Chief Mathers.

He looked tired and stressed and sipped on what Avery was certain was his fifth coffee for the day. He wasn't his usual cheerful self as he greeted the group before him. He had called the meeting to talk about the case and to go over some of the details.

Avery had immediately accepted the invitation to join the meeting. She was eager to recap all the evidence and bring some conclusion to her notes, which were in various notebooks and scattered all over the place at that point.

The mood in the room was serious and tired. And Chief Mathers wasted no time in getting the meeting started.

"Let's discuss our suspects so far," he said, pulling out three files from the stack in front of him. "I'll start with Collette. What do we know about her in relation to this murder? We know that she wore a red ribbon in her hair on the day of their wedding. That could be a symbol for something."

"Well, she has a motive," Charles said. "We know that she has a debt she can't pay off and that their relationship was rocky. He had a large life insurance policy that she would get when he died."

"Have we learned anything new about this policy?" Chief Mathers asked.

A young officer cleared his throat. "I learned from Mr. Davis' mother that Collette had pushed the victim to seek a policy. But other than that, it seems like any normal life insurance policy. In the end, he apparently happily signed the paperwork."

"I see, so he didn't have it before she asked him to take one out?" Chief Mathers asked.

"Not as far as I know," the officer said. "But the information is vague."

"Right, and she has no provable alibi," Chief Mathers said.

"Well, we know from the alarm company that the alarm hadn't been turned on until around three o'clock in the morning, likely meaning that she was home at the time," another officer said, handing over a piece of paper with the information on it.

"Well, she could have left and just not switched it on," Chief Mathers said. "So, I wouldn't really count that as evidence."

"She didn't seem too emotional when she was being questioned,"

Charles said. "What have the officers seen who have been keeping an eye on her?"

"Nothing much," Chief Mathers said. "They say she barely leaves the house other than to go to the store for groceries."

"She could be grieving," Charles said.

"Yes," Chief Mathers agreed. "And that's all we have on her. Moving on to Audrina, the ex-wife otherwise known as Red."

"Well, we know that she was in the midst of a pretty nasty custody battle with the victim," an officer said. "We've got the recordings of the voice messages that she left for him. They were pretty nasty."

"That's a strong motive," Charles said quietly. "She also has no provable alibi."

"That's correct," Chief Mathers said. "And as far as I know, she's carried on with her life as if nothing has happened. She is socializing frequently and all-in-all is having a good time."

"It's not unheard of for an ex-wife not to be all that bothered by the death of her ex-husband," Charles said. "But she has a decent motive. Mothers will do just about anything if they think they're protecting their children."

"Well, from what I understand, she loves her son, but she doesn't exactly behave in a needy way with him," Chief Mathers said. "Our sources say that he spends most of his time at friends' houses and out at parties. She seems to be a pretty chill mother."

Chief Mathers sighed and rubbed his eyebrows before tossing her file aside. "Now, we're left with Gregory Marsh, the cyclist with a doping problem."

"It's well-known that doping can make people unreasonably angry, and often they'll act aggressively," one of the cops said. "And there are countless tales of his aggressive behavior."

"Yes, friends and family have confirmed that he would have scary outbursts and he often lost control of his temper," Chief Mathers said. "Which, according to him, is why he went to hide out in that tent. He says he threatened his mother with no recollection of the event."

"Perhaps the same happened with the victim. He might have murdered the man and forgotten about it?" an officer said. "Let's not forget to mention the red ribbon on his second-place medal. Perhaps he stuffed it in the victim's mouth because he felt Mr. Davis should have come second?"

"It's entirely possible," Chief Mathers said. "And just like the first two, we have no alibi for him either."

"In my mind, it is suspicious how much time he spent in that tent," an officer said. "Why didn't he just go to a psychologist?"

"Well, we can't really think of it that way," Chief Mathers said. "We can only look at the facts. The what-ifs of each suspect don't help us in any way. Each of them could have done things very differently, but we can only focus on what they did do."

"His motive does seem the weakest of the lot," Charles said. "The others had something physical to gain. They'd get money or custody. When we look at Gregory, there's only jealousy and anger, and this doesn't strike me as an angry crime."

"I have to agree with you there," Chief Mathers said. "There's no sign of rage. There's no stabbing or excessive beating. Perhaps we should look at what we know about the murder itself."

"Well, one thing I can say is that each suspect seemed very cooperative with the police," said Charles. "And at this point, we have no conflicting stories; their stories seem to remain the same, and all three of them seem confident in their answers during the interrogation."

"Yes, that is something important to note," Chief Mathers said as he reached for the next file in the stack.

He opened it up and handed out some copied pages to each person at the table. Avery reached for hers and saw that it was an autopsy report on the victim's body. She scanned through it but wasn't entirely sure what she should be looking for.

"Here we have the autopsy report," Chief Mathers said. "One important thing to note is that there are no defensive marks on the body. That means that Mr. Davis did not put up a struggle at the time of the murder. Although, the murderer seemed to want us to think that he did."

"Why do you say that?" one of the officers asked.

"All the items that were thrown across the floor," Chief Mathers said. "I've been wondering why that was done, and I think the killer wanted us to think there was a struggle."

"Yeah, but why?" the officer asked.

Chief Mathers shrugged. "To have us looking in a different direction? I don't know... the entire case is odd."

He then reached in and removed another page from the file. He scanned over it and placed it to the side.

"Then there's the building itself," he said. "This report says that no locks were broken, and there was no sign of forced entry to the shop. That tells me that whoever did it was invited inside."

"So that means it wasn't someone unexpected?" Avery asked.

"Precisely," Chief Mathers said. "It means that whoever it was, they would have knocked on the door and he would have happily let them in. The people living upstairs reported no strange sounds from the shop. There was no shouting or arguments. Everything seemed pretty normal."

"A quiet murder," Charles mumbled. "Those are far and few between."

"Indeed," Chief Mathers said. "Then, there's the matter of the cheese. Has anyone looked into this like I asked?"

"Yes," one of the officers said. "That particular wheel of cheese weighs about twenty pounds. Never mind how cumbersome it would be to hold."

"Right, so not an easy attack to pull off," Chief Mathers said. "And he was hit on the back of the head while his back was turned."

"That's correct," the officer said. "And the cheese hit him in just the perfect place to kill him. The coroner reported that perhaps the intention of the blow was just to hurt him and that the murder was accidental."

"That seems believable," Charles said.

Avery took countless notes as she listened to them all talk back and forth about it. It was refreshing to get a clear look at the case up until that point, but it did nothing to make it any clearer. The more they discussed it, the more confusing it became.

"What if the cheese wasn't lifted?" Charles said. "What if it was pulled off a shelf or shoved or something, and it was dropped onto his head?"

"I suppose it isn't impossible," Chief Mathers said. "Can we get our hands on a wheel of cheese of the same size and dimensions?" he asked one of the officers, who nodded. "Get one for me and arrange for some tests to see if it is possible for that to fall hard enough to have killed him."

"If it was pulled off the shelf or pushed, then either of the ladies could have done it as they wouldn't have had to lift it," Avery said.

"Well, we're forgetting about the weight of the victim himself," Chief Mathers said. "Once the murder was committed, the body was wrapped and lifted into a display cabinet. That is no easy task. Dead bodies are heavy and cumbersome and not as easy to maneuver as the movies would have you believe."

"It also means that whoever did it, they had to have had some time to do it in," Charles said. "All that staging and wrapping would have taken a fair amount of time. They must have been pretty certain that they weren't going to be caught or interrupted."

Chief Mathers sighed. "We are no closer to solving this case, are we?" he asked.

There was a silence in the room that answered his question perfectly. "We have three plausible suspects and nothing to point a clear finger in any of their directions," Chief Mathers continued. "This is starting to look like the kind of case that might turn cold."

With that, the meeting came to an end. Avery had pages of notes with lines drawn to show where all the connections were, and it just looked like a mess. She closed her notebook with a sigh as she joined Charles in the hallway.

"Are you hungry?" he said. "I've got all the ingredients for our lunch today, and I bought double of everything, so you better be."

Avery smiled. "After all of that, it might take me a few minutes."

Charles laughed. "I forget that you're not quite as seasoned as the rest of us."

Avery and Charles walked into the bright autumn sun outside and climbed into his car. And as he drove them to his house, Avery wondered about Cederic Davis' last moments. He had known his killer well enough to unlock the door and let them in.

To her, that was a tragic truth.

Chapter Seventeen

Avery sat at the table in Charles' kitchen as she watched him fumble over the food he was preparing. To say it was an entertaining event would be an understatement. There was one pot already boiling on the stove and one pot that seemed to have eluded him entirely.

It looked like the cartoons she had watched as a child. And it was a noisy affair. There was clanging and banging as he dropped pots and pans around clumsily. Charles was doing his best not to get irritated with himself, but Avery knew it wouldn't last long.

He searched every cupboard and cabinet, muttering, "I know it was here somewhere," over and over again until he eventually found it in the drying rack where he had done the previous day's dishes. He had scratched his head so many times that some of his hair stood upright.

But Avery appreciated the effort. He'd even gone as far as to put an apron on to keep his shirt clean. He had opened a good bottle of wine, and Avery was happy for the entertainment. Still, it took a lot of her control not to step in and take over. He needed the help, and she had looked at the recipe. It should have been simple, and it looked delicious. She knew she could have it prepped and cooking in no time if she did it. But she pushed her hunger aside and allowed him to figure it out without her interference.

Charles seemed pretty stressed about cooking the meal, but eventually, he had it all coming together. It smelled fantastic and was quickly becoming the perfect meal for the bright autumn day that they were experiencing.

Avery had cleared her afternoon to fulfill her promise of having a meal with him.

So, she was in no rush. She had become comfortable in his home over the recent months of their friendship and had spent at least one night a week there, most weeks, to have dinner.

Charles read each instruction of the recipe at least three times before he carried it out and checked with Avery every few minutes to make sure that he had understood it correctly.

And at the end of the debacle, he produced a perfectly cooked meal.

They sat outside in his backyard while they enjoyed it together. Avery was impressed with the food, and he seemed pleased with the result too. It had been a recipe that his mother had cooked for him, and while he ate it, he seemed sentimental.

"That was lovely," Avery said as she finished the last bite.

"You don't have to say that just to be polite," Charles said. "But I think it tasted just like my mother used to make it."

"I'm not being polite," Avery said. "You followed the recipe, and it turned out great! Besides, I'm just pleased not to have been the one to cook this time."

Within a matter of minutes, dark clouds filled the sky, and Avery and Charles had to run inside to hide from a sudden downpour.

"I guess it's only fair that I help you with the dishes, then?" Avery joked.

Charles looked at the kitchen, saw for the first time the mess that he had created, and gratefully accepted her offer. It took them almost an hour to complete the task, and when they were done, the warm day had become chilly.

"Why don't I make a fire?" Charles said as they watched the sky get even darker.

"Excellent idea," Avery said, taking a seat on the sofa.

They sat in each other's company with the warmth of the fire. It was cozy, and as they talked about everything and anything, Avery completely forgot about the case and all the work she had to do. She was able to just sit back and enjoy the afternoon.

Charles joked with her and told her about his mother and some of the stories of what he and his brother were like growing up. And she enjoyed hearing them. It seemed to her that they might have been friends when they were younger, too, had they known each other.

She found herself laughing easily around him.

"You grew up in Los Robles, didn't you?" he asked.

"Yeah," Avery said, taking a sip. "My parents bought the vineyard when I was quite young. But it was different from what it is now. I mean, you know, you've been there for every change that I've made."

"Oh, yeah," he said. "I mean, I worked for your parents before. But I must say, you're a better boss."

Avery laughed. "Is that so?"

"Yes!" Charles laughed. "Your parents never cooked a meal for me. I just went to work, and I went home."

"You might be lucky there," Avery said. "Neither of my parents are very good at cooking."

"So, the skill wasn't inherited?" Charles asked.

"No," Avery said. "It was learned out of necessity. I took over the cooking when I was just a teenager in a desperate attempt to eat better food."

Avery looked out the window behind Charles and saw that the day was getting late. She felt a little sad about it. She was enjoying his company and the conversation, but she knew she would soon need to leave.

She thought about what Tiffany had said and noticed that Charles laughed easily at her jokes. But she no longer knew if it was because she was genuinely funny or just because he liked to laugh around her. She remembered his reaction to her spending time with Chief Mathers.

She didn't want to go home, but she didn't want to seem too comfortable with him. The entire situation was confusing for her. "I should probably go," she said, putting her empty glass down on the coffee table. "Thank you so much for a wonderful meal."

"Are you sure you have to go?" Charles asked. "I'm having such a good afternoon."

"Me too," Avery said with a smile. "But I still have to do some work today. Otherwise, the rest of my week is just a mess."

"I understand," Charles said. "Let me send you home with some left-overs, at least."

Avery gladly accepted, and a moment later, she had a small tub of left-overs with her as she waited for the arrival of the cab to take her home.

"Let's do this again soon?" Charles asked. "I feel like once a week just isn't enough for food this good."

"Sure," Avery said gladly.

She knew Tiffany would have said accepting an offer like that was a bad idea. But she liked the idea of having another afternoon like the one she'd had that day.

She said goodbye to Charles and hopped in the cab, waving happily to him as she drove away from his house. He stood outside and watched her leave until she had disappeared from his sight.

On the ride home, she pondered everything that hadn't bothered her before. If she had apparently accepted a date with Chief Mathers without knowing it, how could she know that she hadn't done the same with Charles? It was getting all too confusing, and she missed the days when there had to be a formal invitation and when men had to specify that they wanted to go on a date. Her head hurt at the thought of it. She worried about what she should do if Chief Mathers wanted a second cup of coffee with her.

Should she ask him first if it was a date? Would that be embarrassing? She couldn't just say no. She liked him as a friend and was eager to get to know him. She lived in the small town of Los Robles, and the only way to survive a small town was to make friends.

She needed a distraction from her thoughts, and she knew just where to go to get it. When they arrived at the vineyard, she instructed the cab driver to drop her outside of her parents' house. And when they answered the door to see her smiling face, she was eagerly ushered inside.

"Coffee?" her mother asked.

Avery shook her head. "Do you have some wine?"

Her mother stared at her blankly. "No," her mother answered sarcasti-cally. "We live here on a vineyard, and we have no wine in this house."

Avery rolled her eyes. "I'll take a glass of shiraz, if you have an opened bottle."

Her mother reached for the bottle and poured Avery what seemed to be the smallest glass of wine she had ever seen.

When her father entered the room, his eyes lit up at the sight of wine.

"I'll take a glass of that," he said, kissing Avery on the head to greet her.

"Half a glass," her mother said. "Otherwise, you'll be asleep at the table in a minute, and I can't carry you to bed."

"Fine, but then I'll pick the glass," he said.

Her mother painfully agreed, and her father reached for a glass that was borderline large enough to be considered a vase.

"That's not funny," her mother said.

"Well, if I let you choose, you'll give me a glass thimble like you've given Avery," her father argued. He poured himself half a vase of wine and then winked at Avery, switching their glasses around.

"You can't give her that much wine!" her mother screeched. "She still needs to walk home."

"She's fit and young," her father said. "She's not like us. She can drink and walk. Don't be so tough."

Her mother joined them at the table as she poured herself her own thimble-sized glass of wine and sipped on it slowly.

"Well then, how was your day?" her father asked.

"I'm tired," Avery admitted. "We had a meeting about the case, and it's all so confusing. When I think about it, my head feels like it's being swarmed with bees."

"Have you tried some vitamin B?" her mother asked.

"What?" Avery asked.

"Vitamin B!" her mother said. "It's excellent for helping with concentration and things like that. You should try it. Perhaps then the answer will come to you."

"Don't listen to your mother," her father laughed. "She believes everything she sees in commercials!"

"It's true!" her mother cheered. "My friend Lucy has been taking it for a week. She says she's reading a book a day now! Her mind works at super speed levels. Just think what you could do if you took it at your young age."

"I don't think that's how it works, Mom," Avery said.

"I'll go buy you some tomorrow," her mother said. "You'll see. And then you'll thank me, I bet."

Her father reached for the bottle and topped up his tiny glass of wine under the angry glare of her mother. Her stares didn't seem to bother him much anymore. Avery liked the idea that someday she might be old enough to no longer care about others' emotions toward her.

"You know, I've found in all my years of experience that when things seem so confusing, the truth is usually simpler than it seems," her father said. His advice wasn't entirely more useful than her mother's, but it seemed to have a little more logic behind it.

"I still think it's the vitamin B that she needs," her mother said under her breath.

"Oh, stop it," her father argued. "We're talking about a murder case, not a book that she's read a hundred times already."

"Lucy has never read those books before!" her mother snapped.

Avery laughed, thanked her parents for their help, finished her wine, and headed home. It hadn't been a helpful visit to her parents, but it had served its purpose in distracting her, and she was eager to get home.

But she walked into a house where work awaited her. She hadn't been lying to Charles. She had some work she needed to get through, so she brewed herself a cup of tea and got to it. She worked easily without distraction until the early hours of the morning.

Finally, she was able to crawl into bed with Sprinkles, who had already been asleep for hours on end. She slept right through the night, and when she woke up way too late the next morning and stepped out the front door to greet the day, she found a bottle of vitamin B capsules waiting for her at her feet.

Next to it was the newspaper. She lifted it and unfolded it and immediately wished that she hadn't. On the front page was the title, "Police Still Stumped on Cheesy Murder."

Chapter Eighteen

B y the time Avery made it back home after a long day in the vineyard, her feet ached, and she had little energy left. The Cellar Vie Guest House was quietening down as Los Robles went into the cooler season, and she found herself with a couple of hours of free time.

Avery rolled her head from side-to-side to stretch her stiff shoulders. She felt as if she was being worn thin by it all. Still, she liked the idea of staying busy. Her mother thought she was using work as a distraction from her sadness or loneliness. Avery had been insulted by that.

It didn't seem to her like a distraction. She merely saw herself as a driven woman. Her dreams were big, and she finally had the means to move forward with them. She simply didn't want to miss the opportunity.

Still, she was eager to have a quiet night to herself.

She had finally found the dull moment that she had wished for just a few days before, but now that she was there, she didn't want it anymore. She sat on the couch with a cup of tea for a few minutes and then realized that she was bored out of her mind.

Avery considered putting on some music to listen to but couldn't choose anything that she felt she was in the mood for. In the end, she decided to be productive instead. She gathered all the notes she had made on the murder case so far and went through them.

She took a few new, blank pages and started to build the characters for her book. The story was still supposed to iron itself out, but at least she had somewhere to start. The three main suspects had the largest lists of character traits.

She pulled her laptop closer and did some further research on the suspects. She went through their social media pages and learned that all three of them had been in the public eye at some point. Audrina had a name for herself as a socialite. She went to fancy parties and seemed to be involved in almost every new business venture that the town of Los Robles had to offer. Collette had been extensively involved in charity work up until a few months before her husband's murder, and most of her large donations had been enough to make it into the news. Then, of course, there was Gregory and his cycle race.

When Avery looked him up, she found multiple interviews from the day of the race and multiple news articles. She decided to switch her tea out for a glass of wine and watch any footage that she could find on the race.

There were many to choose from, so she started at the beginning. She watched as the cycle race began. Cederic Davis was not a good cyclist by any means. She noticed how other cyclists easily passed him. But because the race was smaller, and the town was a small one, only the beginning and the end of the race had been filmed.

Avery understood why it was easy to believe that Cederic had cheated. When she watched the start of the race again, she noticed that all of his gear and his bicycle were brand new. There were no marks or scratches, which she felt meant that it hadn't been used much.

There had been a fairly large crowd gathered outside, and the town had been decorated in celebration of it. From what she could tell, everyone was excited for the event, and every business had a stall outside to give food or water, except for Cederic. None of his businesses were present, despite the fact that he had enrolled in the race.

Then, she noticed some footage where the first, second, and third place cyclists were interviewed. She went through the footage, and it was no surprise that the cyclists coming in second and third didn't seem too impressed.

She watched Gregory as he tediously answered the interview questions. He looked so different from the man she had found in the tent. In the footage, he was immaculately groomed. It even seemed as if he had been to a salon to have his eyebrows evened out.

He was covered in sweat and already had patches all over his body to soothe his aching muscles. He looked exhausted and had bags under his eyes. And the man who had come in third looked similarly exhausted.

Then, she clicked on the thumbnail that showed Cederic's interview. He seemed as if he hadn't done any physical labor at all. There wasn't a single bead of sweat in his hair, and he didn't seem to have the same muscular pain as the rest.

She was certain he had cheated in the race, and he wasn't doing a convincing job of it either. But she felt a tug in her stomach. She had never seen the victim moving and talking before. She'd only ever known him after his death. It seemed eerie to see him that way compared to the way she had found him in the cheese shop that morning. She was staring intently at the screen when her phone rang, startling her.

"Charles, hi," she greeted as she clutched her chest.

"I didn't wake you, did I?" he said.

"It's not even seven o'clock yet, and I won't be asleep for very many hours still," she answered with a laugh. "What's up?"

"I'm cooking something," he said with a sigh. "And I have no idea what this means. The recipe says that I need to julienne the carrots. I've never even heard of such a thing."

Avery laughed as she talked him through the method. And she listened to him struggle on the other end of the phone.

"What are you cooking, anyway?" she asked.

"I am trying to make a stew of some sort," he said. "But this is harder than I thought. I have no confidence in this whatsoever."

"Well, the good news is that it is very difficult to make a bad stew," Avery said. "You're probably doing better than you think."

"Thanks," he said sheepishly. "I'm trying to practice so that I can cook better meals in the future. I thought it might relax me to cook a meal. You're always saying how relaxing it is for you. But I gotta tell you, I'm feeling kinda stressed."

Avery left the footage playing on mute as she walked to the kitchen to refill her glass of wine.

"I just get so confused, and I have a hard time concentrating on everything," Charles said.

"Have you tried taking vitamin B?" Avery asked, making a joke that only she would understand. "I have a bottle if you want it."

"What?" Charles asked. "No, I don't think that's a thing. Anyway, what are you doing tonight? Snowed under with work?"

"Actually, no," Avery said cheerfully. "It's a quiet night. I thought I'd just try to make some headway on the new book."

"Well, if you're hungry, I'm cooking, and there's always a space at my table for you," Charles said.

Avery considered it. It wouldn't be a terrible way to spend the evening. She always enjoyed Charles' company, and even just speaking on the phone with him had brightened up her evening. She was about to accept his offer when she glanced over to her bookshelf and caught a glimpse of one of her late husband's books. Then, her feelings toward another dinner with Charles changed.

"No, thank you for the offer, though," she said. "I need to make some headway here. I'm sorta stuck in it, and I could use an early night."

"An early night in your world means midnight instead of two o'clock in the morning," he laughed.

Avery chuckled. "I know, and trust me, I try to get to bed earlier, but it just never works."

"Maybe you should try taking some vitamin B," Charles said, throwing the joke back at her.

Avery laughed. She looked over at the bottle of vitamin B capsules that still stood on the shelf and wondered what she was going to do with them. Her mother would be sure to ask her any day whether or not they had helped her, and she'd have to explain that she never took a single one. Avery knew that it would initiate an argument.

While Charles asked her a few more questions about his stew, Avery glanced over at the footage that was playing silently on her laptop. She saw various silent interviews of people that she didn't know. There was also some footage of the crowd enjoying some food and drink from the food stalls.

Then there were some scenes where the sponsors of the event were allowed to talk and advertise whatever their product was. She watched as

Cederic happily accepted his gold medal while the second and third place cyclists accepted their own medals in a disgruntled manner.

Then she saw the footage of the final moments of the race. Cederic went over the finish line with a wide smile as the crowd celebrated. Well, some of the crowd celebrated. Most of the crowd seemed to look on with confusion. That's when Avery spotted something in the background of the footage. She couldn't be certain why her eye had been drawn to it, but it was enough to make her go back a few seconds in the footage and watch it again.

She saw what looked like two women in the crowd, celebrating wildly as Cederic crossed the finish line. They cheered and hugged each other and shouted out his name. They seemed to be significantly more excited about his win than anybody else around them. She paused for a moment, but they had been jumping too much, and she couldn't see clearly who they were.

So, she let the footage play as the rest of the cyclists made their way over the finish line. She tried to get a better look at the women, but the angle changed. Avery wasn't sure why she had become so stuck on that moment, but she really needed to know who had celebrated his win that much. She wasn't sure it had anything to do with the case, but her curiosity couldn't be helped. Eventually, as the last of the cyclists crossed the line, she saw them clearly. And she immediately recognized who they were.

Side-by-side, at the finish line of the race, Audrina and Collette stood together like friends and cheered Cederic on. They were dressed as glamorous as ever, with large hats and sunglasses. Avery paused the footage. She wanted to take a screenshot, but she couldn't remember how, and she was so afraid she would lose that moment that she opted to take a photograph on her phone.

"Charles, I'm going to have to call you back," she said, interrupting him mid-sentence. "But I'm sure it will be soon. I think I've found something important about the case."

"Really?" Charles asked. "Alright, well, let me know as soon as you've figured it out. I'll be waiting eagerly."

Avery hung up the phone and snapped the photograph, zooming in to make sure she was right.

Chapter Nineteen

Avery couldn't believe what she was watching. Her entire idea of what the women were like had to change. She had believed that they were not friends, and in fact, both women had been so eager to point the blame at each other that she had assumed they were enemies.

She thought back on the interrogations of the two women and how they had spoken about each other. She thought about her own friends and wondered if she could ever speak that way about them, even if she had been pretending.

Her wine sat untouched on the table beside her as she stared at the footage. She didn't even care to take another sip. Her mind was racing as she tried to piece the truth together. It was the last thing she was expecting to see that day.

It was uncommon for the ex-wife and the new wife to be close friends. And neither of the women had mentioned it, that was sure. She simply couldn't understand why they would have hidden their friendship. The race hadn't happened too long before Cederic's murder. It wasn't impossible that something had happened in the meantime to pull them apart. But that didn't seem likely.

Avery looked over all the notes she had taken about the two women and realized that, despite the way they had been linked to each other, they were a good match to be good friends. They had a lot in common. They were both equally glamorous and seemed to be into the same things. They behaved similarly, and when she looked at them on paper, it made perfect sense that they would be good friends.

She sent the photograph to Charles without a caption. She needed him to confirm for her that they saw the same thing. Within a matter of moments, he had phoned her back again.

"Charles, hello again," she greeted him.

Charles didn't greet her. Instead, he carried on talking as if they had never hung up the phone in the first place.

"I've got the photograph that you sent me," he said. "What exactly am I looking at?"

She could hear the sound of intrigue in his voice. He seemed more cheerful than when he'd been struggling to julienne the carrots. It was as if she'd shown him something massively entertaining. And as he spoke, she could hear the smile on his face.

"I'm hoping you can tell me what you think you're seeing so that way I can confirm my suspicions about it," Avery said.

"Well, it looks like Audrina and Collette," Charles said. "But I find it a little hard to believe."

"Yes, I think it is," she responded.

Charles went quiet for a moment. "Where did you find it?" he asked. "Are they smiling?"

Avery chuckled as she looked at the photograph she had sent him. She had paused the footage at just the right time, so both women were linked arm-in-arm with wide smiles on their faces. It was a grainy photograph, but there were only a handful of women quite that glamorous in Los Robles. And Avery couldn't think of any other women who would go to watch a bike race in heels.

"I was going through some of the footage from the race to get an idea of Gregory's character for the book," she said. "I had it playing silently in the background while I was talking to you. I saw them in the crowd together, cheering him on."

"That surprises me," Charles said.

"Let me show you all of it," Avery said. "There's even a moment where they bring their coffee cups together as if they're clinking wine glasses."

She copied the link to the video where she had found it and sent it to him via email. She waited patiently for him to open the link and watch it.

"Go to around the two-minute mark," she said. "And watch the crowd."

Charles did as she asked, and a short while later, he let out a confused, "Hmmmm."

She could hear the sound of the video in the background of their call and wished she could see his face as he was watching it. She knew he would be wearing the same frown he always had when he was looking at a screen of some kind.

"They look like friends to me," she said. "I don't know many enemies who hug quite that tightly."

She watched the footage again too. The women seemed to have quite the party when Cederic crossed the finish line.

"Have we missed something?" Charles asked. "I mean, they look as if this is a normal thing to happen between the two of them. We've definitely not got the whole picture here."

"Clearly," Avery laughed. "I mean, up until now, I've been convinced that these two women are enemies. They keep trying to pin the murder on each other."

She thought of how Audrina had been so quick to say that she believed Collette had done it. And how Collette had not batted an eye to pull the rug out from underneath Audrina. Then, Avery thought of her own friends. It would take a lot for her to accuse any of her friends of murder. Then again, she was vastly different from the two women in the photograph.

"Yes, that's what I've been thinking too," Charles said. "We need to show this to Chief Mathers."

"I think so too. But should we wait until tomorrow morning?" Avery asked.

"This case really needs some new information," Charles said. "I can see that it is getting to Adrian. Perhaps we should show him sooner rather than later."

He was right. She had seen how frustrated Chief Mathers had been at their meeting and knew that he would be eager for some new information. But she didn't know how important it would be to the case. Still, it did change the way they needed to look at the two women's relationship.

"Alright," Avery said. "I think you're right. We'll have to show him this. Should I send it to him?"

"No," Charles said. "I'd like for us to be there when he watches it. He's a brilliant officer and detective, and I want to know his immediate thoughts."

"Me too," Avery said. "When should we take it to him to watch?"

"Have you had some wine tonight?" Charles asked.

"Do you even know me?" she joked. "It's after six. Of course, I've had some wine!"

Charles chuckled. "Well, I haven't had a glass yet. I've been too focused on this recipe. So, I'll pick you up, and we can go to the police station to discuss it there with Chief Mathers. Why don't you give him a call, and I'll be at your house in a few minutes."

"Sounds like a plan," Avery said, ending the call.

She closed her laptop and packed it in its bag as she dialed Chief Mathers' number. It didn't ring for long before he answered.

"Avery, what a pleasant surprise to get a call from you tonight," he greeted cheerfully.

"Hi, Adrian," she said. "I'm so sorry to interrupt your evening. Do you have a moment?"

"It is really no problem at all," he answered. "I've got all the time in the world for you. To what do I owe the pleasure?"

Chief Mathers sounded entirely casual, and in the background, she could hear the sound of a child's laughter. She had interrupted something fun, and she felt bad about it.

"I'm afraid it's work-related," Avery said. "I've found something that might be important to the case."

"Oh?" he said. "I like a bit of good news."

"Well, I've spoken to Charles, and he's suggested that we all go through it together at the station. He's on his way to pick me up. Will you be able to meet us there?" she said.

Chief Mathers went quiet for a while. "Yes, I'll just drop my son off at his grandparents; I'm sure they won't mind. I'll meet you there as soon as I can."

"I'm so sorry to have disrupted your night like this," Avery said, feeling a pang of guilt.

"It really is no problem at all," Chief Mathers laughed. "I'm the Chief of Police. This is normal. Don't worry about it."

"Alright, then, I'll see you soon?" Avery asked.

"See you soon."

Avery hung up the phone and let Charles know that all was in order. She had to get out of her pajamas and brush the smell of wine from her teeth. Then, she stepped out of the house just in time for Charles to arrive to give her a ride.

"What about your stew?" she asked as she hopped into his car.

"I took it off the heat. I was happy to give up on it," Charles said.

"I'm sorry," Avery said. "This has really been a disruption, hasn't it?"

"Disruption?" Charles laughed. "You saved me from the stress! I was not having a good time in the kitchen. I wasn't ready to attempt cooking on my own yet."

Avery laughed. "Oh dear, that bad?"

Charles shrugged. "Perhaps I'm just not a chef at all. I don't know. I'll try again, but not without your help."

"Alright then," Avery chuckled. "So what will you be doing for dinner then?"

"I'll just get takeout," Charles said. "Maybe on the way home. I'll get some for you, too, if you're hungry."

"That depends entirely on how long this is going to take," Avery laughed.

They pulled into the police station, and Avery walked inside and knew exactly where to go. She had spent so much of her time there lately that it almost felt as if it was her workplace. She sighed and took a seat at the boardroom table while Charles ran off to get them each a cup of coffee.

Chapter Twenty

C hief Mathers arrived looking sharp. He had clothes on that had
 been neatly ironed, likely for the next day's work. But he looked
tired. He had bags under his eyes, and it didn't seem as if he was all that
impressed to be called into work at that time of night.

He clutched a cup of coffee in his hands so tightly that his knuckles
had turned white. He sipped it as the steam fogged up his glasses. Despite
the tiredness on his face, he seemed ready to get to work.

"Hello, everyone," he said with a gruff voice. "Let's get straight to it."

"Absolutely," Charles agreed.

"And let's hope that whatever you've found helps us crack this case
wide open. We have too many questions and not enough answers," Chief
Mathers continued.

It took Charles a moment to get his laptop ready, and he opened the
video and moved to the right moment. Then, he played it without saying a
word. Chief Mathers rubbed his eyes and asked Charles to play it again.

"I don't get it," Chief Mathers said.

"In the crowd," one of the other officers remarked. "Pay attention to
the crowd."

Charles played it again, and Chief Mathers leaned forward. Then he
motioned for it to be played yet again. Charles did so happily. Avery strug-

gled to conceal her smile. The silence in the room confirmed that what she had found was of some importance. The officers had gathered around in a small crowd to try and watch it on the small screen, and some of them, it seemed, struggled to see. Chief Mathers sighed.

"Let's get this on the large monitor over there," he instructed Charles. "I want to watch this a few more times, and I want everyone to see it before we start coming up with any conclusions regarding this."

Charles did exactly as he was instructed. Avery didn't watch the screen. She had seen the footage enough times. Instead, she watched everybody's facial expressions as the image of the two women cheering and embracing played on the large screen.

Chief Mathers smirked as if he'd just learned a little secret while some of the other officers rummaged through their notes and paperwork as if they'd missed something. It was an enjoyable sight, despite the fact that it was already fairly late at night.

"Well," Chief Mathers said as the footage ended. "Clearly, the two wives have not been as forthcoming about their relationship as I'd like them to be. Up until now, we've been under the impression that they did not get along."

"Yes, and they've clearly put the blame on each other," Charles said.

"And those two women on that screen do not look like enemies to me," Avery said. "They were both there to support Cederic. That's not common for a wife and an ex-wife."

"That's my thinking," Chief Mathers said. "And I'm glad that you've arranged to show me this. This is helpful. We've missed something here, and it could potentially be vital."

"What should we do?" another officer asked.

Chief Mathers leaned back and rubbed his eyes. "Well, it might be nice to give the press something new to report on," he said. "I don't want to waste too much time on this. I want to interview both women again first thing in the morning."

There was a murmur of agreement in the room. Chief Mathers pointed at one of the officers. "John, why don't you round up the two ladies tomorrow morning before they start their day? By now, we have a good idea of their routine, so you can work the times around that," Chief Mathers said.

"Of course," John answered.

"I'd like to be here to see it," Avery said.

"You're more than welcome," Chief Mathers said. "After all, you're the one who discovered this footage. Excellent work!"

Avery smiled and nodded.

"And John," Chief Mathers continued. "Put the two women in the same car."

John frowned. "Are you sure about that, sir?" he asked.

"Yeah," Chief Mathers answered. "Let them sit together in the back seat and watch them closely. I want to know how familiar they seem with each other. Any detail that sticks out to you, I want to hear about it, understood?"

"Yes, sir," John answered.

"And putting them together in the car has an added benefit," Chief Mathers continued. "If they do have something to hide, being picked up together like that might make them a little nervous. Hopefully, it is enough to make one of them talk. That's if they have anything to tell me, anyway."

"That's a great idea," Charles said. "We'll see you all tomorrow, then."

Avery and Charles said goodbye to them all and headed back home. Avery was sleepier than she'd been in a long time when she finally arrived home. It meant that for the first time in ages, she was able to put her head down on her pillow and go right to sleep.

She would have an early start in the morning if she wanted to see the questioning of the two women. That would mean that she would have less time to work at the vineyard. She opened her eyes again, groggy from the brief sleep, and reached for her notebook.

Find Assistant.

That's what she scribbled down. Hoping that she'd find the note in the morning, she went right back to sleep and slept through the night. Sprinkles spent the night snuggled up to her leg, and not even his snoring would wake her up that night.

By the time Avery walked into the viewing room next to the interrogation room, Collette was already there, and she was tapping her foot impatiently against the floor. She was dressed in various shades of silver and blue that matched her eyeshadow. Her hair was pulled back into a braid, and her sunglasses were on top of her head.

Chief Mathers entered the viewing room with John, who had been responsible for escorting them to the police station.

"Tell me what happened on the drive," Chief Mathers said.

John shrugged. "Not much," he answered. "The women didn't say a word to each other."

"Nothing?" Chief Mathers asked. "Not even a greeting?"

"Not one word," John said. "They took their phones out and texted the entire time. I am pretty certain that they were texting each other."

"Yeah?" Chief Mathers asked, "How sure are you about that?"

"Well, one would type, and the other's phone would make the sound of a message. Then the other one would type, and a message would come through on the other phone," John explained. "The timing just made sense that they were texting each other."

"Got it," Chief Mathers said. "They don't realize how obvious it really is. Thank you, John. Did they give you any trouble at all?"

"Not at all," John answered. "They were happy to come with me, despite the fact that Mrs. Davis hasn't had her coffee yet."

Avery looked back at Collette. She was clearly frustrated and on edge. Chief Mathers' plan of making them nervous seemed to have worked. But something still bothered her about it all.

"They really didn't say anything to each other?" Avery asked.

"Not even a hello," John said again. "They looked out of their own window, and it seemed as if they weren't interested in each other. You know, except for the constant texting."

"That strikes me as odd, don't you think?" she said. "I just think that women like Audrina and Collette, who were so eager to put the blame on each other would say something if they were put in a room together. If they hated each other, surely they would have made some kind of mean remark or something?"

"That's what I was thinking too," Chief Mathers said. "But we can't base our investigation off of that. We can only say it's odd and move on from that."

Avery agreed. She found it strange, but it didn't make either of them guilty. Chief Mathers prepared himself and then left to begin the questioning.

"There's something odd going on here," Charles said quietly as Chief Mathers entered the room.

"Absolutely," Avery agreed.

Chief Mathers did his usual routine of sitting down and shuffling his papers around, but Collette was in no mood for that.

"What's this all about?" she barked. "If you have more questions, then let's speed it up. I have an appointment today for my hair, and I had to book it weeks in advance. I don't want to miss it."

"We're talking about your husband's murder here, Mrs. Davis," Chief Mathers said, unamused. "I'm sure that's more important than a hair appointment."

Collette looked as if she wished she could swallow her words. She glanced down and straightened her back.

"What can I help you with?" she said. "The other officer said there were a few more questions that you needed to ask me on the record."

Charles chuckled a little. "That's what happens when you make them nervous. They forget to act."

Collette was clearly on edge. She was not the friendly woman who had been in that room before. That might have been because she'd been forced to take a ride with her late husband's ex-wife. Still, the difference seemed a lot bigger than just that.

"I wanted to ask you about your relationship with Audrina," Chief Mathers cut straight to the chase.

Collette scoffed. "What relationship?"

"Well, I want to find out about your dynamic. You know, as wife and ex-wife," Chief Mathers continued. "Do the two of you get along at all?"

Collette forced a roll of her eyes. "Get along?" she said. "She's the ex-wife. Half of his money went to her and her child, who I had to care for some of the time. Besides that, she was always trying to get more money from him. It drove me nuts. No, we didn't get along at all."

She sounded so certain of it. She had answered with no hesitation at all. To Avery, it almost seemed as if she had expected the question.

"Well, we know she's lying at least a little bit," Charles said.

"Really?" Chief Mathers said. "I've met both of you. It seems to me like you'd have a lot in common."

Collette didn't even respond. She checked her nails and made sure her hair was tucked back into place. Chief Mathers made some notes and then continued on.

"Have the two of you ever been friends?" he asked. "Like, before your marriage to Mr. Davis?"

Collette shifted uncomfortably when he asked that question. Everybody in the viewing room and Chief Mathers in the interrogation room seemed to notice.

"Never," Collette answered. "I only met her once I married her ex-husband. It's not a good way to make friends."

"So, you've never really spent time together?" Chief Mathers asked.

His persistence seemed to be frustrating Collette. She folded her arms.

"No," she blurted out. "We don't get along. I don't know how else to say it. You could almost say that we're sworn enemies. If anything I said or did gave you the opposite impression, then let me confirm with you that you're wrong. Besides, I don't understand what all of this is about or how this helps to solve my husband's murder."

Avery watched Collette as she snapped at Chief Mathers. "That seems like a strange reaction," Avery said. "He wasn't blaming her for everything, and yet, she seems almost defensive."

"It's hard to tell," Charles said. "Grief makes people behave in all sorts of strange ways. This must be very stressful for her. And, like John said, she hasn't had any coffee yet. I'm not surprised she's a little short-tempered."

"I suppose you're right," Avery said. "I'm not exactly great when I haven't had my morning coffee."

The questioning continued, and Collette carried on answering in a frustrated manner. But there was no conclusion to it. Chief Mathers could not get her to admit to being friends with Audrina. She remained adamant that the two of them had never spent more than a minute together and that they hated each other.

Chapter Twenty-One

"Thank you for your time, Collette," Chief Mathers said.

"Not a problem," Collette said, eagerly getting up from her seat.

"Unfortunately," Chief Mathers said, stopping her in her tracks as she headed for the door. "You're going to have to miss that hair appointment."

Collette dropped her shoulders in frustration. "I thought we were done here," she said. "I don't need a ride home. I am more than happy to call a cab if that's the problem."

"There is no problem," Chief Mathers said. "We'd just like you to wait here while we question Audrina. That way, if we need to ask you any further questions, you're not too far away. I'm sorry, but until we're done with both of you, I need you to stay here."

Collette's face changed completely. She looked like a teenager that had just been told she couldn't go to the concert of her favorite band.

"Oh, of course," she said nervously.

She tried to smile, but there was concern behind her eyes. "Will you be asking her the same questions?" she asked.

"Unfortunately, I can't answer that," Chief Mathers said.

Collette nodded and walked out of the room. Waiting for her outside of the door was an officer who was likely assigned to keep an eye on her and make sure that she didn't leave. A few moments later, Chief Mathers stepped back into the viewing room.

"She seems a little on edge, doesn't she?" he asked with a short laugh. "And we know she is lying to us about her friendship with Audrina."

"I mean, maybe they're enemies now. But in the footage of the race, the two of them do not look like enemies. At the very least, they were friends at one point. I just don't understand why she won't tell us about it unless she is hiding something bigger," Charles said.

"She is strangely nervous," Avery said. "And a little too defensive, if you ask me."

"Well, I was trying to make her nervous, and it worked," Chief Mathers said. "And I agree with you. It is an odd thing for them to be lying about."

"It kind of puts their eagerness to blame each other into a whole new light, doesn't it?" Charles said. "That kind of behavior is normal for enemies. But certainly not for friends."

Chief Mathers nodded. He looked through his notes from the interrogation. Avery caught a glimpse, and almost all of them had to do with her body language. He wrote down how she had physically reacted to all of his questions.

She wondered what he was looking for exactly. He had noted signs of discomfort and nervousness. He had also mentioned that she had lied to him. But what kind of body language precisely was he looking for?

She was about to ask him when he spoke again, stopping her in her tracks. And perhaps that was better. If she had asked him, she would have given herself away for snooping through his interrogation notes.

"I think we should take a little break," Chief Mathers said.

"We haven't been here very long," Avery said with a chuckle.

"I know," Chief Mathers answered. "But the longer they wait, the more they begin to sweat. Let's make them both a little more nervous while we're at it. I want them on edge. Once they're really concerned, they are bound to slip up somewhere."

"I see," Avery said.

"So, let's take a thirty-minute break and meet back here to question

Audrina," Chief Mathers said. "And then, let's see if Audrina has the same story."

"The truth is there somewhere," Charles said. "You just have to find it."

"And if they don't want to come out and say it, then I'll simply show them the footage," Chief Mathers said.

"Why not show them the footage now?" Avery asked.

"If they're lying, then they'll have talked themselves into a corner," Chief Mathers said. "When I show them the footage, then they'll know they're caught. I've found that often, once you catch a suspect in one lie, the rest of the lies follow soon after."

"He's right," Charles said. "It's a method that works well."

Avery made a note of that. It made sense to her. Chief Mathers would give them the opportunity to be forthcoming. But he'd also give them the opportunity to lie. And once they'd had that chance, they would be presented with the truth.

Avery was excited to see how the day would end. Whatever the outcome would be, she was certain that it would be highly entertaining.

At that moment, an officer came in with a file. He seemed eager to speak with the chief.

"I have the feedback regarding Gregory Marsh's phone signal," the officer said.

"Excellent," Chief Mathers said. "I've been eager to hear about this."

"What's this?" Avery asked.

"We decided to get the records of where Gregory Marsh's phone connected to the cell towers over the days leading up to and after the murder. It's a way to track his whereabouts. We wanted to do it for the two women as well, but we need warrants for all of it, and Gregory's is the only one that has come through so far."

"Brilliant plan," Charles said. "Not only can you track where he's been, but it serves as a potential alibi for him."

"That's what I was thinking, too," Chief Mathers said. "It's just a pity that it takes so much time to get the information."

"Well, what does it say?" Avery asked eagerly.

Chief Mathers flashed Avery a charming smile as he opened the folder. He looked at all the paperwork, circling some bits of information. He looked almost as if he was calculating something. But he was looking for something specific. And the tap of his pen on one particular part of the page signaled that he had found it.

"Here it is," he said softly. "He was nowhere near the shop on the night of the murder."

"Really?" Charles asked. "I thought he was a good suspect."

"This shows that he made a phone call at more-or-less the time of the murder and that it was coming from the area in which his tent was found," Chief Mathers said. "So, he wasn't lying. He was already out there at the time."

"You know what that means," Avery said. "The only two remaining suspects are the two women you've got waiting for you now."

"That's exactly what it means," Chief Mathers said. "Finally, we're making some progress here."

Chief Mathers closed the file and handed it back to the officer who had brought it to him. He then instructed the officer to spread the word that neither of the women was allowed to go anywhere in the station without a chaperone.

"Well, let's take that break," Chief Mathers said excitedly. "And then we'll ask Audrina some questions while Collette sits nervously and waits. Sound good?"

"Sounds great," Charles said. "I'm in need of some coffee anyway."

Charles and Avery went to stand on the sidewalk for a while to get some fresh air. Charles disappeared into a nearby coffee shop to get them both a cup of coffee while they waited. And, with perfect timing, Tiffany phoned.

"Hey, Tiff," Avery answered.

"What are you up to?" Tiffany asked. "I mean, I know you're probably doing some work, but how busy are you exactly? Would you like to meet for a cup of coffee?"

Avery looked back at the station. "Can we meet a little later?" she asked. "I'm at the police station, and Charles has just gone to get me a coffee. We're here because of the case." Tiffany snorted as she tried not to laugh loudly. "Are you sure you're not on another date?" Tiffany teased.

Avery had to laugh. "An interrogation isn't much of a date, is it?"

"Not for us," Tiffany said. "But maybe for Charles. He loves that kind of thing."

"Oh, stop it," Avery chuckled. "I told you, it wasn't a date!"

"If you say so," Tiffany sang. "Well, let me know when you want to get a cup of coffee. I have a quiet week this week, and I'm bored because of it."

"Not much happening at work?" Avery asked.

"Not for a while now," Tiffany said. "If I'm honest, I'm worried about the company. I'm not sure what I'll do if the business shuts down. This is a small town, and there isn't that much work available. And my parents don't own a vineyard."

Avery sighed. "Well, Charles is on his way back. I'll call you later?"

"Okey dokey!" Tiffany answered before hanging up the phone.

Avery thought about the note on her bed about needing to hire an assistant and wondered if she'd be able to work with Tiffany every day. But her thoughts were interrupted by Charles.

"Why are you blushing so brightly?" he asked. "Who was that on the phone?"

Avery hadn't even realized she was blushing, but when she thought about it, her face had warmed when Tiffany was making fun of her about her potential date with Chief Mathers.

"Tiffany was teasing me," Avery said.

"Listen, if there's a reason to tease you, I want to know about it," Charles laughed.

Avery sighed. "It's about Chief Mathers," she said.

The smile dropped from Charles' face. "Why is she teasing you about that?" he asked.

"Do you remember I told you we went for coffee the other day?" Avery asked. "Tiffany says it was a date. But I disagree."

"You don't think that was a date?" Charles asked.

"No!" Avery whined. "I thought we were just, you know, getting a cup of coffee and getting to know each other. Have I missed something? Isn't he supposed to officially ask me and use the word date?"

"Those days are over," Charles laughed.

"Well, I haven't been on a first date since before I was married," Avery said. "I guess I've missed a lot."

"So, you really didn't think it was a date?" Charles asked as if to confirm.

"No," Avery said. "I just thought it was coffee, and now I'm worried I've given him the wrong idea. I really don't know what to do."

Charles looked almost as if he had let out a sigh of relief as he sipped his coffee. "Do nothing," he said. "If the chief wants to go out with you again, he'll ask you. And the next one will be a little more extravagant, like dinner or something. Then, you can tell him that you're not interested."

"I suppose that's the best idea," Avery said.

"I also thought it was a date," Charles said quietly. He burst out laughing a few moments later. "Now that I know that you didn't know it was one, I understand why Tiffany is teasing you! That's hilarious!"

Charles laughed so hard that he almost had tears in his eyes. All Avery could do was sip her coffee and wait for the teasing to come to an end. She realized that, even if she was ready to date again, she no longer knew how to.

"It's alright, Avery," he continued. "My last date wasn't all that great either."

Avery wanted to argue with Charles, but an officer came out to let them know that Audrina had been taken to the interrogation room and that Chief Mathers was waiting for them before he started the questioning.

Avery and Charles rushed inside and stood side-by-side again in the viewing room as Chief Mathers shuffled his papers around as he always did. The steam from their coffee still swirled through the air as they waited for something exciting to happen.

Chapter Twenty-Two

Audrina was in stark contrast to Collette when it came to her body language. Collette had been nervous and defensive, but Audrina was calm, collected, and confident. She leaned comfortably back in her chair and waited patiently for Chief Mathers to finish rummaging through his pages.

"Your officers have been treating me very well," she said before he could speak. "Maybe my next husband should be on the force. It might be nice to be treated well for a change."

It was a clear attempt at flirting with the chief, and it provided much entertainment for all who watched. Chief Mathers raised his eyebrows and shrugged while Avery and Charles chuckled on the sidelines.

"She's coming for the chief," Charles said.

"He better be careful," Avery laughed. "She's an expensive wife."

Avery could tell by the way he was piling the pages together that Chief Mathers was about ready to start his questioning.

"Whatever you need from me, I am happy to talk to you about it," Audrina said, stopping Chief Mathers in his tracks. "I just want this case to be solved so I can leave and go on a long vacation."

"Her behavior is calm," Charles noted. "But she is speaking like someone who is on edge or nervous."

"What makes you say that?" Avery asked.

"She seems to be awfully chatty, don't you think?" Charles continued.

He was right. She was on the verge of rambling, and that could certainly have been a sign of a nervous woman.

"I want to talk about your relationship with Collette Davis," Chief Mathers said, cutting right to the point.

"What about it exactly?" Audrina snapped.

"I want to know if the two of you are friends and how well you know each other, that kind of thing," Chief Mathers said casually.

Audrina pursed her lips, and her expression hardened. "There is no relationship of any kind," she answered. "We've just never gotten along well. You could say that we're sworn enemies."

Chief Mathers made some notes, and Avery wondered if they were about her body language and if he had also noted her chatty responses.

"I mean, there are hardly two people who get along any less. And I'm sure she would tell you the same thing. Have you asked her yet?" Audrina continued. She straightened her shirt and her hair and smiled. "There's no secret there," she said. "Everybody knows how she and I fight with each other often."

Chief Mathers carried on writing as she spoke.

"She should keep rambling," Charles said. "People who talk without pause often say something they don't mean to. This should be interesting."

Avery understood she needed to pay close attention to every one of Audrina's words. And then, Audrina moved for the first time since she had sat down. She shifted ever-so-slightly and pressed her hand to her stomach.

"Do you think she feels ill?" Avery asked.

"She might if she's nervous or stressed," Charles asked. "Or perhaps she's just ill today."

"Collette has only ever made things difficult for me," Audrina said. "I could barely get a word in with Cederic. She answered every phone call and would just go off on me for no reason. She would give my son foods that I don't like for him to eat, and she knows that."

Audrina folded her arms, and it was becoming quickly clear that she was getting more and more worked up the more she spoke about it.

"She's such a selfish woman," Audrina continued. "Even when she landed Cederic in huge amounts of debt, she kept on spending. He had to work twice as hard to earn enough money to keep them afloat while she sat around and did nothing."

Chief Mathers opened his mouth to ask the next question, but he didn't get the chance. Audrina was ready to carry on complaining.

"I tried to be kind to her, but she wouldn't hear it," Audrina said. "She just always decided I was an enemy and that she would always treat me that way. It's ridiculous, pathetic even. If she told you that we're friends, she is lying. And if she's lying about that, then what else is she lying about?"

"Were the two of you always such enemies?" Chief Mathers asked.

"Oh, absolutely, "Audrina said. "In fact, I was always sure that she was seeing my husband romantically before we were even divorced. I wouldn't be surprised if she was the one who put the idea of divorce in his head."

"Well, I don't know about that," Chief Mathers said. "But it does give me some insight into your relationship."

"I can't wait for him to show them the footage," Avery said. "They're going to have to eat all their words."

"Collette stole my husband, my style, and then she tried to take my son," Audrina said bitterly.

"Your ex-husband was the one who tried to get custody of your son," Chief Mathers corrected her.

"Yes, but I'm sure it was her idea," Audrina said. "It's just the kind of thing she would do to get at me."

Charles let out a sigh. "I think they're both lying about this," he said. "There's just something weird about their behavior today."

"I agree," Avery said. "Being interrogated is terrifying. Surely she wants to just answer the questions she's being asked and leave? Instead, she seems to be dragging Collette over the coals here."

Chief Mathers made some more notes and looked as if he was eager to get it all over with. It was still early in the morning, and Audrina had brought a lot of energy into the room.

"She's like an evil stepmother to my son," Audrina said. "She doesn't treat him badly outright, but from a distance, I can see that she doesn't like him or love him. And you'd think that if you marry someone with children, you'd accept that child into your life openly. Otherwise, don't marry them, you know?"

"And what about your ex-husband?" Chief Mathers asked. "Were you on good terms with him at any point after your separation?"

"Well, yeah," Audrina answered. "Until he filed for custody of our son. That would make any mother upset. And then Collette got in the middle of it all, like always, and it just turned completely sour."

Audrina clenched her jaw. "I was perfectly willing to play nice with him until that point. After that, everything became really ugly between us. That's no secret. I blame him entirely for my unhappiness."

"She certainly is making a point of saying that there are no secrets," Charles said. "That's twice now. Sounds like something someone with a secret would say."

It was becoming clear to Avery that the questioning she was watching now was intricate. It relied on a slip of the tongue or a particular physical response to a question. She still had a lot to learn, and she was learning it quickly.

"And who made it ugly?" Chief Mathers asked. "I mean, there are legal routes to take in a custody battle. It doesn't need to get personal. Who made it personal?"

"I did," Audrina said. "When I took it personally. He came after my ability to care for our son. It was outrageous. And I couldn't believe it when Collette agreed with him."

"Why couldn't you believe that if the two of you are such foes?" Chief Mathers asked.

Charles let out a satisfied chuckle. "Mistake number one," he said.

"I just didn't think she'd get involved in matters when it came to our son," Audrina answered.

Chief Mathers looked at her for a while, and it was clear on his face that he didn't entirely believe her. Audrina did her best to remain calm, but she pushed her back into the backrest of the chair as if she had been backed into a corner. Then, she folded her arms in front of her.

"I wouldn't be surprised if Collette is the murderer," Audrina said.

"And why do you say that?" Chief Mathers asked. "That's a pretty huge accusation."

"It's like I said last time," Audrina answered. "She wants the life insurance policy. They're probably just waiting to pay her out, and she's probably already picked out her shopping list."

Chief Mathers raised his eyebrows, but he didn't get a chance to speak.

"Besides, murder suits her, don't you think?" Audrina said. "I've watched crime documentaries. She fits the character of a murderous wife perfectly. She's got a big enough ego to think she'd get away with it. That's for sure."

"Well—"

"I don't think she ever cared about him as a person," Audrina interrupted the chief. "I think she was always in it for the money, right until she killed him."

"Some people think the two of you are pretty similar. That means you also fit the character description of a murderous wife, wouldn't you say?" Chief Mathers said.

Audrina scoffed. "Please, I don't have the time!" she said. "I can just picture Collette doing it. I mean, she has a key to his shops, if I remember correctly. My son had to get one from her once when Cederic had locked himself out."

"She has keys to the businesses?" Chief Mathers asked.

"Of course she does!" Audrina answered. "She was supposed to be helping Cederic to run them all, but she just never did a thing. She didn't lift a finger for those businesses. I bet you half the staff at his shops have never met her."

"Interesting," Chief Mathers said as he made a note of it.

"You should have seen her when I got into the car and had to sit in the back seat with her," Audrina said with a laugh. "I thought she would swallow her teeth! She looked so frightened of me."

"Does she have a reason to be frightened of you?" Chief Mathers asked.

"Of course not," Audrina said. "I would never do anything to hurt her. I have better things to do than that."

"Well, Collette seems to think you are the murderer," Chief Mathers said.

"Why is he telling her that?" Avery asked.

"I think he wants to see how she reacts when she is accused again,"

Charles said. "He's going to make sure that their questioning from today and their original questioning match."

"I see," Avery said. "What is he looking for, exactly?"

"He's looking for an inconsistency in their stories," Charles said. "If he gets nothing out of Audrina, he will likely bring Collette back in. Then, he'll try to exhaust them and see if they slip up when they're tired."

"This could be a long day, then," Avery said.

"That depends," Charles said. "If they are hiding something, they'll likely slip up soon. If they aren't hiding anything, then yes, this will be a long day."

"In that case," Avery said. "I'll get the next cup of coffee."

"Is that a date?" Charles teased with a childish smile.

"Oh, stop it," Avery said, nudging him in the ribs.

Audrina checked the state of her nails and rolled her eyes. "I can just see her there, standing behind him and deciding that he needed to die so she could go shopping," she said. "She's such a dramatic person. And she would probably convince herself that he deserved it."

"Do you think?" Chief Mathers asked, prompting her to keep talking.

Chief Mathers leaned back at that point and stopped writing. It looked almost as if the two of them were having a conversation in a coffee shop somewhere. He wanted to sit back and listen to her ramble and hoped that she would talk herself into a hole.

"Oh yeah, I think she probably resented him the moment he tried to restrict her spending," Audrina said. "I think she decided to teach him a lesson and killed him, and I think she enjoyed it. I bet her favorite moment was when she stuffed that red wedding ribbon of hers in his mouth."

Chapter Twenty-Three

"Gotcha!" Charles said quietly.

There was clearly shock in the viewing room between everyone who had been watching the interrogation. Audrina had just said something that made her look like the strongest suspect they had. Nobody moved. Avery didn't even want to blink out of fear of missing something important.

"How do you know about the ribbon in his mouth?" Chief Mathers asked. He leaned back and tapped the end of his pen against his knee.

Audrina shrugged. "I saw it in the news," she answered nonchalantly.

Chief Mathers looked at her silently for a while as he paged through his file. He pulled out the image of her and the page with all her information and put it on top of the pile.

"You see, the problem I have with that, Audrina, is that we never released that information to the public," Chief Mathers said. "In fact, we've gone out of our way to keep that small bit of information quiet."

He looked at her with a pleased smile. Everyone knew she had been caught, including Audrina herself. Charles took a step closer to the glass as if it would help him hear and see better. It was like watching a thriller movie.

"Um, well, you see," she started saying, but she quickly fell quiet.

Audrina's hands began to shake, and she swallowed. Her face paled, and her eyes widened as she realized that she had caught herself out in her own lie. It couldn't have been a good feeling.

"The only way you could have known about the red ribbon in his mouth is if you were there at the crime scene," Chief Mathers said. "And I know you weren't there after the body was discovered. So, it would have been before that."

Avery remembered the way she had found Mr. Davis' body. It had been a shocking discovery. The crime scene was so ugly, and the person who currently seemed responsible for it was so beautiful. It was an odd yet satisfying juxtaposition.

Audrina would need to think of something really good if she was going to talk her way out of it.

"I was there," Audrina confessed. "I'll say that. But I didn't take part in the murder. I had nothing to do with that. But I did witness it."

"Why didn't you come forward?" Chief Mathers asked.

"I didn't want to be next," Audrina said. "I was worried that if I talked, I would be the next person found dead."

Audrina didn't seem afraid to Avery, though. She seemed frustrated that she was having the conversation at all.

"That would mean you know who the murderer is," Chief Mathers said. "And you haven't told us until now. We're talking about the death of a man that you once loved, and you didn't say anything?"

"I do know who did it," Audrina said. "But as I said, it's too dangerous for me to tell you. I was there, but I had nothing to do with the murder itself. I only saw it happen."

"Let me make this clear," Chief Mathers said. "You're in trouble here. You're likely already going to jail. You might as well tell us everything that happened, Audrina."

Audrina seemed to be thinking it over. Then, she closed her eyes and sighed. Her confident demeanor changed entirely as if she had suddenly deflated and slowly come back down to Earth with the rest of the world.

"It was Collette," she said. "That's why I keep trying to point the finger at her. It's because I know she did it."

"I thought you just said you couldn't tell us who did it out of fear?" Chief Mathers said. "Yet, you've been blaming her the entire time."

"Yeah, but I wasn't like using evidence or anything," Audrina said.

"I don't have to tell you that this is a weak story," Chief Mathers said. "You know that this isn't convincing. You're smarter than that."

Audrina regained the stern look she had before. She knew he was right. And instead of looking afraid of the possible repercussions, she looked annoyed that she'd been caught.

"We know the wheel of cheese is too heavy for Collette to have lifted over her head," Chief Mathers said. "And we know she definitely wouldn't have been able to lift his body into the display case. She would have needed help."

Audrina's leg began to twitch, and she pressed her nail between her teeth as she thought. She had nothing else that she could lie about, and it was quickly becoming clear to her and everybody else that the more she lied, the worse her lies became.

"We did it together," she eventually confessed.

Once she had said it, she seemed entirely calm again as if a weight had lifted off her shoulders.

"There you go," Charles said in a satisfied manner.

"When we brought you in here, we knew of your friendship," Chief Mathers explained. "We saw the footage of the cycle race, and we could see the two of you celebrating in the background."

"I see," Audrina said, sounding completely defeated.

"Your story was falling apart the moment you walked in here," Chief Mathers said. "So, I suggest you start talking, and you talk honestly. Because I am tired of this, and I'd like to get this case solved and off my plate."

Audrina chuckled slightly. "Yeah, well, nothing creates a close friendship like a shared hatred toward another person."

"That's so true," Avery said, breaking the silence in the room filled with stunned people.

"Well," Charles said. "Now we know it will be a shorter day than we thought."

Charles smiled excitedly. He looked like a child watching his favorite film as he watched Audrina's story unravel in front of her. Avery felt excited too. Finally, she was reaching the peak of the story at hand, and there were so many questions still unanswered.

It finally looked like they might get some answers.

"Collette and I bumped into each other at a bar one night," Audrina explained. "We had both gone there to drink away our sorrows. At first, I thought about leaving, but I quickly learned that our sorrows had the same root cause."

"And that's where the friendship began?" Chief Mathers asked.

"Yeah," she said. "She was asking me if he had been that mean when he was married to me too. And I assured her that it was just the way that he was. She was really upset, and so was I. I bought her a shot, and she bought the next round. Before we knew it, it had been hours, and we were still enjoying each other's company."

"So you could say that you bonded over your frustrations with Cederic?" Chief Mathers asked.

"I know it seems silly," Audrina said. "But I don't have many friends, and she was just looking for someone who understood what she was going through. In the end, I realized that she was not the terrible person that I thought she was."

Chief Mathers looked completely taken aback.

"I don't understand women," one of the officers remarked.

"I knew what it was like to be married to him," Audrina said. "He was terrible in arguments. He had a way of making things personal, and he'd be ugly about it too. So, I knew what she was talking about, and she could take pity on me too. It was a pleasant change for the two of us."

"When was it decided that a murder needed to take place?" Chief Mathers asked.

Audrina shrugged. "We were talking about what we wanted from Cederic," she said. "I wanted custody of my son, and she wanted some money. He had all but cut her off from spending. She had wanted him to support the lifestyle that he had promised her when they got married."

Audrina looked down as she rested her hands in her lap. "We understood the only thing in our way was Cederic," Audrina said. "Collette had told me she had taken a massive life insurance policy out on Cederic. And I knew that if he wasn't around anymore, he couldn't possibly get custody of my son."

Chief Mathers sat patiently as he waited for her to continue his story. "So, what was the plan exactly?" he asked.

"Well, we knew he had to go," Audrina said. "But we didn't immediately jump to murder. We did think we could reason with him at first. We thought that maybe if we spoke to him together, as a team, he'd be more likely to listen."

Avery and Charles stood silently at each other's sides as they watched her confession. There was such a complication to the motives and emotions involved that Avery soon had multiple pages of notes written down.

"We couldn't carry on and let him control our happiness like that," Audrina said. "We were bursting at the seams, and he didn't seem to care at all. All he cared about were his shops." Audrina shifted to make herself more comfortable. "It was Collette's idea to murder him," Audrina said. "She wanted the life insurance, and she convinced me it was the only way for me to get custody of my son. Eventually, she threatened to turn on me and help Cederic in the custody battle if I didn't go through with it all."

"She manipulated you into taking part in the murder?" Chief Mathers asked, hoping for her to confirm it.

Audrina nodded silently. "It was her idea to pretend that we were enemies, too," she said. "But I should have known that our farce had failed when you put us in the same car. She hoped that it would cause a diversion if we put the blame on each other."

Avery thought of her own friends and wondered how she would react if they had asked her to help them commit a murder. It seemed crazy to her, and she knew with certainty that she would reject the offer.

"She thought if we pretended we weren't friends, we couldn't possibly be looked at as a team. So, we started early. We created arguments between ourselves and pretended to hate each other. That part was actually kind of fun. Then, in secret, we would get together to go through the plan."

"And what was the plan, exactly?" Chief Mathers asked.

"To slowly murder him," Audrina said. "She would add poison to his food to make him ill until he died."

Everyone in the viewing room looked at each other as Chief Mathers shuffled his file around. He pulled out a photograph of the crime scene and placed it in front of Audrina to look at.

"That doesn't look like a poisoning," he said.

Audrina shook her head. "It wasn't supposed to happen that night," she said. "We just wanted to talk to him and convince him to change his ways. We wanted to try one last time before we decided for certain that he would die."

"How did that result in such an elaborate murder?" he asked.

"The conversation got heated," she explained. "It got nasty, and eventually, we hyped each other up too much. There was a kind of hysteria between the two of us, and before I really knew what we were doing, he was on the floor and wasn't breathing."

"Once he was dead, what happened?" Chief Mathers asked.

"Collette started throwing stuff everywhere, and she asked me to help her stage the scene that you found," Audrina explained. "She wanted to make it as confusing for the police as possible."

"Well, that worked," Chief Mathers said.

It almost looked as if Audrina was going to give him a proud smirk. But before she could, Chief Mathers reached for his handcuffs and stood up. Avery, Charles, and the rest of the officers in the room watched as he read her rights to her and tightened the cuffs around her wrists.

Chapter Twenty-Four

Audrina barely struggled as Chief Mathers handcuffed her. Avery wondered if there had ever been a more fabulous criminal. Chief Mathers instructed Audrina to take a seat again and left the interrogation room.

"What is he doing?" Avery asked.

"I dunno," Charles shrugged.

A few moments later, the door to the viewing room opened, and a very pleased-looking Chief Mathers entered.

"We've got one," he said. "Now, we just need to get the other one."

"What do you want us to do with Collette?" one of the officers asked.

Chief Mathers took a moment to think about it. Then, he looked back at Audrina.

"Let's make sure the door to the boardroom is open. Collette is in there, and she is probably very nervous by now. I'd like to see how she reacts when she sees Audrina in handcuffs," he said.

"Got it," the officer said.

"I'll follow close behind as you lead Audrina past the door. After that, I'll continue Collette's questioning right there in the boardroom," Chief Mathers continued.

"That's an great idea," Charles said quietly.

Avery didn't care what the plan was, but she knew she would follow them. The day was quickly becoming highly entertaining to her, and she was eager to see how it all came to an end. They were on the verge of the entire case coming to an end, and it was becoming rather dramatic.

"Right, I'll go get Audrina," one of the officers said.

Avery and Charles moved out into the hallway and waited for the handcuffed Audrina to pass them. As she was led down the hallway, her eyes caught Avery's.

"You," she said quietly. "From the vineyard. What are you doing here?"

There was no time for an explanation. Audrina was hurried down the hall and passed the boardroom just a moment after the door had been opened. She was pushed past the door and looked inside, her eyes likely meeting the eyes of Collette.

There was a gasp from inside the boardroom, and then Collette started to cheer.

"I knew it!" she screamed. "I knew you were the one behind this!"

Audrina scoffed, and within a matter of moments, she had disappeared into the station where she would likely be put in a cell.

"You crazy woman!" Collette shouted. "You took everything from me! I knew you were behind this. You've ruined my life!"

Chief Mathers entered with two officers, Avery and Charles close behind. Each of them filled a seat around the table, and the ambushed Collette sat back down in her seat.

"Mrs. Davis," Chief Mathers said. "Audrina has been arrested for the murder of your husband. It seemed she had information that would only have been known to us or someone who was there when the murder took place."

It looked as if Collette was trying to decide how she should react. Her eyes looked around the room as she judged the reactions of everyone around her. Then, the corner of her mouth turned downward, and she frowned.

Collette dropped her head into her hands and began to sob loudly. "My poor Cederic," she said through sobs. "I knew it was her. She's an evil, evil woman."

When Collette looked up, she wiped her cheek with her hand. But it was clear to Avery and everyone else present that there were no real tears present. Her face had turned red, and it had sounded like sobbing, but there were no real tears there.

"Why are you sobbing?" Chief Mathers asked coldly.

Collette shrugged. "What do you mean?" she asked. "I'm crying because it is finally over. My husband has been murdered, and the person responsible has been caught. It's normal for me to cry over this." Collette sniffed loudly and wiped away more invisible tears. She looked dramatically out the window.

"It's just been so stressful, you know?" she asked before sniffing again. "I've been so scared that whoever killed Cederic would come after me. Not knowing who did it was just awful."

"If you were concerned about your life, then why did you not contact us for protection?" Chief Mathers asked.

Collette was momentarily stunned. It quickly became clear anticipated that she'd have to think further than that.

"I-I didn't want to keep you guys away from the case," she answered feebly. "I wanted all your focus on finding the murderer. If I made it about me, then Cederic would be forgotten."

Chief Mathers sighed deeply. He didn't look at all concerned about her tears or fears, and that alone had made Collette feel taken aback.

"Collette, is it true you have keys to each of your husband's businesses?" Chief Mathers said.

"Yes," Colette said. "My *late* husband had given them to me so that he didn't lose them."

"Right," Chief Mathers continued. "And where are those keys now?"

"I-I don't know," she said, flustered. "I haven't needed them in quite some time. They should be where I left them last, in the drawer of my desk. Unless they've been stolen."

"Have you been burglarized recently?" he asked.

"Not that I know of," Collette said.

"Then I am assuming that they are still in the drawer at home then," Chief Mathers said, writing it all down.

"Why is this so important?" Collette asked.

It did not go unnoticed by those in the room that her crying antics had come to a sudden end. Her eyes were not red or puffy, and she'd stopped sniffing.

"I'm just trying to clear up some information," Chief Mathers said. "There are some loose ends that need tying up."

"Loose ends?" Collette asked. "You've got Audrina. Everybody knows she did it. What do the keys have to do with it?"

"We're just trying to understand how she got access to the shop," Chief Mathers said.

"He let her in, obviously!" Collette said.

It seemed that Chief Mathers' line of questioning was causing her to lose her temper. She frowned and folded her arms. She looked suddenly unamused and annoyed by the fact that nobody felt any pity toward her.

"Audrina gave us a full confession just a few minutes ago," Chief Mathers said. "I am sure there is still more to uncover about all of this, but we have a pretty good idea of what happened that night."

"I'm glad she decided to come clean," Collette said. "Cederic deserved to get justice for this crime. Some people might not have gotten along with him, but that doesn't mean he deserved to die."

"I agree with that," Chief Mathers said.

It wasn't the reaction Avery had expected. She'd assumed Collette would be stressed at the idea of Audrina having told them about her involvement. The women must have been better friends than they thought. It looked as if Collette was convinced Audrina would never have told on her. Did she think her good friend would protect her when it came to the confession of the murder? Avery knew many close friends, but none that she thought were that close.

"How long did she think she would get away with it?" Collette asked, still certain that she could convince the officers of her act.

"I'm not sure," Chief Mathers said. "But, as I said, she told us everything. It's likely she'll be put away for quite some time."

"Good!" Collette said with a frown. "I hope she never sees the outside world again. She deserves to sit and become ugly in a jail cell somewhere."

Chief Mathers sighed. "Collette," he said despairingly. "You're smart enough to know what I'm saying here."

Collette just sat quietly and stared at him as if she was the most unintelligent woman on the planet. "I'm not sure what you're implying," she said.

"You know that if Audrina told us everything, then we're already aware of your involvement in the murder," Chief Mathers said. "We know the two of you went to confront Cederic about what it was you wanted from him. We know that the argument got out of hand, and we know the two of you, together, killed him."

"Typical," Collette scoffed. "She couldn't get to me in time to kill me, so now she's trying to take me down with her." It was a feeble attempt at shifting the blame away from herself again.

"We're enemies," Collette said. "Why on Earth would we work together?"

Chief Mathers reached for the television remote and turned on the monitor. The footage of the two of them cheering together in the crowd was still up there and ready to be played. He played it for her.

"You don't look like enemies here," he said. "In fact, you two look like very close friends."

He turned the television off, and Collette remained quiet. She seemed entirely stunned at the footage that she had seen. It had undone all her attempts at lying.

"Audrina told us how the two of you had bonded over your hatred for Cederic. It seems the two of you were far from happily married," Chief Mathers said.

"Well, we were friends then," she argued. "But we haven't been friends for a very long time; I can promise you that."

"Is that so?" Chief Mathers asked plainly.

"We hung out together like once or twice, but then after the whole custody battle thing, we've been sworn enemies," Collette said. "And if you don't believe me, I have voicemails and emails to prove it."

"Yes," Chief Mathers said, frustrated with her. "We're also aware of the part of your plan where you pretended to hate each other in order to divert police attention."

Collette's mouth hung open with shock. Her eyes had turned cold and dark, and she seemed to lose all signs of emotion completely. For the first time, Avery felt they were looking at the real Collette. It seemed as if she had finally dropped all pretense.

"So, we know the two of you are actually friends," Chief Mathers continued. "We know your hatred of each other is nothing more than an act, and I'm sure we can prove that by going through your recent messages. And we know that the two of you worked together to commit this crime."

There was silence in the room as everyone waited for Collette to react.

"Audrina says it was all your idea," Chief Mathers said. "But that is still up for debate, according to me."

"All you have is her story; I see no facts here," Collette argued.

"The fact of the matter is that Audrina couldn't have done it alone," Chief Mathers said.

It was the same conversation he'd had with Audrina, which had been what had finally caused her to break under the pressure.

"The cheese was too heavy, and the body was too heavy for her to have lifted it on her own," Chief Mathers said. "So, it is perfectly believable that the two suspects we have, you and Audrina, who have no alibi and have the strongest motives, might have worked together on this."

Collette rolled her eyes. "Always blame the wife...isn't that how it goes?" she said. "I've seen the crime shows. It's always the wife's fault."

"I suppose it wouldn't be too difficult to prove that you were there," Chief Mathers said.

Colette glanced at him out of the corner of her eye. She seemed more nervous than before.

"All we have to do is prove that the red ribbon that was stuffed into his mouth is the one that was tied in your hair at your wedding," Chief Mathers said. "You two women are not professional killers in any way. You're bound to have left some kind of evidence or DNA somewhere."

Collette clenched her jaw and looked back out of the window. She seemed cold and unfeeling to Avery. So much so that Avery suddenly was scared of Collette.

Eventually, Collette turned to face everyone in the room and leaned forward. "I want my lawyer," she said.

Chapter Twenty-Five

A very sat in the back of the courthouse as she waited for the jury to read out their verdict. The jury had taken only forty-five minutes to deliberate. It had been a short trial. In the end, neither woman was a good liar. Once Chief Mathers had the right direction to look in, it was quick enough for him to find the evidence that placed both women at the scene of the crime.

Most of the trial consisted of the lawyers trying to prove whose idea it was to murder in the first place.

The courthouse had fallen completely silent as everybody in attendance listened carefully. And when the guilty verdict was called out for both women, a cheer erupted throughout the courtroom. It was as if they'd been watching sports, and everybody's favorite team had won.

In a row ahead of her, Avery watched as Audrina's son and Collette's daughter embraced each other with tears in their eyes. They had lost their parents. Cederic was dead, and their mothers would likely spend most of the rest of their lives in prison.

Between the excited chaos, they were the only two people who seemed unhappy with it all. Avery felt bad for them. They had been dragged through television interviews and had been the victims of multiple verbal attacks. They were collateral damage for the bad ideas of their mothers.

In the end, the trial had been nothing like what Avery's husband had written about in his books. There had been no courtroom drama and no dangerous people on the stand. No witnesses had been murdered, and nobody had attempted to escape incarceration.

In fact, she had found it to be really boring. She had sat through the entirety of the trial as she worked on the end of her book. She wanted to see it through to the end, and she was grateful that it was finally over.

She looked forward to having at least one day that didn't involve something to do with the murder case. The more she learned about the women, the less she liked them. As their truths came to light, they seemed less glamorous. And then, eventually, after having been refused bail, they really started to look uglier. They had been unable to color their hair or style it in any way. They'd been unable to get their hands on makeup or have their nails done. The two women who were found guilty that day were vastly different from the two women who had been arrested at the police station.

They were facing the rest of their lives behind bars. And, in some ironic twist of fate, they wouldn't get anything that they'd set out to achieve. The custody of Audrina's son was handed over to his grandmother on his father's side. Collette wouldn't see a penny of his life insurance money.

Their plan had been their downfall, and they had lost what they loved most about their lives in the process.

When Avery stepped out of the courthouse, she was met with a wall of journalists who were already waiting for the lawyers to leave the room. The story had made national news. In a way, Audrina and Collette had become celebrities, and Avery wondered how long it would be before a movie was made about them. She knew that there'd be television deals, interviews, and book deals and that both women would likely still make a fair amount of money from their prison cells. It was a strange world to Avery.

The camera crews and journalists waited impatiently, and Avery had to weave her way through them. Not a single one of them was willing to give up their spot and move out of her way. She was just glad she had left before the lawyers. She knew that once they found someone worth interviewing, it would be pure chaos outside of that courthouse.

The sun was only about an hour from setting when Avery finally made it into the light. She took a moment to enjoy the sunshine on her skin.

She thought about how the two women had become a media sensation and remembered her favorite news headline from the trial.

THE FABULOUS FATALES FACE THEIR FUTURES

That had become their name in the media, and it had stuck. The women were a complete sensation, and everyone had become fascinated by the two fabulous women who had created such a crazy murder. Avery didn't blame the public for becoming so invested in it all.

It had been weeks of sitting in trials and listening to questions, and following the case closely. It had been exhausting, but Avery hadn't missed a minute of it. She was eager to leave it behind her now. Her book had been finished the week before and was already at the publishers.

With the trial done, it meant that Avery would have a lot more time on her hands. And with Tiffany acting as her new assistant, she'd have even more time to move on and write her next book. Still, she would have more free time than she'd had in a while, and part of her worried that she'd get bored.

Avery made her way down the stairs and searched to see if there was anywhere nearby that was still open to get a cup of coffee. She felt odd, as if it had all taken too long and also as if it had all been too short. It was over and that was almost unbelievable.

The street was filled with cars. The town hadn't been that busy in a long time. Ever since the story broke on national news, Los Robles had seen more tourism than ever. In the end, the murder had been very fruitful for all of them. The businesses had made a lot of money, and it seemed that nobody was concerned about the upcoming down season. As macabre as it was, they had to see the bright side of it. Cederic's businesses had all been sold, and that money had gone to his mother and son.

"Avery!" She heard her name called.

She looked in the direction of the voice and was looking into the sun. She squinted to see who it was as she took a few steps closer. As the building in the distance moved in front of the sun while she walked, she started to see clearly.

Charles waited with a wide smile, two coffees in hand and Sprinkles, who wagged his tail enthusiastically at his side.

"Oh, I am happy to see you," she said with a smile. "And I am so happy for this coffee. Thank you." She lifted the cup to her mouth and sipped. "This is shiraz," she whispered.

"Yes," Charles said with a wink. "We're here to take you home. I thought you might be ready to unwind."

"Bless you," she said with a wide smile.

Sprinkles wagged his tail wildly and pushed his nose against her hand to greet her. She bent down and kissed him on the head gently. "Good boy," she whispered. Sprinkles licked her hand and smiled.

"Bad news is...we had to park all the way down on the other block," Charles said. "There isn't a spot anywhere nearby."

"That's alright," Avery said. "I've been sitting for hours. It will be nice to stretch my legs."

She sipped her shiraz in her coffee cup as she told Charles all about the proceedings of the day. He listened closely.

"I was watching from the coffee shop nearby," he said. "It was showing on the news, but you know what the media is like. They pick and choose the parts they like, and then they only show that."

"Yeah," Avery said. "They're all waiting outside the courthouse. It's absolute chaos in there. I feel so bad for those children."

"With parents like that, I don't think they ever had it easy," Charles said. "I can only imagine how dramatic those women must have been as mothers."

They walked slowly down the road beneath the canopy of the trees. The dappled sunlight cast moving shadows that Sprinkles chased as if they were moving animals. With the world consumed by the current event at the courthouse, the rest of the town seemed quiet.

"So, what are you going to do now?" Charles asked.

"Now that this is all over?"

"Yeah, you're going to have so much more free time on your hands. What will you do with it all?" he asked.

CHAPTER TWENTY-FIVE

"Maybe I'll learn to relax," Avery said. "Or maybe I'll teach you how to cook."

Charles laughed. "How much time do you have?"

Avery chuckled. "Truthfully, I don't know. I haven't really thought that far ahead."

"That seems unusual for you," Charles said. "You've always got a plan for what's coming next."

"I know, but I'm tired of that now," she said. "There's the opening of the new waterside wine tasting coming up. And that will still take up some of my time. But after that, I think I might want to take it a little easy."

"That's progress," Charles said. "I'm proud of you for saying that."

Avery gave him a weak smile. He was right. She had been keeping herself busy as a pleasant distraction from the things she didn't want to think about. If she remained busy, she might not feel so lonely, or she might not think about her husband so often. But in the end, she still felt those things despite how busy she had been. She was finally feeling ready to take things easy again. She wanted to travel and enjoy her afternoons. Avery dreamed of a day when she had nothing to do and could sit out in the backyard and read a book.

"I'm excited to read this next book," Charles said. "I can't wait to see what you've done with this story."

"I've changed it quite a bit," Avery said. "It didn't feel right. I don't want anyone thinking I profited off Cederic's death."

"Of course not," Charles said. "You're a decent human being."

"But I've made sure the murderers are as fabulous as ever," she said. "That was one detail I wasn't ready to let go."

"As long as you're happy with the book, I am sure that it will be great," he said kindly.

They had finally reached his car. Avery happily hopped in while Charles helped Sprinkles into the back seat. Within moments, she was headed for home. She couldn't wait to get into bed with a movie. She wanted something to take her mind off the case for a short while.

"So, when you've got all this time off, do you think you'll find some time to have dinner with me?" Charles asked.

"Absolutely," Avery said. "Are you cooking?"

"I thought perhaps this time we could go somewhere together,"

Charles said. "There's a new restaurant on the main road that I'm dying to try."

"I'd like that," she responded.

Charles smiled. "It's a date, then."

Avery didn't correct him. For reasons she didn't understand yet, she didn't mind if it was a date. The feeling of guilt she had briefly anticipated never came. As she wondered what James might think, she discovered that she felt he wouldn't mind at all.

"It's a date, then," Avery said happily.

The End.

∾

If you loved this book, you'll definitely want to check out *Murder at the Cellar!*

A recently widowed city girl. A curious note found by mistake. It's about time this small town's cold case mystery is finally solved.

When Avery Parker comes home following her husband's untimely death, all she wants is the familiarity and security of her peaceful hometown. All is good until she unexpectedly stumbles upon a cryptic note. Just twenty-six words hastily scrawled on a forgettable piece of paper and that's all it took for everything in her life to be turned upside down.

As Avery scours the town to solve the mystery with old friends and new, she soon learns that in working to solve the case, her own life is in danger. With her trusty golden retriever pup unearthing clues, will she find the perpetrator before he finds her? The clock is ticking and there is no time to spare.

With more twists than the vines at Le Blanc Cellars, *Murder at the Cellar* will have readers guessing until the very end.

Murder at the Cellar is best paired with a bold cabernet sauvignon. So, grab a glass of your favorite cab, cozy socks, and sleuth it out with the gang from Le Blanc Cellars!

As usual, wine pairings and irresistible recipes included!

For this free book and to hear about upcoming releases, visit
www.DaniSimms.com

Recipes

Creamiest Cheesy Scrambled Eggs (serves 2)

4 large eggs
4 tablespoons cottage cheese
½ cup of your favorite cheese, shredded (I like to use Gruyere,
sharp cheddar, or Colby Jack)
1 tablespoon butter
Salt and pepper to taste

- Heat a large pan to medium-high.
- In a medium bowl, whisk eggs, cottage cheese, and shredded cheese until mixed well.
- When the pan is hot, melt butter and pour in egg and cheese mixture.
- As eggs are setting, use a spatula to move eggs from the outside of the pan toward the center.

- Continue moving eggs around until cooked to desired consistency.
- Finish with salt and pepper to taste.

Pair with pinot blanc or your favorite dry white wine.

Nacho Regular Sheet Pan Nachos (serves 6)

1 bag tortilla chips* (16 ounces)
1 ½ cups Mexican cheese blend (or you can make your own with
½ cup each of cheddar, Monterey Jack, and Colby)**
1 cup tomatoes, diced
½ cup red onion, diced
¼ cup cilantro, chopped
1 avocado, diced
Salsa, sour cream, and pickled jalapeños to garnish

- Set the rack to the middle position and preheat oven to 375°F.
- Line a large sheet pan with foil and cover with non-stick spray.
- Arrange chips in a single layer and top with cheese blend.
- When the oven is ready, bake for 6-7 minutes (cheese should be melted by then).
- Remove the pan and top with tomatoes, onions, cilantro, and avocado.
- Serve alongside salsa, sour cream, and pickled jalapeños.

This is a versatile base recipe where you can allow your creativity to run wild! Here are some toppings and combinations I've enjoyed in the past:

- Roasted duck with brie
- Shredded rotisserie chicken with mozzarella (with a touch of blue cheese and sprinkled with Frank's Hot Sauce)
- Crab with Monterey Jack
- Bulgogi (Korean BBQ beef) with mozzarella (sprinkled with gochujang), replace cilantro with green onions
- BBQ pulled pork with Monterey Jack

*I'm partial to using my favorite tortilla chips from Taco Works in San Luis Obispo, CA. If you get the chance to try them, definitely do. It will undoubtedly elevate your nacho game!

** Feel free to add more cheese to suit your taste.

Pairings depend on what kind of nachos you're making:

- *Spicy or beefy nachos - pinot noir*
- *Poultry - chardonnay*
- *Veggie - rosé*

G's Mac and Cheese (serves 8)

1 package elbow macaroni (16 ounces)
6 tablespoons butter, divided
3 tablespoons all-purpose flour
2 cups low-fat milk
1 cup heavy cream
½ teaspoon salt
½ teaspoon pepper
4 ounces cream cheese, softened at room temperature and cut into ½" cubes
10 ounces white cheddar cheese, shredded
10 ounces Gruyere cheese, shredded
1 ¼ cups panko breadcrumbs

- Preheat oven to 350°F.
- Bring a large pot of water to a boil and cook pasta according to package directions. Drain and transfer to a large mixing bowl.
- Melt 3 tablespoons of butter in a large saucepan until bubbly.
- Create a roux by adding 3 tablespoons of flour.
- Whisk mixture until golden brown (about 2-3 minutes).
- Add in milk and heavy cream, slowly whisking until mixture is smooth.
- Add salt and pepper and mix to combine.
- Add cream cheese to the mixture and stir to melt.
- Add cheddar and Gruyere cheeses slowly, mixing to combine (about 5 minutes).
- Pour cheese mixture over prepared macaroni.
- Transfer mixture to a parchment lined 9x13 pan.
- Melt remaining 3 tablespoons of butter and mix with panko breadcrumbs.
- Top macaroni and cheese with breadcrumb mixture.
- Bake in the oven uncovered for 25 minutes.

Pair with pinot noir or grenache.

Mini Strawberry Cheesecake Cups (48 mini cheesecake cups)

1 package vanilla wafers (12 ounces)
2 blocks cream cheese (8 ounces each), softened at room
temperature
¾ cup granulated sugar
2 large eggs
1 teaspoon vanilla extract
Fresh strawberries, sliced

- Line a mini muffin pan with mini cupcake liners.
- Preheat oven to 350°F.
- Place one vanilla wafer into each mini cupcake liner.
- In a large bowl, beat cream cheese with sugar, eggs, and vanilla extract until smooth.
- Fill each cup with cream cheese mixture ⅔ full.
- Bake for 15 minutes.
- When cool, top with sliced strawberries.

Pair with ruby port or coffee.